CHURCH MUSIC
IN
HISTORY AND PRACTICE

Studies in the Praise of God

HALE LECTURES

THE PRAISE OF GOD. By the Rev. Winfred Douglas, Mus. Doc., Canon of St. John's Cathedral, Denver, Colorado. 1935. (Published under the title "Church Music in History and Practice.")

THE SOCIAL IMPLICATIONS OF THE OXFORD MOVEMENT. By the Rev. William George Peck, Rector of St. John Baptist, Hulme, Manchester, England. 1933.

PASTORAL PSYCHIATRY AND MENTAL HEALTH. By the Rev. John Rathbone Oliver, M.D., Ph.D., Associate in the History of Medicine at the Johns Hopkins University. 1932.

CHRIST IN THE GOSPELS. By the Rev. Burton Scott Easton, Ph.D., S.T.D., Professor at the General Theological Seminary. 1930.

NEW HORIZONS OF THE CHRISTIAN FAITH. By the Rev. Frederick C. Grant, D.D., Th.D., Dean of Seabury-Western Theological Seminary. 1928.

SOME ASPECTS OF CONTEMPORARY GREEK ORTHODOX THOUGHT. By the Rev. Frank Gavin, M.A., Ph.D., Th.D., Professor at the General Theological Seminary. 1921.

THE ETHIOPIC LITURGY. By the Rev. S. A. B. Mercer, D.D., Ph.D., Professor at Trinity College in the University of Toronto. 1915.

BIOGRAPHICAL STUDIES IN SCOTTISH CHURCH HISTORY. By the Rt. Rev. Anthony Mitchell, D.D., late Bishop of Aberdeen and Orkney. 1913.

THE NATIONAL CHURCH OF SWEDEN. By the Rt. Rev. John Wordsworth, D.D., LL.D., late Bishop of Salisbury. 1910.

CHURCH HYMNS AND CHURCH MUSIC. By Peter C. Lutkin, Mus.D., A.G.O., late Dean of the School of Music, Northwestern University. 1908.

CHURCH MUSIC

IN

HISTORY AND PRACTICE

Studies in the Praise of God

BY

WINFRED DOUGLAS, Mus. Doc.

Canon of Denver

NEW YORK

CHARLES SCRIBNER'S SONS

1955

TO THE HONOURED AND BELOVED MEMORY OF

PETER CHRISTIAN LUTKIN

THE FIRST HALE LECTURER, WHOSE ENTIRE LIFE
WAS HUMBLY DEVOTED TO THE PRAISE OF GOD,
THESE PAGES ARE INSCRIBED BY HIS FOLLOWER
AND FRIEND

"*Had we but true understanding, what duty would be more
perpetually incumbent upon us than to hymn the Divine Power,
both openly and in secret, and to tell of all his benefits?* . . .
*Ought there not to be some to fulfil this duty, and sing the
praise of God on behalf of all men? What else can I do that
am old and lame, but sing hymns to God? Were I a nightingale, I would do the part of a nightingale: were I a swan, I
would do as a swan. But I am a reasonable being, and I ought
to praise God. This is my work. I do it. I will never desert
this post as long as I am permitted to hold it: and I beseech
you to join in this self-same song.*"

Epictetus in Arrian, *Discourses* I, xvi.

FOREWORD

A VAST literature has been developed, both in Europe and in America, on the subject of Church Music. During the past century, the entire body of existing Choral Music of the earlier Christian ages has been subject to the processes of comparative analysis. A treasure of musical praise which had long been lost to the world has been restored to practical use, largely through the religious devotion and the technical skill of the French Benedictine Congregation of St. Pierre, Solesmes, and of the Plainsong and Mediæval Music Society in England. Similar care in allied fields of research has provided us with a scientific Liturgiology, and with exhaustive studies in the development of the Christian Hymn. We have at the present day no lack of authoritative source books available for the further research of scholars. Nor do we lack a flood of popular books about Church Music; either small technical manuals for the organist and choirmaster, or stories about the Hymns and their writers, and the better known religious composers, for both Clergy and laity.

We do lack a book, solidly based on the scientific research of scholars, and yet free from needless professional technicalities, which treats of both the text of the liturgical services and the words of the hymns, together with the music which has grown up with them, as parts of an indivisible whole attuned to one high purpose, the worship of God in the One, Holy, Catholic, and Apostolic Church.

The invitation of the Committee of the Hale Lectureship Foundation to deliver a series of lectures on Church Music encouraged me to attempt this extensive synthesis, which necessarily involved some treatment of three of the subjects prescribed in the bequest, (*a*) Liturgies and Liturgics, (*b*) Church Hymns and Church Music, and (*c*) Treatment of events happening since the beginning of what is called the Oxford Movement, in 1833. The lectures were delivered at Seabury-Western Theological Seminary to an audience of Clergy, Seminarians, Church Organists, and interested laity. They were fully illustrated by the kind assistance of the A Cappella Choir of Northwestern University, Mr. Oliver Seth Beltz, Conductor; of the Seminary Choir, Mme. Edith Bideau Normelli, Director; and of Mr. Lester W. Groom, F.A.G.O. In addition, many phonographic records were played, and the Congregation joined extensively in the singing of illustrative Hymns.

The considerable amount of time necessarily occupied by these illustrations involved a condensed treatment of the lectures themselves. After a delay caused by long and serious illness, they have now been put into proper form for publication as chapters of this book.

Since the element of practical illustration is essential to the profitable use of the book, I have compiled a fairly complete list of European and American phonographic records now available, and illustrative of the various periods, types of music, and individual compositions cited in the text. A collection of such records should form part of the equipment of every Seminary, of every College giving courses in Music, and of other Musical

Conservatories, especially those giving courses in Church Music. It is hoped that the complete phonographic references in the text will enable such institutions, as well as private persons, to form collections of real educational value.[1]

In addition to the use of records for illustration, the chapters throughout cite the works on Church Music set forth under authority of General Convention of the Protestant Episcopal Church, by the Joint Commissions on the Hymnal and on Church Music. These are *The Hymnal,* edition of 1930; *The Choral Service,* 1930; *The Congregational Choral Service; The American Psalter;* and *The Plainsong Psalter.*[2] I strongly recommend that the book be read in connection with these publications; that the last four chapters be studied in sections, Hymnal in hand; and that each Hymn referred to be *sung,* not merely played over.

In preparing the work, I have had primarily in mind the need of Clergy, Seminarians, and Organists to learn the underlying principles of musical worship; too often either forgotten, or never acquired. But outside of these groups, whose relation to the subject is professional as well as personal, the book may appeal to that very large public whose growing interest in musicology is attested by the rapidly increasing titles in this department on the shelf-lists of our public and institutional libraries. Apart from highly technical publications, no branch of musicological study has suffered such neglect as that which is here attempted. This book traces the relationship between

---

[1]All records may be obtained of The Gramophone Shop, 18 East 48th Street, New York.

[2]*The Hymnal* is to be had of the Church Pension Fund, 20 Exchange Place, New York; the other publications of the H. W. Gray Company, 159 East 48th Street, New York.

worship and music from the beginning of the Christian Church to the present time. Its object is not to give a detailed history of music as an art, but rather to trace the development of Christian liturgical worship and of Christian Hymns, with the music which expressed them at significant periods of Church history, in order to arrive at practical and intelligent conclusions regarding the present musical worship of the Church; and to bring out and illustrate the principles which should govern the composition, the choice, and the performance of liturgical Church Music today.

No effort has been made to introduce any original theories. I therefore wish, in estimating the gratitudes which spring up in the heart on the completion of a long task, first of all to thank the personal instructors in America, England, France, and Germany, who have taught me what I here transmit, and the authors of the books cited; then the Committee of the Hale Foundation for the great honour and privilege they have conferred upon me; Dean Frederick C. Grant of Seabury-Western Seminary for wise counsel and unfailing kindness and long patience; the members of the Faculty and student body for great helpfulness; and those good friends previously mentioned who prepared and gave the original illustrations.

My thanks are also due the Denver Public Library and the Library of Denver University for much aid during absence from my own technical library; to Miss Alice Ward of Denver for typing a difficult manuscript; and to the Reverend Frank Walter Williams for practical suggestions, sound criticism, and the laborious task of compiling indexes.

WINFRED DOUGLAS.

Denver, March 12, 1937,
Feast of Saint Gregory.

CONTENTS

CONTENTS

CHAPTER III

THE MUSIC OF THE EUCHARIST FROM THE RISE OF POLYPHONY TO THE PRESENT TIME

CONTENTS

CHAPTER IV

THE MUSIC OF THE OFFICE BEFORE THE REFORMATION: GREGORIAN PSALMODY

CHAPTER V

OFFICE MUSIC SINCE THE REFORMATION

CONTENTS

CHAPTER VI

THE PRE–REFORMATION LITURGICAL HYMN

[xiv]

CONTENTS

CHAPTER VII

ANGLICAN ECLECTIC HYMNODY: LATER PRE-REFORMATION SOURCES

CHAPTER VIII

ANGLICAN ECLECTIC HYMNODY: POST-REFORMATION SOURCES

CONTENTS

CHAPTER IX

A CENTURY OF REFORM

CHURCH MUSIC IN HISTORY AND PRACTICE

STUDIES IN THE PRAISE OF GOD

CHAPTER I

FOUNDATION PRINCIPLES OF CHURCH MUSIC

THE NATURE OF WORSHIP

WORSHIP is the primary and eternal activity of redeemed mankind. So basic a statement of the attitude of the Church toward God should need no defense: but as we shall see later, the word 'worship' is quite generally misinterpreted. Worship may be simply defined as the offering of all our faculties to the glory of God. An increasing awareness of God almost inevitably results in some degree of adoration, a prayer of out-going to the Supreme Good, unmindful of self: for adoration is the movement not of the mouth only, but of the heart, of the mind, and of the will, as well: in short, of the entire being toward God. From the time of Josiah, when a Book of the Law (parts of Deuteronomy) was found in the house of the Lord, the Jews continually heard that great word which was later to become the Credo of the Synagogue, the *Shema'*. "Hear, O Israel: The Lord our God is one Lord: and thou shalt love the Lord thy God with all thine heart, and with all thy soul, and with all thy might." Repeated a dozen times in the Biblical literature of that period, our blessed Lord made the phrase his own, and taught it to his Church. Since 1718, it has appeared in Communion Offices of the Anglican rite. Its use every Sunday is universal in the American Church: and well may it usher in, as a sort of fixed Introit, our most solemn act of divine service; for to "love the Lord thy God with all thy heart, and with all thy soul, and with all thy mind" is to "worship the Father in spirit and in truth"; and only such loving worship can enable us to "love our neighbours as ourselves," and truly to serve them in the spiritual and corporal works of mercy which today wear the slightly distorted mask of 'social service.'

All worship must spring from such a sense of God's presence, and of the paradoxical mysteries wherein alone we can apprehend him. His presence in my heart, or where two or three are gathered together in his Name: and his simultaneous presence in the utmost bounds of remotest nebulæ. His inexpressible fulness in both the material universe and the world of life: "Heaven and earth are full of the Majesty of thy Glory," but yet, "Thou didst not abhor the Virgin's womb." The splendor of the illimitable stars is contained in God; yet that God, for very love of us, was personally embodied in a single fertile cell in the womb of a young girl. Truly, as was said by Proclus, the scholastic of Neo-Platonism, "God is the synthesis of infinite and boundary." God in the awe and wonder of the numinous, the *'mysterium tremendum et fascinans'*: yet God in the near, the dear, the familiar. God's freedom, the spontaneous, joyous self-expression of a limitless and perfect nature, which makes him Holy, Holy, Holy; and awes and humbles us, who, like Isaiah, are a people of unclean lips: and yet God in his assumed Human Nature, 'tempted in all points like as we are, yet without sin,' and able to take away our iniquity and purge our sin. God's infinite impassible joy: and yet the Agony, the Cross and Passion of our Redeemer, who is God incarnate.

[4]

Such considerations, vividly conceived, make us, both as individuals and as living members of the corporate organism of the Church, more aware of God, more sensible of our profound need of him; more conscious of the fact that out of his awe-inspiring immeasurable difference from ourselves, he can and will supply all our need superabundantly. That difference is so great that we cannot be content with speaking to him in repentant sorrow, or in petition for his gifts, or in thanksgiving for them; necessary as these movements of the soul must be. No, we must worship, we must adore, our whole being with all its faculties must move toward him in some form of expression, without thought of self at first: and so moving toward him, become a little more like him, a little more the image and likeness of himself which he wills us to be, and therefore a little more able to serve our fellow men to their benefit. "In earthly worship man does not merely secure for service that which alone can make it serviceable; he anticipates the essential and all-engrossing activity of eternal life."[1]

Does the phrase, Divine Worship at 11 A.M., suggest such thoughts as these to the average American, or even to the average Christian? Is the average Church Music which one hears all over our country consonant with such ideas? One cannot think so. In both cases the reason is very simple. The main activities and the music of the average eleven o'clock service are directed manward and not Godward. I quote from a well-known American writer, Elmer Rice. "The drama presents the same elements of appeal as does organized worship. We find, in both, the same attack upon the senses and the emotions, through the use of lights, of music, of rich vestments, of resonant voices, of

[1]Kenneth Kirk, *The Vision of God*.

[5]

decoration, and of a more or less stylized pantomime." For him, organized worship is the presentation before an audience of an artistic performance well acted out, for their edification. The whole action is manward, though its subject matter may have to do with God. The audience is passive. They have come to receive; not to give, not to do; just to get. What is lacking? Good intention? No. Sense of duty? No. Merely that the primary attention is turned from God to self. We thank him for favours received, we ask him for favours renewed. We hear, read or sung, the words with which some saint of older time has praised him for himself, and think them beautiful and enjoyable. All we do is referred to self. What we need most is to forget self, and in the depth of our being to apprehend, to realize, to see God, and generously pour forth with all our heart and with all our soul and with all our mind our *Te Deum* of rapt praise.

> *Te Deum laudamus;*
> *Te Dominum confitemur;*
> *Te æternam Patrem*
>   *omnes terra veneratur.*
> *Tibi omnes Angeli,*
> *Tibi Cæli et universæ Potestates,*
> *Tibi Cherubim et Seraphim,*
>   *incessabili voce proclamant:*
> *Sanctus, Sanctus, Sanctus Dominus Deus Sabaoth.*
> *Pleni sunt cæli et terra majestatis gloriæ tuæ.*

> *Thee,* O God, we praise;
> *Thee* we acknowledge as Lord;
> *Thee,* O Father eternal,
>   all the earth doth worship.

To *thee* all Angels,
To *thee* the Heavens and all the Powers
therein,
To *thee* Cherubim and Seraphim
cry out with ceaseless voices,
Holy, Holy, Holy Lord God of hosts:
Heaven and earth are full of the majesty of thy glory.

For such profound outpouring from the depths of the spirit words alone are insufficient. They need to be vitalized and intensified by that most spiritual of all the arts of self-expression, music.

MUSIC EXPRESSES HUMAN LIFE

Music is an art of human expression which *directly* voices the human soul in tone governed by rhythm. It can really utter the voice of the spirit through the flesh; and make the spoken word more intensely vital, more sincere, truer. In its combination of the sensible and the spiritual, it corresponds to the nature of man, and to the sacramental idea characteristic of the religion of Jesus. Both religion and art are *qualitative* expressions of the nature of being, and therefore allied. Science, on the other hand, is *quantitative* in its approach to reality.

What are the sources of the unique art of music?

Music has a double source in man's very existence, springing from the co-ordination of two quite diverse human impulses. The first is the impulse of emotional self-expression, the external manifestation of life as personal feeling. It is this which produces *tone,* sustained sound, the material out of which music is made. The high wandering sounds of a baby's voice communicate directly the baby's inner mood, long before speech. We may call this the *song* impulse. The second is an impulse of ordered law which corresponds to his own individual life processes, but is also significant because it relates them to the universe outside of himself. The beat of the baby's heart, the steady rise and fall of his breath, correspond in kind with the sequence of day and night, with the ordered swing of planets and suns. The baby will very early yield to this impulse by making rhythmic movements which express his delight in corresponding to something outside of himself. We therefore call it the *dance* impulse. The rattle, the drum, will take the baby's rhythmical expression into the realm of sound. A little later in life, when sustained tone is wedded to ordered rhythm, *music* is created; music, which is the most human of all the arts, because it can *directly* express personality in action; or life. It is necessary to lay stress on this unique characteristic of music itself before we can rightly estimate the nature of Christian music.

A widespread belief, not always wholly conscious, exists in America that music, far from being an essential art of life, is merely a surface decoration. People think of music as an escape from silence, of which they are unconsciously afraid: as an excitant whose exaggerated mechanical rhythms take the place of a calm which they cannot attain: as a sensuous pleasure which they can buy, paying the highest prices to the best purveyors of it, and estimating its excellence merely by the objective delight which it gives: as an emotional intoxicant, a spiritual drug whose emotion leads to no action, and therefore leaves the spirit weakened as by an opiate: as a superior sort of circus, which astonishes them by a display of mechanical or of intellectual dexterity. I have heard every one of these misuses of music in churches of our Communion. This is perhaps not strange in a civilization but recently out of the pioneer stage, and still in the commercial stage, intensely preoccupied with material things. But as life becomes more deeply conscious of spiritual values, so the expression of life in religious music must become more real, more sincere; it must become true *worship* music, in which the ordered tone, whether sung or only heard, will be the veritable voice of the worshipper's prayer. No valid Church music was ever made merely to be listened to as a sensuous pleasure.

It is a grave impoverishment of our culture that so many classify music as an amusement; and not as a collective voice of mankind that unites men on a higher level of spiritual sensitiveness than they could otherwise attain. Music is not merely a succession of pleasing sound-patterns formed of sensuous tone; but is essentially an utterance, an elemental utterance of the whole man. Its message is not primarily addressed either to the intellect or to the emotions; but to the complete personality of the listener: and that message, to be valid, must spring from the complete personalities of both composer and performer. In it, heart speaks directly to heart, mind to mind, life to life. To singer or to listener, the message becomes as his own voice speaking within; not only an external revelation of beauty, but also the vital utterance of his own soul; so that he adores with the voice of Palestrina, prays with that of Bach, rejoices in the mighty tones of Beethoven, loves and suffers in the surging crescendos of Wagner.

Music is thus not only closely related to life by its power of personal utterance, but still more by its essential character as rhythmic flow; for our life is a continuous movement, of which we are conscious through periodic recurrences of experience. Life is never a state, but always a process; never a being, but always a becoming. Of Music alone among the arts is this wholly true. The Drama and the Dance possess rhythmic flow in varying degree, but they remain external to all but the participants. Other arts are static in their relation to the life of man. Architecture permanently shelters and expresses the various manifestations of his social activity; Painting records his interpretation of the world which he sees; Jewelry and Clothing adorn his body; Sculpture perpetuates the forms of that body in its more perfect or passionate states; Poetry delineates particular aspects of his thought and feeling. Only Music moves and changes as his whole being moves and changes, lives parallel with his life, agonizes with his struggle, mourns with his grief, exults with his joy, prays with his adoration. From the far dim dawn in barbarism of that 'Light which lighteth every man that cometh into the world,' the sense of divine vision has evoked the mysterious power of music to express man's reaction to the numinous, to vitalize and supplement speech in the utterance of worship.

CHURCH MUSIC EXPRESSES THE LIFE OF THE BODY OF CHRIST

SUCH being the relationship of music in general toward life itself, how did the Catholic life of the first Christian centuries manifest itself in music? That life was not the sum total of individual human lives combined in an organization for purposes of church government and administration. It was the life of the mystical Body of Christ. Jesus, the God-Man, brought into this world a new kind of human life. His perfect Humanity, body, soul, and spirit, was for ever and indissolubly united to his divine Person, the second Person of the ever blessed Trinity. The individual members of his Church were 'born again' of water and of the Spirit into a new supernatural life, the life of God incarnate; a life nourished, not by ordinary food and drink, but by the gift of the very being of Jesus in the Sacrament of his Body and Blood. They are members of his Church, not as a man can be a member of a human society, but as being grafted into his life: so that the Church is rightly called the Mystical Body of Christ, in which all partake of his life, as my hand or my foot partakes of the life of my body. Thus the Catholic Church is not an organization, but a living organism. "An organism is a whole whose parts are reciprocally means and ends, and partake of a common life."[2] In the Church, Jesus is the end we seek, and we are a corporate end which Jesus seeks; that in a life common to him and to ourselves, we may be for ever united to God the Father through God the Holy Spirit.

It is this *organic* life which the Church Music of the early Christian centuries expresses. The object of redeemed life is the praise of God. The chief end of man is to glorify God. We cannot really serve our fellow man apart from some vision of a God to be glorified in thought, word, and deed; and the service which we men can mutually render each other now is but temporary; since all our needs, individual and social, will be satisfied when we shall attain in heaven to the perfect vision of God which is perfect union with him. Church Music is therefore the earthly form of an eternal and primary activity of redeemed mankind.

> We come unto our fathers' God:
> Their Rock is our salvation;
> The eternal arms, their dear abode,
> We make our habitation;

[2]Laurence Gronlund, *The Co-operative Commonwealth.*

We bring thee, Lord, the praise they brought,
We seek thee as thy saints have sought
   In every generation.

Their joy unto their Lord we bring,
   Their song to us descendeth;
The Spirit who in them did sing
   To us his music lendeth:
His song in them, in us, is one;
We raise it high, we send it on—
   The song that never endeth.

Ye saints to come, take up the strain,
   The same sweet theme endeavour;
Unbroken be the golden chain!
   Keep on the song for ever!
Safe in the same dear dwelling-place,
Rich with the same eternal grace,
   Bless the same boundless Giver.[3]

EARLY CHRISTIAN MUSIC IS A BLEND OF HEBREW, GREEK, AND LATIN ELEMENTS

THE formative period of early Christian music was extraordinarily brief, after the bitter persecutions of the Roman state came to an end. Soon after the Edict of Milan, a Song-school for the training of Church musicians existed in Rome. Within three centuries, the period of experiment, assimilation, and codification had ended with the establishment, in the time of Pope St. Gregory the Great, of the first complete corpus of fully artistic

[3]Hymn 424: Thomas H. Gill. Unless otherwise indicated the hymn numbers referred to throughout this book are those of *The Hymnal* as authorized in 1918 by the Protestant Episcopal Church. References to *The Hymnal* are to this book also.

music which the world had ever known; in which the enduring principles of relationship between Church Music and Catholic Worship were perfectly and permanently set forth. Let us first consider this period of experiment, assimilation, and codification, and afterward the principles then established; which ought to underly all our worship music at the present time, and which are for ever valid in the Church on earth.

Both experiment and assimilation were inevitable. Christianity began in a Jewish environment in the midst of a Græco-Roman culture. In a rapidly changing world, it became a growing force that was to become dominant, and to bring about a unification.

Not until this unity had been in some degree achieved could the Christian Music of the West reach its first culmination under St. Gregory the Great; in which a perfect fusion of Hebrew, Greek, and Roman elements formed a new embodiment of artistic expression comparable only to the culmination of Greek Sculpture in the Periclean age. Let us consider each of these elements in turn, as well as some probable lesser influences.

The Hebrew Element

THE Christians in Jerusalem undoubtedly continued attending the Temple worship until at least about 60 A.D., when, as we read in Acts xx:16, St. Paul was so anxious to be in Jerusalem with thousands of other pilgrim Jews, for the feast of Pentecost, the celebration of the giving of the Law. At the Temple worship they heard, after the *Shema'*, "Hear, O Israel," the singing of the daily Psalm, ushered in by organ music from an instrument with ten rows of pipes, the magrephah, and by ceremonial trumpet calls, and accompanied by the Temple orchestra. The liturgical Psalms were sung in three parts:[4] the trumpets were blown[5] and the people prostrated themselves after each part. With this gorgeous and elaborate ceremony Christian psalmody has little relationship, nor have we any indication as to the nature of the music used. But one thing should be known. The congregation repeated the first verse of the psalm as a refrain after each verse was chanted; and on festivals when the *Hallel* Psalms were sung, they interpolated Hallelujah after each clause, according to the *Mishnah,* or book of traditions compiled by Rabbi Jehuda at the close of the second century. Thus the important principle of the congregational refrain, too much neglected in our day, is a heritage from the Temple worship. It is most improbable that any of the Temple psalm melodies have come down to us, or that they resembled either the tones of the Ambrosian or of the Gregorian Chant. Indeed, we may be reasonably certain that Folksong, a wholly different type of music, was characteristically used in the Temple psalmody. In Isaiah lxv:8 we have such an ancient song quoted, a vintage song: "When wine is found in the cluster, one saith, 'Destroy it not, for a blessing is in it.'" We find the melody of this song, *'Al-tashhîth,* "Destroy it not," prescribed in the titles of Psalms 57, 58, 59, and 75.

But when we come to the music of the Synagogue, we are on surer historical ground, thanks to recent research along sound critical lines. There was at first a close relationship between the music of the Temple and that of the Synagogue. The Synagogue or Meeting-house doubtless had its origin during the Babylonian captivity, in the need of the exiles for a place of worship

[4] *Sukka* iv:5.　　　　　　　　　　[5] *Tamid* vii:3.

and instruction. Its antiquity is cited by St. James at the Council of Jerusalem, Acts 20:21: "Moses of old time hath in every city them that preach him, being read in the synagogues every sabbath day." Synagogues were the scenes of our Lord's worship and preaching, and of much of St. Paul's Christian proclamation to the Jews of Asia Minor. Before the destruction of the Temple, A.D. 70, there were over four hundred synagogues in Jerusalem. The *Mishnah* mentions one of them as being in the precincts of the Temple itself.[6] Rabbi Joshua ben Hananiah, who had been a member of the Temple Levitical Choir, told, toward the close of the first century, 'how the Choristers went in a body from the orchestra by the Altar of the Temple to the Synagogue and so participated in both services,'[7] which would indicate that the system of singing in the Temple was adopted (without instruments) as Synagogue music.

Now the structure of the ancient Synagogue Liturgy is well known through modern research: with its Scripture readings, or cantillations, from the Pentateuch and from the Prophets; with its great Credo, the *Shema'* (Hear, O Israel, the Lord our God is one Lord), framed in Benedictions; with its Prayers, including the *Kedûshah* or *Sanctus;* and with its special Psalms for each day of the week, besides proper Psalms for various feasts. Much of the detailed proof and of the presumptive evidence is set forth in W. O. E. Oesterley's volume, *The Jewish Background of the Christian Liturgy.* Doctor Oesterley has also written of "The Music of the Hebrews" in the *Oxford History of Music.* This essay was prior to the monumental and search-

---

[6]*Yomah* vii:1; *Sotah* vii:7, 8. Otherwise interpreted by Edersheim.
[7]Babylonian Talmud, tractates *'Arakhin* 11b and *Sukka* 53a. See also F. L. Cohen in the *Jewish Encyclopædia* IX:120a.

ing investigations of original sources by A. Z. Idelsohn, Lazare Saminsky, and other recent musicologists. Its admirable learning in certain fields is, quite unblameably, not paralleled in others, in which his argument has been vitiated by a presumption unrelated to the facts now known. He regards "the music of the Arabs as our most important source of information" as to the ancient music of the Hebrews. Now Saminsky points out[8] that "during the Middle Ages the cultural life of the Jews and the Arabs of Spain and the near East intermingled so utterly that both poetic and musical forms of the Jewish people underwent a sharp process of orientalization. The Arabic *Hedjaz* or Hebrew *A'avo rabo* mode has become the popular scale of the Oriental highway, and has . . . contaminated the Jewish religious melody." As our earliest Hebrew melodies in manuscript date only from the twelfth century, it is absolutely essential for our estimate of Synagogue music in its relationship to early Christian music, that we should have earlier and pre-Arabian sources. These are to be found in the living tradition of the Georgian, Persian, and Yemenite Jews, and of the Babylonian Jews as handed down in Iraq. Obviously, Jewish orthodoxy, and therefore Hebrew tradition, tended to be better preserved among the Jews of the strong Babylonian settlement with its Semitic speech than among the Greek speaking Alexandrian Jews. And the Jews of Babylonia, far from the wrath of Rome, developed a high degree of political security in the Parthian Empire. Their head, the titular 'Prince of the Captivity,' had secular authority. Strong traditional Rabbinical Schools grew up there: and there was developed the immensely important Babylonian Talmud. In this early collection of tractates, Rabbi Jo-

[8]*Music of the Ghetto and the Bible*, 1934.

hanan condemns those "who read the Scriptures without sweetness, and learn them without the Chant."[9]

In another tractate (*Berachot* 62a), the martyr Rabbi Akiba, who saw and described the worship of the Temple before its destruction in 70 A.D., tells about a significant feature of the ancient Biblical cantillation, which relates it at once to early Christian usage. He says, "The hand is used for leading and showing the meaning of the text." Cheironomy,[10] closely related to both the music and text of Scripture passages sung in Divine Service, is a very ancient heritage. We shall see, in a later chapter, its immediate relationship to the structure and performance of early Christian Chants.

The Babylonian and Persian groups of Jews were kept quite remote from European Hebrew groups. At present, very primitive Persian Synagogues are found in Trans-Caucasia, as well as the more numerous Georgian Synagogues in the neighbourhood of Tiflis and Kutais. Such groups all came from the northern part of the ancient Median kingdom along the Caspian Sea, the earliest arriving before the Christian era. Now these oriental Jews, as far as their domestic and secular music is concerned, show the common characteristics of their Christian or Mohammedan neighbours. But in their religious song, the cantillation of the Bible, and the various liturgical units of Synagogal worship, they are utterly uninfluenced by their age-long proximity to differing systems. This typically Oriental branch of Israel knows of *no* sacred song built on the favourite Oriental scale,[11] the so-called *Hedjaz* mode; which points to a high antiquity in their chant.

[9]*Megilla,* English transl., M. Rodkinson.
[10]See page 56.   [11]Saminsky, *Op. cit.*

Such a conclusion is vastly reinforced by the remarkable relationship of the Trans-Caucasian music to that of the Yemenite Jews. This group has been until recently the most detached, and probably the most persecuted part of the *Diaspora*. They settled in Arabia Felix, the modern Yemen, soon after the destruction of Jerusalem, safe from Roman persecution. Both Eusebius and St. Jerome mention a probable visit of St. Bartholomew to the region, with the Gospel of St. Matthew. At any rate, Christianity obtained a precarious hold there. It was practically stamped out by massacre in the year 523 A.D. under Yusuf Dhu Nuwas, a Jew, but a vassal of Abyssinia. Elesbaan, King of Abyssinia, invaded Yemen and revenged the martyrs by a terrible slaughter of the Jews: after which time, they remained in complete isolation and under frequent persecution, until the British occupation of Arabia during the World War. They are now settling more and more in Palestine, and there are Yemenite Synagogues in Jerusalem itself. Their music has been extensively recorded by A. Z. Idelsohn.[12] An examination of much of the Bible music of this group, completely isolated from the Babylonian Jews since the fall of Jerusalem, and consequently from the Persian and Georgian group, reveals an astonishing similarity of method, of mode, and of melody: we can only conclude that we possess, through both groups, a true contact with Hebrew sacred music of the early Christian period.

Christian Plainsong derived from Jewish Bible song many enduring features. They may be stated as follows:

I The basic principle of monotonic recitation with cadences, or chanting.

---

[12]A. Z. Idelsohn, *Thesaurus of Oriental Hebrew Melodies, 1923.*

II The principle of inflected monotone, corresponding accurately to the various rhetorical pauses of prose: such as we have in the ancient tones of Lessons, Gospels, and Epistles.

III Congregational refrains in the singing of the Psalms: the precursors of the Antiphon and of the Respond.

IV Elaborate festal jubilations of many notes at the end of some phrases, or passages, like the brilliant melodic exfoliations on the vowel 'a' in the Alleluia Responds of the Mass.

V The principle of the indivisible note unit; which indeed may be ornamented by a shake or a grace note, but which is the equivalent in time of a syllable: hence, that most characteristic quality of Christian Chant, prose rhythm in music.

VI A certain number of definite melodies, some of which I shall quote in subsequent chapters.

VII A musical style of noble and grave dignity, sharply distinguished from secular or domestic song; a fit vehicle for the utterance of inspired liturgical worship.

The Greek Element

WE now turn to consider the contributions of Greek music toward the early Christian song. They were twofold, direct and indirect. In the Græco-Roman world in which Christianity developed, it is evident that the Greek language was pre-eminently the language of culture. The vast empire of Alexander the Great had begun a Hellenizing of both East and West, which continued for centuries. Not only was Judaism profoundly affected by this change, which necessitated the Greek version of the ancient Scriptures, the Septuagint: but Christianity itself, under the providence of God, became a world religion through its contact with Hellenism. After the destruction of Jerusalem, Syria, Asia Minor, Greece, Italy, and Egypt became the burgeoning roots of its growth. For three hundred years Greek was the language of the youthful Church, even in Rome. Not till the middle of the third century did the use of Greek begin to die out in Italy, in Gaul, and in Africa. But long before that time, the bi-lingual Tertullian, in Africa, had amazed the educated world with his Latin tractates.

Now the classic Greek mind, which had perfected so marvellous and subtle a vehicle of thought as the Greek tongue, was also the first national mind to apply itself to the problems of music. For the first time in the history of mankind, the various tones which he can utter in song or produce from instruments were subjected to scientific analysis of the keenest kind. Varying modes were named: and varying scales within those modes. The names, Lydian, Phrygian, Æolian, Dorian, and Iastian or Ionian, plainly indicate an origin in Asia Minor. The relation of Greek music to Gregorian has been confused by the unscientific adoption of some of these names for the scales of Plainchant. But there is no question that the general diatonic scale system, out of which the Gregorian modes were eventually formed, is Greek. Christianity rejected the chromatic and enharmonic modes of the Greeks, which contained microtonal intervals, smaller than the semitone.

The Greeks also invented a precise interval notation, using the letters of their alphabet to express the seventy possible notes of their system. One set of alphabetic signs was used for voices, another for instruments. We are thus able to decipher with approximate accuracy the very meagre remains of actual Greek music. These consist of three hymns carved in stone, three man-

uscripts on parchment, and a few fragments on papyrus. One of
the songs[13] cut in stone is from a memorial column erected by a
man named Seikelos at Tralles in Asia Minor. The music bears
a close resemblance to that of the Antiphon *Hosanna filio David*
for Palm Sunday. It is probably of the first century A.D.

One of the Oxyrhynchus papyri[14] contains parts of a Christian hymn, ending with a Doxology, πατέρα χ᾽ υἱὸν χ᾽ἅγιου πνεῦμα,
Father, Son, and Holy Spirit. The music is in pure Greek
modality, with the characteristic microtonal intervals of the
enharmonic scale, which never entered Christian music in the
West.

It is to be noted, moreover, that both Greek music and Roman
music of the first three centuries were metrical, not rhythmical.
The definition of Remigius of Auxerre (ninth century) shows
the distinction. "Metre is melody in mathematical measure:
while rhythm is melody without mathematical measure, deter-
mined by the number of syllables."

Thus the *direct* influence of Greek music was slight; it supplied the diatonic scale; a form of alphabetic notation which
was demonstrably used in the West; and a few probable melodies.

The *indirect* influence was momentous: for the vast Jewish
contribution passed through the Greek language, through the
Greek mind, and could not possibly have failed to be modified
by Greek music as well. This is definitely asserted by Josephus[15]
and by Clement of Alexandria.[16] It is unquestionable that

---

[13]*Musici Scriptores Græci*, p. 450 ff. See phonograph record, Parlophon
B 37022–1.
[14]Part 15, No. 1786. Before 300 A.D.
[15]*Antiquities* xv:8.   [16]*Pædagogus* ii:4.

Greece first made music an art resting on a secure basis of accurate thought; and the debt of Christian music to Greek, often minimized, is therefore very great.

Minor Miscellaneous Elements

BEFORE coming to the great fusing element which gave final form to the Church Music of the West, popular Latin speech, we should perhaps consider for a moment some minor subsidiary influences.

It is increasingly evident that the vast Psalm literature of ancient Babylonia uncovered by archæological discovery must have profoundly influenced Hebrew Psalmody from the exile on; although scholars today regard an increasing number of the Jewish Psalms as Pre-exilic. But similar literary form and similar ethical content appear in the Babylonian writings. The acrostic form, so common in the Hebrew Psalms, is characteristic of the Babylonian. Many of them are penitential in character, and of touching sincerity. Is it not probable that Babylonian melodies became incorporated in the Psalmodic Liturgies of the Second Temple, and somewhat influenced the musical heritage of Eastern Christianity?

Again, Aramaic, the common speech of our Lord's time, had its characteristic song forms; some of them have left traces in New Testament passages, such as the *Nunc dimittis* and the song quoted in Ephesians v:14, "Awake thou that sleepest, and arise from the dead, and Christ shall give thee light." The music of such songs would obviously become part of the Jewish musical treasure which contributed to Christian song.

One more brief note. Did the Church of Alexandria, whose

great Bishop St. Athanasius gave certain directions as to Church music, receive any part of an Egyptian musical tradition? At any rate, Newlandsmith's long research into the very ancient music of the Coptic Church[17] has convinced him that such is the case, and has revealed at least one melody whose themes are again and again used in Gregorian antiphons.

The Latin Element

THE sovereign catalyst which blended into homogeneity the various elements of primitive Christian song was the Latin tongue as it developed from the close of the third century to that of the sixth. The majestic language of Cicero and Cæsar, of Horace and Virgil, had carried on, in another medium, the tradition of Greek culture. But later, classical Latin became more and more an artificial vehicle of preciosity within a limited group of literary men; and a younger and more flexible Latin became the speech of the people. Both in Greek and in Latin, the old learned conception of quantity was gradually superseded by the new convenience of accent. Practical Latin ceased to be metrical, and became rhythmical. St. Augustine, the great Doctor of the West, stood at the parting of the ways. In his unfinished work *De Musica,* he defines the Iambic foot used by St. Ambrose as consisting "of a short and a long, three beats." Yet St. Augustine himself wrote his abecedarian *Psalm against the Donatists* in the rhythmical style, depending solely on accent and devoid of quantity. This was to become a characteristic feature of Christian poetry.

Latin prose made the same change. In this new Latin were

[17]Ernest Newlandsmith, *The Ancient Music of the Coptic Church.*

made the first translations of the Bible; including the old *Itala* version, which was to supply the vast majority of texts for the Gregorian music. A translation based on the Greek Septuagint and using the rhythms of popular speech helped to make a transformed Latin. "The mystical fervour of the prophets, the melancholy of the penitential Psalms or of the Lamentations, could not be rendered in Latin without giving that severe and logical language a strange flexibility, an emotional and symbolical quality which had been foreign to its nature."[18] In this marvellously expressive and musical tongue were composed the non-biblical elements of the Liturgy as well.

Two characteristics of the new rhythmic prose had a profound formative influence on all music to which it might be sung. They were the tonic accent, and the *cursus*.

We are familiar with the tonic accent in English. Every English word, however polysyllabic, has one primary accent. As an accented syllable naturally tends to a higher pitch, the tonic accent gives a word a melodic tendency. It was thus in Latin. And words combined in phrases, and phrases combined in sentences, give increased rhetorical emphasis to important accents; so that well-spoken prose is in itself melogenic. Analysis of the Christian music of Rome at the opening of the seventh century shows that this formative principle has everywhere governed the relation between melody and sentence.

The *cursus* was a system, not named till much later, which regulated the word rhythms at the close of sentences. It appears in metrical form in much classical Latin. But from the fourth century to the seventh, it is enormously prevalent in liturgical Latin, in its rhythmical form. Its effect was to make a har-

[18] F. J. E. Raby, *Christian Latin Poetry.*

monious close by the use of a longer rhythmical foot before the last. There were four chief formulas. They were as follows, the upright stroke marking the beginning of the *cursus*.

Cursus Planus of 5 syllables:

cle|*ménter exáudi*
tibi | *sóli peccávi*
sine | *fíne dicéntes*

or in English

take | cóunsel togéther
a|gaínst his Anóinted
to | áll his Apóstles

Cursus Tardus of 6 syllables:

| *cárnis appáruit*
| *méntis et córporis*
instau|*ráre dignátus es*

or in English

with |Ángels and Árchangels
be|cáuse of thine énemies
the | beáuty of hóliness

Cursus Velox of 7 syllables:

|*prǽmia prǽstitísti*
|*sánguine dedicásti*

or in English

his most | glórious Resurréction
from gener|átion to generátion

[25]

Trispondiac *Cursus* of 6 syllables:

a|*móre roborémur*
|*dúce revelásti*

or in English

|práising thee and sáying
|présence with thanksgíving

It is evident from systematic examination of the music that some two hundred musical cadences commonly used, not only in the pure Gregorian music, but also in the Milanese or Ambrosian, and in the Spanish or Mozarabic, are definitely based on the literary *cursus;* higher notes being invariably assigned to the accented syllables of the formula. These cadences range from the greatest simplicity, with one note only for a syllable, to a high elaboration in which each syllable is sung to a melodic group.

Time does not permit the citation of other illustrations of the close nexus between the melodies of the Gregorian age and the liturgical Latin which came to its perfection at that period, but soon after deteriorated. It must suffice for the present to say that at the beginning of the seventh century A.D., the Church at Rome possessed a vast body of music completely homogeneous; ideally wedded to the basic liturgical texts which were to continue in Western Europe; of thrilling beauty as an expression of pure worship; and embodying certain principles which have proved to be perennially valid. To these principles, as to standards, contemporary Church music needs from time to time to be compared: and rectified when it departs from them.

North Italy, Spain, and Gaul had also their local develop-

ments parallel in kind, but not in perfection. Later ch
refer to them; and the growth of various types of
music will be examined in some detail.

But now at the close of this necessarily elaborate introduction, let us enumerate the main enduring principles of liturgical
worship music embodied in the Gregorian repertory of the
year 600 A.D.

PRINCIPLES DEDUCED

I THE music, whether solo or choral, was sung to the glory
and praise of God, and not to man; except in those parts of the
Liturgy where Bishop and Congregation carried on a lofty dialogue, as at the *Sursum corda*.

II The music was an integral part of each service, not a
decorative addition. The sung worship was not individualistic
prayer, but the voice of the whole Church. In it, the expression
of personal devotion was taken up into the ordered prayer of
the mystical Body of Christ.

III Due provision was made for each member of the Body
to join in the active praise of the whole in accordance with his
own degree of musical skill. The dialogue between Bishop and
Congregation clothed the essential framework of the Liturgy
in simple recitation and cadence. Scripture lessons were read
by the clergy in melodic formulas whose cadences brought out
natural accents and pauses. The Congregation was supplied
with refrains and with simple melodies suited to their vocal
ability. For the Choir, there were more elaborate compositions,
in some of which skilled solo Cantors found opportunity to
exercise their best powers in God's praise.

IV In the music, no slightest change was made in the liturgical words for musical reasons. The music was subordinate to the text. No phrase or word might be repeated unless the Liturgy itself called for the repetition for devotional reasons, as in the Greek response *Kyrie eleison,* whose older form was altered by St. Gregory himself to include *Christe eleison.*

V Prose texts were set to prose rhythms, either through chanting, that is, monotonic recitation with cadences; or through melodies following the natural vocal curve of prose sentences, and keeping their free unbarred form.

VI The musical style was purely religious, and unrelated to that of secular music.

VII The first music so completely synthesized and ordered was that of the Holy Eucharist, in the Gregorian *Antiphonale Missarum.* Then, as now and ever, the very center of Catholic worship was that great Sacrament in which the one Sacrifice of Calvary is offered and pleaded before the Father for all our needs; and in which Christ-given life is sustained in the members by their feeding on the offered Sacrifice, the sacramental Body and Blood of God Incarnate.

VIII The music of the subsidiary Offices, preparatory to and reminiscent of the Eucharist, although not fully completed in St. Gregory's time, was worked out along similar lines: and its more important portions are undoubtedly part of the original treasure.

This corpus of the strictly Gregorian music at the beginning of the seventh century is the most complete artistic treasure bequeathed to us by antiquity. It is not an "undeveloped and rudimentary form of musical art," although barbaric distortions of it occasionally heard might lead one to think so. It is the world's primary treasure of wholly artistic melody. In its æsthetic importance, it is only comparable to the monumental sculpture of the age of Pericles. That marvellous flowering of serene beauty five centuries before Christ was made to give men a vision of the god-like, imperfectly apprehended through a mythology already obsolescent; yet its shattered remnants can still raise men's hearts to things divine. But the perfect, the unmarred choral song of the seventh century after Christ uplifts the mind into a perennially vital expression of worship directed to the one true God, as revealed through his eternal Son in words inspired by the Holy Spirit.

CHAPTER II

THE MUSIC OF THE EUCHARIST
BEFORE POLYPHONY

THE GREGORIAN "ANTIPHONALE MISSARUM"

IN the previous chapter, we saw that a blending of Hebrew, Greek, and other musical elements passed through the unifying influence of the Latin tongue just at the period when the great change was being made from learned classical metre to popular accentuated rhythm; and that by the beginning of the seventh century, the Church possessed in the Gregorian *Antiphonale Missarum* a full collection of music for the Holy Eucharist which is the most complete treasure of antiquity bequeathed to us by any art.

Out of the cruder and less organized music of earlier days had been produced a body of song, homogeneous, coherent, logically designed, of marvellous correspondence with the Latin liturgical text, and of noble and thrilling beauty. The bald and abrupt simplicity of some earlier choral forms had become models of dignified euphony and cunningly balanced proportion. The long, confused, ornate solo melodies of the Milanese type, without much form and often musically void, had taken on structure, justly distributed accent, stirring climax. Due and

[30]

proper provision had been made in this body of music for every individual or group of individuals participating in the common worship: for the Bishop at the altar, and other clergy assisting him; for skilled solo singers; for the Choir of ecclesiastics in general; and for the Congregation of the faithful, men, women, and children. Liturgy and music, so reformed and unified, stood as a complete model and standard for the worship of the Church. Its principles are as valid today as they were in the year 604 A.D. when St. Gregory died. Its actual melodies are heard today throughout the habitable earth, instead of only in the basilicas of pontifical Rome.

In a striking essay recently published[1] by Mr. Artur Schnabel, the eminent pianist, he speaks of Europe beginning "to erect a new art edifice from the shambles of a collapsing civilization," an edifice based on "an idealistic faith in an esoteric glory, an indestructible power that is identical with humility, a power within the grasp of every one, if only he be guided by love, kindliness, abstinence, and the willingness to suffer." "The elevation of music took place in that small part of Europe which owes the colorful variety of its creations . . . to the cross-breeding of Paganism, Hellenism, and Christianity. Here music was raised from a means of private pleasure, from a secondary, servile, merely ornamental rôle . . . to sovereignty. It proceeded from a recognized spiritual necessity." Such was the music of the *Antiphonale Missarum.*

What was contained in this great collection?

Primarily, portions of the Psalms, in the old *Itala* version, the predecessor of St. Jerome's Vulgate, with music for solo voices, choir, and congregation. The element of elaborate

[1] Artur Schnabel, *Musical Reflections,* 1934.

Psalmody was predominant. Psalms, with or without refrains, were sung before the Eucharist began, between the various Lessons from the Old and New Testaments, at the Offertory, and at the Communion. The Psalms with their refrains varied with the Seasons and Feasts of the Liturgical Year. But the music to which these liturgical Psalms were sung in the Eucharist was invariably more elaborate than the simple chants which had been in use for a long period in the subsidiary Offices. This was a matter of principle, evidently. At the Eucharist, it was deemed fitting that the Choir should sing music of the greatness richness and perfection: while that of the Celebrant and Congregation was at this time simple to the extreme. We will take up the various types of Psalmody in the order of their occurrence in the Liturgy.

MUSIC OF THE CHOIR

The Introit

THE earliest records of the Western Church indicate that the Mass was preceded by a processional Psalm. Apparently at first it was sung as a solo with a choir refrain after each verse, the form taken from Jewish tradition, and known as *Cantus Responsorius*. But according to the *Liber Pontificalis*,[2] Pope Celestine I, who died A.D. 432, "ordered that the Psalms of David be sung *antiphonally* by all before the Sacrifice, which was not done before." This was the *Cantus Antiphonus,* a method of alternate singing between two Choirs, which had been introduced in Rome by Damasus I and in Milan by St. Ambrose toward the close of the previous century. Curiously enough, this alternate mode of singing the Psalms gave the name "Antiphon"

[2]A series of biographical notices of the Popes, not too dependable for the early period.

to the refrain which was sung by all before and after the Psalm, and in earlier times between verses. *Ordo Romanus I,* a document of about St. Gregory's time, tells us that after the lighting of the candles, the Choir enters and stands before the altar on either side, and the leader begins the *Antiphona ad Introitum,* the Antiphon for the Entrance of the Celebrant with his Ministers. At this time the Psalm was continued only till the Celebrant signaled that his preparation was over: when *Gloria Patri* was sung, and the Antiphon repeated. The *Antiphonale Missarum* contained 150 Introits. They are rich and expressive, but not elaborate.

Illustrative Records:

Victrola Album M 87, Solesmes Abbey Choir:
   7348 A, *Spiritus Domini,* Whitsunday.
   7348 B, *Da pacem,* 8th Sunday after Pentecost.
   7342 A, *Requiem æternam.*
Victrola Album M 177, Pius X Choir.
   11529 A, *Requiem æternam.*
Semen, Phonedibel Choir:
   S. N. 1004, *Puer natus est,* Christmas.
Christschall, Choir of White Fathers, Treves:
   *60, *Ad te levavi,* 1st Sunday in Advent.
      Gaudens gaudebo, Conception B. V. M.
Christschall, Choir of Maria Laach Abbey:
   13, *Ecce advenit,* Epiphany.
   20, *Resurrexi,* Easter.
Christschall, Missionary Congregation of Steyl:
   132, *Gaudeamus,* All Saints Day.
Electrola, Choir of Beuron Abbey:
   EH 456, *Exsurge,* Sexagesima.
Columbia DFX 156, Choir of Notre Dame d'Auteuil.
   Spiritus Domini.
                  In Introit form.
His Master's Voice C 2087, *Asperges me,* Ampleforth Abbey Choir.
Victor, 25820 A, *Asperges me,* Children's Choir.

The Gradual Respond

THE reading of Scripture Lessons followed by Psalms was a universal heritage of the Church from the Service of the Synagogue. Prior to the fifth century, the usual number of lessons had become three: an Old Testament Lesson, an Epistle, and the Gospel. Two Psalms were then sung, one before the Epistle, one before the Gospel. After that time, the Old Testament Lesson was ordinarily omitted, and both Psalms sung before the Gospel, in shortened form. They were sung by a soloist in *Cantus Responsorius,* with a refrain for the people. We read in the "Apostolic Constitutions," "The readings by the lectors being finished, let another one sing the hymns of David, and the people sing the last words after him." Later on, these refrains became highly elaborate, and only the skilfullest singers could join in them. The soloists stood on the step, *gradus,* of the *ambo* or pulpit whence the Lesson was to be read; and thus the name "Gradual" was later applied to the composition. There were 110 Gradual Responds in the Gregorian collection.

Illustrative Records:

Gramophone Shop Album 132, Dortmund Choir:
Polydor 90057, *Christus factus est,* Maundy Thursday.
Victrola Album M 87, Solesmes Abbey Choir:
7343 A, *Christus factus est,* Maundy Thursday.
7343 B, *Qui sedes,* 3d Sunday in Advent.
Dirigatur oratio mea, 19th Sunday after Pentecost.
Montserrat Album, Montserrat Abbey Choir:
Disco Gramofono AE 3347, *Convertere,* Ember Saturday in Lent.
Victrola Album M 177, Pius X Choir:
11529 B, *Requiem æternam,* Mass for the Dead.
Semen, Phonedibel Choir:
S. N. 1004, *Viderunt omnes,* Christmas.

Semen Album I, Maredsous Abbey Choir:
S. M. V, *Constitues eos,* Sts. Peter and Paul.
Christschall, Missionary Congregation of Steyl:
132, *Timete Dominum,* All Saints Day.
Christschall, Maria Laach Abbey Choir:
15, *Propter veritatem,* Assumption, B. V. M.
2000-Jahre Musik, Curt Sachs:
Parlophon B 37023-1, *Misit Dominus verbum suum,* 2d Sunday
after Epiphany.
[The last records a horrible example of how *not* to sing plainsong; by the *Gregorianische Arbeitsgemeinschaft der Staat-
liche Akademie für Kirchen und Schulmusik zu Berlin!*]

With the hundred Alleluia Responds of which I shall now
speak, they formed the very climax of the musical art of antiquity. Such masterpieces as the Graduals *Christus factus est,
Constitues eos,* and the Alleluia Responds *Justus germinabit* and
Assumpta est are in the very forefront of inspired melody for
all time.

The Alleluia Respond

THIS joyous form of the *Cantus Responsorius* is a definite
heritage from the *Hallel* Psalms of the Synagogue. The Respond is on the word Alleluia. It was sung by the soloist, repeated by the Choir, and extended by a long Jubilus on the final
vowel "a"; another Hebrew inheritance. St. Gregory himself
added the Verse, not always taken from the Psalms or even
from the Bible, to the Alleluia. It was sung by the soloist. The
close of the Verse took up the Alleluia melody, after which all
repeated the Respond, Alleluia, with its Jubilus.

Illustrative Records:

Gramophone Shop Album 132:
Polydor 90056, *Alleluia: Assumpta est,* Assumption B. V. M.,
Dortmund Choir.

Polydor 22197, *Alleluia: Adorabo,* Dedication Festival.
Polydor 22197, *Alleluia: Post dies octo,* Low Sunday, Paderborn
  Cathedral Boys.
Victrola Album M 187, I, II, Solesmes Abbey Choir:
  7344 A, *Alleluia: Justus germinabit,* for Doctors.
  7350 B, *Alleluia: Ascendit Deus,* Ascension.
    Alleluia: Assumpta est, Assumption B. V. M.
Montserrat Album, Montserrat Abbey Choir:
  Disco Gramofono AE 3302, *Alleluia: Veni Sancte Spiritus,* Pen-
  tecost.
His Master's Voice, Ampleforth Abbey Choir:
  H. M. V., C 2088, *Alleluia: Veni Sancte Spiritus,* Pentecost.
Columbia DF 102, *Alleluia: Pascha nostrum,* Easter. Paris Schola
  Cantorum.
Semen Album I, Maredsous Abbey Choir:
  S. M. III, *Alleluia: Dies sanctificatus,* Christmas.

In the Christian East, the use of Alleluia was not restricted
to joyous seasons such as Eastertide, nor was it at first so restricted in Rome.[3] Damasus introduced it into the Sunday
Mass, following the custom of Jerusalem. But before St. Gregory's time, Alleluia was omitted in Penitential seasons, and in
its place was sung an older form of elaborate Psalmody, the
Tract.

The Tract

THE *Psalmus Tractus* was sung straight through by the soloist; to use the Latin expression, *"tractim."* This was the oldest
method of solo Psalmody at the Mass, and was from the first,
before the adoption of the jubilant Alleluia Respond, the characteristic way of singing the second of the Psalms between
Lessons. There were twenty-three Tracts in the Gregorian collection.

[3]Atchley, *Ordo Romanus* I: 78–79.

Illustrative Records:

Victrola Album M 87 I, Solesmes Abbey Choir:
7342 A, *Absolve Domine,* Mass for the Dead.
Victrola Album M 177, Pius X Choir:
11529 B, *Absolve Domine,* Mass for the Dead.

The Offertory

DURING the offering of the Oblation of the bread and wine which were to be consecrated, there was sung a solo Psalm with a Responsorial refrain; the Offertory. Its length was originally regulated by the amount of time occupied by the Deacons in gathering and presenting the Oblations. Later, the whole piece was shortened, the refrain grew more elaborate, and became a solo Chant: and finally, the Psalm was omitted. There were 102 Gregorian Offertories.

Illustrative Records:

Gramophone Shop Album 132, Solo:
Polydor 90056, *Ave Maria,* Conception B. V. M.
Victrola Album M 87 I, II, Solesmes Abbey Choir:
7342 B, *Domine Jesu Christe,* Mass for the Dead.
7345 A, *Ad te levavi,* Advent Sunday.
7345 A, *Meditabor,* 2d Sunday in Lent.
7345 B, *Custodi me,* Tuesday in Holy Week.
7349 A, *Precatus est Moyses,* 12th Sunday after Pentecost.
7349 B, *Jubilate Deo,* 2d Sunday after Epiphany.
Victrola Album M 177, Pius X Choir:
11530 B, *Domine Jesu Christe,* Mass for the Dead.
Christschall, Abbey Choir, Maria Laach:
13, *Reges Tharsis,* Epiphany.

The Communion

THIS was an Antiphonal Chant, sung during the Communion of the faithful, and again regulated in length by the time consumed in that action. It was similar in form to the Introit, and the number of these melodies was the same, 150.

Illustrative Records:
Victrola Album M 87, I, II, Solesmes Abbey Choir:
7343 A, *Hoc corpus,* Passion Sunday.
7344 B, *Memento verbi tui,* 20th Sunday after Pentecost.
7344 B, *Quinque prudentes,* For a Virgin.
7344 B, *Pascha nostrum,* Easter.
7348 A, *Spiritus Sanctus docebit,* Whitsun Monday.
7348 A, *Spiritus qui a Patre,* Whitsun Tuesday.
Victor V 6199 A, Beuron Abbey Choir:
Lux æterna, Mass for the Dead.
Victrola Album M 177, Pius X Choir:
11531 B, *Lux æterna,* Mass for the Dead.
Columbia DF 102, Paris Schola Cantorum:
Passer invenit sibi domum, 3d Sunday in Lent.

Psalm 34 was used in Jerusalem early in the fourth century. The ancient Roman Psalm was the twenty-third. The Communion Psalm was commonly sung in Africa in St. Augustine's time. Centuries later, the Psalm verses were dropped from the Communion, although one Psalm verse and *Gloria Patri* were retained in the Introit. The Communion Antiphons and Introit Antiphons well repay the musician's close study; together with the Alleluias, they represent melody composed throughout, with no element of recitation, and they are picturesquely expressive. The other chants, even the most elaborate, are Psalmody, based upon the combination of Intonation, Reciting Note or Dominant, and Cadence, quite as much as the simpler Psalm Tones of the Office, with which we are familiar.

These 645 melodies form the musical deposit of the Gregorian *Antiphonale Missarum.* It will be noticed that they are *all* music for the Choir; and for a skilled choir of well-trained singers, including soloists capable of artistic flexibility and sustained smoothness in the long, flowing phrases of the Graduals, Alleluias, and Tracts. Again it is to be noticed that these elaborate compositions were performed at points in the service where no *action* was being performed; unlike the Introits, Offertories, and Communions, whose length was regulated by the time consumed in the Celebrant's Preparation, in the gathering of the Oblations, and in the Communion of the People.

And now let us turn for a moment to the present. Due provision is made in the Communion Service of the Episcopal Church for all of the Choir devotions of the Gregorian Mass. Hymns, or Anthems, in the words of Holy Scripture or of the Book of Common Prayer, may now be lawfully sung before the Service (the Introit), after the Epistle (the Gradual, Alleluia, or Tract), at the Offertory, and at the Communion. May we not well consider whether the point of most elaborate musical praise should not be now, as then, between the Epistle and the Gospel: and whether the character of the Offertory as an offering of the Oblations to God, and not a mere collection of money, should not be kept in the nature of what is then sung? And there is no reason why the ancient scriptural Propers should not be fully restored to use, where Choirs are adequate to sing them.

MUSIC OF THE CELEBRANT, ASSISTANTS, AND CONGREGATION

At this point we note that in leaving the music of the Choir, we leave all elaborate music. The framework of the Eucharistic Service was a Dialogue between Celebrant and Congregation, marked by grave dignity and utter simplicity.

Two portions of this Dialogue are of supreme importance:

[39]

the Preface, with the *Sursum corda,* and the *Pater noster,* also
with its introductory phrases.

Sursum corda and the Preface

THE *Sursum corda* is very ancient. It occurs in the earliest
sources, such as the Canons of Hippolytus (A.D. 220–230), and
in writings of St. Cyprian in the middle of the third century.[4]
There is every reason to believe that the traditional chant of all
these dialogues, in its simpler forms, long antedates St. Gregory;
and that by his time, the richer festal forms had been developed.
It is of the *Sursum corda,* so developed, that Mozart spoke in
deep admiration, preferring it to any melody he had ever composed.

The Preface, which follows the *Sursum corda,*[5] was far more
widely used in pre-Gregorian times than in later ages. The so-
called Leonine Sacramentary, representing a pure Roman use
with no Gallican element, is dated by Msgr. Duchesne[6] in the
middle of the sixth century. It contained no less than 267 Prefaces. They are of the later type, in which the element of thanksgiving for God's many benefits, so characteristic of Eastern rites,
and suggested in the Epistle of St. Clement, the fourth Bishop
of Rome, is very much shortened; although the universal mention of angels remains, as at the present time. In Gregorian
times the number of Prefaces was greatly reduced. But it is here
particularly that the musical influence of the literary *cursus* is
shown. All of the cadences of the ancient chant are directly

[4]*De Orat.,* 31.
[5]See *The Choral Service,* pp. xviii, 26–33. This is the official manual set forth by
the Joint Commission on Church Music under Authority of General Convention.
It is to be had of The H. W. Gray Company, 159 East 48th Street, New York.
[6]*Origines de Culte Chrétien,* 129–137.

based upon it; and the result is a gracious flow, a perfect correspondence between words and music, which makes the Latin
Preface a model of simple but eloquent song. The butchery of
these noble phrases by modern Clergy, both Roman and Anglican, is one of the great abuses in worship to be ceaselessly
corrected.

Illustrative Records:

> H.M.V. C 2087, The Festal chant, Ampleforth Abbey.
> Victrola Album M 69, Pius X Choir:
>> 7181 A, The Festal chant, Rev. V. C. Donovan, O.P.
> Victrola Album M 177, Pius X Choir:
>> 11531 A, The Ferial chant.
> Columbia DB 1568, Preface of Easter Day.
> See also *The Hymnal,* No. 689.

The Pater noster

THE Lord's Prayer had formerly followed the Communion
of the People, at Rome. St. Gregory himself moved it to the
position which it now occupies in the Roman Mass, and to
which it has been restored at the last revision of the American
Book of Common Prayer. In one of his letters, he tells John of
Syracuse: "We say the Lord's Prayer immediately after the
Prayer (of Consecration). It seems to me unsuitable that we
should say the Prayer composed by some scholar over the oblation, and not say the Prayer handed down by our Redeemer
himself over his Body and Blood."

Illustrative Records:

> Columbia DB 1568, Festal *Pater noster,* Rev. M. D. Willson, O.S.B.
> Victrola Album M 69, Pius X Choir:
>> 7181 B, Festal *Pater noster,* Rev. V. C. Donovan, O.P.

Victrola Album M-177:
  11531 A, Ferial *Pater noster,* Rev. V. C. Donovan, O.P.
See also *The Choral Service,* p. 34, Festal, 57, Ferial; and *The Hymnal,*
No. 695, Festal, 696, Ferial.

The traditional music of the Lord's Prayer is unquestionably a part of our oldest musical inheritance. It is a chant which is used not only with the *Pater noster,* but also with the sung endings of certain prayers which had been said in a low tone by the Celebrant. This *Ekphonesis,* a common feature of the early Greek Liturgies, was also used in the Gregorian Mass, where it introduced both the *Sursum corda* and the *Pater noster.*[7] We find the older form of this melody occurring also in the primitive chant of the *Te Deum,* and of the earliest Latin *Gloria in excelsis.* Arthur Friedlander has discovered the practical identity of this music with that used in the Jewish Biblical cantillation of Zechariah ii:10, "Sing and rejoice, O daughter of Zion: for lo, I come, and I will dwell in the midst of thee, saith the Lord." Dom Germán Prado,[8] O.S.B., quoting this melody, with the *Te Deum* and the *Gloria in excelsis,* says, "All three belong to the musical tradition of the primitive Judæo-Christian Communities."[9]

Besides these great Dialogues between Celebrant and Congregation, there were the lesser Dialogues involved in the Prayers and in the reading of the Scripture lessons. The Congregation was never considered as other than an essential factor at the Eucharist. The expression "to hear Mass" is absolutely uncatholic. The very framework of the Eucharist is the ordered

[7] *The Choral Service,* pp. xviii, xix, 34, 56.
[8] *Mozarabic Melodics,* R. P. Germán Prado, O.S.B. Translated by Walter Muir Whitehill, Jr.
[9] See page 47.

series of invitations from the Celebrant and responses from the Congregation, which indicate that both together do the work of worship in the Lord. Hence at every new section of the Service occurred the solemn mutual greeting, *Dominus vobiscum, Et cum spirito tuo;* "The Lord be with you," "And with thy spirit." A simple monotone generally sufficed for this, except at that high point where the Congregation is bidden to enter the very worship of heaven itself, with Angels and Archangels. Here the Dominical greeting partook of the exalted solemnity of the *Sursum corda,* which it preceded.

The Scripture Lessons

THE melodic formulas to which the Epistle and Gospel, and also any other Bible readings were sung, consisted of plain recitation with cadences corresponding precisely to the various rhetorical pauses. With their use, the Scriptural words stood out in bold relief, and were heard and understood as they would seldom be without the chant. At the Gospel, the Lesson of chief importance, the preliminary dialogue consisted of the Dominical salutation, the Announcement, and the Response *Gloria tibi, Domine;* all sung to the same melodic formula.[10]

The Collects[11]

THE Collects and the Postcommunion Collects had also their formal inflections, simpler than those of the Lessons; and their Dialogue; consisting of the Dominical salutation (recently restored to the American Prayer Book) before the Collects, and

[10]*The Choral Service,* pp. xvi, 21, 55, 71.
[11]*The Choral Service,* pp. xiii, xiv, 19, 20, 49, 50.

"Amen" sung by the people after them. Above all, the people sang "Amen" at the close of the great Eucharistic prayer, the Consecration.[12]

It is this sung Dialogue between Priest and People which constitutes the Choral Service. A Eucharist in which the Congregation is silent except for a modern hymn or two; in which the Celebrant reads his part in a conversational voice, not even in monotone; and in which the Choir alone sings all Responses and Amens, besides elaborate anthems: is not a Choral Mass, but a nondescript hybrid intrinsically unworthy of the worship of God. Many Churches with good Choirs conscientiously perpetuate this maimed inartistic worship through sheer lack of knowledge, and faulty tradition.[13]

MUSIC OF THE CONGREGATION

In St. Gregory's time at Rome, this consisted of three numbers only, *Kyrie eleison, Gloria in excelsis,* and *Sanctus.* Remember that the Congregation had to some extent joined with the Psalmody of the Choir in singing certain refrains: and that it had fully participated with the Celebrant in the structural Dialogue of the rite. But in these three numbers, one purely Greek, one adapted from Greek sources, and one adapted from Hebrew sources, the people had their simple part of the music, as against the elaborate part of the skilled choir. We will consider these numbers, chiefly from the musical point of view.

Kyrie eleison

At a very early period, Christian litanies in the East had a response for the faithful, *Kyrie eleison,* Lord, have mercy. Dom

[12]St. Justin Martyr, *First Apology,* 65 A.D., 150–155.   [13]See page 51.

Suitbert Bäumer traces it to the first century. We have it fully described in the fascinating description of worship at Jerusalem in the fourth century by the pilgrim Etheria. It does not seem to have been a part of Eucharistic worship in the West until the beginning of the sixth century.[14] St. Gregory speaks of the introduction of the alternate *Christe eleison,* Christ have mercy; and says that it is sung alternately between clergy and people. It is quite clear from his words that at daily Masses, the litany petitions to which this was the people's response were omitted; and *Kyrie* alone sung. It was not till the eighth century, however, that the number of repetitions was finally settled as nine: *Kyrie* thrice, *Christe* thrice, *Kyrie* thrice. This arrangement was perpetuated in the first Prayer Book of 1549; and is set forth in the official Hymnal of the American Episcopal Church,[15] as well as in the present English Prayer Book.

Obviously, as this chant was for the people alternately with the clergy, its music had to be simple. We possess an exceedingly ancient melody,[16] of wide dispersion in slightly varied forms, which probably comes down from the early period. Note that in the *Kyrie,* we have a Greek text which has remained unaltered in the West; not only in the Roman Church, but elsewhere. The Greek *Kyrie* is found in the present English Prayer Book and in several Protestant Liturgies. It should be added to the Book of Common Prayer for permissive use: one liturgical feature of the Eucharist binding together East and West.

An artistic detail of great interest in the historic music of the Eucharist is the unifying musical recapitulation of the *Kyrie*

[14]Duchesne, *Origines*, p. 183.   [15]*The Hymnal*, No. 681.
[16]See *The Saint Dunstan Kyrial*, H. W. Gray Co., *Kyrie* 8, pp. 29, 105.

melody which began the Mass, for the *Ite, missa est* or *Benedicamus Domino,* which, with its Response *Deo gratias,* concluded it. Those who know the beauty of musical form will appreciate the devotional value of this feature. These Dismissals have been published for use with the Anglican Eucharist both in England and in America.[17]

Gloria in excelsis

THIS very early Greek hymn did not find its way into the Eastern Liturgies, but became a part of the Morning Office. Its first section, at least, was written prior to 150 A.D. A Benedictine writer[18] regards its translation into Latin as being the work of St. Athanasius. At any rate, the treatise *De virginitate,* somewhat uncertainly attributed to him, alludes to this hymn. One form of it is found in the fifth century *Codex Alexandrinus,* with other Canticles and with Psalms. But about the beginning of the sixth century, Pope Symmachus ordered its use on Sundays and on the Feasts of Martyrs. By this time, the translation into the vernacular Latin was in use. Its position in the Liturgy, directly after the *Kyrie,* was retained in the first English Prayer Book.

As regards its early music, we are on sure ground. The very simple congregational melody which I cited as common to the Lord's Prayer, the *Ekphonesis,* and *Te Deum,* was sung also to *Gloria in excelsis.*

Observe this melody: first as set to the Lord's Prayer in the Spanish *Missale Mixtum Mozarabicum* compiled from ancient

[17]*The Ordinary of the Mass:* The Plainsong and Mediæval Music Society, London. Winfred Douglas, *The St. Dunstan Kyrial;* H. W. Gray Co., N. Y.

[18]*Stimmen aus Maria-Laach,* LXXIII, iv, 43.

sources by Cardinal Cisneros at the close of the fifteenth century.[19]

Pa-nem nos-trum co-ti-di-a-num da no-bis ho-di-e.

Next, as printed by John Merbecke in the *Book of Common Praier Noted* in 1550.

Thou-sit-test on the right hand of god, in the glo-rye of the fa-ther.

And finally, as in the earliest manuscripts of *Gloria in excelsis.*

Qui tol-lis pec-ca-ta mun-di, mi-se-re-re no-bis.

Here we have a melody preserving its identity in such diverse times and places as Italy, Spain, and England; in the tenth, fifteenth, and sixteenth centuries. The long tradition back of its appearance in each of these places (and of many others), points to a very early original.

It is probable that in *Gloria in excelsis,* as certainly in *Kyrie eleison,* the phrases were sung antiphonally between Clergy and People as component parts of the Congregation.

Sanctus

THIS great hymn, with its Scriptural antecedents in Isaiah and in the Apocalypse, and with its frequent use as the primitive *Kedúshah* of Jewish worship long before the Christian Era, is

[19]See page 42.

undoubtedly a very ancient, as it is a most important, part of Eucharistic worship. St. Clement alludes to it in the first century,[20] in such a way as to indicate it as a song for the entire congregation: "And we, . . . gathered together in one place in concord, cry to him as from one mouth." The fourth century Apostolic Constitutions mention it as sung by the people; as does St. Gregory of Tours, who died A.D. 593. We may safely conclude that the *Tersanctus* was in general a Congregational Chant, notwithstanding *Ordo Romanus I,* which directs it to be sung by the subdeacons.

We are so accustomed to the *Tersanctus* as the culmination of the *Sursum corda* and Preface that it may seem puzzling to some to hear that this was not always the case. Thus in the early *Apostolic Tradition* of St. Hippolytus, the *Sursum corda* leads directly to the Eucharistic Prayer, in the same way that it precedes the blessing of the font in our present Baptismal rite. Many liturgical scholars regard the *Sanctus* as an interpolation in the ancient and natural order of the Eucharistic Prayer. Dom Cagin[21] adduces arguments showing that this interpolation was made at Rome in the second century.

The primitive music of the *Tersanctus* is of great simplicity. It survives in the music of the Requiem; and is seen to be a normal continuation of the Preface.

Illustrative Records:

  Victrola Album M 177, Pius X Choir:
  11531 A *Sanctus,* Mass for the Dead.
  Victor 24819, B, *Sanctus* XVIII, Ferias in Advent and Lent, sung by American School Children.
  Victor 21621 A, *Sanctus,* Mass for the Dead, Palestrina Choir.

[20]I Cor. xxxiv: 6, 7.   [21]Schuster, *The Sacramentary* I, p. iii.

LATER ADDITIONS TO THE CONGREGATIONAL MUSIC

Two portions of the Congregational Ordinary of the Mass are not included in the Gregorian *corpus:* but for practical reasons, we will consider them briefly at this point. They are the *Credo* and the *Agnus Dei.*

The Nicene Creed

THE introduction of the Creed into the Liturgy was late; in the East it began in the fifth century at Antioch; in the West, the third Council of Toledo in 589 A.D. ordered its use in the Eucharist before the Lord's Prayer. The Mozarabic rite still keeps it in that position. Its use slowly spread through Gaul, Britain, and Germany. Rome did not adopt it permanently till five hundred years later.

The purpose of introducing the Creed into the Liturgy was specifically that of preserving and confirming the faith of the people, which had been endangered by a prevalent Arianism in Spain. It was obviously Congregational. For centuries, but one melody was in use; and the very wide dispersion of that melody with a minimum of local variation convinces that it is the venerable tune going back to Gregorian times; but in Spain, not Rome. It is widely in use up to the present time: and its very nature suggests that always, everywhere, the Creed should remain Congregational.

Illustrative Records:

Victor Album, Grand Séminaire, Montreal: 6-B, Credo I.
Victrola Album M 69, Pius X Choir:
 7180 B, Credo I, The most ancient melody.
See also *The Choral Service,* pp. 23–25.

Agnus Dei

THIS touching hymn, obviously derived from the central section of *Gloria in excelsis,* carries us back to the fifty-third Chapter of Isaiah, and to the reading of it by the Ethiopian eunuch of Queen Candace, when Philip the Deacon began at the passage, "Like a lamb dumb before his shearer, so he opened not his mouth," and preached unto him Jesus. We remember John the Baptist, with his great word, "Behold the Lamb of God, which taketh away the sin of the world." We recall some of the thirty references in the Apocalypse to Jesus as the Lamb of God. We cannot but be thankful that in the year 687 A.D., Pope Sergius I directed that clergy and people together should sing *Agnus Dei* at the time of the breaking of the consecrated Host. The words "Grant us thy peace" were substituted for the last "Have mercy upon us" four centuries later.

The oldest melody of *Agnus Dei,* like that of *Sanctus,* antedates the modal system, and is unquestionably primitive. It was used not only in the Mass, but in the ancient Litany as well.

Illustrative Record:
Victrola Album M 177, Pius X Choir:
11531 B, *Agnus Dei,* Mass for the Dead.

Contrast, for a moment, the musical plan we have been examining with that very frequently carried out in our Churches.[22] On the one hand, a service in which a framework of familiar and simple musical Dialogue is provided between Clergy and Congregation, into which the more important liturgical units are fitted; some with simple music for all, and some with elaborate music for a skilled Choir. On the other hand, a service in which

[22]See page 44.

the Celebrant speaks his part of the Dialogue, the Choir alone answers with more or less elaborate Responses, and sings all of the great units of liturgical worship: while the Congregation is passive and mute throughout, except for half-hearted participation in a few non-liturgical hymns. Can there be any question as to which of these two plans best achieves the high ideal of a worshipping Church?

THE ROMAN SCHOLA CANTORUM

THE unique and complete collection of ancient worship music which we have been considering did not achieve its perfection fortuitously, through blind chance: nor was it the work of a single inspired genius, St. Gregory, or any other. It was undoubtedly the work of a definitely organized musical body, the Roman *Schola Cantorum.*

This great institution, which preserved its identity and organization unbroken for almost eight hundred years, had the double aim of sustaining a group of ecclesiastical musicians capable of producing, improving, and singing the very devotional and beautiful music which we have been considering; and of supporting or aiding schools to train a continuous supply of singers to the fullness of religious understanding, the excellence of technical facility, and the completeness of repertory, which could create a standard for the whole Western Church; throughout which it disseminated the music during the following three centuries.

Its Formation

THERE is a highly probable tradition, that a Song School was founded at Rome early in the fourth century. Gerbert says:[23]

[23]*De Cantu et Musica Sacra,* I, 36.

"Although at the time of Pope Silvester there were several large basilicas in Rome, . . . they did not possess the income necessary to support colleges for singers. So a *schola cantorum* was founded which was common to the whole city; and if a procession or feast was celebrated in a basilica, all the singers went there and performed the Office and the Mass." To grasp the full significance of this statement, one must recall certain dates and facts. Silvester was Bishop of Rome from 314 to 336 A.D. The last and most terrible persecution of the Christians began with the fourth edict of Diocletian, February 23, 303. After Diocletian's abdication two years later, Galerius and his colleagues continued his dreadful policy for six years more; and this was the climax of some two hundred years of intermittent persecution, during which the religious emotions of a constantly increasing multitude of men had been kept from all public musical expression. Repressed emotion is one of the mightiest forces in the world; tragically destructive if strained beyond human power to control; gloriously creative if liberated at the right time and place by men who have bravely developed their own power of restraint. A great collective emotion, fusing countless thousands into one throbbing life, must, if liberated at such a time, produce an artistic expression of immense significance. Such was the case with Church Music when, first under Galerius' edict of toleration, April 30, 311, and more fully two years later under the edict of Milan, Christians were freed from persecution. At the great liberation, all this repressed emotion poured forth to begin the formation of the earliest considerable body of beautiful religious music of which we know; and under the rule of the first Bishop of Rome after its occurrence, the *Schola Cantorum,* "common to the whole city," doubtless had its origin.

The next chapter of our story brings us to a solid historical basis. St. Hilary, Bishop of Rome from 461 to 467 A.D., established a definite body of ecclesiastical singers, seven in number, to which alone the name *Schola Cantorum* was thereafter applied in Rome; and which continued its corporate existence and essential organization until the close of the fourteenth century. It was the duty of these seven Sub-deacons to be responsible for the music of all services at which the Bishop officiated, wherever held. Gregory the Great, in A.D. 595, issued a decretal forbidding Deacons to fill the office of chief singer at the Mass, and confining it to the lesser Orders of the Ministry. To supply the necessary singers, he developed two previously existing schools, and founded two new ones of a different character. The older institutions were what we should call theological seminaries. One had long existed; the other had been newly opened by the Benedictine monks of Monte Cassino, who took refuge in Rome after the destruction of their monastery by the Lombards in 580 A.D. Seminarians at that time, and for long afterwards, were required to memorize not only the words, but also the appointed music, of the major part of the Church's services. There were thus facilities in these schools for the training of specially talented youths in the musical duties of the inferior Orders of Lectors, Cantors, and Sub-deacons.

Its Extension

But St. Gregory did not rest content with this source of supply for the remarkable movement in Church Music of which he was the undoubted center; he founded and endowed two houses (*orphanotrophia*), one near the Church of the Lateran, the

other near St. Peter's, for the express purpose of training or-
phans in the duties of the *Schola Cantorum,* and of other allied
bodies of singers which were appointed for the Churches of St.
Peter, St. Paul, St. Mary the Greater, and St. Lawrence outside
the walls. The lads were given a sound general, musical, and
religious education by the members of the *Schola Cantorum,*
which thus became a self-perpetuating body. So highly successful was this foundation in supplying competent religious musicians that the Schola itself came to be popularly called, after the
orphanages, the *Orphanotrophium.* It was the first musical
Conservatory.

But let us turn to the actual accomplishments of the institution. It assisted vitally in the creation of the first great body of
worship music, definitely based on sound artistic and liturgical
principles. The most important part of this work was undoubtedly carried out during St. Gregory's pontificate, in closest connection with his reform of the Liturgy. The formative period
ensuing upon the liberation of Christianity had gradually
blended traditional Jewish methods of sacred song, Greek musical science, and Latin rhythmical idioms into a musical medium
that needed only the unifying touch of genius and of trained
skill to produce master-works. In the *Schola Cantorum* the
genius and the skill developed; for we possess the master-works
in the Gregorian *Antiphonale Missarum,* and the verdict of
modern scholarship is that they cannot be assigned a later date
than the beginning of the seventh century. Liturgy and music,
so unified, stood as a complete model and standard for the worship of the Church; and though this work was primarily under-
taken for the city of Rome alone, its very excellence brought

about a very wide dissemination, not only of the actual services and music, but as well of the method of organization that had made them possible.

Dissemination of the Chant

ENGLAND was the first country to receive the Gregorian music from the lips of the little company of forty men sent out by Gregory himself with St. Augustine. We possess the very tune which they sang as they marched in procession into the presence of King Ethelbert of Kent in 596 A.D. Less than a century from this time, Pope Agatho sent John, the First Singer of the *Schola Cantorum,* to conduct a school of Church Music in the Abbey of Wearmouth, whither came a multitude of students from all parts of England during the two years prior to 680 A.D. Under the monarchs of the Carolingian dynasty, permanent *Scholæ Cantorum* based on the Roman model were founded among the Franks, of which the most famous was that of Metz. The Synod of Aachen in 803 A.D. enjoined on the Frankish Bishops the duty of instituting such schools. From Metz the movement spread to St. Gall in Switzerland, where the *Schola Cantorum* became justly famous for its close following of the methods so successful in the Roman *Schola,* and for the fostering of new and vital creative activity which enriched the world with a fresh treasure of musical devotion. This widespread diffusion of its musical ideas and of its practical plan of organization for putting them into practice was of immense service to the Christian world. As a result, liturgical choral music became an integral part of the devotional and intellectual life of all Europe, having been ineffaceably stamped upon it during the formative period when the mediæval world was being slowly molded throughout the so-called Dark Ages. In all that welter of migration, war, political turmoil, and social transformation, the Song Schools of many a monastery and cathedral, faithful children of a great mother, preserved the ideals and advanced the practice of purely religious music. We are in their debt today for a very large part of what is best in our choral worship.

Development of Notation

Was the Chant disseminated throughout Western Europe by means of manuscripts with musical notation? Undoubtedly not. Our earliest manuscripts with notes date from the middle of the ninth century. But we possess six manuscripts and some fragments, of the eighth century, which not only tend to delimit the Gregorian repertory from later additions, but which also, to some extent, classify texts in the order of the musical modes, corresponding precisely with the later musical versions. But consider that the Cantors of the *Schola Cantorum* spent ten years in the mastery of the music, memorizing all of it; that they taught by means of the old cheironomy (to which I referred in the previous chapter), a very graphic form of conducting which outlined melodies both as to rhythm and pitch; and that when the earliest notations appear in the ninth century, the manuscripts from every part of Europe agree with startling unanimity. Consider also that the old Greek notation by means of letters of the alphabet was preserved not only by the early theorists, but also by practical musicians and choir leaders. Thus Odo, second Abbot of Cluny, who had been a musical pupil of Remigius of Auxerre, at the end of the ninth century, had later been master of a choir school and was himself a composer of hymn and antiphon melodies. In the *Musica Encheiriadis* attributed to him, and certainly of his time, the familiar Psalmody of the Introit is precisely noted by the letter system. A tradition existed at St. Gall, whence our best early manuscripts emanate, that in Charlemagne's time a Cantor sent from Rome by Pope Adrian I used the Greek notation. But more important yet in this connection is the famous *Tonarium* of Montpellier, the Rosetta stone of early music notation, in which a letter notation is placed immediately beneath the neum notation of the older type, thus giving precise intervals.

Now the neum notation, one of the most ingenious inventions of the human mind, expressed not only rhythm and phrasing, but at times the most minute expressional nuances, by the addition of certain marks and letters to the ordinary musical signs: in fact, it showed everything about a melody and its artistic rendition except the pitch of the notes. By the year 1000 a line notation had been evolved, on which at first were placed the hooks and curves and points of neumatic notation; but later, the familiar square notes, which have constituted the ecclesiastical notation since it reached its perfection in the thirteenth century. Remember that the time unit in all these notations was the length of a syllable of well read prose, and was indivisible. Longer notes were built up as needed by combination of units, but there was no shorter note. The rhythm therefore was absolutely the free flowing rhythm of prose: and Plainsong might be called prose music.

Practically no new compositions were added to the Gregorian Eucharistic repertory until the tenth century. As new Feasts were added to the Calendar, music from the Gregorian deposit was adapted to their Propers. Thus the great Introit *Gaudeamus* from the Gregorian Mass of St. Agatha was adapted for All Saints Day, and for several other Feasts. What new Propers were composed were less perfect musically. It is the minute study of these adaptations, as also of the early adaptations from Greek text to Latin, which enables the scholar of the present day to adapt the old melodies to English liturgical texts without impairing their musical characteristics.

NEW TYPES OF PLAINSONG DEVELOPED LATER

FROM the tenth century on, the music of the Eucharist was enriched with two classes of compositions wholly different in type from the Gregorian repertory.

The Sequence

ONE of these was the so-called Sequence, appended to the Alleluia Respond. As this form bore an important part in the development of Hymnody, and was, in fact, the introduction of the popular hymn into the Mass, we shall consider it in the chapter on the Pre-Reformation Hymn.[24]

The other new type was that of more elaborate melodies for the Ordinary of the Mass.

The Ordinary of the Mass

IT is evident, as is the case again and again throughout history, that liturgical units intended for the Congregation have been gradually usurped by the Choir. This is notably true in the Anglican Communion at the present time, when *Gloria tibi, Sursum corda,* even *Amen* after the Prayer of Consecration, are

[24]See page 179.

sung by Choirs alone. Apparently, by the beginning of the tenth century, singers in various Choirs began to compose new melodies for *Kyrie eleison, Gloria in excelsis, Sanctus,*[25] and *Agnus Dei.* Over a hundred such settings were made in the succeeding six centuries. From the first, some were highly elaborate, while others were capable of congregational use, and from time to time received it. Some of the settings probably reflect a new musical influence from the East. The ninefold *Kyrie*[26] offered wonderful opportunities in the development of fascinating musical form: and opened up a new world of artistic composition. Similar principles built up true structural music in the other numbers. As a result, we have in the melodies of the Ordinary the great secondary treasure of Eucharistic Plainsong: which is today far more widely known and appreciated than is the earlier Gregorian repertory.[27]

Tropes

ONE fascinating subject must be mentioned briefly in conclusion because of its momentous bearing on post-Reformation English Church Music. With the increased elaboration of the melodies of the Ordinary, came a movement that went to amazing lengths in the way of practical simplification of them. I refer to what are called Tropes. These consisted of additional words supplied to the liturgical text, making a devotional com-

[25]See *The Hymnal,* No. 694, for a fourteenth-century *Sanctus,* which is also adopted in *The Pilgrim Hymnal* and *The Presbyterian Hymnal.*
[26]See *The Hymnal,* No. 681.
[27]See Winfred Douglas, *The Kyrial;* H. W. Gray Co., N. Y. Also *Kyriale Romanum,* George Fischer and Brothers, N. Y. At the close of this chapter is appended a list of records illustrative of the later Plainsong of the Ordinary of the Mass.

mentary on it; and at the same time providing one syllable for each note of the florid melody; and also for new additional melodies, possibly of Byzantine origin. Thus the words of an early Trope on the *Sanctus* are:

> *Sanctus ex quo sunt omnia;*
> *Sanctus per quem sunt omnia;*
> *Sanctus in quo sunt omnia*
> *Dominus Deus Sabaoth,*
>   *tibi gloria sit in sæcula.*

The practice became a serious liturgical abuse; but the Tropers, or great collections of music so treated, represent the main *musical* advance for some centuries. "All new developments in musical composition, failing to gain admission into the privileged circle of the recognized Gregorian service-books, were thrown together so as to form an independent musical collection supplementary to the official books."[28]

The opening words of a Trope gave names to the various Kyrie melodies, quite naturally: names still retained. Thus, *Kyrie fons bonitatis,* of the tenth century, opens with this melody:

[28]W. H. Frere, *The Winchester Troper.* See page 67, following.

Its Trope, one syllable to a note, is as follows:

Ky - ri - e fons bo - ni - ta - tis, Pa - ter in - ge - ni - te,

a quo bo - na cunc - ta pro - ce - dunt, e - le - i - son.

On this theme, with the detached notes of the Trope, Johann Sebastian Bach was to compose one of the greatest of his organ Preludes.[29]

The use of Troped or Farsed Kyries continued in France and England up to Reformation times:[30] and there we must leave for the time being the consideration of the music of the Eucharist. In the next chapter, we will examine it from the Rise of Polyphony to the present time. We may be sure that the centuries of testing and development, the new impulses toward experiment and extension of methods, the shorter periods of true creative musical vitality, have not been wasted: they make possible today a richer and nobler Eucharistic music than the world has yet seen. It is our part to learn the lessons of the past, and to apply them practically in advancing the progress of the future.

Illustrative Records of the Ordinary of the Mass from the tenth century on:

Victrola Album M 87, I, II, Solesmes Abbey Choir:
    7341 A, *Kyrie Lux et origo,* X Century, *Missa Paschalis.*
    7341 A, *Agnus Dei,* X Century, *Missa Paschalis.*

[29]*Kyrie Gott Heiliger Geist,* in which the pedal bass is this melody.
[30]The Responses to the Commandments are practically a Farsed *Kyrie.*

7341 B, *Gloria in excelsis,* X Century, Easter.

7341 B, *Sanctus,* X Century, *Missa Paschalis.*

7347 A, *Sanctus,* XIV Century, *Missa Marialis.*

7347 A, *Agnus Dei,* XIII Century, *Missa Marialis.*

7348 B, *Kyrie Orbis factor,* X Century, *Missa Dominicalis.*

Victrola Album M 69, Pius X Choir:
  7180 A, *Kyrie Alme Pater,* XI Century, Feasts B.M.V.
  7180 A, *Gloria in excelsis,* XI Century, Feasts B.M.V.
  7181 A, *Sanctus,* XIV Century, *Missa Marialis.*
  7181 B, *Agnus Dei,* XIII Century, *Missa Marialis.*
  7181 B, *Ite, missa est,* XI Century, *Missa Marialis.*

Victrola Album M 177, Pius X Choir:
  11529, A, *Kyrie,* XI Century, *Requiem.*

Gramophone Shop Album 132, Dortmund Choir:
  Polydor 90054, *Kyrie de angelis,* XIV Century, *Missa de angelis.*
  Polydor 90054, *Gloria in excelsis,* XVI Century, *Missa de angelis.*
  Polydor 90055, *Credo III,* XVII Century, *Missa de angelis.*
  Polydor 90055, *Sanctus,* XI Century, *Missa de angelis.*
  Polydor 90055, *Agnus Dei,* XV Century, *Missa de angelis.*

Montserrat Album, Montserrat Abbey Choir:
  Disco Gramofono AE 3302, *Kyrie altissime,* XI Century, Festal
  (The finest plainsong record I know. W.D.)

His Master's Voice C 2087, Ampleforth Abbey Choir:
  Sanctus, XIV Century, *Missa Marialis.*
  Kyrie cum jubilo, XII Century, *Missa Marialis.*

Victor 21621 B, Palestrina Choir:
  Kyrie cum jubilo, XII Century *Missa Marialis.*

Columbia DFX 156, Choir, Notre-Dame d'Auteuil:
  Kyrie Lux et origo, X Century, *Missa Paschalis.*
  Gloria in excelsis, X Century, Easter.

Victor Album M 212, Dijon Cathedral Choir:
  11678 A, *Kyrie Orbis factor,* XVI Century, *Missa Dominicalis.*
  (With alternate settings by Victoria.)

Lumen, Choir of St. Eustache, Paris:
  30.040, 32.025, *Missa de angelis.*

Semen Albums I, II, Maredsous Abbey Choir:
S. M. 1, *Kyrie Cunctipotens,* X Century.
 Sanctus IV, XI Century
S. M. 5, *Kyrie de Requie,* XI Century.
S. M. 10, *Kyrie, Sanctus, Gloria, Missa Paschalis.*
S. M. 11, *Kyrie, Agnus, Missa Marialis.*
S. M. 12,.*Kyrie, Agnus, Gloria, Missa Dominicalis.*

Semen, Averbode Abbey Choir:
S. A. 3, *Kyrie Deus Genitor alme, Missa Penitentialis.*
 Sanctus IV, XI Century.
 Agnus, Missa Marialis.

Christschall, Choir of White Fathers, Treves:
CH 55, *Kyrie Alme Pater,* XI Century.
 Gloria, XV Century, *Missa Marialis.*
 Credo III, XVII Century, *Missa Marialis.*
CH 56, *Sanctus X,* Modern.
 Agnus X, XII Century.

Electrola, Beuron Abbey Choir:
E. G. 1727, *Sanctus, Agnus, Missa Dominicalis.*
E. G. 1728, *Kyrie, Gloria, Missa Paschalis.*

Columbia, Dutch Franciscan Friars:
DHX 6, *Kyrie XVII,*[2] XIV Century, Lent.

Victor Album, Grand Séminaire, Montreal:
1 A, *Kyrie Cunctipotens,* X Century.
 Sanctus II, XII Century.
 Gloria XI, X Century.
3 A, B, 5A, B, *Missa de angelis.*
6 A, *Kyrie, Sanctus, Agnus, Missa Dominicalis.*

CHAPTER III

THE MUSIC OF THE EUCHARIST FROM THE RISE OF POLYPHONY TO THE PRESENT TIME

THIS book is in no sense a history of Music, or even a history of Church Music. It constitutes a treatment of Church Music from a practical point of view based upon historical data. We may not therefore dwell upon the long and fascinating story of the evolution of Polyphony, and thereafter of modern Harmony; but must press on to examine the permanent and practical results of these new procedures as they affect the Eucharistic Music of the Anglican Communion. For a Priest to meet his necessary responsibility with regard to the oversight of the music of his Parish, it is not necessary that he should be a technically trained musician, however helpful such training might be. It *is* necessary that he should thoroughly understand the principles governing the relationship between music and worship; and it is equally necessary that his organist or Choir director should know those principles. Moreover, both Priest and Choir director should, as far as the outward circumstances of their environment permit, develop a formed taste for 'the things that are more excellent' in Church Music, and be able to distinguish the profound differences in style between the sacred and the secular. No one could possibly confuse the old sacred Plainsong with its contemporary secular Folksong; but very much music put forward for worship in recent centuries and at the present time is indistinguishable in style from the music of the world. True worship music could never possibly be mistaken for anything else.

THE EVOLUTION OF POLYPHONY

FROM the tenth century on, we have the genesis and development of a new type of sacred music which culminated in the glorious Polyphony of the Reformation period. Six hundred years were required to produce the first fully developed body of artistic worship music, the Gregorian Plainsong: and from the first feeble experiments in the tenth century six hundred years were necessary to evolve the masterpieces of the second great school, the Classical Polyphony or many-voiced music.

The Plainsong, pure melody, was not in one sense homophonic: for it was sung in octaves whenever men and women or men and children joined in singing the same melody; which had to be limited in range, so that the lower voices could sing the higher notes, and *vice versa*. The first part-singing besides octaves came when, as is still the case in Russian country Churches, some of the singers sang the same tune beginning on the dominant instead of the tonic; that is, a fourth below. This duplication of melody at a different pitch was known as 'organum.'

Illustrative Records:
Columbia History of Music, Terry Choir:
5710 *Veni Sancte Spiritus* with organum, 11th Century.
Victor 20897 B, Organum, Palestrina Choir:

Scotus Erigena, who died A.D. 880, describes it. It is recorded in the theoretical work *Musica Encheiriadis,* probably by the Abbot Odo of Cluny, which I cited in relationship to the preservation from antiquity of Gregorian Music in a derivative of Greek notation.[1] In early Gregorian music, the *melodic* use of f natural and b natural in close proximity was a common procedure.

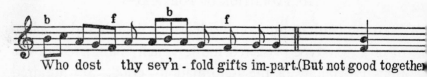

Who dost   thy sev'n - fold gifts im-part.(But not good together)

But when simultaneously sounded in the Organum, the effect was displeasing. It came to be regarded with such aversion that it was picturesquely described as *diabolus in musica*: and this bad name has so persistently clung to the interval that in our day, Richard Wagner and Richard Strauss have both used it to express the diabolical.[2] Odo records a method of avoiding this interval by keeping one part stationary for a time. This is our first instance of the use of two simultaneous but differing melodies.

Illustrative Record:
Columbia History of Music Album, Terry Choir:
C 5710, *Mira lege,* XII Century.

It is only to be compared to the momentous occasion when Wilbur Wright, at Kittyhawk, flew for the first time in a self-propelled airplane. That invention permanently transformed the journeyings of man about his planet home; and ever since with a swelling tide of fascinated study which now carries along millions of children, the improvement of the airplane has been ceaselessly pressed forward.

It was precisely so with the art of music. The novelty of

[1]See page 56.   [2]Fafner in *Siegfried: "Also sprach Zarathustra."*

simultaneously sounded intervals brought about the discovery of discords and concords, and the experimenters were soon deducing rules to make the movement of the additional part more pleasing. By the year 1000, we find extant in Cornwall a crude two part setting of the Hymn for St. Stephen's Day. Contrary motion was discovered, one voice moving up, while the other moves down. It is found in the very early Winchester Troper. You will remember that the Tropes were interpolations in the liturgical text so arranged that each syllable of the interpolation took up one note of music. This was the fruitful field which the experimenters cultivated.[3] Bishop Frere says of it, "The Tropers practically represent the sum total of musical advance between the ninth and twelfth centuries." These novelties were heavy and clumsy and inartistic: but they were the sources of all that we have today in glorious many-voiced music. But note, that they continued for a long time the idea found underlying the Tropes; that it is somehow easier to sing one note to a syllable than several.

No attempt was made at first to compose any new melodies, or to establish any rhythm other than the prose rhythm of Plainsong. Even when Plainsong with groups of notes to a syllable was thus embellished, the additional part kept the same grouping, reflected as in a mirror.

Mensurable Notation and the Consequent Decay of Plainsong

BUT soon, the additional part or parts began to be more independent, to move with a freer flight, to possess a different rhythm from the Plainsong itself. This produced a double result. It made necessary a new feature in Church music, mensurable

[3]See page 60.

rhythm, to be expressed by a mensurable notation. This was nearly as momentous a discovery as was that of music in more than one part. The advance in the musical quality of the parts was great: but on the other hand, the Plainsong basis was practically destroyed as music: for a melody without its characteristic rhythm is dead. From this time on, Plainsong, which had attained its height of perfection, began to decay. It was moribund in the sixteenth century, and continued only in debased and corrupt forms until the great revival not yet a hundred years old.

At the close of the twelfth century we find the Plainsong, in notes of intolerable length, wholly devoid of any melodic sense, used as a basis for several free flowing parts, which have now become so independent that one voice will, as we say, imitate another, repeating some melodic figure at a different interval. I have twice heard such a work, the composition of Pérotin the Great, as he was called, choirmaster and organist of Notre Dame de Paris at the close of the twelfth century. As sung by the *Schola Cantorum* in New York, it was so effective that its repetition was demanded the following year. Pérotin edited and revised the settings of the Propers of the Mass composed by his predecessor and master, Léonin.

Illustrative Record:
    Lumen 32011, Léonin, *Organum duplum.*
        32012, Pérotin, *Conductus.*

Not only the organ, but other instruments, especially of brass, are in use at this time; and thenceforth we have two streams of composition, one for the human voice alone, and another lesser one which was to develop later, for the human voice with instruments. With the former only are we concerned until after the Reformation.

A monk of Reading, John of Forncett, wrote a remarkable work before 1240 A.D., unmatched in quality among the scarce remnants of that time, *Sumer is i-cumen in.*

Illustrative Records:
  Columbia History of Music, 5715, The St. George's Singers.
  Roycroft Living Tone 159, The English Singers.

It is a Canon or Round, a song of spring sung by four voices over two lower parts. It gave such pleasure that they wanted it in Church, and somebody wrote sacred words for it. This is the first instance I know of a very great abuse common in our day. Sacred words cannot make a secular composition a fit vehicle for worship. Yet in the period we are considering, and for long after, a reprehensible custom grew up among composers of basing a polyphonic work, not on a plainsong melody, as at first, but on the music of some popular song. This abuse went even to the length of permitting one of the many voices to sing the actual secular words, sometimes ribald words, of the song. Later on, many composers were fascinated with what might be called the ingenuities of composition, the combining of themes in all manner of intricate relationships, rather than with problems either of musical beauty or of divine worship.

The Church was little inclined to permit these abuses, however widely they were practiced in parish Churches. Pope John XXII, in the bull *Docta sanctorum patrum,* 1322, reprehended them severely. He says that composers of the *Ars nova,* all intent on measuring the time, forget the old ecclesiastical modes: that they substitute for the traditional melodies their own tunes, or mix profane parts with the liturgical chant; that in the imitations, or 'chases' as they were called, part pursues part, running on and never finding repose: and that such an art, however satisfying to curiosity, cannot give peace to souls, nor incite them to devotion.

The Musical Form Known as a Mass

NOTWITHSTANDING such abuses, it was about at this time, in the fourteenth century, that a highly significant step was taken in the development of music for the Eucharist. It was the first appearance of the art-form which we know as a Mass: that is, the combination of *Kyrie, Gloria, Credo, Sanctus,* and *Agnus* in a single work.[4] The composer was Guillaume de Machaut, Canon of Rheims in 1337 A.D. The Mass was probably composed in 1364 for the Coronation of Charles the Fifth. The *Kyrie* is ingeniously built about the famous tenth century *Kyrie Cunctipotens genitor Deus* composed by Tutilo, the monk of St. Gall. The music is in four parts, not three, as had generally been the case up to that time. Thus out of the mere fact that the intercalated Tropes of the *Kyrie, Gloria, Sanctus,* and *Agnus* made experimental composition easy, has arisen a new art-form completely destroying the old and necessary balance between the music of the Choir and that of the Congregation. Heretofore, the Propers of the Mass had been the field of the Choir, the Ordinary of the Mass that of the Congregation. It should be evident that in some way this balance must be restored, that means must be found to give the Congregation a proper part in the actual music of the Eucha-

[4]The many Plainsong melodies of the Ordinary have never been combined in fixed Masses, although, for convenience sake, modern editors have so grouped them. But these groups are purely arbitrary, and vary in all the different editions.

rist itself. The first effort must be to restore to the Celebrant and Congregation the musical Dialogue of the Eucharist, and to the Congregation at least the Nicene Creed. There is the greatest need for settings of the *Kyrie, Sanctus,* and *Agnus Dei* in which Choir and Congregation can unite or alternate: and the persistence of the not too musical "Old Chant"[5] proves the rightful eagerness with which the Congregation welcomes opportunity to sing *Gloria in excelsis.* On the other hand, the true future place for elaborate compositions for the Choir will be at the Introit, the Offertory, and between the Epistle and Gospel, as of old.

Yet we cannot regret the adoption of the five-fold art form of the Mass; for it has enriched the world with its greatest treasure of Choral music, comparable in importance only with the parallel treasure evolved from popular instrumental dance music; the Symphony. The culminating masterpiece of choral art, the B minor Mass of Bach, whose two hundred and fiftieth anniversary has recently been celebrated, is truly descended from the Mass of Machaut: and like it, interweaves, at least in the *Credo,* the ancient plainchant from which it originally sprang.

Machaut's Mass was in the repertory of the Church of St. Quentin at Cambrai, which possessed an excellent Choir School. One of the young choristers in 1412 was Guillaume Dufay, who later on joined the Pontifical Choir in Rome, where Machaut's Mass also became known. In 1436 Dufay became Canon of Cambrai Cathedral, and later, choir director there. We may hear his very characteristic and fascinating *Gloria in excelsis:* two boys' voices singing in Canon, to an unvarying naïve accompaniment of two trumpets.

[5]*The Hymnal,* No. 699.

Illustrative Record:
2000 Jahre Musik Album, Berlin Academy Choir:
  Parlophon B 37025-1, *Gloria ad modum tubae.*
The musical form is that of *Sumer is i-cumen in* 200 years earlier.

Hitherto ingenuity, often very pleasing ingenuity, as in the Dufay *Gloria,* has characterized the slowly developing music of the Mass, rather than real musical creativeness. But in the Fleming, Josquin Des Prés[6] (1445–1521), arose a true genius, who broke through the scholastic complexities of his earlier style to greater simplicity and expressiveness, culminating in works of true devotional beauty, whose flowing melody was equalled by a highly expressive harmonic richness. Such were his last two Masses, *Da pacem* and *Pange lingua.*

Illustrative Records:
2000 Jahre Musik Album, Berlin Academy Choir:
  Parlophon B 37025-11, *Et incarnatus est, Missa Da pacem.*
Christschall 119, Munich Cathedral Choir:
  Sanctus, Sanctus, Missa Pange lingua.

INFLUENCES OF THE REFORMATION

JOSQUIN died the year after Martin Luther was excommunicated by the worldly Pope Leo X. Incidentally, Luther was a warm admirer of Josquin's compositions. But I mention him, because the great period of Polyphonic Composition which gave the world an unparalleled treasure of true worship music, not only for the Eucharist, but also, as we shall see later, for the other Offices of the Church, is synchronous with, and intimately related to, that vast movement of human thought and impulse, to

[6]From the Flemish group, and especially from its culminating figure, Des Prés, a completely mastered Polyphony spread throughout Europe. Flemish composers settling in Rome, Venice, Austria, Bavaria, Spain, and elsewhere, were the founders of the great schools of composition in those regions.

[72]

which we ordinarily refer as the Reformation. The movement was really one: Ignatius Loyola was as important a factor in it as was Martin Luther; Francisco Quiñones as Thomas Cranmer; Pius the Fifth as Henry the Eighth. All sides, Roman Catholic and Protestant and Anglican, suffered terrible losses and made glorious gains: but it can truly be said that in the field of Church Music, it was a period of amazing, of almost miraculous advance. This vast transformation drew to a close early in the seventeenth century: and in England, as well as on the Continent of Europe, the golden age of sacred Polyphony ended then with the oncoming of new inventions and far lesser triumphs of Christian praise. The great masters of this golden age were, almost without exception, deeply religious men; some, like Guerrero and Palestrina, saintly men. Morales and Victoria, the Spaniards, were devout Roman priests: Tye, the Englishman, became an Anglican priest. Some, like Orlando di Lasso in Munich, and Tallis and Byrd in England, though practicing and convinced Romanists, composed superbly in the vernacular, as well as in the liturgical Latin. The better influences of the Reformation, taken in its widest sense of a spiritual rebirth of European religion, formed their work, now the common treasure of the Christian world.

All of these great composers except the Englishmen took part at one time or another in the musical life of Rome. The Fleming Orlando di Lasso was head of the Choir at the Roman Cathedral, the ancient Basilica of St. John Lateran, while the Italian Palestrina was master of the Julian Choir at St. Peter's in 1554. St. Ignatius Loyola had just founded the *Collegium Germanicum* for the training of priests for Bavaria and the Rhine country. Thither came, a little later, the young Spanish priest, Tomás

Luis de Victoria, as Chaplain. Doubtless he had been profoundly influenced by a previous personal acquaintance with St. Teresa: an influence showing to the end of his life in the mystical tenderness of his music. It can seldom have happened in history that the three greatest living exponents of an art were within a decade or so displaying it in the same city. Palestrina stayed in Rome in various capacities: di Lasso went to Munich. After long lives of ceaseless musical production, they both died in 1594. Victoria returned to Madrid as Chaplain to the widowed Empress Maria. He lived on till 1608 A.D. The extent of their compositions is amazing. Victoria published 180, Palestrina about 700, and di Lasso over 1200. Among these, together with the numerous compositions of the almost equally great Englishman, William Byrd, who died A.D. 1623, are found hundreds of master-works which form the very crown and climax of all that has been composed for the use of skilled musicians in the worship of God. In the work of di Lasso, we find a superb architectonic power, combined with a noble and rugged expressiveness of detail which rises far above mere picturesqueness; in that of Victoria, a mystical and passionate tenderness, unmatched among others; in that of Byrd, a sturdy vigour coupled with deep sincere feeling; in that of Palestrina, a high serenity of spirit and a perfection of both musical and liturgical form which makes his music truly angelic.

Records illustrative of Classic Polyphony for the Eucharist:

Ordinary of the Mass

Guillaume de Machaut †1377

L'Anthologie Sonore, Vol. IV, 31, 32:
  Credo, Sanctus, Agnus Dei, Ite, missa est.

Guillaume Dufay †1477 (See also p. 72)
L'Anthologie Sonore, Vol. IV, 35A:
Kyrie Se la face ay pale.

Josquin Des Prés †1521 (See p. 72)
Orlando di Lasso †1594

Victor 80160 A, B, *Missa octavi toni,* Berlin Cathedral Choir:
Kyrie, Sanctus, Benedictus, Agnus.

Giovanni Pierluigi da Palestrina †1594

Victor Album M 212, *Missa Assumpta est,* Dijon Cathedral Choir:
11680 A, *Kyrie,* B, *Agnus Dei.*
11681 A, *Sanctus,* B, *Benedictus.*
Columbia History of Music Album, Terry Choir:
5712, *Missa Papæ Marcelli, Sanctus.*
2000 Jahre Musik, Berlin Cathedral Choir:
Parlophon B 37027–1, *Missa Papæ Marcelli, Sanctus.*
Victor, *Missa Papæ Marcelli,* Westminster Cathedral Choir:
35942, *Gloria in excelsis.*
35943, *Credo.*
35944, *Sanctus, Benedictus.*

Tomás Luis da Victoria †1608

Victor Album M 212, Dijon Cathedral Choir:
11678 A, *Kyrie Orbis factor.*
Christschall 143, St. Michael's Choir:
Gloria in excelsis from *Missa Vidi speciosam.*

William Byrd †1623

Columbia Album, XVI Century Songs, The St. George's Singers:
5547, *Agnus Dei,* The five part Mass.

Antonio Lotti †1740

Victor 20410 B, *Crucifixus est,* Princeton Westminster Choir.

Propers of the Mass

Giovanni Francisco Anerio †1620

Victor Album M 182, The Sistine Choir:
Victrola 7814 B, Introit, *Requiem æternam.*

Palestrina

Victrola 7812 A, Tract *Sicut cervus,* Easter Eve.
Victrola 7813 A, Offertory, *Super flumina,* 10th Sunday after Pente-
cost.
Victrola 7813 B, *Improperia,* The Reproaches, Good Friday.
Victor 20898 B, *Improperia,* The Reproaches, Palestrina Choir.
Victor 20898 A, *Sicut cervus,* Palestrina Choir.

Victoria

Polydor 27117, *Improperia,* St. Hedwig's Choir, Berlin.

The story that Palestrina was the saviour of polyphonic music
by specially composing the *Missa Papæ Marcelli* for the audition
of the Fathers of the Council of Trent, who upon hearing it
withdrew their action excluding such music from the services
of the Church, is completely apocryphal. The Mass was composed at an earlier period; it was sung at a solemn Mass celebrated by St. Charles Borromeo, a member of the Commission
appointed by Pope Pius IV to push reforms already decreed by
the Council.

But Palestrina was a true reformer of Church Music. He
brought about in his own work the elimination of all secular
themes, and of all elaborate ingenuities of contrapuntal device
which could mutilate or distort or obscure the words of the service. As in the Gregorian Plainsong the liturgical words had been
sung straight through to single melodies which brought out their
meaning, so in the Palestrina style they were sung to similar
melodies for many parts, each of which sang the text with a
minimum of repetition.[7] Plainsong had a single rhythm. Polyphony is primarily a combination of rhythms like the surging

[7]See also page 116.

waves of the sea, each bringing out the sense of the words. Palestrina, the penitent of St. Philip Neri, the friend of St. Charles Borromeo, wrought a true spiritual reform in the purifying and perfecting of the Praise of God.

But we must turn from the influence of the so-called Counter-Reformation on the Music of the Liturgy to that of the English Reformation.

England had produced one masterly polyphonic composer, John Taverner, who wrote eight Masses and many motets before the Reformation. He was Choirmaster of Cardinal's College at Oxford, Wolsey's foundation. He resigned in 1530, ceased all musical work, and became a fanatical adherent of the extreme anti-Catholic party. Cromwell employed him in the suppression of the monasteries: and in a letter from Boston in 1538, he writes his master, "according to your lordship's commandment, the Rood was burned the seventh day . . . and a sermon at the burning of him which did express the cause of his burning and the idolatry committed by him." We learn that "this Taverner repented him very muche that he had made songs to Popish Ditties in the time of his blindness." Among these "songs" were the eight Masses, two of which were adapted to English words, quite crudely, before the publication of the first Book of Common Prayer; a recently elicited testimony to the overwhelming urge for the vernacular which was one of the major features of the English Reformation.

THE ENGLISH REFORMATION AND CHURCH MUSIC

WHAT was done about Church Music at the English Reformation? Disregarding the enormous political forces involved in that complex movement, and the external influences of a Continental Protestantism which had rejected the Apostolic Ministry of the Church, we may say that the purely religious effort of *Ecclesia Anglicana* was toward the restoration of Catholic life as in the early centuries, and also toward its normal expression in choral worship. Gross popular misconceptions and real abuses concerning the Mass had led to very infrequent reception of Holy Communion. Grave superstitions had vitiated in many the old and devout cultus of the Saints, which had truly expressed our acknowledged communion with them. The liturgical language, Latin, had once been the vernacular; it was such no longer: and an ever increasing desire for the services of the Church in English had become irresistible. The conscious effort of the Church was toward correcting such abuses and meeting such contemporary conditions by a return to the principles of Christian antiquity.

In Church Music, also, there were distortions to correct, abuses to end, and altered circumstances to meet. For over five hundred years, the art of music in more than one part had been developing to its high culmination in contrapuntal Polyphony: an art of simultaneous independent melodies for voices alone, which at its best has never been surpassed as a vehicle for religious worship. But this great art, just coming to its perfection in England, in Spain, and in Italy, had too extensively replaced large portions of the classical Plainsong, or so obscured it in a web of woven parts that its values were lost. Only the dialogues between Priest and People and the simple chants of the Psalms were left unaltered. Moreover, for every great religious composer of Polyphony, there were scores who were carried away with mere intellectual ingenuities, or based their work on popular worldly tunes, sometimes of a ribald association. Even among the good composers, there was often disregard of the liturgical text. Thus, in England, large portions of the Nicene Creed were habitually omitted by the best composers; and what had been earlier the solemn profession of Christian faith, sung by all to a familiar melody, had become a mere musical commentary by the choir on a portion only of the historic words. Nevertheless, at the Reformation, English Polyphony had risen to lofty heights of devotional expression.

Now, what readjustments were actually made at this period? On June 11, 1544, Archbishop Cranmer set forth "in our natvye Englisshe tongue, the Letanie with suffrages to be songe in the tyme of processions." The music, derived from the old, was of extreme simplicity, so that all could join in singing it.[8] At the Royal Chapel, it was sung in a five-part setting. Six months later, Cranmer submitted to the King further translations looking toward a book of Processions before Mass, regarding which he wrote, "If your grace command some devout and solemn note to be made thereunto, I trust it will stir the hearts of all men to devotion and godliness. But in mine opinion, the song that shall be made thereunto would not be full of notes, but, as near as may be, for every syllable a note, so that it may be sung distinctly and devoutly. . . . I have put the Latin note unto the same. Nevertheless they that be cunning in singing can make a much more solemn note thereto: I made them only for a proof to see how English would do in song."

When the Parliament of Edward VI was opened, a complete English Mass set to simplified Plainsong was sung. Early in

[8]See *The Choral Service,* pp. 10–18, 64–68, 98; or *The Congregational Choral Service.*

Edward's reign appeared ten English Masses containing *Kyrie, Gloria,* Creed, *Sanctus* and *Agnus Dei,* in four or five parts, besides the Taverner adaptations previously mentioned. Finally, a year after the publication of the first English Prayerbook in 1549, was printed *The Booke of Common Praier Noted,* the work of an excellent musician, John Merbecke, organist of St. George's Chapel, Windsor, who himself had composed a superb polyphonic Mass in five parts.[9] In this publication, obviously set forth as a standard for parish churches, Matins, Evensong, the Communion Service, "commonly called the Mass," the Burial Service and the Requiem were supplied with music from ancient sources in strict accord with Cranmer's injunction, which had been officially set forth on the accession of Edward VI, that "no anthems are to be allowed but those of our Lord, and they in English, set to a plain and distinct note, for every syllable one."

The real origin of this restriction was undoubtedly the development of the Trope, or syllabic commentary inserted into the liturgical texts, with the idea that they would make long melodies easier to sing.[10] We have seen how these syllabic Tropes influenced early part writing, and became the real reason for developing the musical form known as a Mass. The Tropes, especially the farsed Kyries, were sung right up to the Reformation in England. I have no doubt that they suggested to Archbishop Cranmer his injunction of simplicity.

It may be parenthetically suggested that, as not infrequently happens when the reverend clergy dictate musical rules without skilled musical advice, the Archbishop's excellent inten-

[9]*Missa Per arma justitiæ.*   [10]See pages 59–61, 67.

tion of making the services easy for congregations to sing and understand was largely defeated by a faulty method: for music of the syllabic type is far harder to sing well than that of a more flowing movement, in which several notes often occur to a single syllable. I remember well a Bishop on the Hymnal Commission suggesting the elimination of the triplets in the famous tune *Ton-y-botel*,[11] and the substitution of single notes for them. Much of the impoverishment of English religious music, including that of the hymn tunes, has been due to this practical error.

The musical provision for the Holy Eucharist in Merbecke's book was most interesting. The Introit Psalm, without any Antiphon, was set to an ordinary Psalm Tone. The Nine-fold *Kyrie eleison* was simplified from that of the oldest extant Mass, that for the Dead. *Gloria in excelsis,* which immediately followed it, had its familiar Intonation by the Celebrant, as did also the Nicene Creed: but what follows in each, although in ancient modal style, was wholly his own composition. Fifteen Offertories were drawn from earlier Antiphon melodies. *Sursum corda* and the Preface were to be sung, followed by *Sanctus* (with *Benedictus*) from the older Sunday Mass. *Amen* was sung after the sung close of the Prayer for the Church. At the end of the Prayer of Consecration, the Celebrant sang the *Ekphonesis,* "World without end"; and after the congregationally sung *Amen,* the Introduction and Lord's Prayer as in our present American service, except that the Congregation alone sang "But deliver us from evil" as a Response. The Priest sang "The peace of the Lord be always with you" and the Congregation responded, "And with thy spirit." *Agnus Dei* followed, adapted

[11] *The Hymnal*, No. 433.

from an earlier Sarum melody. Sixteen Postcommunion Antiphons ensued: and then, after "The Lord be with you" and its Response, the Postcommunion Collect "Almighty and most merciful Lord, we heartily thank thee" was sung. The Blessing was said, with its *Amen*. For the Requiem, Merbecke chose different settings of the *Kyrie eleison, Sanctus,* and *Agnus Dei,* those of the daily Sarum Mass for the Dead.[12]

Re-assertion of Ancient Principles

It is evident from this brief analysis that the Church of England, far from making any new departure in Church music at the Reformation, was merely re-asserting the ancient principles which we considered in the first chapter.

I The English Liturgy and its suggested music were formulated together, and the sung service set forth as the standard worship of the Church as a whole.

II Due provision was made for varying degrees of skill: the simple Plainsong for Priest and People; harmonized music in parts for "Queres and placys where they sing." But in both, the liberty of art was unduly restricted by Cranmer's arbitrary limitation of one note only to a syllable.

III The music was kept purely liturgical, subordinate to the text, without repetition or alteration.

IV Primary consideration was given to the full choral celebration of the Eucharist, both in Plainsong and in harmonized music.

V The lesser services of Matins, Evensong, Litany, and Burial were fully provided for along these same lines.

[12]Merbecke's Communion Service will be found in the present edition of *The Hymnal,* numbers 671, 679, 686, 690, and 697.

Their Decline

WHAT was the fate of this careful reassertion of the ancient principles of Christian worship music? I quote Bishop Frere, whose words regarding the general situation apply also to that in Church Music: "The central body of Catholic minded Bishops and Clergy, who were willing enough for reform, but did not want a revolution, were soon drowned in the clamour of extreme men goaded on by the extravagance of foreign divines and the shamelessness of rapacious politicians." Merbecke's book was little used and soon forgotten. But English had become the liturgical language of a young and vigorous nation, and was destined to attain an unforeseen expansion.[13]

Much music for parts of the English Communion Service was composed before the death of Queen Elizabeth. The Reverend William Harrison, Canon of St. George's, Windsor, in a paper published in 1587, indicated that in Cathedral and Collegiate Churches, only the Psalms were sung at Matins and Evensong, the rest being read "as in common Parish Churches": but that "In the administration of the Communion, the quier singeth the answers, the creed, and sundry other things appointed, but in so plaine and distinct manner that each one present may understand what they sing, everie word having but one note, though the whole harmonie consist of many parts, and those very cunninglie set by the skillful in that science."

[13]In 1582, Richard Mulcaster, Edmund Spenser's master, wrote, "The English tongue is of small reach, stretching no further than this island of ours, nay, not there over all." Less than 5,000,000 human beings spoke it then, or for two hundred years afterward. It is now the language of about 200,000,000 men, a forty-fold increase in two centuries.

English Polyphonists

WE must mention briefly several of "the skillful in that science," for the greatest choral masterpieces of English music were composed *after* the Reformation, and for the then proscribed Latin service.

John Merbecke, after his editorship of *The Booke of Common Praier Noted,* abandoned music, and prepared a concordance of the Bible. Christopher Tye, choirmaster of Ely until 1561, wrote three fine Masses. He became an Anglican Priest and abandoned the public profession of music: it is recorded of him in a contemporary document, "He is a Doctor of Music; but not, however, skilful at preaching." On playing some elaborate but dry organ music to Queen Elizabeth at one time, she sent a message by a verger, "Doctor Tye, your music is out of tune." He sent the verger back with the reply, "Your majesty, your ears are out of tune."[14]

But the two great figures of Thomas Tallis and of William Byrd are in another category. Tallis had been organist of Waltham Abbey at the dissolution of the monasteries, in 1540. Subsequently, he served the Royal Chapel under Henry, Edward, Mary, and Elizabeth. He composed two Latin Masses, and two English Communion Services, besides a world of beautiful music apart from the Eucharist. William Byrd, by common consent the greatest of English musicians, was wholly a post Reformation composer. Although a Roman Catholic, he became

[14]Anthony Wood: "Doctor Tye was a peevish and humoursome man, especially in his latter days, and sometimes playing on ye Organ in ye chap. of qu. Elizab. wh. contained much musicke, but little delight to ye ear, she would send ye verger to tell him he play'd out of Tune: whereupon he sent word yt her eares were out of Tune."

organist of Lincoln Cathedral in 1563, and within a few years joint organist with Tallis at the Chapel Royal. Queen Elizabeth, a lover of good music, not only tolerated him, but granted to him and to Tallis jointly a twenty-one year monopoly for printing and selling music. For the Latin Mass, he composed three settings, besides many settings of the Proper. His English Eucharistic Music is incomplete, consisting only of *Kyrie* and *Credo,* according to the very bad custom of the late sixteenth century. But Byrd was a great instrumental composer as well; and in his long life put forth an amazing body of superior music of all kinds, most of which has only become known of recent years. Canon Fellowes, at the Byrd Tercentenary in 1923, wrote of him:

"If we consider Byrd's versatility alone, and the fact that he produced work of the highest class in every field that he explored, it becomes abundantly clear that he stood above his contemporaries."

With the magnificent climax of William Byrd and of his contemporary, Orlando Gibbons, the great period for English Eucharistic music came to an end. Before they died in 1623 and 1625, the Choral Eucharist practically disappeared; and the mediæval Roman Catholic practice of celebrating the Holy Mysteries without music became general in the English Church. In the days of Charles II, Bishop Cosin restored a full Choral Celebration at Durham: and both there and at Exeter, its monthly use continued unbroken throughout the worst days of Georgian coldness and apathy. The Choir music, in addition to the Dialogue, consisted, however, of only *Kyrie, Credo,* and *Sanctus:* and the few eighteenth-century settings which we possess are of slight moment.

THE RESTORATION OF THE SUNG EUCHARIST

THE general restoration of the Choral Eucharist during the past century has led to highly controversial developments in its musical treatment. It is sad that music, ideally a blender of men's hearts, should often, in this connection, prove to be a divider of their minds. Men otherwise gentle and kindly will grow fierce with resentment over what they like or dislike as the music for this primary service of the Church. Perhaps we can best avoid rancour if we put away from our thought all questions of liking or disliking, and endeavour to appraise the different solutions of the problem that have appeared in the experimental course of the nineteenth century by reference to standards: the standards so clearly established in the sixth, and reaffirmed with but little change in the sixteenth.

The revival of the Sung Eucharist in Parish Churches followed inevitably upon the return to primitive principles set forward by the Oxford Movement. Strangely enough, the first instance was in Ireland, in the County of Limerick. The second was at the Consecration of Leeds Parish Church in 1841, where it was repeated monthly. Samuel Sebastian Wesley, grandson of Charles Wesley, became organist there the following year, and composed his fine Communion Service in E with organ accompaniment; containing, however, only *Kyrie, Credo,* and *Sanctus.* The plan of a weekly Choral Eucharist was soon begun in the Chapel of Margaret Street, London, which was later replaced by All Saints Church. This normal Christian use spread with amazing rapidity in England: and led to a vast volume of new compositions, of adaptations from Latin services, and of revivals of ancient music.

Merbecke's unison music was reprinted after the lapse of three hundred years, and edited in many forms, with either vocal or instrumental accompaniment. It has made its way so amazingly as to become the music of the Eucharist at the opening of Lambeth Conferences. It is officially set forth by the Episcopal Church in America. Byrd's beautiful five voice Mass[15] was published in 1841; for concert use, to be sure. But that was the beginning of the great revival of polyphonic Mass music which is now moving on with accelerated pace.

In the new compositions, invariably with organ accompaniment, *Gloria in excelsis* soon found its place again, and later, two numbers not in the current English Prayer Book, although they had been in the Book of 1549: *Benedictus qui venit* and *Agnus Dei.*

But the standards of contemporary English Church Music were then at a low ebb, both artistically and devotionally. *No* standards were set, as of old, by the Royal Chapels. At Queen Victoria's Coronation alone, among all Anglican crownings, the Eucharist was said, not sung. Popular taste was at its lowest in all the arts. The great impulse of the Romantic Movement seemed in some ways to bring an advance: but unfortunately its weaker elements chiefly influenced English Church Music. A tendency toward the sentimental or the dramatic, rather than the devotional; a loosening of due correspondence with the form and text of the Liturgy; a shifting emphasis from the Congregation to the Choir; were unnoticed in a non-critical age when people were carried away with the pleasure of passive listening to, instead of actively sharing in, vocal worship.

Moreover, the center of gravity for many composers during

[15] See list of Records, pp. 74–76.

this period had passed from the choir to the organ; and in a very great number of settings, musical themes based upon impulses apart from the liturgical text led to meaningless repetitions of phrases and even of separate words. The total effect might be pleasing to the hearer: but the Liturgy was not adequately sung. No Eucharistic music of a consistently high order characterized this period. With the notable advance of recent years, we shall deal in the final chapter.

On the Continent, the ebb of the Polyphonic tide had been followed by the long, slow rise of a type of Mass music with orchestral accompaniment, which had culminated in such unparalleled masterpieces as Bach's B minor Mass and Beethoven's great Mass in D.

Illustrative Records:
  Victor Album M 104, Philharmonic Choir, London Orchestra:
    9955-9971, The B minor Mass, Bach.
  Victor Album M 29, Orfeo Catalá of Barcelona:
    9133-9144, *Missa Solemnis,* Beethoven.

But noble as these works are, they are for the concert hall, not for the Sanctuary. A host of lesser works, whose length permitted their use in Church, came to be considered typical Catholic music. Adaptations of them for English words and for organ accompaniment came into extensive use both in England and America. The great names of Haydn, Mozart, Weber, and Schubert gave them an almost irresistible appeal. Their prevalence in England was largely due to the good Roman Catholic publisher, Vincent Novello, who issued them in cheap editions. When performed with adequate orchestras and soloists, they were sometimes charming music: but it was essentially worldly music, not worship music. Their cheerful strains had not infrequently been written as vehicles for the opera singers and orchestras of their composers' noble patrons, who desired to be entertained by the same sort of music on Sundays as on weekdays. Some such Masses were sincere work, some were mere pot-boilers; all of them failed lamentably in liturgical correspondence with the service. They were symphonic in structure, not liturgical. When sung with English text and organ accompaniment by inadequate choral forces, they were musically as well as devotionally disastrous. They have no proper claim to be considered as Catholic music. As Sir Richard Terry, for long musical director of the Roman Westminster Cathedral, has pointed out, they are essentially Lutheran in form and spirit.

Illustrative Records:
    His Master's Voice, Philharmonic Choir, London:
      D 1875, *Kyrie eleison,* Twelfth Mass, Mozart.
      D 1478–1480, Mass in G, Schubert.
      DJ 100, *Crucifixus, Messe Solennelle,* Rossini (Caruso).
      DB 120, *Domine Deus, Messe Solennelle,* Rossini.
    Victor Album M 96, La Scala Chorus:
      9831–9840, *Requiem,* Verdi.

Let me quote from the 1922 Report of the English Archbishops' Committee on Music and Worship. "In this connection it may be well to say something about the custom of employing during the Choral Eucharist big works written for the Latin Rite during the eighteenth and nineteenth centuries. Such music is used with the laudable desire of offering the best that can be found. But the writings, though bearing the names of distinguished composers, seek, in great measure, to excite emotion by a kind of expression that is essentially mundane. Frequently both their structure and their length make them unsuitable for the Anglican Service. And, with reason, their use is forbidden in the Roman Church. More recent Masses, of which Gounod's *Messe Solennelle* may stand as an example, frankly exploit the idioms of the opera and the concert room, besides being also subject to the above objection. The dignity and the mystery of the Eucharist demand a different treatment. The great traditions of the past have set a fine example in the ascetic beauty of plainchant and in the timeless purity and religious art of the polyphonic period. Each age must find its own expression while retaining what is best in the past. But all such music ought to be characterized by a noble simplicity, an eloquent reticence, and a religious awe combined with the expression of deep inner feeling."

Illustrative Records:
 Victor 11154–11158, Societé Bach, Paris:
  Requiem, Gabriel Fauré, a modern work of transparent serenity.
 His Master's Voice, Philharmonic Choir, London:
  D 1147–1149, *Requiem,* Mozart, a classical Mass of true religious
  feeling.

These qualities are found to the full in the last great school of Liturgical Music, which has produced many works worthy to be considered the equal, both artistically and devotionally, of the sixth century Plainsong and the sixteenth century Polyphony. I refer to the noble modern Russian School. Based on ancient Slavic traditional melodies and choral methods, as the Polyphony was based on the Plainsong, perfect correspondence with the old liturgical principles has found expression in the settings of the Liturgy of St. John Chrysostom by such composers as Kastalsky, Kalinnikoff, Tchesnokoff, Gretchaninoff, and Rachmaninoff. Mention should also be made of settings by Bortniansky and Glinka, the notable predecessors of this school.

Illustrative Records:
    His Master's Voice, G–L 1005, Russian Metropolitan Choir:
        Cherubic Hymn No. 7, Bortniansky.
    Polydor R 65006, 65007, Ural Cossack Choir:
        Cherubic Hymn, Musichenko.
    Victor 20358 A, Russian Symphonic Choir:
        Cherubic Hymn, Glinka.
    Victor 36040 A, Russian Metropolitan Choir:
        Nicene Creed, Gretchaninoff.
    Victrola 7715 A, Russian Metropolitan Choir:
        Nicene Creed, *Liturgia Domestica,* Gretchaninoff.
    7715 B, Russian Metropolitan Choir:
        Nicene Creed, Archangelsky.
    Victor 20-68970 B, Russian Symphonic Choir:
        Nicene Creed, Gretchaninoff.

With English Text:
    Columbia DX 133, St. George's Chapel Choir:
        Angel spirits ever blessed, Tchaikovsky.
    Victor 22709, St. Bartholomew's Choir:
        How blest are they, Tchaikovsky.
    His Master's Voice, B 3731, St. Paul's Cathedral Choir:
        Contakion of the Departed, edited by Walter Parratt.
    His Master's Voice, B 3763, Westminster Abbey Choir:
        Veneration of the Cross, Rachmaninoff, edited by Winfred Douglas.

These works form a priceless treasure for us, not merely because they are available with English text for the use of our choirs; but still more so because they prove that the great human fountain of consummate praise to God in the words of the Eucharistic Liturgy has not run dry; and that devout composers of the time to come have at least three ideal models to rouse their emulation in the heavenly work of musical worship. Of the creators of these three great treasuries of beauty, we may say,

> Their joy unto their Lord we bring,
>   Their song to us descendeth;
> The Spirit who in them did sing
>   To us his music lendeth:
> His song in them, in us, is one;
> We raise it high, we send it on —
> The song that never endeth.[16]

[16]Hymn 424.

CHAPTER IV

THE MUSIC OF THE OFFICE BEFORE THE
REFORMATION: GREGORIAN PSALMODY

THE GROWTH OF THE OFFICE

WE must now turn to the music of the subsidiary Offices, preparatory to, and reminiscent of, the Eucharist. Their origin and
development are shrouded in greater obscurity than is the case
with the Liturgy proper. It cannot, I think, be assumed, as is
commonly the case, that the Offices are a direct inheritance from
Synagogue worship, or that the melodies and method of our
singing of the Psalms are Jewish; although the early Plainsong
doubtless inherited a few melodies from other portions of
Hebrew musical tradition, one of which I shall cite later. Undoubtedly the earliest Christians joined in the Synagogue worship. They would continue some of the old forms of Hebrew
piety with little change, when later on they were thrust out of
the Synagogue. And these old forms, the reading of Scriptures,
preaching, prayers, and psalmody of some sort, must have been
constituent parts of Christian worship, apart from the Eucharist,
from the very beginning. The original purpose of the Synagogue
was for Scripture reading and exposition; though doubtless the
element of worship was found in some degree in very early times.

In the first half of the second century, Psalms cxlv–cl were said in the daily Synagogue service.[1] Certain other Psalms were prescribed for special days. But there was nothing corresponding to the much later Christian plan of Offices built primarily from the Psalter. The old Jewish hours of prayer were kept privately by Christians from the first. The early third century *Canons of Hippolytus* prescribe them, and add prayers at bed time and at midnight. But by the close of the fourth century, the *Apostolic Constitutions* very definitely describe two principal daily public services with prescribed Psalms, besides lesser Offices at the other accustomed hours of prayer. The Spanish pilgrim, Etheria, in her fascinating account of services at Jerusalem and Bethlehem about the year 385 A.D., indicates the singing of Psalms at Morning and Evening Offices (which were better attended than the lesser hours), congregational Responses, and the use of special Psalms and Scripture Lessons for Holy Week and for Festivals. And these services were definitely for all the clergy and faithful, not merely for the monastic groups. We do not know what music was used for the Psalms at these Eastern Offices; but we do know that the antiphonal method of singing them was already familiar there. Might this in some form, date back to Apostolic times, when St. Paul could twice refer[2] to the Asiatic Christians as 'putting one another in mind in psalms and hymns and spiritual songs'? Possibly; however, Socrates, the church historian who died A.D. 440,[3] speaks of this custom having been introduced at Antioch, by St. Ignatius, probably martyred in the reign of Trajan. The method was thoroughly familiar to St. Basil the Great. This custom of alternate singing

[1]Rabbi Jose ben Chalaphta, *Sopherim* xvii:11.
[2]Col. iii:16; Eph. v:19.   [3]*Hist. Eccles.* vi:8.

of the Psalms, with the interpolation of a refrain sung by all, spread through the entire East. Its real origin in Temple and Synagogue we have already discussed. It was introduced at Rome by Damasus I; and at Milan by St. Ambrose, at the time of his persecution by the Arian empress Justina. St. Augustine tells us expressly that this was *"secundum morem orientalium partium,"* "after the custom of the Eastern Churches." He takes delight in the melodic sweetness of the new music, and yet hesitates, almost afraid to accept the feeling of personal pleasure from the song addressed to God. Few worshippers of our day are troubled with so sensitive a conscience in the matter of enjoying church music! Paulinus, the Deacon, speaking of the innovation, says, "Then, for the first time, Antiphons . . . began to be part of the use of the Church in Milan: which devout use lasts to our day . . . in nearly every province of the West."

CENTRAL IMPORTANCE OF THE PSALTER

ONE fact germane to our purpose stands out clearly in the history of the Office at Milan. At an early date, it included the singing of the entire Psalter every two weeks: which is still the custom of the Ambrosian rite.

At Rome, there is evidence that prior to the sixth century, the *weekly* recitation of the Psalter became the basic principle of the Offices. This is very definitely the case in the order of worship set forth about A.D. 530 by St. Benedict in the Holy Rule, with complete detail. Doubtless his plan was based upon the Roman order, which he modified and enriched to suit the needs of a body of laymen living in Community with a wholesome alternation of liturgical prayer and physical work. Eleven of his seventy-three chapters are occupied with explicit directions for this public prayer: and he makes it a primary consideration that the whole Psalter be said in the course of a week. St. Benedict also added two Offices, Prime at early morning, and Compline at the close of the day: and included one wholly novel element: *Ambrosiani*, or Hymns, one of which was to be included in each Office. The Hymns, however, we shall consider in a later chapter.

From this time on, we have a completely developed scheme of public Offices in the West, of which the Roman and Benedictine forms differ but slightly in detail. Both came to England; and, subject to various developments and alterations, continued in use until the Reformation. The greatest changes in the Roman Office were due to the Franciscan movement. A radical shortening of Scripture and other lessons, and an immense increase in the number and rank of Festivals, which practically resulted in the almost complete neglect of the ancient regular weekly recitation of the Psalms, and the orderly continuous public reading of Holy Scripture. The Offices became more and more a matter for the Clergy only. Public attendance at divine worship, apart from the Mass, was practically limited to presence at the singing of the old Morning Office before Mass and of Vespers at night, on Sundays and Holy Days: and such public attendance became passive rather than active. The Franciscan innovations made less headway in England than on the Continent: and the old non-monastic uses in England, such as the Sarum rite put forth by St. Osmund in the eleventh century, and the somewhat similar uses of York, Bangor, and Hereford, largely retained their pre-Franciscan character; and were closely allied to the Mediæval Dominican use, both in text and music.

But from this hasty survey of change and decay, let us return to consider the music of the Office in the golden age of Plain-song. The greater part of the music, as of the Office itself, was devoted to the Psalms: not only were *all* of the Psalms to be sung in the course of a week, but the words of the Antiphons which so beautifully frame each Psalm and clarify its devotional pur-pose, were generally chosen from the Psalm. The musical dia-logue between Officiant and Choir was chosen from the Psalms. The words of Psalms formed most of the Responds: both the elaborate solo Responds used between lessons at Matins and occasionally at Vespers, and the simple Short Responds of the lesser Hours. And furthermore, there were incorporated into various Offices Psalm-like Canticles from both the Old Testa-ment and the New.

EARLY METHODS OF PSALMODY

BUT this overwhelming preponderance of Psalmody, although it includes the various types of music which we have already considered in the Psalmody of the Mass, is in every case far simpler. Within the bounds of its simplicity, however, there is the most delicate musical discrimination, the finest and most artistic distinction, in the means used to bring out the relative importance of portions of the Service. We will consider each type of Psalmody in turn and note its relationship with the corresponding Psalmody of the Mass. The methods there, you will remember, were three: and each is represented in the Chant of the Office.

Direct Psalmody

THE first, *Cantus directaneus,* is so called because the chorus sings the Psalm straight through, *in directum.* without any alternation. It is of extreme simplicity, having a musical inflection only at the central pause of the verse. The method is that of the Tract at Mass, but the Tract is elaborate solo Chanting, and the *Psalmus in directum* the acme of simple chorus Chanting.

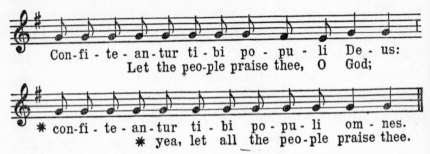

Con-fi - te - an-tur ti - bi po - pu - li De - us:
Let the peo-ple praise thee, O God;

* con-fi - te - an-tur ti - bi po - pu - li om - nes.
* yea, let all the peo-ple praise thee.

Responsorial Psalmody

RESPONSORIAL Psalmody, the alternation between a soloist and Choir, was sung in three forms in the Office; all of them less ornate than the rich solo Psalmody of the Gradual and the Alleluia Respond in the Mass. The simplest is that known in modern parlance as the Short Respond. In the Sarum and Roman Offices, it occurs in the Little Hours; in the Monastic Office, at Lauds and Vespers. It is a delightful little form. An example taken from Compline is very familiar in the American Episcopal Church, and well illustrates the Responsorial method, with its charming contrast of melody and refrain.

1ˢᵗ time, Cantor: the Choir repeats   Mode **vi**

In-to thy hands, O Lord, *I com-mend my spi-rit.

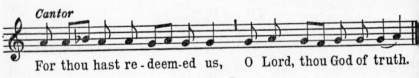

Cantor

For thou hast re - deem-ed us, O Lord, thou God of truth.

The next form in elaboration, the Invitatory Psalm *Venite exultemus Domino* at the beginning of Matins, is of unusual interest to us because of the recent restoration, in the American Prayer Book, of permissive use for both the unmutilated version of Psalm 95, and of nine of the ancient Responsorial refrains.[4] With methods for present day musical use, we shall deal in the fifth chapter; but the original method was set forth by St. Benedict in the Holy Rule. The refrain, which has come to be liturgically known as the Invitatory, was sung by the soloist, then repeated by the Choir. Its music was moderately elaborate. The soloist then sang the *Venite* alone, while the Choir interpolated the Refrain in whole or in part, after the second, fourth, seventh, ninth, and eleventh verses, and after the *Gloria Patri*. Each of the *Venite* melodies is long enough for two verses of the Psalm. The whole formed a glorious porch to the structure of the daily Office, a prelude unsurpassed in dignity and musical

[4]See *The Choral Service*, pp. 41–45, 85–91; *The Congregational Choral Service*, pp. 15–18.

fitness even by the famous introduction to Beethoven's Seventh Symphony. Those who have been fortunate enough to hear Matins sung by a good monastic Choir will never forget either the musical or the devotional experience.

The third Responsorial form corresponded in function to the Gradual and the Alleluia Respond between the Eucharistic Lessons of Epistle and Gospel, but it was somewhat simpler in character. The early service of Vigils, which developed into the Night Office, or Matins, was rather informal; but was characterized by the reading of Scripture lessons of greater length than those at the dawn service of Lauds and the evening service of Vespers. In the developed Matins, three groups known as

Nocturns each contained, first, several Psalms; then Scripture or other Lessons divided into sections. Between these sections occurred the great Responds: the Verses sung in elaborate Psalmody by the soloist, the Choir joining in the richly ornate refrain which was sung wholly or in part after each verse. The earlier manuscripts give 800 of these Responds. In the Sarum and other older Offices, one was sung after the single short Lesson at Vespers. Msgr. Battifol, in his *History of the Breviary*, compares the greater Responds interpolated between the Lessons of Matins in the Office of the Season to the eloquent comment of the Chorus in the classical tragedies of ancient Greece. A few Anglican religious houses still sing them in part, but they are unlikely to be sung elsewhere, notwithstanding their beauty, except at *Tenebræ* on the three days before Easter.

Illustrative Records:
    Victor Album M 87, I, II, Solesmes Abbey Choir:
        Victrola 7346–A, *Ecce quomodo*, Respond VI, *Tenebræ*, Easter Eve.
        Victrola 7346–B, *Tenebræ factæ sunt*, Respond V, *Tenebræ*, Good Friday.
        Victrola 7350-A, *Descendit*, Respond IV, Christmas Matins.
        Victrola 7351-A, *Media vita*, Respond IV, Septuagesima.
        Victrola 7351-B, *Christus resurgens*, Respond III, Wednesday in Easter Week.
    Victor Album M 177, Pius X Choir:
        Victrola 11528-B, *Subvenite*, Burial Office.
        Victrola 11531-B, *Libera*, Burial Office.
    Columbia DFX 155, Choir of Notre Dame d'Auteuil:
    Media vita, Christus resurgens.

Antiphonal Psalmody

BUT the main body of the ancient Choir Offices was sung to the most important and permanent form of chanting, Antiphonal Psalmody: a form which has continued to the present day in its completeness in the Latin rite; and in a mutilated form in the Anglican Communion and among the Lutherans. The last revision of the American Prayer Book contains evidence of a growing desire to restore Antiphonal Psalmody to its true form. We find a series of Antiphons, so named, printed with their Psalms in the Office of the Visitation of the Sick; an Office, I should judge, little likely to call for musical efforts on the part of the Clergy, the Choir, or the sick person being visited: but nevertheless the recognition of the Antiphon is made openly in the Prayer Book.

Principles of Antiphonal Psalmody

WHAT is the principle of Antiphonal Psalmody? It is not merely that of chanting Psalm verses by answering choirs; but of completing the alternate musical chant with a refrain sung by all; a refrain which not only brings the music to a satisfying close, but also affords an enrichment to the Psalm itself, subtly reinforcing the devotional purpose with which its words are sung on that particular occasion.[5]

This brings us to the very practical matter of the Gregorian Psalm Tone, which is what most people mean when they speak of Plainsong. What *is* a Psalm Tone? Like all chants, it is a combination of monotone recitation and melodic cadence.

The simplest such combination we know is that of the Versicles and Responses at Evening Prayer, taken directly from the ancient Dialogue of the Office.

[5]See pp. 106, 134.

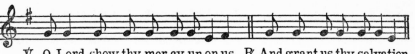

℣. O Lord, show thy mer-cy up-on us. ℟. And grant us thy salvation.

℣. O Lord, save the State. ℟. And mer-ci-ful-ly hear us when we

call up-on thee. ℣. En-due thy Min-is-ters with right-eous-ness.

℟. And make thy cho-sen peo-ple joy-ful. ℣. O Lord, save thy peo-ple.

℟. And bless thine in-her-it-ance. ℣. Give peace in our time, O Lord.

℟. For it is thou, Lord, on-ly, that mak-est us dwell in safe-ty.

℣. O God, make clean our hearts with-in us.

℟. And take not thy Ho-ly Spir-it from us.

Illustrative Record:

His Master's Voice Album 24, Choir of St. George's, Windsor:
D 965, The Versicles and Responses.

[103]

Such must have been the early method under the recommendation of St. Athanasius, that the simplicity of the inflection should make the chant resemble a recitation rather than a melody.

In the Milanese Chant, which doubtless dates back to St. Ambrose, we have slightly more elaborated cadences; but as in the Responses, only a single cadence for the verse.

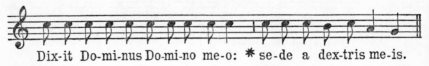

Dix-it Do-mi-nus Do-mi-no me-o: * se-de a dex-tris me-is.

These simple methods were insufficient in two respects: they were not definitely placed in any scale, and were therefore vague musically; and they failed to correspond with the characteristic two-fold form of the Psalm verse, with its distinct central pause.

The Gregorian Psalm Tone remedied the first fault by adding an Intonation, several notes which definitely placed the Chant in one of the eight ancient scales, and made the reciting note the dominant of the scale: it remedied the second fault by adding a medial cadence, or rather semi-cadence, at the close of the first half of the verse, and a fresh recitation followed by the final cadence for the second half.

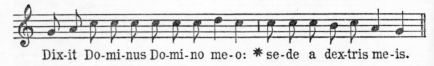

Dix-it Do-mi-nus Do-mi-no me-o: * se-de a dex-tris me-is.

The Antiphons

BUT an examination of the ancient Psalm Tones shows that very few of the final cadences ended on the final note of the scale in which the Chant was placed. Such tones are musically incomplete. They leave the singer or the listener as unsatisfied as though a modern composer should end his song on an unresolved discord. Therefore the Antiphon, or final refrain, which cleverly dovetailed into the final cadence of the Psalm Tone at the end of the last verse, and brought the whole piece to a satisfying close with a simple flowing melody resting at last on the final of the scale, was an absolutely necessary integral part of the plan. Whoever has never heard Gregorian Psalms chanted with Antiphons has never heard Gregorian Tones; but only a mutilation of them.

Illustrative Records:

Victor Album M 177, Pius X Choir:
Victrola 11528-A, Ant. *Si iniquitates,* Ps. 130.
Victrola 11528-B, Ant. *Exsultabunt,* Ps. 51 Lauds of the Dead.
Victrola 11531–B, Ant. *Lux æterna,* Verse, *Requiem æternam.*
Victrola 11532-B, Ant. *Ego sum,* Cant. *Benedictus.*
His Master's Voice, Ampleforth Abbey Choir:
C 2088, Ant. *Miserere mihi,* Ps. 134.
C 2087, Ant. *Asperges me,* Ps. 51.
Victor 24820-A, Ant. *Asperges me,* Ps. 51, School children.
Victor 24820–B, Ant. *Adoremus,* Ps. 117, School children.
Victor V 6199–A, Ant. *Lux æterna,* Verse, *Requiem æternam,* Beuron Abbey Choir.
Victor Album M 87, I, II, Solesmes Abbey Choir:
Victrola 7345-B, *Montes Gelboe.*
Victrola 7347-B, *Salve, Regina.*
Victrola 7351-B, Easter Antiphons of Blessed Hartker.
Gramophone Shop Album 132, Paderborn Cathedral Boys:
Polydor 22198, *Alma Redemptoris, Regina cæli, Ave, Regina, Salve, Regina,* Antiphons after Compline.
Victor V 6199-A, *In Paradisum,* Beuron Abbey Choir.
His Master's Voice, Ampleforth Abbey Choir:
C 2087, *Salve, Regina.*
Victor 24820-B, *Ave Maria,* School children.
Victor Album M 177, Pius X Choir:
In Paradisum.

There were over two thousand of these golden nuggets of pure melody in the Office. They are classified into forty-seven distinct types, of which the common characteristic feature is the delightful ingenuity with which each opening coalesces with the close of the proper Psalm Tone Ending. Many attain a degree of musical expressiveness which makes them little master-pieces of song: and when the regular swing of the chanted Psalmody from side to side of the choir closes at the *Gloria Patri,* and both sides unite in the surging phrases of such an Antiphon, bringing all the singers to a satisfying final close, we realize that here is a simple form of human praise which for ever settles the musical problem of the prose text. Such a form must neither be allowed to die out, nor to become mutilated. Its use (that is, the use of the old melodic refrains with the Gregorian Chant; and as we shall see in the next chapter, of refrains in harmony, with the Anglican Chant, when suitable) may be one of the means in restoring Chanting to the rightful place which it has largely lost in the American Episcopal Church.[6]

Method of Prose Chanting in Plainsong

THE great problem of singing prose texts (and practically all of our liturgical texts in the Prayer Book are prose) is beau-tifully solved by the ingenious construction of the Psalm Tones, which permits expansion by the addition of notes for extra un-accented syllables, and contraction by the omission of notes, to correspond invariably with verbal accents. A Gregorian Tone is not a little tune sung over and over mechanically, as the

[6]A recent example in very wide use may be found in the Wellesley Compline, in which *Nunc dimittis* with its proper Antiphon is set to modern music. The pamphlet may be had of the Church Periodical Club, New York.

Anglican Chant has been for almost a century: it is a flexible formula sensitive to every rhythmical variation of a prose text, and assuming its precise form.

The means whereby this lovely correspondence is attained are very simple. We saw in the first chapter that the tonic accent, both in Latin and in English, is the rhythm-producing element in speech; and that a syllable, so accented, naturally tends to a higher pitch. In the two cadences of the Psalm tone formula, therefore, whenever the first note of the cadence rises *above* the reciting note, it attracts to itself an accented syllable. As accent recurs normally at every second or third syllable, in the latter case an extra note must be interpolated for the extra syllable. The following verses from the 51st Psalm exemplify the method.

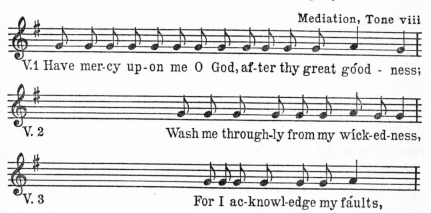

Mediation, Tone viii

V.1 Have mer-cy up-on me O God, af-ter thy great góod - ness;

V. 2 Wash me through-ly from my wíck-ed-ness,

V. 3 For I ac-knowl-edge my fáults,

Should the cadence be a longer one, rising above the reciting note, not at the last metrical foot, but at the one before the last, the same flexible process is carried out in both feet.

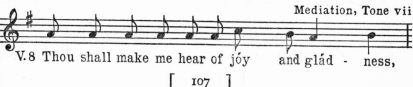

Mediation, Tone vii

V. 8 Thou shall make me hear of jóy   and glád - ness,

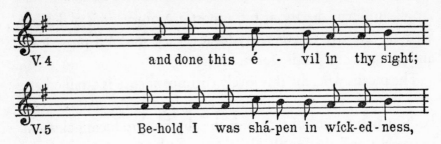

For the purpose of always bringing a preponderant accent in the text to the corresponding note in the chant, a phrase may be contracted, by the omission of a note.

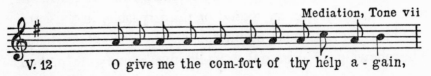

Of course, the final syllable of the whole verse must fall on the last note of the final cadence, or ending. Only the central cadence, or mediation, may be left incomplete.

In a very short verse, not only may a contraction occur, but a recitation or even part of a cadence may be entirely omitted. These processes of expansion and contraction are illustrated in two verses of *Nunc dimittis*.[7]

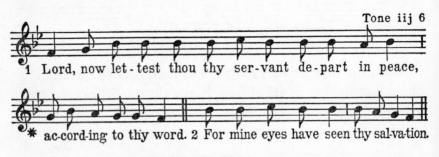

We must do no more than give the foregoing very brief sug-

[7]See *The Hymnal*, Chant 635.

gestion of this subtle artistic method of chanting a prose text.[8] It is evident that it involves constant attention on the part of the singers to the normal reading of the words, so as to bring out their meaning; the importance of this fact in the devotional use of music cannot be sufficiently emphasized. Ralph Waldo Emerson was probably unacquainted with the Gregorian Psalm Tones, but nevertheless, in an essay of his,[9] I find the most perfect description of how to sing them. He says "The secret . . . is, that the thought constructs the tune, so that reading for the sense will best bring out the rhythm."

Musical Origin of the Chants

WHAT was the musical origin of these chant formulas, and of the actual Antiphon melodies which completed them? A comparison of the chants with those of the Ambrosian tradition, shows that most of the endings were developed from that source. And that source leads us, as we have seen, directly to the East. It does *not,* however, lead us to any ancient Hebrew melodies for the Psalms: but I cite an instance of precise correspondence between a melody of the oldest Hebrew musical tradition, that of the Persian Jews, and a Gregorian tone.

The Persian melody is not for the Psalms, but for the Shema'.[10]

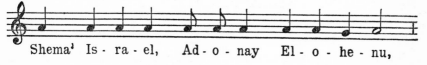

Shema' Is - ra - el,   Ad - o - nay   El - o - he - nu,

[8]It may be studied more fully in *The Hymnal,* pp. 723 and 725 and completely exemplified in *The Plainsong Psalter.*

[9]*On Reading Shakspere.*

[10]Lazare Saminsky, *Music of the Ghetto and the Bible,* p. 16.

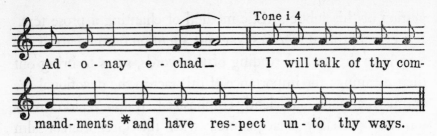

Not only do the Tones, whatever their ultimate sources, reflect perfectly the rhythms of the Latin Psalter: but the Antiphon melodies, many of which doubtless came also from the Orient, were re-formed melodically to bring out the Latin sentences in their own rhythm and rhetorical expression. Doubtless not all of them were Eastern: one famous Antiphon melody in particular, set most cleverly to scores of different prose texts, shows every evidence of having been a popular Roman song. It does not fit into any of the usual classifications, but keeps its highly individual character with all texts.[11]

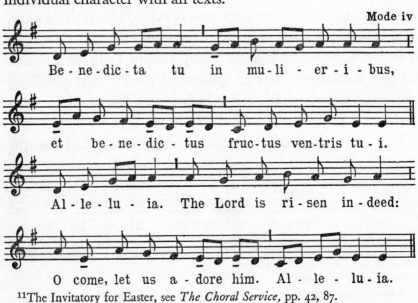

[11]The Invitatory for Easter, see *The Choral Service*, pp. 42, 87.

The Chant of the Gospel Canticles

THE music of the Gospel Canticles was of the same antiphonal type, but was much richer, both in the character of the Psalm Tones and of the Antiphons. Ornamental Intonations, Recitations, and Medial Cadences, and in some cases special Final Cadences, enriched the Tones: and the corresponding Antiphons, often developed from the simpler Ambrosian forms, were models of expressive flowing melody. A brief example may be one of the great Antiphons sung on successive days before Christmas, with its special Psalm Tone for Magnificat.[12]

₁₂See also *Magnificat*, Chant 618, *The Hymnal*.

Such a delicate sensitiveness as to liturgical proportion, as to the relative *devotional* importance of the various units of the Liturgy, is sadly lacking in most modern composers of sacred music: and alas, in the minds of a large proportion of the clergy and choir directors who have the responsibility of choosing music for their services.

Comparing the Antiphonal Psalmody of the Office with that of the Mass, we find, as might be expected, that the Introit Antiphons and Psalm Tones are still more fully developed than those of the Gospel Canticles, and along the same lines.

The Canticle *Te Deum laudamus* stands apart from all of the other music of the Office. One section of its music is related to Antiphonal Psalmody: but because of certain analogies in literary form, I will discuss this great Hymn and its ancient music with other Hymns in the sixth chapter.

For the other liturgical units of the Office, the same simplicity, as compared with the Mass, obtained. We are all familiar with the Dialogue, the Versicles and Responses. Anciently the Lessons were sung to very plain formulas less elaborate than those of the Epistles and Gospels, but sometimes enriched on Festivals.

Illustrative Record:

Gramophone Shop Album 132, Dortmund Choir:
Polydor 90057 *Quomodo sedet,* Lesson I, Matins, Maundy Thursday.

When the Collect of the Mass was also introduced into the Office, it doubtless brought its own musical intonations into the two principal Offices of Morning and Evening; and was monotoned at the other Hours.

THE DECLINE OF THE PLAINSONG OFFICE

Rhymed Offices

SUCH were the elements of the musical Office when Plainsong was at its best. But after the golden age, although much new music was composed for Offices later introduced into the Liturgy, the genius for this type of composition was gone. A decadent fashion set in for Offices in metre or rhyme, and was carried to unbelievable lengths. Thus Stephen, Bishop of Liège, composed music for such an Office of the Holy Trinity at the close of the ninth century. It was very dull. The first Antiphon was as follows:

Gloria tibi Trinitas
Æqualis, una Deitas,
Et ante omnia sæcula,
Et nunc, et in perpetuum.

Glory to thee, O Trinity
Co-equal, onely Deity,
Ere yet the worlds began to be,
And now, and through eternity.

The Franciscan Archbishop of Canterbury, John Peckham, who died in 1292 A.D., just before Pope John XXII ordered the Feast of the Most Holy Trinity to be observed throughout the Western Church on the Octave of Pentecost, wrote a still more elaborate rhymed Office of the Trinity, of considerable beauty. The later Middle Ages were full of ceaseless experiment, both liturgical and musical. This particular experiment was unfruitful; though it was to be repeated *ad nauseam* after the Reformation in the metrical Psalters.

Descant and Faux-bourdon

BUT the great experiment, that of inventing and developing many-voiced music, was extraordinarily fruitful in the Office, as in the Mass. Two of its earlier and simpler methods were destined to become of lasting importance in the music of the Office; the forms known as Descant and Faux-bourdon. Descant, originally, was simply the art of adding one or more flowing, contrapuntal parts in measured music to the notes of a given Plainsong melody so modified rhythmically as to be also mensurable.

Records illustrative of Descant:

Victor 20897 B, Example 3, Palestrina Choir.
Columbia History of Music, I, Terry Choir.
Columbia 5710, *Mira lege,* with Descant.
2000-Jahre Musik Album, Berlin Academy Choir, *Congaudeant Catholici,* 12th century.

Tallis' Festal Responses illustrate the developed form. Singers were trained in the art of adding such a part or parts by rule: so that with only the notes of the Plainsong before them, they could improvise the Descant. This practice continued in England right through the Reformation period. It has suggested the idea of adding a free part for the trebles of the Choir above some portions of any well-known congregational melody; and this device has greatly increased our simpler musical resources at the present time.

Faux-bourdon was originally a method by which the Plainsong melody, instead of being the lowest part, was transferred by the singer an octave higher, and became the highest. Dufay, whose quaint *Gloria in excelsis* was cited in the previous chapter, developed this form. Later on, the term came to signify a type of harmonized chant with simple polyphonic cadences, in which the Plainsong melody, more or less disguised, generally appeared in the tenor part.

Records illustrative of Faux-bourdon:
    Victor 20897-A, Palestrina Choir:
      Magnificat.
      Gloria Patri, Palestrina.
    Columbia History of Music I, Terry Choir.
      Columbia 5711, *Christe Redemptor,* Dufay.
      Columbia 5711, *Conditor alme siderum,* Dufay.
      Columbia 5711, *Nunc dimittis,* Anonymous.
      Columbia 5711, *Nunc dimittis,* Palestrina.
    l'Anthologie Sonore II, Vocal Quartet.
      A. S. 30, Psalm 25, Claude Goudimel, 1505-1572.
      A. S. 31, Psalm 42, Claude Le Jeune, 1528-1600.
    Victrola Album M 182, The Sistine Choir.
      Victrola 7813-B, *Improperia,* The Reproaches, Good Friday, Palestrina.
    Victor 20898-B, *Improperia,* The Reproaches, Palestrina Choir.

The immense usefulness of this device came with the practice of singing alternate verses of a Canticle or Psalm in the congregational Plainsong, the Choir taking the answering verses in Faux-bourdon. Thus a new distribution was effected which gives both Congregation and Choir due opportunity for praise. During the contrapuntal period there grew up a vast repertory of such settings. Many of them are available today, and they are quite as effective in English as in Latin. They form an ideal solution of the problem of music for the Canticles. At the opening of a recent Diocesan Convention in Colorado, I heard *Magnificat* and *Nunc dimittis* most effectively sung in this manner.

Continuation of Free Rhythm in Polyphony

WITH the final perfection of counterpoint in the matchless works of the sixteenth century, we find that the great merit of the earlier Antiphonal Plainsong has developed in a new way. Just as the text itself, in its natural diction, was the formative influence in shaping Antiphons and Psalm Tones; so in the masterpieces of counterpoint the phrases of the text shape those of the music with equal simplicity: and we have a resulting woven web of perfect musical phrases in quite independent rhythms: but all built up into a unified form of profound religious expression.[13] It is impossible to judge such music by playing it over on a piano or organ from a modern edition with bar lines. The bar lines *seem* to reduce the whole composition to a regular time counting; whereas the phrases are really perfectly free. Instrumentally, such music can only be performed with strings, as was often the case of old: but the phrases are purely vocal. The soaring voices seem to carry the soul of the devout worshipper to the heaven of heavens, to the rapt contemplation of the eternal God, beyond the limitations of time and space.

It is perhaps significant that so many of these superb compositions are settings of the Responds of the Office. That would be their obvious place. Just as the old Responsorial Psalmody afforded the highly skilled singers opportunity to make their due offering of praise to God, so this new and greater development continued that opportunity. Quite naturally, where choirs could sing music like this, the old elaborate Plainsong was disregarded and almost forgotten. From the twelfth century on

[13]See also pp. 76, 77.

till the twentieth, it practically ceased to be a factor in musical worship. The old framework of the Office in its Dialogue remained. The old weekly offering of the entire Psalter in antiphonal Psalmody remained only in theory: for the vast increase in festivals with a small number of proper Psalms crowded out the ancient orderly course. The Hymns, which we shall consider later, remained, but they ceased to be popular hymns as Latin grew less and less familiar to the ordinary man. The music of the Office, shortly before the Reformation, had become more and more a function of the Choir and Clergy, with the Congregation of the faithful merely passive listeners. Such a distortion of the normal order could not continue without the rise of enormous forces for readjustment; for the truly Christian man must and will have his share in the praise of God. Thus after the six hundred years which brought the Latin Plainsong of the Office to its perfection, and the further six hundred years which developed Latin Polyphony to its glorious climax of beauty, the daily praise of God in the music of the Office was ready for the next great step in England: the return to the native speech, as once before in Rome it had been transferred from the disappearing Greek idiom to the new and popular vernacular Latin.

Records illustrative of the Polyphonic Respond:

Orlando di Lasso †1594

Polydor, 27116, Munich Cathedral Choir:
Tristis est anima mea, Respond 8, Maundy Thursday.
Polydor 22587, *Surrexit pastor bonus*, Respond 4, Easter

Tomás Luis da Victoria †1608

Disco Gramofono AB 578, Orfeó Catalá, Barcelona.
Caligaverunt, Respond 5, Good Friday.
O magnum mysterium, Respond 4, Christmas.

Columbia DFX 18, Choir of the Sainte-Chapelle, Paris.
O vos omnes, Respond 8, Easter Eve.
Victrola Album M 182, The Sistine Choir:
7814-A, *Tenebræ factæ sunt,* Respond 7, Good Friday.

Gregor Aichinger 1565-1628

Victrola Album M 212, Dijon Cathedral Choir:
11679 B, *Ubi est Abel,* Respond 11, Septuagesima.

Records illustrative of Polyphony in the Office:

2000-Jahre Musik Album, Berlin Cathedral Choir:
Parlophon B 37027, *Miserere,* Ps. 51, di Lasso.
Polydor 22528, Palestrina, Paderborn Cathedral Choir:
Antiphon, *O admirabile commercium,* Circumcision.
Victor 20410-A, Palestrina, Princeton Westminster Choir:
Ant., *Hodie Christus natus est,* Christmas.
Montserrat Album, Montserrat Abbey Choir:
Disco Gramofono AE 2033, Ant. *Ave Maria,* Victoria.
Victor Album M 182, The Sistine Choir:
7812-B, Ant. *Ave Maria,* Jacob Arcadelt †1575.
Victor 21622-A, Palestrina Choir:
Ant. *Ave Maria,* Arcadelt.
Polydor 27107, Sweelinck, St. Hedwig's Choir, Berlin:
Ant. *Hodie Christus natus est.*

CHAPTER V

OFFICE MUSIC SINCE THE REFORMATION

ABSOLUTE AND APPLIED MUSIC

Absolute music, that is, music in its purest form, existing by itself apart from all conditioning connection with ideas expressed in another medium, has been but little used in the service of the Church. In the ancient music of the Mass, it appeared in the rich jubilations sung to the vowel 'a' in the Alleluia Respond. Certain strange melodies, the *Sequelæ,* introduced later on for pure vocalization without words, were similar. In modern times, while we possess priceless treasures of pure instrumental music congruous to spiritual aspiration, no great amount of it is susceptible of Church use. Its beneficent impact on the human soul almost invariably takes place in the concert hall or in the home. Even the great Chorale Preludes for the organ by Johann Sebastian Bach,[1] the very summits of religious instrumental music, are not absolute music. They are conditioned by the words and associations of the hymns from which they are named.

With these rare exceptions of pure wordless vocal melody, or of organ or other instrumental music unassociated even by implication with any other art, but productive of religious emotion, Church Music is *applied* music, which can only attain its true characteristic excellence in being the faithful and subordinate handmaid of the liturgical words to which it is sung.

[1]See p. 233 and list of records, p. 240.

Church Music is a means to an end: the end being the Praise of God, the external expression of the God-ward side of vital religion.

This being the case, so cataclysmic a change as that, not merely to another language, but to a different type of language, with a different rhythmical balance, could not fail to be a disintegrating force, at first. The earlier change from Greek to Latin had been far less difficult, because of the exceedingly close rhythmical relationship between the two tongues. But it was Latin which shaped the Gregorian Plainsong, and it was Latin equally which shaped the miracles of devotional expression created by the polyphonic masters. What would be the effect on Church Music of services in German, or in French, or in English?

URGES TOWARD CHANGE AT THE REFORMATION

THERE were three great urges affecting the Offices of Divine worship in the Reformation period, quite apart from the urge to eliminate whatever might be considered as false or superstitious. They were the urges toward the use of the vernacular, toward simplicity, and toward uniformity.

Toward the Vernacular

BY all odds the most powerful was that toward the use of the vernacular. Both in England and in northern Europe, where popular speech was more remote from Latin than were the Romance languages of Italy and Spain, this tendency had brought about a series of vernacular public devotions called the Prone, in connection with the Sermon at High Mass. It contained a bidding prayer for intercessions, a confession and abso-

lution, the Creed, the Lord's Prayer, and the Ten Commandments with explanation, and the Church notices. Archbishop
Peckham, to whose elaborate rhymed Office of the Holy Trinity
I referred in the previous chapter, particularly enjoined the
Decalogue with instruction in 1281 A.D. Inevitably, the Prone
prepared the way for the adoption of native speech in the services
themselves. On the Continent, Martin Luther at first yielded
to this tendency by having the Lessons read in German: but in
1526 he put forth an Order of 'Divine Service in German,'
followed a few years later by a German Litany. The Sunday
Offices contained Psalms, Lessons, a Collect, the Gospel Canticles, and *Te Deum laudamus* in German; on weekdays both
Latin and German were used. The use of modified Plainsong
melodies began at that time; it has continued ever since among
the Lutherans. But the German movement chiefly affected
Church Music in the matter of rhymed metrical versions of
liturgical units, as we shall see later. In this it followed the
pre-Reformation practice of using Offices in verse.

In England, you will remember that Cranmer's Litany, with
its exceedingly bald and simple music,[2] was set forth in 1544
for use on Wednesdays and Fridays. The following year Cranmer abandoned his idea of an English Processional, and ordered
the English Litany as the Procession on Sundays and Feasts
also. The way was now prepared for English Offices, with
appropriate music.

Toward Simplicity

AND at this juncture, we shall observe the operation of the
urge to simplicity pushed very far. This urge had been power-

[2] See *The Choral Service*, pp. 10–18, 64–68, 98; or *The Congregational Choral
Service*.

fully felt in Rome. Francisco, Cardinal Quiñones, a distinguished Franciscan, was also a born reformer. Incidentally, it was he who, in 1524 A.D., sent as a missionary to America Father Juarez, destined to become the first Roman Bishop within the present territory of the United States. Commissioned by Clement the Seventh to complete a revision of the Breviary already begun on rather silly pseudo-classical lines, he produced in 1535 A.D. a work so radical in the way of simplicity that some modification was forced on him in the second edition. He omitted all Antiphons and all Hymns, though later permitting both for Choir use. Each Office had three Psalms, and the 150 Psalms were to be read through in their fixed order each week, regardless of festivals. The Bible was to be read through in the Lessons each year. The book passed through over 100 editions and was permitted for private use, by both regulars and seculars. In a few places in Spain it was used in Choir. It was abolished by the Pope in 1568: but meanwhile, it had profoundly influenced liturgical revision in England. That it was known to Archbishop Cranmer is very evident. Vernacular experiments had been made with the singing of English Compline in the Royal Chapel in April, 1547; with English Matins and Evensong at St. Paul's Cathedral the following year; and in wide variety at other Cathedral and Parish Churches throughout England, giving rise to much confusion and scandal. A commission of six Bishops and six divines was appointed to assist Cranmer in the preparation of a book of services in the vernacular. Undoubtedly Cranmer had already prepared the draft; and based it, with regard to simplifications, on the essential parts of Quiñones' first reformed Breviary. He retained the reading of the entire Psalter, which had been from the earliest days the very essence of the Office: but distributed it over the month instead of over the week. As in Quiñones, the 150 Psalms were to be read in unbroken order regardless of Feasts; most of the Bible was to be read through in order in a yearly course; all Antiphons and Hymns were omitted, as well as all Responds and Invitatories.

Toward Uniformity

With the preparation of this book, the urge to uniformity, which in Rome was to impose the Pian Breviary of 1568, came into full play in England. In appointing his liturgical Commission, the King urged the need of "one uniform order throughout the realm." By the first Edwardine Act of Uniformity, the first English Prayer Book came into exclusive use on Whitsunday, 1549.

Cranmer's avowed objective in the revised Office was a return to the principles of Christian antiquity: "Here you have," he wrote, "an order of prayer much agreeable to the mind and purpose of the old fathers." The need of instruction and edification was undoubtedly great, and the means were at hand in the vernacular Bible and Offices. But one may question whether the true proportion of divine Service, as established by the ancient fathers, was well preserved under the stress of the times. In the judgment of many, there was a swing back to the old didacticism of the Synagogue. The Offices became incidental to the teaching of the congregation, rather than being primarily the lifting up of the people into the worship of God. The good seed of the Word of God was sown; but with it were planted the tares of an over-emphasis on self, as though God existed for Man rather than Man for God. However, the Reformation is not yet over, either in Religion or in Church Music. We stand midway in a process which, please God, will in his good time restore the just balance between edification and worship.[3]

The Booke of Common Praier Noted

MUSICAL expression of the new Services was immediate. We have seen that the publication of Merbecke's *Booke of Common Praier Noted* followed in 1550. But before that time, in addition to the English Masses mentioned in a previous chapter, many settings of the Gospel Canticles in English had been composed, and a surprising number of English Anthems. One set of manuscript part books at Oxford contains over a hundred of these.

Merbecke's book reaffirmed and expressed the ancient principles we have been considering, as far as was possible with the omission of all Antiphons, and with Cranmer's arbitrary and ill-advised limitation of one note to a syllable. The Versicles and Responses were practically unaltered, the Psalms and Canticles were set to easy Gregorian Psalm Tones on the rhythmical principles outlined in the last chapter, and *Te Deum* kept a simplified form of its ancient melody. All of the music was purely liturgical, subordinate to the text, without repetition, omission, or alteration.

Doubtless this book was intended for the normal use of Parish Churches. In the Royal Chapels, and in Cathedrals and Collegiate Churches, some of the characteristic devices of polyphony were put into play almost at once: thus leading to the much discussed form which we call the Anglican Chant.

[3]See Chapter IX, p. 242.

THE ANGLICAN CHANT

THERE is perhaps no department of Church Music more utterly misunderstood, not simply by the ordinary parishioner, but by Clergy, Choirs, and Choirmasters, than this much-abused system. We shall perhaps arrive at sounder ideas about it through some historical investigation. The process of these chapters is to cite facts, to deduce principles, to suggest practice. In the case of the Anglican Chant, which as ordinarily performed, especially in America, is frequently a distortion of a distortion of a perfectly reasonable and artistic devotional practice, the facts and the principles must be grasped before improvement can be expected.

Its Formation

WE are all probably familiar with the Choral Responses at Evening Prayer as set by Thomas Tallis; or at least with some of the many arrangements of them. They consist of Merbecke's Plainsong, the melody of the Congregation, harmonized with either three or four additional parts. The melody, which of course should be sung by the Congregation, is set in the Tenor part. The Soprano is what we might call a Descant, an additional ornamental melody sung by the Choir above the real tune. It is rather absurd to hear men and women trying to sing this part instead of their own tune, as is often the case.[4]

Precisely what was done in the Choral Responses (that is, the writing of additional free parts both above and below the melody,

---

[4]See *The American Psalter,* pp. 6 and 7: *The Choral Service,* pp. 95–97. Note the tenor part, which is the People's tune.

yet corresponding absolutely to its rhythm) was also done by Tallis, Byrd, and others with the older Psalm Tones. The Plainsong rhythms were unchanged: duple and triple units freely alternated as before in the unison chant, an extra note being added for the extra weak syllable of an occasional dactyl. The typical retard was made at the close of each of the two cadences. In writing or printing the notes, no bar lines were used, since all rhythmical qualities come solely from the words themselves. Each side of the Choir sang an entire alternate verse, not a half verse. In short half verses, the recitation, or even part of the mediation or of the final cadence, was omitted. In short, this harmonized chant preserved the precise form of the prose sentence just as did the old Plainsong Psalm Tone.[5] The final note was always set to the final syllable, in a majority of cases a weak one. Thus the typical cadence was trochaic, with a frequent dactylic variation. An examination of the rhythmic endings of the English Psalter shows that the number of unaccented finals, 1376, is considerably greater than that of accented finals, 1132: although the proportion is not as great as in Latin. The typical musical cadence adapts itself perfectly to the occasional verses closing with an accent in either tongue. There is therefore no linguistic or musical principle involved which either necessitates, or tolerates as artistic, a fixed accent on the final note of a Chant, which is the main modern abuse.

Its History

THE Chants so harmonized, or else in plain unison, continued in use until the Great Rebellion. It is interesting to note that Canon Harrison of Windsor, writing in 1587, speaks of the

[5]See pp. 106–108.

chanting of the Psalms in this manner as being the only part of Choral Matins and Evensong then in use; thus reasserting the ancient belief as to the primary importance of Psalmody in the Office. In 1641 the Rev. John Barnard of St. Paul's Cathedral published many of the harmonized Chants, including those of Tallis. After the Restoration, Edward Lowe, Professor of Music at Oxford, printed all of the Gregorian Tones as he had sung them at Salisbury Cathedral before the Rebellion. Some of them were harmonized; as were also four in a similar work by the Rev. James Clifford of St. Paul's published in 1664. Ten years later John Playford, in his "Order of performing the Divine Service in Cathedrals" printed seven Psalm Tones, of which two were harmonized in this manner. Within a century, the old Plainsong tunes began to appear in the soprano part instead of in the tenor: and are so printed in Doctor Boyce's "Cathedral Music," in 1760. His pointing is unchanged from the ancient method, and for the first verse of *Venite* is precisely that of the Hymnal (No. 569) and Psalter used by the Episcopal Church in America. In 1864, Heywood's *Anglican Psalter Noted* followed the same system.[6] Moreover, I possess Chants printed in Ithaca, New York, in 1824, and in Troy, New York, in 1846, which show the same immemorial tradition of the relationship between the words and musical cadences of a Chant.

Let us pause to refer again to the ancient Jewish melody of the Shema', which was quoted in the last chapter (p. 109) and then to its gradual transformations into the modern Anglican Chant.

[6]Still later examples are A. H. Brown's *Anglican Psalter,* 1878; The S. P. C. K. Psalter edited by James Turle, organist of Westminster Abbey; and the Psalter edited by the Reverend Sir Henry F. Baker and Doctor W. H. Monk, who gave us *Hymns Ancient and Modern.*

Ancient Latin Chant

Tone i 4

Ec - ce con - cu - pi - vi man - da - ta tu - a:

*in æ - qui - ta - te tu - a vi - vi - fi - ca me.

Tallis, 1550

Melody in the Tenor

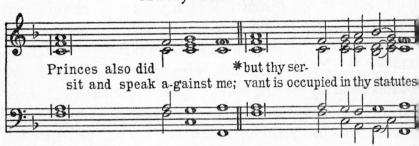

Princes also did | *but thy ser-
sit and speak a-gainst me; vant is occupied in thy statutes

Christ Church Tune, Clifford, 1664
Melody in the Tenor
(*Note antique pronunciation of final word*)

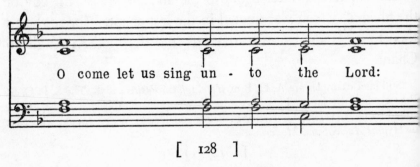

O come let us sing un - to the Lord:

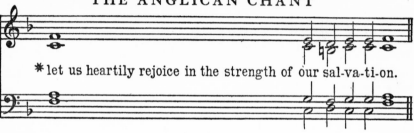

Boyce, 1760

(Melody in the treble: "salvation" as at present)

Compare with this the same verse as sung at Chant 569 in *The Hymnal* or at Chant 1 in *The American Psalter*. It will be seen that they are identical.

Its Corruption

But this seemingly continuous tradition of the rhythm of chanting began to be disregarded in Restoration times; and in the last half of the nineteenth century suffered almost complete collapse. The Chant began to be rigid instead of flexible in the time of Charles II. That lively monarch was a musical modernist in his day. He loathed the solemnities of the old contrapuntal style, and as we shall see further on, his taste for the latest thing in music led to the introduction of four and twenty fiddlers[7]

[7]"I went today to the Chapel Royal. . . . Instead of the grave and solemn organ was introduced a band of twenty-four fiddlers, after the French way—better suiting a play-house or a tavern than a Church. We heard no more of the organ. That noble instrument, in which our English Musicians do so excel, is quite left off."— *Evelyn's Diary.*

into the Chapel Royal, and profoundly modified the development of the Anthem. Like many another person more moved by the physical aspect of music than by the spiritual, he liked to beat time. In Pepys' Diary, there is an entry on November 22nd, 1663. "At Chapel: I first perceived that the king is a little musical, and kept good time with his hand all along the Anthem." One cannot beat time to sound chanting.

As this was the period when, after the long break of the Comonwealth, the attempt was being made to restore chanting as well as monarchy, it does not seem improbable that a time-beating monarch should have given the first impulse toward that deadly mediocrity, strict time chanting: in which a little tiresome tune unrelated to the natural rhythm of the words is played and sung over and over in meaningless iteration till the welcome "Amen." This mechanical tendency was increased by the many Chant composers of the eighteenth century and later who introduced short notes into the parts, in such a way as to prevent any possibility of singing except in strict time.

The culmination of the abuse came with the introduction of the modern bar line into the printed Chant, with its implication of an accent following the bar. In the whole history of chanting, we have seen that accent normally fell on the penultimate note, or in the case of a dactylic ending, on the antepenultimate: but by implying an invariable accent on the final note, the whole historic and artistic plan of pointing was distorted in the nineteenth century, and the entire cadence moved a foot forward, to close with what has been called the 'Anglican thump.'

Let me illustrate the change with an example or two. Look back to the setting of Tone I 4 by Thomas Tallis, the tune being in the tenor (p. 128).

Here is the same tune and verse, as pointed in a Psalter still in American use.

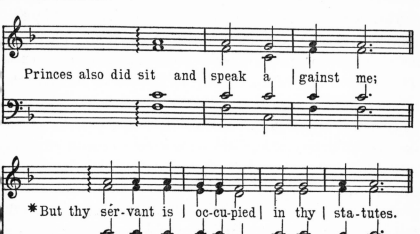

The ending of the next verse shows even greater contrast:

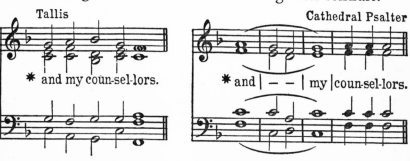

What has happened here? The free plastic Chant, in which each syllable gave the rhythmic value to its accompanying note, has disappeared: in its place, seven bars of music are played over again and again, and the poor syllables are drawn out or hurried up to fit the deadly monotony of this unyielding rhythm. The syllables before the so-called accented syllable are almost invariably rushed. The lovely rhythmic cadence of the old Chant has been exchanged for a jerky snap on the last word.

This calamitous change has been brought about, first by the introduction of the bar lines; then by their misinterpretation, as involving fixed measures with invariable equidistant accents. Thus the last note of the melody, lengthened by the old rule of graceful delay at the cadences, has come to be considered as a measure always begun with an accent. If the verse ends with one or two unaccented syllables (as it does in a majority of cases) the whole melody is moved backward to make this falsely imagined musical accent coincide with the last accented syllable of the text.[8] Perhaps the musical absurdity of this procedure can be best shown by illustrations from well-known hymns.

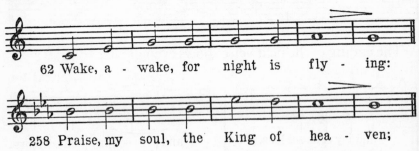

Had the same rhythmic displacement been made in these typical cadences as in the similar cadences of the Chant, they

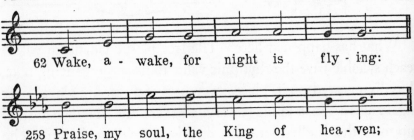

[8]See illustrative records, p. 146.

would have become what precedes: Beckmesser could do no worse.

Captain Tombs, a Victorian defender of the ancient tradition against the mechanical novelties of the Cathedral Psalter, gives us a delightful secular illustration, which I cannot forbear quoting.

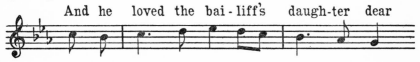

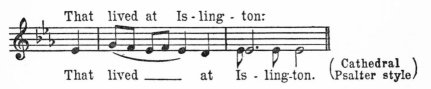

Quite obviously, when a Recitation consists of a single syllable only, it should not be made to fill a whole bar, as in the system here condemned.

Its Historic and Proper Method

It is a matter of deep satisfaction that the American Episcopal Church has set forth the historic method of Chanting in four of its official publications: *The Hymnal, The Choral Service, The Plainsong Psalter,* and *The American Psalter.* Every Candidate for Holy Orders, every Priest, every Organist or Choir Director, and every Choir singer should study practically the principles set forth in these books; and should certainly know two of them by heart:

1 The words should be sung at the *same pace* in the Recitations and Inflections. The Recitation is as rhythmical as the Cadences.

2 All accents, without exception, should be merely those of good reading.

Where these principles are carried out, there may be at least reverent and distinct chanting: which may soon be made artistic and beautiful as well.

POSSIBLE ANTIPHONS IN HARMONY

THE alternate chanting of Psalms and Canticles to the Anglican Chant may be made truly Antiphonal, by the use of refrains composed in harmony for the whole choir, to be sung before and after the Chant. An obvious place for this is in connection with *Venite, exultemus Domino.* The American, Scottish, and English Prayer Books now supply a certain number of the old Invitatories. As we have seen, these were anciently sung responsorially, a soloist singing the Psalm and the Choir interpolating the refrain in whole or in part. But for Parish use, they are more effective when sung antiphonally. Antiphon settings in Plainsong to be sung before and after the Canticle are officially provided in *The Choral Service.*[9] But for use with the Anglican Chant, several simple Choral settings, both polyphonic and homophonic, have been provided in America.[10] They should be sung *after,* as well as *before,* the *Venite,* which

[9]See p. 99.
[10]By Richards, Holler, Warner, Matthews, Sowerby, and Douglas.

should have an appropriate Chant. And this form, a new one, may become of immense value in our worship.

IMPORTANCE OF THE PSALTER IN WORSHIP

You will not have failed to note that the orderly singing of the whole Psalter is historically the very center of the music of the Office. Every fortnight in the Ambrosian rite, every week in other ancient rites, every month in the Anglican rite, this continuous act of praise to God has gone on. We should have great searchings of heart that it has so nearly disappeared in America. Few Churches sing the Psalms at all. Fewer follow any order which insures the regular use of the entire Psalter. The last revision of the American Prayer Book, far from abandoning such a use, directs it, imperatively, in certain places. "In places where it is convenient, the Psalter *shall be* read through once every month." I do not believe that this refers *only* to Cathedrals. I know of at least one small country church where for years the daily Evensong Psalter has been *sung* through every month, and the Matins Psalter read. A certain degree of adaptability to conditions, of reasonable flexiblity, is good: but the permissions granted in the rubric have often worked out disastrously in our Offices. Not only our people, but some of our clergy, are slowly losing any spiritual knowledge of the Psalter as a whole. That spiritual knowledge has therefore, in every age, been the main sustainer of the soul of man apart from the Sacraments and Prayer; and the main vehicle of the praise of God, even in the Sacraments. The Christian Psalter is not identical with the ancient historical Psalms in their literal original meanings. It brings to the worshipper's heart and lips the perfect devotional life of Jesus, who lived and died by it. Furthermore, it joins him to the vast company in heaven and in purgatory and on earth who day by day, week by week, month by month, year by year, have striven to form their lives on Jesus' life, and to praise the Father as he did in his holy Manhood on earth.[11] Do we clergy choose a single Psalm, almost invariably the shortest available, for each of our public Offices? Do we permit it to be carelessly and hastily read, instead of reverently sung, where that is feasible? Do we thus suggest that the Psalter is an outmoded encumbrance, to be perfunctorily dealt with, until we gain sufficient iconoclastic courage to abandon it, and substitute a Gospel hymn? If so, we strike at the very life of all sound Church music, because we cut off the main stream of Christian praise. St. Benedict called the singing of the Divine Office *Opus Dei,* the Work of God, the primary spiritual labour "to which nothing is to be preferred." Was he right? Is the Praise of God elementary, or merely accessory, in the services of the Church? Is their object primarily didactic, and, to use a horrible word, 'inspirational'? or is it primarily to render our due service of joyous adoration to the God who created us with our miraculous faculties for aspiring to him; to the God who redeemed us by 'taking upon him Manhood for our deliverance,' and as Man passing through the death of the Cross for love of us; to the God who descended upon his Church to breathe into it the very Breath of the divine, that the eternal worship of heaven

[11]On the devotional and practical value of the Psalter, note the following passage from John Donne, Dean of St. Paul's Cathedral, London, 1621–1631 A.D.

"The Psalmes are the Manna of the Church. As Manna tasted to every man like that that he liked best, so doe the Psalmes minister instruction and satisfaction, to every man, in every emergency and occasion. David was not onely a cleare Prophet of Christ himself, but a Prophet of every particular Christian; He foretells what I, what any, shall doe and suffer and say."

might at least be attempted by our mortal tongues, whose present stammering imperfections must prepare one day to join in the praises of Angels and Archangels and of all the Company of heaven? Is our prayer man-centered, for our own personal profit, or God-centered, to his greater glory? Do we come to Church to give or to get? On our answer to these questions may depend our decision as to singing the Psalms according to the Church's ancient order in the Praise of God.

Many choirmasters, many clergy, have quite overlooked one important provision of the Episcopal Church in America in this matter: that is, the setting forth of an Annual Cycle of the Psalter for Sundays, on pages ix and x of the Prayer Book. This is probably the maximum now possible in the regular use of the Psalter for all the faithful: it certainly should be the minimum for any ordinary Parish Church. Its omissions are only of those imprecatory Psalms which uninstructed people insist on taking in their literal non-spiritual sense. But it should be no vast task for any large Parish to secure the adequate Chanting of this very limited use of the Psalms in praise, and so to retain in some degree the great Christian tradition of what is central in the Offices.

SERVICES IN ANTHEM FORM

The lofty heights of true beauty and technical perfection which English Church music had reached by the middle of the sixteenth century could not readily be abandoned because of a change of language. To some extent, the old Latin forms remained in the English Church. The first Act of Uniformity permitted Offices to be sung in the College Chapels of the Universities in Hebrew, Greek, or Latin. Elizabeth extended this permission to include the Communion Service in 1560. I haven't heard of any compositions in either Hebrew or Greek: but many leading composers found an outlet for the creative faculty in writing works for the College Choirs along the old lines, in Latin. However, the same men, including some of the greatest, immediately began to compose services, that is, settings of the Canticles in English, for the admirable choirs of many Cathedrals. The daily Chapter Mass of Abbey and Cathedral alike had been discontinued, and Choral Matins and Evensong substituted. The Services so composed were of two types.

The Short Service

THE Short Service conformed strictly, as a rule, to the Cranmerian limitation of a note to a syllable. As an inevitable result, many of the early ones are but dull music. But William Byrd was able to achieve great beauty even under these novel and trying conditions; especially in keeping the purity of the verbal rhythms. In his second Evening Service, he presented a novel treatment destined to revolutionize English Sacred Music. He composed certain verses for solo voices with independent organ accompaniment: and this device was at once taken up by others, and continued to the present day. For some fifty years, Short Services, containing an alteration of solo or duet passages and chorus music, were composed with both devotional and artistic success. Then a blank period sets in till the beginning of the nineteenth century.

The Great Service ⟨of verse service⟩

BUT besides the typical Short Service, master composers like Tallis, Byrd, Morley, Tomkins, and Gibbons wrote what were called 'Great Services,' in which every device of the old counter-point and every forward step in the development of new forms were given free scope. Byrd's Great Service is the finest of all English Services of the old school. In Gibbons' Short Service in F, available for the phonograph in part, you will note that he has already freed himself from the unhappy restriction of a note to a syllable, especially in the flowing *Gloria Patri.*

Illustrative Record:

> Columbia DB 215, Nicholson Festival Choir:
> *Nunc dimittis,* Orlando Gibbons.

The worst effect of syllabic restriction lay in a tendency which, from the Reformation on, has been the pest of religious, or would-be religious music. I refer to the building out of musical forms conceived independently of the text, by repeating words and phrases, sometimes to the point of absurdity. This blemish, which destroys the devotional integrity of any composition, is fortunately less frequent in Service music than in Anthems. Meaningless repetition should be wholly excluded from both. There is a magnificent field for syllabic melody in the Canticles of the Office: but it should be attempted only by the devout composer of high rhythmic skill and impeccable taste. Men of lesser gifts should freely use the flowing forms that will satisfy musically without any distortion or repetition of the text.

The Revival of Service Writing

WITH Samuel Sebastian Wesley and T. A. Walmisley in the middle of the nineteenth century, Service writing took on a new lease of life, although no striking new developments of form have been added. Such notable figures as Charles Stanford, Hubert Parry, Charles Wood, and John Ireland, with others both in England and in America, have kept the standard of Service writing in the Cathedral style at a high level for those who will reject inferior work.[12] For the ordinary Parish Church, it is far preferable to sing the Canticles to congregational Chants, sometimes relieved by verses in Descant or Faux-bourdon: and to reserve as the special offering of the skilled singers to God, the Anthem.

THE ANTHEM

If the Anthem is to benefit the congregation, whose participation in it is passive rather than active, it must be a worthy and sincere act of worship on the part of the Choir. It is a musical meditation on high and holy things; not an entertainment for wealthy persons who hire the singers for their own pleasure.[13] Nor must it go beyond the technical skill and the musical capacity of the singers; it should be a giving of their best, according to their real ability. From the point of view of the Service there is no *need* of an Anthem at all; and hundreds of services would gain in devotion and in musical quality were the Anthem omitted. For instance, last Easter I saw a singer rise, face the congregation, his back to the altar: and alas, I heard him sing a sentimental ditty about 'the flowers and the trees, the birds and the bees' in music with the 'flavour of an over-ripe banana,' to quote Geoffrey Shaw. Such intolerable corruptions of divine service may not be excused, however amiable may be the inten-

---

[12]List of records illustrative of Services in Anthem Form, p. 146.

[13]A parish which has difficulty in raising $500 for Missions, and yet spends $2500 for professional music, is little likely ever to achieve an anthem which is really religious worship. Choirmasters would profit by reading the Introduction to *The Oxford Anthem Book*.

tions of the persons concerned. It is the undoubted duty of both the Parish Priest and his Choir Directer to choose and permit only such Anthems as may be a worthy offering to God from the skilled singers of the Choir.[14]

Its Desirability

SUCH an offering is desirable on both historical and devotional grounds. The ancient Graduals and Alleluias of the Mass, the Great Responds of the Office, have for ever disappeared from our Anglican Parish Churches. The masterly polyphonic settings of these texts are gone too, except as they may be one by one equipped with singable and liturgical English text, or permitted by liberal authorities such as those of the Cathedral of St. John the Divine, New York, in the original Latin. But where these great wonders of music are unavailable, the non-liturgical Anthem *must* take their place, or one of two bad things will happen: either the function of the Congregation will be taken by the Choir, whose skill will be ineffectively used in the wrong place; or else the Choir will be left with no function of its own except as a leader of the Congregation. The first of these evils is the course commonly taken; and it is devotionally disastrous to both Choir and Congregation. The non-liturgical Anthem is not technically part of my theme any more than is the Oratorio or any other form of Religious Music outside the appointed services of the Church. But in view of this vicarious function, of supplying the hiatus opened in the Liturgy at the Reformation by the elimination of all of the old specifically Choir and Solo parts, I feel justified in writing a few further words as to its history and present place in our worship.

[14]See list of records illustrative of the English Anthem, pp. 151, 152.

Its Origin

IN the Pre-Reformation Church after 1500, and in the Roman Church today, the use of non-liturgical or quasi-liturgical compositions for unaccompanied singing, called motets, was and is common.[15] Many supremely beautiful works both in polyphony and in modern style have been of this character. Bach also used it gloriously in the Lutheran Church,[16] and it has found place increasingly in the services of the Anglican Communion during recent years. But although this was one of the origins of the Anthem, it is not the Anthem, strictly speaking. The word 'Anthem' is not other than an Anglicising of our old term 'Antiphon,' banished from the Prayer Book for four centuries, but now again given a courteous welcome, at least in the sick room![17] But in the later Middle Ages, the use of either one of four famous Antiphons became common at the close of both the Morning and the Evening Offices. They were known as the Anthems of our Lady, being in honour of the blessed Virgin Mary. Their popularity was immense, especially in England. Chaucer's "Prioresses Tale" is entirely based on a legend regarding a child singing the first of them:

> This litel childe his little book lerninge,
> As he sat in the scole at his prymer,
> He *Alma Redemptoris* hered singe,
> As children lerned his antiphoner.

All four of the Anthems were set by many great composers of the polyphonic age, in works of surpassing tenderness and

[15]List of illustrative records, pp. 147–149.

[16]List of illustrative records, p. 150. Here may be mentioned the superb Extended Chorales of J. S. Bach, now available with suitable English words.

[17]See p. 102.

beauty. The Antiphon of our Lady came to be considered *the* Anthem, pre-eminently.

Illustrative Records:

In Plainsong

Gramophone Shop Album 132, Paderborn Cathedral Boys:
Polydor 22198, *Alma Redemptoris.*
Polydor 22198, *Regina cæli.*
Polydor 22198, *Ave, Regina.*
Polydor 22198, *Salve, Regina.*
Victor Album M 87 II, Solesmes Abbey Choir:
Victrola 7347-B, *Salve, Regina.*
His Master's Voice, Ampleforth Abbey Choir:
C 2088, *Ave, Regina.*
C 2087, *Salve, Regina.*

In Polyphony

His Master's Voice, Westminster Cathedral Choir:
C 2256, *Alma Redemptoris,* Peter Phillips †1633.
C 2256, *Salve, Regina* (modern) Herbert Howells.
C 1606, *Ave, Regina,* William Byrd †1623.
Montserrat Album, Montserrat Abbey Choir:
Disco Gramofono AE 164, *Salve, Regina,* A. Nicolau b. 1858.
A masterly setting of the famous Plainsong tune.
AB 600, *Salve, Regina,* Pérez Moya. Modern setting.
Polydor 22593, Aachen Cathedral Choir:
Regina cæli, Franz Nekes †1914.
l'Anthologie Sonore, Vol. IV, 35♭, *Alma Redemptoris,* G. Dufay †1474.

Its Authority

But the injunction of Edward VI that "no anthems are to be allowed but those of our Lord, and they in English, set to a plain and distinct note, to every syllable one" put an end to all this. We have already seen what a flood of new compositions in the vernacular appeared in the earliest years of the Reformation. These pieces were sung in the old place, at the close of Morning and Evening Prayer. Queen Elizabeth recognized them; but it was not till the Prayer Book of 1662 that rubrical provision was made for the Anthem; and at the historic place.

Its Secularization

LATER on, the Royal Chapel set the example of a second Anthem, after the Sermon. We have the invaluable Pepys, himself an excellent singer, remarking, "The sermon done, a good Anthem followed." Perhaps this was an added inducement to keep the Merry Monarch in Chapel till after the Sermon. At any rate, Charles the Second saw to it that the music of the Anthem should be thoroughly secularized. He sent Pelham Humfrey, a member of the Choir, to Paris to study under the prominent opera composer, Lully. On his return, he was appointed 'Composer in Ordinary for the Violins to his Majesty': and as such he saw that the four and twenty fiddlers had their part in the Anthem. The great composer Henry Purcell acquired the art through Humfrey, and notwithstanding his genius as a composer, he completed the secularization of the Anthem.[18] The great example of the Chapel Royal was debased to provide acceptable entertainment for the fashionable world when it deigned to attend Church. Alas, this unholy musical alliance between the Church and the world, as far as the Anthem goes, has continued to our own times; and the restoration of the

[18]It must not be thought that I am wholly condemning Purcell's anthems. He was capable of poignant and dramatic expression, and at times of broad and fine choral effects. Some anthems are effective and beautiful small Cantatas for the Concert Hall. But their feeling is often secular, not religious; especially in their use of instrumental *ritornelli*. Such an excerpt as "Let my prayer come up" is in itself devotional and fine. There are other similar examples of right feeling.

Anthem to its high estate as the unadulterated Praise of God
is part of our present task in the Church.

Its Religious Restoration

No betterment in the composition of Anthems came till the
nineteenth century: when with the works of Samuel Sebastian
Wesley, the true devotional note again appears in the English
Anthem. He restored to English Church Music the lost primacy
of the word; and set his verbal texts with extraordinary musical
felicity.

Illustrative Records:

> H. M. V. C 1541, Blessed be the God and Father, Temple Church
> Choir.
> H. M. V. C 2249, Wash me throughly, Westminster Abbey Choir.
> Columbia DB 215, Thou wilt keep him in perfect peace, Nicholson
> Festival Choir.

He also made new formal developments; the use of expressive
recitative, a free organ accompaniment for the choral sections.
In Victorian days, the general decline in religious music deeply
affected the Anthem. The sentimentalities of Spohr and Gounod
were widely and feebly imitated. But some fine compositions
date from this period, and it is unreasonable to condemn all of
its products. Reconstructive forces were then germinating,
which in the past Century of Reform have led to a new synthesis
of what is fine in the past, and prophetic of the future. These
forces, and their products for the Eucharist, for the Office, and
for the non-liturgical Anthem we must consider in the final
chapter of this book. But we should remember that the great
heritage of the skilled Choir, developing through the ancient

Gregorian Propers of the Mass and Responds of the Office, and later through the almost miraculous masterpieces of the golden age of Polyphony, must and shall be continued in the future by religious compositions embodying every device of the living art of music consonant with the pure praise of God.

Records illustrative of the conventional Anglican Chant:

H. M. V. Album 24, Choir of St. George's, Windsor:
D 963, *Venite,* James Nares †1783.
D 964, Ps. 23, George M. Garrett †1897.
D 964, Ps. 111, Thomas A. Walmisley †1856.
D 965, *Benedictus,* James Turle †1882.
D 966, *Magnificat,* S. S. Wesley †1876.
D 966, *Nunc dimittis,* Jonathan Battishill †1801.
The chanting recorded above exemplifies the faulty 'Cathedral' method, well carried out.
Columbia 5428, London Male Voice Octette:
Ps. 65, Benjamin Cooke †1793.
Ps. 85, George C. Martin †1916.
From *The English Psalter:* a modern experimental pointing by MacPherson, Bairstow and Buck.

Records illustrative of Services in Anthem Form:

H. M. V. Album 24, Choir of St. George's, Windsor:
D 964, *Te Deum* in F, Samuel Sebastian Wesley †1876.
His Master's Voice, Westminster Abbey Choir:
B 2911, *Te Deum,* in B♭, Sir Charles Stanford †1924.
C 1812, *Benedictus* in B♭, Sir Charles Stanford.
C 1849, *Magnificat* in B♭, Sir Charles Stanford.
C 1849, *Nunc dimittis* in B♭, Sir Charles Stanford.
Columbia, Nicholson Festival Choir:
DB 214, *Nunc dimittis,* Orlando Gibbons †1625.
DX 639, *Magnificat,* S. S. Wesley †1876.
DB 214, *Te Deum* in B♭, Sir Charles Stanford.
Columbia, St. George's Chapel Choir:
9174, *Magnificat,* T. A. Walmisley †1856.
9174, *Magnificat* in G, Sir Charles Stanford.

DX 357, *Te Deum* in C, Sir Charles Stanford.
4210, *Nunc dimittis* in B minor, T. T. Noble, b. 1867.
Brunswick 20082, Dudley Buck Singers:
Victor 35994, Trinity Choir:
Festival, *Te Deum* E♭, Dudley Buck †1909.
(How *not* to compose Church music.)

Records illustrative of the Latin Motet:

Josquin Des Prés †1521
Victor Album M 212, Dijon Cathedral Choir:
11677-A, *Ave, verum.*
11677-B, *Ave, cælorum Domina.*
Pathé X 93055, *Ave, vera virginitas,* St. Léon IX Choir.

Jachet van Berchem c. 1560
Columbia DFX 18, Choir of the Sainte-Chapelle, Paris:
O Jesu Christe.

Jacob Handl (known as Gallus) †1591
Polydor 22757, *Ecce quomodo moritur justus,* St. Hedwig's, Berlin.

Orlando di Lasso †1594
Polydor 66673, *Tui sunt cæli* (8 voice), St. Hedwig's, Berlin.

G. P. da Palestrina †1594
Christschall 115 *Jubilate Deo,* Munich Cathedral Choir.
Victrola 9159-A, *Adoramus te,* Maestri Cantori of Florence.
Victrola 9159-B, *O bone Jesu,* Maestri Cantori of Florence.
Victor 21622-B, *Adoramus te,* Palestrina Choir, Philadelphia.

Thomas Morley †1603
His Master's Voice B 2892, *Nolo mortem peccatoris,* Westminster
Abbey Choir.

Tomás Luis da Victoria †1608
His Master's Voice, EG 1752, Cologne Cathedral Choir:
O quam gloriosum, Quæ est ista.

Polydor 27123, *Domine, non sum dignus,* St. Hedwig's Choir, Berlin.

Jan Pieterszoon Sweelinck †1621

Polydor 27107, *Hodie Christus natus est,* St. Hedwig's Choir, Berlin.

William Byrd †1623

His Master's Voice, B 2447, *Justorum animæ,* New College Chapel Choir.

His Master's Voice, C 1606, *Ave verum,* Westminster Cathedral Choir.

His Master's Voice, C 1606, *Ave, Regina,* Westminster Cathedral Choir.

His Master's Voice, C 1678, *Exsurge, Domine,* Westminster Abbey Choir.

Columbia Album XVI Century Songs, The St. George's Singers. 5547 *Justorum animæ.*

Gregor Aichinger †1628

Polydor 22588, *Intonuit de cæli,* Munich Cathedral Choir.

King João IV of Portugal †1666

Victor Album M 212, Dijon Cathedral Choir: 11679-A, *Crux fidelis,* for Good Friday.

William Child †1697

His Master's Voice, C 1678, *O bone Jesu,* Westminster Abbey Choir.

J. C. Aiblinger †1867

Polydor 27125, *Jubilate Deo,* Aachen Cathedral Choir.

Karl Greith †1887

Polydor 90064, *Ecce sacerdos magnus,* Munich Cathedral Choir.

Anton Bruckner †1896

Polydor 27119, *Tota pulchra es,* Munich Cathedral Choir.
Polydor 27137, *Christus factus est,* Munich Cathedral Choir.

Franz Nekes †1914

Polydor 22757, *O crux ave*, Aachen Cathedral Choir.

Josef Venantius von Woess b. 1863.

Polydor 27122, *O sacrum conviviom*, Aachen Cathedral Choir.

Gottfried Rudinger b. 1886

Polydor 90064, *Emitte spiritum*, Munich Cathedral Choir.

Charles Villiers Stanford b. 1852 †1924

His Master's Voice B 2447, *Beati quorum*, New College Chapel Choir.

In recent times, compositions for Choir with instrumental accompaniment are often called Motets. The following records illustrate the type.

Wolfgang Amadeus Mozart †1791

Parlophon P 9108, *Ave verum*, Irmler Madrigal Choir.
Parlophon P 9355, *Ave verum*, Vienna Singing Boys.
Polydor 66534, *Ave verum*, St. Hedwig's, Berlin.
Polydor 66863, *Ave verum* (In German), Bruno Kittel Choir.
H. M. V. B 2892, *Ave verum*, Westminster Abbey Choir.

Jakob Ludwig Felix Mendelssohn-Bartholdy †1847

H. M. V. B 3631, *Veni, Domine*, Westminster Cathedral Choir.

Edward William Elgar †1934

H. M. V. B 3631, *Ave verum*, Westminster Cathedral Choir.

Records illustrative of the German Motet:

Gregor Aichinger †1628

Polydor 27152, *Maria uns trost*, Dortmund Choir.

Heinrich Schuetz †1672

Kantorei 4, Schuetz Society Chorus:
Ich bin ein rechter Weinstock, Gott Vater in Ewigkeit.

[149]

2000-Jahre Musik Album, Berlin Cathedral Choir:
Parlophon B 3703, *Ich danke dem Herrn.*

Andreas Hammerschmidt †1675

Polydor 66673, *Machet die Tore weit* (6 voices), St. Hedwig's
Choir, Berlin.

Johann Sebastian Bach †1750

2000-Jahre Musik Album, Berlin Cathedral Choir:
Parlophon B 3703, *Der Geist hilft,* final fugue.
Polydor 66706, *Der Geist hilft,* final fugue, St. Thomas' Choir,
Leipzig.
Polydor 66706, *Du heilige Brunst,* from same, St. Thomas' Choir,
Leipzig.
Polydor 66708, *Singet dem Herrn,* final fugue, St. Thomas' Choir,
Leipzig.
Gramophone Album 14, *Jesu meine Freude,* Bach Cantata Club.

Dimitry Stepanovich Bortniansky †1825

Polydor 27208, *Ehre sei Gott in der Höhe,* St. Cæcilia Choir.

J. Hatzfeld b. 1882

Polydor 27116, *Ihr Felsen hart,* Paderborn Cathedral Choir.

W. Berten (contemporary)

Polydor 27123, *Komm' heil'ger Geist,* St. Hedwig's Choir, Berlin.

French Motet:
Victor Album M 212, Dijon Cathedral Choir:
Victrola 11678-B, *En son temple,* Ps. 150, Jacques Mauduit †1627.

Records illustrative of the English Anthem:

Elizabethan (but probably *not* by Richard Farrant †1580)

Columbia DB 216, Nicholson Festival Choir:
Lord, for thy tender mercy's sake.

Thomas Weelkes †1623

Roycroft 161, Hosanna to the Son of David, The English Singers.
H. M. V. Album 24, Choir of St. George's, Windsor:
  D 963, Let thy merciful ears.

Orlando Gibbons †1625

H. M. V. C 1337, O Lord, increase my faith, York Minster Choir.
H. M. V. C 1337, O clap your hands, York Minster Choir.
H. M.V. C 1337, God is gone up, York Minster Choir.

Henry Purcell †1695

H. M. V. Album 24, Choir of St. George's, Windsor:
  D 966, Remember not, Lord, our offences.
H. M. V. C 2249, Rejoice in the Lord, Westminster Abbey Choir.

Jakob Ludwig Felix Mendelssohn-Bartholdy †1847

H. M. V. B 3733, Judge me, O God, St. Paul's Cathedral Choir.
Victor 35856, Hear my prayer, Temple Church Choir.

Ludwig Spohr †1859

H. M. V. B 3711, As pants the hart, Chapels Royal Choir.

William Sterndale Bennett †1875

Columbia DB 216, God is a Spirit, Nicholson Festival Choir.
H. M. V. E 397, God is a Spirit, British National Opera Chorus.

Samuel Sebastian Wesley †1876

Columbia DB 215, Thou wilt keep him in perfect peace, Nicholson
  Festival Choir.
H. M. V. C 2249, Wash me throughly, Westminster Abbey Choir.
H. M. V. C 1541, Blessed be the God and Father, Temple Church
  Choir.

John Goss †1880

H. M. V. B 3711, O Saviour of the world, Chapels Royal Choir.
H. M. V. B 2543, O Saviour of the world, Canterbury Cathedral
  Choir.

Arthur Seymour Sullivan †1900

H. M. V. E 397, O gladsome Light, Brit. Nat. Opera Chorus.

Charles Wood †1926

H. M. V. B 3103, Hail, gladdening Light, St. Paul's Cathedral Choir.
H. M. V. B 3930, Great Lord of Lords, Westminster Abbey Choir.

Charles Villiers Stanford b. 1852 †1924

H. M. V. C 1612, Glorious and powerful God, Westminster Abbey Choir.

T. Tertius Noble b. 1867

Victor 22709-B, The souls of the righteous, St. Bartholomew's, N. Y.

Henry Walford Davies b. 1869

H. M. V. B 3518, Lord, it belongs not to my care, Temple Church Choir.
H. M. V. B 8348, God be in my head, St. Margaret's Choir, Westminster.

Edward Cuthbert Bairstow b. 1874

H. M. V. B 4013, St. Paul's Cathedral Choir:
Let all mortal flesh keep silence.

Herbert Howells b. 1892

H. M. V. B 3763, A spotless Rose, Westminster Abbey Choir.

CHAPTER VI

THE PRE-REFORMATION LITURGICAL HYMN

ORIGINS

THE pre-eminent claim of the Psalter to be our most important vehicle of praise in the Offices of the Church is based upon its constant use by our Lord Jesus Christ in his own worship. It was his Hymnal. Surely he 'worshipped the Father in spirit and in truth.' If our use of the Psalms be in the spirit of his, we shall be singing Christian Psalms, whatever may have been the circumstances or intentions which led to the writing or use of each during the Jewish dispensation.

Gloria Patri

MOREOVER, at an early age, the Church added to each Psalm the unvarying stanzas, "Glory be to the Father, and to the Son, and to the Holy Ghost: As it was in the beginning, is now, and ever shall be, world without end. Amen." These great phrases have for ever confirmed the seal of Christ upon the use of his Hymnal. As we saw in the first chapter, a similar form has been found in one of the Oxyrhynchus papyri[1] of the third century. By the end of the fourth, *Gloria Patri* was a settled part of Christian Psalmody. Is it not well for us to recall that this epilogue to each Psalm, this great teaching word with which we begin each Office, sets for us the enduring primary standard of Christian

[1] Part 15, No. 1786. Before 300 A.D. See p. 21.

praise? We speak these words more frequently than any other phrases in divine service. Do you wish to improve the music of Morning and Evening Prayer? Then watch yourself. Observe how you utter them, with what inner recollection of their eternal and primary significance they come to your tongue. Does attention immediately flag when your lips reach the familiar formula, and the material vocal organs alone make the sound of it, while your busy mind presses on to the next and less customary phrases of the service? If so, you are tending in the direction of the lamaistic prayer wheel of Tibet, and making of your god-like power of utterance a mechanical thing, divorced from the movements of your spirit. I confess with shame to the singing of those great words many, many times with little immediate consciousness of their solemn implications: and my greatest lesson in Church Music has been in learning to let them heighten my recollection instead of lowering it.

If this be the case with many of us in the sacred Ministry, how much more likely will it be that our Choir singers, men, women, and children, will utter carelessly words which are so frequently repeated. Begin to improve your Hymn singing by a care, spiritual rather than æsthetic, that will bring about a *meaningful* utterance of this age-long stanza, which, in one form or another, became the completion of every Hymn down to the Reformation.

Its fullness of meaning had still another side in its early use: that of being a safeguard against doctrinal error. The allied formula, "Glory be to the Father, through the Son, in the Holy Spirit" seems at first sight to express the nature of our worship as not finally directed toward either God the Son or God the Holy Spirit, but as pressing on to God the Father, the very

Center and Source of being in the eternal Triune Deity. This form, however, was susceptible of another and false interpretation. We may observe, therefore, early in the experience of the Christian Church, a note which characterized much of its later Hymnody: that of accurately expressing divine truth as a shield against insidious error.

Pre-Christian Hymns

BUT the Psalms, even when interpreted in the light of Jesus' use of them, and guarded by the Christian Doxology, could not remain a fixed and exclusive Canon of worship song. The eternal Hymnal of Praise began with man's first dim perceptions of God, and it will only come to perfection in the glory of the Beatific Vision in heaven. Has a generation ever passed into eternity since man was made in the image of God which has produced no song of praise to its Creator? I doubt it. Certainly a deeply ethical and religious Sumerian and Akkadian psalmody long antedated that of the Hebrews. Fourteen centuries before Christ, Akh-en-aten the Egyptian sang of the one and only God, and paralleled our 104th Psalm with his unique Hymn to the Sun. Eight centuries later, while the supreme poet Deutero-Isaiah wrote his great hymn,[2] "To whom then will ye liken God"? the Greek philosopher Xenophanes sang,[3] "There is one God alone, of mortals and immortals greatest, and unlike mankind both in spirit and form." Empedocles (B.C. 495-435) said of God[4]

"Spirit only is he, pure Mind, unspeakable, holy, . . . a divine Flame burning in all things."

[2]Isaiah xl:18–31.   [3]*Die Fragmente der Vorsokratiker,* Berlin, 1912. 1, p. 62.
[4]*Die Fragmente der Vorsokratiker,* Berlin, 1912. 1, p. 274.

St. Paul, preaching to the Athenians, could recall to them the words of their own poet Aratos (*c.* 270 B.C.), "For we are also his offspring," in that hymn[5] wherein he hails God as "the Father, the mighty wonder": and doubtless also the greater words of Kleanthes, a little later;[6] "For we are thine offspring, and, alone of living and moving creatures upon the earth, possess a voice which is thine image: therefore will I sing of thee, and for ever praise thy power." Finally, about at the time that St. Luke recorded the dawn-songs of the religion of Jesus, that "most noble Stoic, Epictetus,"[7] the poor lame slave "dear to the immortals,"[8] spoke the great passage which appears at the beginning of this volume. It may well be the inspiration of every religious musician, as it has been that of the present writer throughout his mature life. Let us read it again.

"Had we but true understanding, what duty would be more perpetually incumbent upon us than to hymn the Divine Power, both openly and in secret, and to tell of all his benefits? . . . Ought there not to be some to fulfil this duty, and sing the praise of God on behalf of all men? What else can I do that am old and lame, but sing hymns to God? Were I a nightingale, I would do the part of a nightingale: were I a swan, I would do as a swan. But I am a reasonable being, and I ought to praise God. This is my work. I do it. I will never desert this post as

---

[5] ΑΡΑΤΟΥ ΦΑΙΝΟΜΕΝΑ, χαῖρε, πάτερ, μέγα θαῦμα.

[6] ΚΛΕΑΝΘΟΥΣ, ΥΜΝΟΣ ΕΙΣ ΔΙΑ, Ἐκ σοῦ γὰρ γένος ἐσμέν, ἰῆς μίμημα λαχόντες
Μοῦνοι, ὅσα ζώει τε καὶ ἕρπε θνήτ᾽ ἐπὶ γαῖαν.
Τῷ σε καθυμνήσω, καὶ σὸν κράτος ἀιὲν ἀείσω.

[7] St. Augustine.

[8] The Epitaph: Δοῦλος Ἐπίκτητος γενόμην καὶ σῶμ᾽ ἀνάπηρος καὶ πενίην Ιρος καὶ φίλος ἀθανάτοις.

long as I am permitted to hold it: and I beseech you to join in this self-same song."[9]

Gospel Canticles

WITH so noble a Gentile heritage of praise, parallel to the glories of Hebrew poetry, it is obvious that new-born Christianity could not but begin an unending progress in Hymnody. St. Luke, the beauty-loving Greek, gave us what only he, with his opportunities of "a perfect understanding of all things from the very first,"[10] could give, the three Canticles of the Incarnation, *Benedictus, Magnificat,* and *Nunc dimittis.* They take absolutely the place of first importance in the praise of the Divine Office: but, of course, they are the glorious culmination of ancient Psalmody, rather than the beginning of a new art. One might point out that *Nunc dimittis,* in its poetic form, bears a close relationship to Aramaic poetry, as does the famous stanza quoted by St. Paul,[11]

> Awake, thou that sleepest,
> And arise from the dead,
> And Christ shall give thee light.

Possibly these hymns had once their own Syrian tunes: but of this we can only conjecture.

Early Christian Greek Hymns

THE early Christian Greek Hymns were also what we should call Canticles. *Sanctus* and *Gloria in excelsis,* which we have

9 Εἰ γὰρ νοῦν εἴχομεν, ἄλλο τι ἔδει ἡμᾶς ποιεῖν καὶ κοινῇ καὶ ἰδίᾳ ἢ ὑμνεῖν τὸ θεῖον καὶ εὐφημεῖν καὶ ἐπεξέρχεσθαι τὰς χάριτας; ... οὐκ ἔδει τινὰ εἶναι τὸν ταύτην ἐκπληροῦντα τὴν χώραν καὶ ὑπὲρ πάντων ᾄδοντα τὸν ὕμνον τὸν εἰς τὸν θεόν; τί γὰρ ἄλλο δύναμαι γέρων χωλὸς εἰ μὴ ὑμνεῖν τὸν θεόν; εἰ γοῦν ἀηδὼν ἤμην, ἐποίουν τὰ τῆς ἀηδόνος, εἰ κύκνος, τὰ τοῦ κύκνου. νῦν δὲ λογικός εἰμι; ὑμνεῖν με δεῖ τὸν θεόν. τοῦτό μου τὸ ἔργον ἐστίν, ποιῶ αὐτὸ οὐδ' ἐγκαταλείψω τὴν τάξιν ταύτην, ἐφ' ὅσον ἂν διδῶται, καὶ ὑμᾶς ἐπὶ τὴν αὐτὴν ταύτην ᾠδὴν παρακαλῶ.

Arrian, *Discourses of Epictetus* i:16.

10St. Luke i:3.   11Ephesians v:14.

already considered in the second chapter, are almost Biblical. Two others were the *Trisagion,* "Holy God, Holy and Mighty, Holy and Immortal, have mercy upon us," and the *Te decet laus,* still in daily use by the Benedictines, "To thee belongeth praise, to thee belongeth song: Glory to thee, Father, Son, and Holy Ghost, for ever and ever. Amen."

Unlike the Response, *Kyrie eleison,* these four pieces, when their use spread to the West, were translated into the Latin vernacular. In the Good Friday services of the Roman Church, the *Trisagion* is still sung both in Greek and in Latin. The principle of translating Hymns into popular speech was thus affirmed from the first: and the characteristic procedures of adapting the Plainsong to another tongue were also clearly defined.

Te Deum laudamus

THE great Canticle *Te Deum laudamus,* similar in form to the Greek praises, was nevertheless purely Latin in its origin. Many scholars have assigned its authorship to a contemporary of St. Jerome, Nicetas, Bishop of Remesiana, in what is now Jugoslavia. But of recent years, such students as Professor Peter Wagner, Dom Paul Cagin, O.S.B., and Clemens Blume, the great hymnologist, argue for an earlier date for the first section of *Te Deum.* During the plague in Carthage in 272 A.D., St. Cyprian wrote a work, *De mortalitate,* from which I quote:[12]

> *Illic apostolorum gloriosus chorus:*
> *illic prophetarum exsultantium numerus:*
> *illic martyrum innumerabilis populus.*

[12]Cyprian, *De mortalitate,* xvii.

Compare this with the following passage from *Te Deum:*

> *Te gloriosus apostolorum chorus;*
> *Te prophetarum laudabilis numerus;*
> *Te martyrum candidatus laudat exercitus.*

It is improbable that this is mere coincidence: it is more likely that St. Cyprian quoted an existent Hymn than that a much later poet was inspired by a little known work of St. Cyprian. Moreover, the whole form of the section is unlike that of fourth century Hymns, and parallels Greek Hymns of the period, especially *Gloria in excelsis.* We have, first of all, two stanzas, the first closing with *Sanctus,* the second with a Doxology different in form from *Gloria Patri,* which came into general use later. In these two stanzas, no attention is paid to the rhythmical *cursus,* which was in general use in the fourth century. The most ancient form of the *melody* always associated with these two stanzas differs from the melodies of the rest of the Hymn.[13] The well-known Jewish musicologist, Arthur Friedlander, has identified this melody as being essentially the ancient cantillation of Zechariah xi:10. The second part of *Te Deum,* beginning *Tu Rex gloriæ, Christe,* exhibits the fourth century *cursus* in every verse. It is set to a typical fourth mode Chant, with a form of intonation discontinued before Gregorian times. Verse 21 is set to a characteristic Antiphon melody corresponding to the Chant, thus giving the second section musical completeness.

Illustrative Records:
Montreal *Grand Séminaire* Album 2-A.
Victor 20896 B, Palestrina Choir, Philadelphia.
(A somewhat later version)

[13]The Solesmes Benedictines have recently published the purest text of the ancient melodies of *Te Deum* in the revised edition of the *Antiphonale monasticum,* Tournai, 1934.

Verses 22 to the end are for the most part quotations from Psalms. It is definitely known that these later verses were appended to the Hymn proper as Versicles and Responses. Such Versicles and Responses were known as the *capitellum*. In the monastic Rules of St. Cæsarius of Arles, 542 A.D., and of Aurelian, 551 A.D., both *Gloria in excelsis* and *Te Deum laudamus* were directed to be said at the close of Matins, with their *capitella*. Later, when *Gloria in excelsis* came to be sung only at the Eucharist, all of these Versicles and Responses were kept on with *Te Deum,* and two more added, thus giving the Canticle its present form.

The action of General Convention in printing *Te Deum* in three sections, therefore, corresponds precisely with its history, its true form, and its devotional purpose. It is much to be desired that permission should be granted for the omission of the *capitellum* when a shorter Canticle is needed, instead of our singing mediocre settings of *Benedictus es, Domine.* Moreover, the twenty-first stanza affords an admirable opportunity for the musical composer to build up an impressive close to the Hymn: whereas the following Versicles and Responses are unsatisfactory as a text for an effective choral *finale.* The frequent procedure of a dynamic climax on "Let me never be confounded," as though *me* were the center of gravity of the work, instead of *thee,* must be condemned on all counts.

But let us hope that *Te Deum,* in its proper form, may again be widely sung either to its own very beautiful ancient Chant, or to *fitting* Anglican Chants, which, for the first time in its long history, have been supplied in the present definitive edition of *The Hymnal,* and in *The American Psalter.*

THE RHYTHMICAL HYMN OF THE WEST

We must now press on to the upspringing of what was to be the wonderful flowering of Christian devotion in a form utterly new, the rhythmical Hymn of the West. The most beloved and oldest of the Greek hymns, "O gladsome Light,"[14] did not come into Western use, so far as I know, until Bishop Andrewes printed a translation in his *Preces Privatæ:* but in the East, its perennial liturgical place is indicated by St. Basil. *The Hymnal* contains a paraphrase of it at No. 12.

A Safeguard of Christian Faith

Two points should here be noted about the rise of this new development of Christian art. The first is that, as previously mentioned with *Gloria Patri,* popular song both East and West was very early used as a safeguard against false doctrine. Thus the Syrian St. Ephraem, 308–373 A.D., said of the Gnostic Bardaisan, that he "clothed the pest of depravation in the garb of musical beauty"; and St. Ephraem proceeded to write his famous Hymns in Syriac as an antidote. St. Gregory of Nazianzus used the same means of combating Arianism; as did the western St. Hilary of Poitiers, after his six years' banishment in the East. A little later the great Bishop of Milan, St. Ambrose, the real father of the liturgical Hymn, was moved to write his truly popular songs during his critical persecution by the Arian

[14] φῶς ἱλαρόν : Authorship unknown: but quoted by St. Basil, 329–379 A.D. *De Sancto Spiritu,* xxix:73. "We cannot say who was the father of those expressions in the thanksgiving at The Lighting of the Lamps; but it is an ancient formula which the people repeat, and no one has ever been accused of impiety for saying, We hymn the Father and the Son and the Holy Spirit of God.'"

Empress Justina in A.D. 385 and 386. You will perhaps recall the passage in St. Augustine, describing his taking refuge from the imperial forces in the Cathedral Church, surrounded by his people. "Then it was first instituted that, according to the custom of the East, Hymns should be sung, lest the people should faint through fatigue and sorrow. From that day to this the custom had been retained; and today almost all thy congregations throughout the world follow us herein."[15]

In Popular Rhythm, Rather Than in Classical Metre

THE second point to be noted is one of great significance, but one very little considered even among students of hymnology. Before the Hymn could attain universal acceptance as an expression of devotion, it had to abandon the old classical metrical conception of quantity, and receive its rhythmical form from the natural word accent. Christian hymnody was originally and essentially the song of the people. The heart of the people could not be reached by classical compositions, however beautiful, which did not echo their living speech. At the time that Christian metrical Hymns began, this rhythmical change in popular speech was well toward its final universal adoption. Regarding the Greek hymns, I quote from Krumbacher's *History of Byzantine Literature*, "Had there not been invented and received at the appointed time another artistic form of expression, the Greek nation would have for ever lost the treasure of a true religious poetry. This effective artistic form which awoke as by magic the poetic genius of the Greeks was *rhythmical* verse." Early in the fifth century, St. Augustine himself composed his

[15]Augustine, *Confessions*, ix:7.

Psalm against the Donatists, to be sung by congregations for a doctrinal safeguard against the heresy of the Donatists. Augustine, the great rhetorician and student of classical Latin verse, adopted definitely the popular rhythmical system.

The change was not instantaneous in the West. But it is significant that only those Hymns which were at least susceptible of accentual rhythm found their way into the liturgical services. St. Ambrose himself wrote in quantitative metre: but "he usually avoids a conflict between the word and accent and the verse quantity, so that his hymns are naturally read rhythmically."[16] And he chose a most popular stanza form, that of four iambic dimeters. Another metre adopted from the first was that of the *versus popularis.* St. Hilary used it. An example in English would be,

> Blessed city, heavenly Salem,
> Vision dear of peace and love.

Illustrative Record:
>Victor Album M 87, II, Solesmes Abbey Choir:
>Victrola 73528, *Urbs Jerusalem beata.*

As has been well said, "Christians were the first to break away from the game of long and short syllables intended for the eye alone; for they wished to reach the ear of the masses. They attained by means of their metrical system that which Luther first achieved in German religious poetry: contact with the people; with their ear; and thus with their heart."[17]

These two conditions gave specific form and purpose to the liturgical Hymn at its very origin. It was a doctrinal Hymn, reflecting theological truths, expressing them in relation to the

[16]Clemens Blume, *The Catholic Encyclopedia* VII, 598.
[17]*Byzantinische Zeitschrift,* xxii:24.

Church's hours and seasons, and later, celebrating the characters of Saints whose lives illustrated such truths practically; and it was a Hymn of the people, for them to sing in the very rhythms of their daily speech.

St. Ambrose

THIS latter quality appears even in the fourteen genuine Hymns of St. Ambrose which we possess, notwithstanding their strictly quantitative metre; since they not only permit rhythmical reading and singing, but as Wilhelm Meyer[18] has pointed out, the stanza "structure follows the rules of the new rhythmical poetry," in the form which has been so widely characteristic of Christian hymnody ever since, of a pair of strophes of two lines each, with a sense pause between. In our own Hymnal, this pause is invariably marked by a double bar in the music: but unfortunately, it is not always observed by choirs and organists.

The immediate effect of the Hymns of St. Ambrose was very great. It was at once felt that they should find a place in the Liturgy, which they speedily did at Milan. Their direct and austere beauty, when sung to the simple tunes which perfectly reflected their form, could stir the hearts of men learned or unlearned. "What tears," says St. Augustine,[19] "did I shed over the Hymns and Canticles, when the sweet sound of the music of thy Church thrilled my soul! As the music flowed into my ears, and thy truth trickled into my heart, the tide of devotion swelled high within me, and the tears ran down, and there was gladness in those tears."

Archbishop Trench says of them:[20] "The great objects of

[18]*Rythmik*, ii:119, note 1.   [19]Augustine, *Confessions*, ix:6.
[20]*Sacred Latin Poetry*, London, 1874, p. 87.

[164]

faith in their simplest expression are felt by him so sufficient to stir all the deepest affections of the heart, that any attempt to dress them up, to array them in moving language, were merely superfluous. The passion is there, but it is latent and repressed, a fire burning inwardly, the glow of an austere enthusiasm, which reveals itself indeed, but not to every careless beholder. Nor do we presently fail to observe how truly these poems belonged to their time and to the circumstances under which they were produced; how suitably the faith which was in actual conflict with the world found its utterance in hymns such as these, wherein is no softness, perhaps little tenderness; but a rock-like firmness, the old Roman stoicism transmuted and glorified into that nobler Christian courage which encountered and at length overcame the world."

These Hymns were the true beginning of Western Christian poetry; and their tunes initiated the most widespread and perennially enduring of Christian musical forms. Earlier poets, and some later ones, merely attempted to give a Christian content to verse of the classical tradition: but in the Hymns of St. Ambrose, the thought controls the form. The beauty is that special beauty pre-eminently characteristic of Greek culture; the very essence of the thought simply and directly expressed in a form wholly free from irrelevant ornament. A German writer, Adolf Ebert,[21] well says of them, "The hymns appear as the ripest fruit of the process of the assimilation on the part of Christianity of the formal education of the ancient world."

As no Hymn by St. Ambrose appears in *The Hymnal*, I append one of high perfection. St. Ambrose uses the great

[21]Ebert, *Allgemeine Geschichte der Literatur des Mittelalters im Abendlande*, i:172.

opening line, *Splendor paternæ gloriæ,* of God the Son in his *De Fide,* iv:9. The translation is that from the *Yattenden Hymnal.* It is by the late poet laureate of England, Robert Bridges. The ancient tune may be found in *The English Hymnal,* No. 52. It remains today one of the noblest, most practical, and most widely sung hymn melodies in existence.

Splendor paternæ gloriæ,	O splendour of God's glory bright,
de luce lucem proferens,	O thou that bringest light from light,
lux lucis, et fons luminis,	O Light of light, light's living spring,
dies dierum inluminans;	O Day, all days illumining,
verusque sol inlabere	O thou true Sun, on us thy glance
micans nitore perpeti,	Let fall in royal radiance,
iubarque sancti Spiritus	The Spirit's sanctifying beam
infunde nostris sensibus.	Upon our earthly senses stream.
votis vocemus et Patrem,	The Father, too, our prayers implore,
Patrem perennis gloriæ,	Father of glory evermore;
Patrem potentis gratiæ,	The Father of all grace and might,
culpam releget lubricam,	To banish sin from our delight:
informet actus strenuos,	To guide whate'er we nobly do,
dentem retundat invidi,	With love all envy to subdue,
casus secundet asperos,	To make ill-fortune turn to fair,
donet gerendi gratiam;	And give us grace our wrongs to bear.
mentem gubernet et regat	Our mind be in his keeping placed,
casto fideli corpore:	Our body true to him and chaste,
fides calore ferveat,	Where only faith her fire shall feed,
fraudis venena nesciat.	To burn the tares of Satan's seed.
Christusque nobis sit cibus,	And Christ to us for food shall be,
potusque noster sit fides;	From him our drink that welleth free,
læti bibamus sobriam	The Spirit's wine, that maketh whole,
ebrietatem Spiritus.	And, mocking not, exalts the soul.
lætus dies hic transeat;	Rejoicing may this day go hence,
pudor sit ut diluculum,	Like virgin dawn our innocence,
fides velut meridies;	Like fiery noon our faith appear,
crepusculum mens nesciat.	Nor know the gloom of twilight drear.

aurora cursus provehit;	Morn in her rosy car is borne;
aurora totus prodeat,	Let him come forth, our perfect Morn,
in Patre totus Filius,	The Word in God the Father one,
et totus in Verbo Pater.	The Father perfect in the Son.[22]

So useful an innovation speedily brought a host of imitators: and Hymns of similar content and metre began to multiply. They were quite naturally called *Ambrosiani;* and in consequence, there has been some uncertainty as to the actual work of St. Ambrose, until the definitive results of recent research. Many of the *Ambrosiani* are of great beauty. Among them are two which appear in John Mason Neale's translations in *The Hymnal:* No. 11, *O lux beata Trinitas,* with its heavenly ancient tune; and No. 28, *Te lucis ante terminum,* set to more recent music. Such Hymns continued to be written during the fifth century, and to find their places in the developing forms of the daily Offices.

Illustrative Record:
   His Master's Voice, C 2088.
      Te lucis, Ampleforth Abbey Choir.

THE OFFICE HYMN

In the Holy Rule of St. Benedict, about 530 A.D., every Office was supplied with an appropriate Hymn in a specific place: for the lesser Hours, a Hymn proper to the Hour; for Matins, Lauds, and Vespers, *Ambrosiani.* The slightly later Rules of Caesarius and Aurelian indicate, in some manuscripts, the inclusion of proper Hymns by St. Ambrose for Christmas and Epiphany; and also his fine Hymn for Festivals of Apostles, *Æterna Christi munera.* From this time on, the liturgical

[22]Quoted by permission of The Oxford University Press.

Hymnal is established at least in monastic houses; although not in the Roman Office.

Its Dissemination and Rich Growth

THE Benedictine cycle came to England with the mission of St. Augustine of Canterbury in 597 A.D. In fact, the earliest known manuscript which attests the Benedictine cycle was written in England early in the eighth century, and contains the superb morning Hymn of St. Ambrose printed on page 166. Scholars are divided in their opinion as to whether this group was the true nucleus of the prevailing and practically permanent collection of liturgical Hymns which has come down to our own day: but this discussion lies in the field of liturgical, rather than of musical research. What does have practical bearing on our subject is, that whatever may have been the older cycle, it was enriched to an extraordinary degree in the early mediæval centuries. What began in Milan, and achieved its permanent recognition at Monte Cassino, was soon to bring about a Mozarabic Hymnal in Spain, a Gallican Hymnal in northern Europe, an Anglo-Irish cycle in Britain: and from all these sources various increments not only enlarged the growing Hymnal, but also richly diversified it. Let us examine some of these enrichments.

The Spanish magistrate Prudentius,[23] who could remember the pagan days of Julian the Apostate, and who received a court appointment from his fellow Spaniard, the Emperor Theodosius I, was a true poet. The first to follow Ambrose in point of time, and like him a master of metrical form, the whole spirit and purpose of his poetry is different. His muse is romantic, not

[23]Aurelius Prudentius Clemens, 348–413 A.D.

classic; a lovely human tenderness, an emotional warmth, a wealth of symbolism, and a free use of Old Testament types fill his two collections of poems. They were literary and personal poems, not, like the Hymns of St. Ambrose, designed for singing. Yet selections from them soon entered the Mozarabic Hymnal, and others are among our permanent treasures. We are all familiar with the exquisite *Corde natus ex parentis*,[24] "Of the Father's love begotten," which found its way into English Breviaries in the eleventh century. A brief example will illustrate the poetic qualities which have so endeared Prudentius to the worshipping Christian.

O sola magnarum urbium[25]	O more than mighty cities known,[26]
major Bethlem, cui contigit	Dear Bethlehem, in thee alone
ducem salutis cælitus	Salvation's Lord from heaven took birth
incorporatum gignere.	In human form upon the earth.
quem stella, quæ solis rotam	And from a star that far outshone
vincit decore ac lumine,	The radiant circle of the sun
venisse terris nuntiat	In beauty, swift the tidings ran
cum carne terrestri Deum.	Of God on earth in flesh of man.
videre postquam illum Magi,	The wise men, seeing him, so fair,
eoa promunt munera:	Bow low before him, and with prayer
stratique votis offerunt	Their treasured orient gifts unfold
thus, myrrham et aurum regium.	Of incense, myrrh, and royal gold.
regem Deumque annuntiant	The fragrant incense which they bring,
thesaurus, et fragrans odor	The gold, proclaim him God and King:
thuris Sabæi, ac myrrheus	The bitter spicy dust of myrrh
pulvis sepulcrum prædocet.	Foreshadows his new sepulchre.

A poet of the fifth century, Cælius Sedulius, may be mentioned, from whose *Pæan alphabeticus de Christo* two centos,

---

[24]*Liber Cathemerinon*, ix. *The Hymnal*, No. 74.
[25]*Liber Cathemerinon*, xii: see also Caswall's translation, Hymn No. 93.
[26]Winfred Douglas, *The Midnight Mass*, Oxford University Press, 1933.

one for Christmas and one for Epiphany, early entered Western liturgical use.[27] The abecedarian idea, an inheritance from the Psalms, in nine of which it is employed, had appeared in St. Augustine's *Psalm against the Donatists,* and in a poem of St. Hilary of Poitiers. The form is too artificial for our times, and has not been retained by translators. But an ancient tune, known in England in Anglo-Saxon days, and still earlier on the Continent, has from the first been associated with the poem: and is a real treasure of melody.[28]

The sixth century produced a true liturgical poet in Venantius Fortunatus.[29] Trained in the artificialities of court life at Metz and elsewhere, he eventually turned his literary gift to the service of religion, and settled for life near the Abbey of the Holy Cross, which had been founded at Poitiers by his friend Queen Rhadegonda. There he became Priest and eventually Bishop. His mystical imagination was profoundly stirred by the legends which had grown up about our Saviour's Cross since its reputed discovery by St. Helena: and still more by the gift of a relic of the holy wood, made to the Abbey by the Emperor Justin II. Fortunatus wrote many poems in honour of the Cross. One of them, *Vexilla regis prodeunt,* was composed, with its tune, for the reception of the holy relic from the hands of the Bishop of Tours, who had brought it in solemn procession to the little village of Migné on November 19, 569 A.D.[30] The Hymn, then

[27] *A solis ortus cardine: Hostis Herodes impie.*

[28] *Antiphonale Romanum,* Christmas Lauds, Epiphany Lauds: *English Hymnal,* 18.

[29] Venantius Honorius Clementianus Fortunatus, 530–609 A.D.

[30] "Eufronius, Bishop of Tours, came with his clergy with much singing and gleaming of tapers and fragrance of incense . . . and brought the holy relics." — Gregory of Tours, *Hist. Franc.,* ix:40, in Migné, *Patrologia Latina* I, xxi:518.

sung for the first time, soon entered the liturgy as the Vesper Hymn in Passiontide. Here it is, in part, with the superb translation by John Mason Neale, found in *The Hymnal* at No. 144. There were originally eight stanzas.

Vexilla regis prodeunt:
fulget crucis mysterium,
quo carne carnis conditor
suspensus est patibulo.

The royal banners forward go,
The cross shines forth in mystic glow;
Where he in flesh, our flesh who made,
Our sentence bore, our ransom paid.

quo vulneratus insuper
mucrone diræ lanceæ,
ut nos lavaret crimine,
manavit unda et sanguine.

There whilst he hung, his sacred side
By soldier's spear was opened wide,
To cleanse us in the precious flood
Of water mingled with his blood.

impleta sunt, quæ concinit
David fideli carmine,
dicendo nationibus
'Regnavit a ligno Deus.'

Fulfilled is now what David told
In true prophetic song of old,
How God the heathen's King should be;
For God is reigning from the tree.

arbor decora et fulgida
ornata regis purpura,
electa digno stipite
tam sancta membra tangere!

O tree of glory, tree most fair,
Ordained those holy limbs to bear,
How bright in purple robe it stood,
The purple of a Saviour's blood!

beata cuius bracchiis
pretium pependit sæculi!
statera facta est corporis,
prædamque tulit tartari.

Upon its arms, like balance true,
He weighed the price for sinners due,
The price which none but he could pay,
And spoiled the spoiler of his prey.

Here, we cannot but recognize, we are moving in a different world of religious expression. The old world of austere classicism is gone. A new pathos is here, a new richness of symbolism, a new reflection of ways of thought which were mediæval, not antique. The mediæval restatement of Christianity as received from the ancient Fathers involved a rich emotionalization of its content, the filling of it full of the human elements of pity, fear, and love. Mediæval men strove to make religious faith enter into all life, to join to itself every emotion and experience of life. Fortunatus was the first great poet of this early dawn. Thus it must ever be, if the praise of God is to be real. Although the rich treasure of the past should, and doubtless will, be retained in part, man must praise God also in the expression of his own times in the life of the world. The Divine Objective is unchanged: but the human approach must vary as man by varying steps approaches that

> one divine far-off event
> To which the whole creation moves,[31]

the Beatific Vision of God in the perfect praises of heaven.

Examples in The Hymnal

CONSIDERATIONS of space forbid the further detailed consideration of the growing body of mediæval Office Hymns. Their main tendencies have already been indicated. But brief mention should be made of certain examples found in *The Hymnal*. First among these is the only Hymn given a definite liturgical place in our services, the famous *Veni, Creator Spiritus*. Two English versions appear, both in the Book of Common Prayer, and also in the Hymnal, Nos. 375 and 455. Although the poem quotes from the Christmas Hymn of St. Ambrose the couplet

> *infirma nostri corporis*
> *virtute firmans perpeti,*

it is now generally ascribed to the authorship of Hraban Maur,[32] the pupil of Alcuin, and later, the Archbishop of Mainz. Hraban

---

[31]Tennyson, *In Memoriam*.   [32]Magnentius Rabanus Maurus, 780–856 A.D.

was addicted to such quotations, or appropriations. Other considerations make the attribution probable.[33] But the tune, more sung than any other Plainsong tune throughout the world, antedates the Hymn: it is that of St. Ambrose's Easter Hymn.

Illustrative Records:
Victor 20896-B, Palestrina Choir, Philadelphia.
Victor 24819-B, American School Children.

Another tune in *The Hymnal,* No. 155[II], illustrates the metrical variety of the old Office Hymns. It was the setting of tenth century words from the Monastic Office.

Ecce jam noctis tenuatur umbra	Lo! the dim shadows of the night are waning;
lucis aurora rutilans coruscat:	Radiantly glowing, dawn of day returneth:
nisibus totis rogitemus omnes	Fervent in spirit, to the mighty Father
Cunctipotentem.	Pray we devoutly.

This modification of the famous stanza of Sappho, by way of its Latin imitators, was destined to provide the form of an ever-increasing number of fine Hymns, and to give us perennially singable tunes. We may note also the beloved Christmas tune at 328[II], and the richly ornate contemporary melody (No. 556[II]) of the Easter Hymn of St. Fulbert of Chartres, composed about the year 1000 A.D. Later writers not infrequently imitated their predecessors, or wrote for already existent tunes. Such was the case with St. Thomas Aquinas, when he composed Hymns for the new Office of Corpus Christi in 1263 A.D.

The first, represented by two of its stanzas at No. 331, was based upon a very early Advent Hymn: but it was written for the florid Ascension Day tune No. 331[II].

[33]Dreves, *Analecta Hymnica,* L 193, 194.

Illustrative Records:

His Master's Voice C 2088 (Ascension tune), Ampleforth Abbey Choir.

Victor 24819-A (another tune), American School Children.

Another beloved Hymn of St. Thomas Aquinas which appears in modern Anglican Hymnals is the following:

Victrola Album M 87 I, Solesmes Abbey Choir.

Victrola 7347-B, *Adoro te devote.*

The other and greater poem, No. 338, was modelled after the superb Passion Hymn of Venantius Fortunatus, and utilized his tune, one of the noblest ever composed. Its rhythm is the very rhythm of the popular Roman soldier's songs. St. Hilary had used this stanza form in his poem,

Adæ carnis gloriosa et caduci corporis.

How touching to think that the very rhythm to which we sing the words,

> Now, my tongue, the mystery telling
> Of the glorious Body sing,
> And the Blood, all price excelling,
> Which the Gentiles' Lord and King,
> Once on earth among us dwelling,
> Shed for this world's ransoming,

may have been heard from the lips of the guard casting dice for the seamless robe at the foot of the Cross!

This inspiring rhythm occurs also in the very early Hymn for the Dedication of a Church, No. 508. The contemporary seventh-century tune is the first Plainsong melody I ever heard. It was sung in procession on the streets of Albany, New York, led by brass instruments, as Bishops, Clergy, Choir, and Congregation marched from the old iron foundry which had long been used for worship to the Dedication of All Saints' Cathedral on November 20, 1888.

Proper Office Hymns Should Be Restored to Use

AT the fullest development of mediæval worship there were about one hundred and fifty such Hymns appointed for their specific places in the Choir Offices of the West: a veritable Christian Psalter. We may be glad that *The Hymnal* has been enriched by such excellent examples as those we have been considering: but it is much to be desired that at the next revision of the Book of Common Prayer, Proper Hymns, as well as Proper Psalms, should be appointed for a specific place in Morning and Evening Prayer, both for the Seasons and for the various Holy Days. Many more of these may profitably be drawn from the venerable Offices which gave us the liturgical Hymn. At least, an augmented number of Office Hymns with their proper tunes should be included at the next revision of the Hymnal, after the example of conservative Hymnals in England.

LITURGICAL HYMNS OF THE HOLY EUCHARIST

THE Roman Church in early ages was notably cautious in the matter of admitting to the Eucharist Hymns not found in Holy Writ. The Psalms, as we have seen, formed the text of the various Propers, with slight exceptions: and even the semi-biblical *Gloria in excelsis* and *Agnus Dei* were not fully received for many centuries. This conservative tendency was less noticeable in the Gallican, Mozarabic, and Celtic rites.

A Primitive Irish Communion Hymn

IT is not surprising, therefore, to find the earliest metrical
Hymn, in the modern sense, appearing in Ireland. A very early
legend assigns its authorship to Sechnall, nephew of St. Patrick.
It is contained in the Bangor Antiphoner, a manuscript written
about 690 A.D.; and there headed, *Ymnum quando commoni-
carent sacerdotes.* Another early writing, the *Leabhar Breac*,
calls it "the first Hymn that was made in Ireland." The character of the Latin, *Sancte, venite, Christi corpus sumite,* bears
witness to its very early date, prior to the introduction of rhyme.
We are all familiar with Neale's translation (*The Hymnal*
No. 330), "Draw nigh, and take the Body of the Lord." Thus
the custom of singing a Hymn at the Communion is of very
ancient standing.

The Processional Hymn

BUT far more significant than this single example of a Communion Hymn was another form, the Processional Hymn; not
the meaningless singing of some military march or sentimental
ditty as the Choir enters the Church or leaves it; but the true
Procession, starting from the Altar and returning thereto, for
a specific devotional purpose on a given occasion.[34] Such Processional Hymns almost invariably had the popular feature of a
congregational refrain, answering to the verses sung by the
Choir. This plan we should put into far wider practice, if we
really desire to improve our congregational singing. Our failure
to do so is largely the result of the complete pre-occupation of
the organist with the music of the Choir only; and this can be
corrected by no one but the Parish Priest, in whose hands respon-

[34]See *Report of the Joint Commission on Church Music,* Part II, Section B.

sibility finally rests. Our Hymnal contains fifty-six such compositions, just one tenth of its contents. Yet how rarely is any one of these sung as intended!

A notable example of this failure is found in the Palm Sunday Processional of the Carolingian poet Theodulf, Bishop of Orleans (d. 821 A.D.). Probably during his lifetime, this became the liturgical Procession after the Blessing and Distribution of the Palms. A choir of children sang the verse

Gloria laus et honor tibi sit, rex Christe, redemptor,
cui puerile decus prompsit Hosanna pium.

Illustrative Record:
Semen S.M. VII, Schola of Maredsous Abbey.

This was repeated by all, and then sung as a refrain after the children sang each of the subsequent stanzas. But in most of our parishes, when we sing Doctor Neale's well-loved translation, Hymn 143, everybody sings everything, and much too fast. It is a breathless and undignified performance. Instead, the Choir alone, or possibly only a part of it, should sing the numbered stanzas, and the Congregation should respond after each,

> All glory, laud, and honour
>   To Thee, Redeemer, King!
> To whom the lips of children
>   Made sweet hosannas ring.

Neale translated more stanzas than appear in *The Hymnal;* among them this quaint one:

> Be thou, O Lord, the rider,
>   And we the little ass,
> That to God's holy city
>   Together we may pass.

The ancient Processionals for Easter Day, Ascension Day, and Whitsunday, appearing in *The Hymnal* at Nos. 168, 184, and 195, are all drawn from the third book of Venantius Fortunatus, written prior to 582 A.D. These three centos from the one poem, so tellingly describing the springtide of the Christian year, were early arranged in the same form as the preceding, for Processional use. The Choir sings the first couplet, which is then repeated by the Congregation as a refrain, and follows each succeeding couplet by the Choir. All three refrains are printed at No. 195, for the convenience of the Congregation when Selby's tune, the most practical one, is sung. Archbishop Cranmer essayed the translation of this Hymn, but unsuccessfully, to his own critical judgment. He wrote, in 1544, "But by cause my English verses want the grace and facility that I would wish they had, your majesty may cause some other to make them again, that can do the same in more pleasant English and phrase." Several such adequate translations now exist: it is to be hoped that at the next revision of the Hymnal there may be chosen versions in the flowing metre of the original, which will permit the use both of the ancient melody and of the fine modern tune by Vaughan Williams.

One more of the ancient Processionals may be mentioned, although it does not appear in our books. It is the greatest poem of Fortunatus, the *Pange, lingua gloriosi, prœlium certaminis,* which formed the basis for the Eucharistic Hymn of St. Thomas, as we have seen. It was early introduced into the Gallican Liturgy for use on Good Friday, and its tenderly beautiful eighth stanza was used as the refrain. Rome adopted it later.

Here are the eighth and ninth stanzas, with Neale's translation. The original and contemporary tune is that at No. 338[1].

Crux fidelis, inter omnes	Faithful Cross! above all other,
arbor una nobilis,	One and only noble tree!
nulla talem silva profert	None in foliage, none in blossom,
flore, fronde, germine,	None in fruit thy peer may be;
dulce lignum, dulce clavo,	Sweetest Wood and sweetest Iron!
dulce pondus sustinens!	Sweetest Weight is hung on thee.
flecte ramos, arbor alto;	Bend thy boughs, O Tree of Glory!
tensa laxa viscera,	Thy relaxing sinews bend;
et rigor lentescat ille,	For awhile the ancient rigour
quem dedit nativitas,	That thy birth bestow'd, suspend;
ut superni membra regis	And the King of heav'nly beauty
mite tendas stipite.	On thy bosom gently tend!

The Sequence

ONE more type of Hymn, the Sequence, already mentioned in Chapter II, must be considered briefly: both because it was a means of introducing popular Hymn singing into the Mass by a very ingenious form, and because it gave to the world, as a permanent treasure, the final perfection of mediæval rhymed and rhythmical poetry in a few Sequences, three of which are contained in *The Hymnal*. There has been much confusion as to the origin of the Sequence: but thanks to the minutely careful scholarship of such men as Bannister, Hughes, Frere, and Blume, the question seems to be definitely answered.[35]

You will remember that in pre-Gregorian times the word *Alleluia* was sung after the Gradual Respond, with a Jubilus or melodic extension on the final vowel "a," an inheritance from Jewish music. This brought choral melody out of the realm of self-expression through sung words into that of emotional

[35]Henry Marriot Bannister, Clemens Blume, S.J., *Analecta Hymnica*, Vol. liii, Introduction. Anselm Hughes, O.S.B., *Anglo-French Sequelæ*, 1934. Walter Howard Frere, C.R., in Grove's *Dictionary of Music and Musicians*, 1927.

expression through pure tone and rhythm; that is, the ideal realm of absolute music. The purest and most vocal of sounds was prolonged in phrases of intense vitality to express a joy too deep for words. St. Augustine speaks of this in his comment on Psalm 95. "He who sings a Jubilus speaks no words; it is a song of joy without words; it is the voice of a heart dissolved with joy, . . . its joy is too great to put into words." St. Jerome uses similar expressions in commenting on Psalm 32.

To the *Alleluia,* St. Gregory added a Verse, generally scriptural, after which the *Alleluia* melody with its Jubilus was repeated as a Respond. In the seventh century, other Alleluias were provided with Verses. But in the eighth century, in northern France, began a custom of adding to the Jubilus still another wordless melody of strange construction, called a *Sequela.* This was divided into phrases of irregular length, each of which was repeated; which were therefore called *Sequentiæ.* To some parts of these novel strains, words were set, and thus the first step taken toward the later Sequence. The word *Prosa* was applied to these words; but it probably had no relation to their literary form, being merely an abbreviation of *Pro S[equenti]a.*

The upspringing of new intellectual life in the Carolingian empire gave a forward impulse to the art of music: and in the composition of such melodies we find the beginnings of "an artistry which will develop in steady and surely marked progress until the superb architecture of the great classical polyphonists has reached its climax."[36]

A theory that these melodies were of Byzantine origin is unsubstantiated by any definite proof. No Byzantine melody

[36]Hughes, *Anglo-French Sequelæ,* p. 12.

has been found which parallels any one of them. On the other hand, most of them begin with the recapitulation of at least part of a Gregorian *Alleluia.* Of course there was definite Greek influence at the Carolingian Court, which may have somewhat affected the beginnings of this new art of melody.

After the sack of the Benedictine Abbey of Jumièges in A.D. 852, one of its monks came to St. Gall in Switzerland with a manuscript in which these *longissimæ melodiæ* were written out, sometimes with words. The famous Notker Balbulus, the Stammerer, reputed inventor of the Sequence, having thus received the idea from Northern France, proceded to compose words for others of the *Sequelæ:* but he made the characteristic error which we considered while discussing the Tropes, in the second chapter, of providing a syllable for each note; thereby depriving the joyous Jubilus of its characteristic flow. He attributes this plan to his master Iso, who had written a commentary on Prudentius. Some doubt has been cast upon the accuracy of the account, which occurs in a letter addressed by Notker to Liutward, Bishop of Vercelli; but the letter is now accepted as authentic by leading scholars. The French origin is acknowledged in it: and we may at least assign an honorable place to Notker as the chief early figure in the development of the German Sequence.

As soon as texts were written for the pre-existing melodies in their completeness, the characteristic musical form of successive pairs of stanzas, each with its own tune, was developed. In performance, the stanzas usually alternated between men's and boys' voices: but the form is admirably adapted to alternation between Choir and Congregation: and it gives a richer opportunity to the Congregation than was found in the unchanging refrains of the Processional Hymn. The words of the early Sequences were balanced verses of unrhythmical prose: but all the devices of poetic form were gradually introduced in the rapid development of this new popular Hymnody. Rhyme, especially, which had slowly become familiar and then almost necessary since its tentative and partial introduction in the days of Fortunatus, blossomed to full perfection late in the eleventh century, when it is always at least two-syllabled. By then, also, the word-accent rhythm is perfectly regular, the *cæsura* occurs invariably at the end of a word, and the stanzas are generally of equal length: in a word, the formerly irregular Sequence has become a modern Hymn. An accessible example of this fully developed form is found in the so-called "Golden Sequence" for Whitsunday, *Veni, Sancte Spiritus,* Hymn No. 196[1].

Illustrative Records:

His Master's Voice C 2088, Ampleforth Abbey Choir.
Columbia History of Music Album 5710 (with Organum), Terry Choir.

Its history is of interest. The Gregorian Verse of the Whitsuntide Alleluia Respond, *Spiritus Domini,* was replaced in the eleventh century by another, *Veni Sancte Spiritus, reple tuorum corda fidelium.* There is reason to believe that this was written and composed by Robert the Pious, King of France, who died A.D. 1031. He was one of the few monarchs accustomed to don the cope, and act as Cantor in a church Choir. The Gallican music of the Reproaches, still in use on Good Friday, gave him the theme of his Alleluia. This theme is extended and characteristically developed in the Golden Sequence: which is often attributed to Pope Innocent III, but regarded by the Solesmes

Benedictines, on what seems excellent proof, as the work of Stephen Langton, Archbishop of Canterbury, 1207–1228 A.D. Archbishop Trench[37] calls it "the loveliest of all the Hymns in the whole circle of Latin sacred poetry." The music is worthy of the poem.

But another Sequence not, unfortunately, as yet in our Hymnal, will not only illustrate the earlier type, but will also indicate lines on which the future praises of the Church were to develop, as we shall see in the next chapter. It is the famous Easter Sequence, *Victimæ paschali,* traditionally assigned to Wipo, the Burgundian Chaplain of two Emperors. He died 1050 A.D. Here is the text, with the translation from the English Hymnal, No. 130; which also gives the fascinating music.

Illustrative Records:

Polydor 22647, Paderborn Cathedral Boys.
Christschall 63, Treves White Fathers.
Columbia DFX 184, Choir of Notre Dame d'Auteuil, Paris.

Victimæ paschali laudes	Christians, to the Paschal Victim
immolent Christiani.	Offer your thankful praises!
agnus redemit oves,	A Lamb the sheep redeemeth:
Christus innocens patri	Christ, who only is sinless,
reconciliavit peccatores.	Reconcileth sinners to the Father;
mors et vita duello	Death and life have contended
conflixere mirando,	In that combat stupendous:
dux vitæ mortuus regnat vivus.	The Prince of Life, who died, reigns immortal.
dic nobis Maria	Speak, Mary, declaring
quid vidisti in via?	What thou sawest wayfaring?
sepulchrum Christi viventis	'The Tomb of Christ, who is living,
et gloriam vidi resurgentis.	The glory of Jesus' Resurrection:

[37]*Sacred Latin Poetry,* 1864, p. 195.

angelicos testes	Bright angels attesting,
sudarium et vestes.	The shroud and napkin resting.
surrexit Christus spes mea	Yea, Christ my hope is arisen:
præcedet suos in Galilæa.	To Galilee he goes before you.'
credendum est magis Mariæ veraci	Happy they who hear the witness,
	Mary's word believing.
quam Judæorum turbæ fallaci.	Above the tales of Jewry deceiving.
scimus Christum surrexisse	Christ indeed from death is risen,
a mortuis vere,	Our new life obtaining.
tu nobis, victor rex, miserere!	Have mercy, victor King, ever reigning!

It is hard for us to realize the immense popularity of this composition for the following five hundred years, or the widespread and lasting results of that popularity in the fields of drama and music. Its character as a dialogue at the sepulchre on Easter morning led to its being sung not only as a Sequence at Mass, but also as a little music-drama before *Te Deum* at Matins, with choristers as angels and deacons in dalmatics as the three Marys. "From this tiny seed, and not from the classical stage, which had perished centuries before, has grown the drama of today; first the miracle plays, then the moralities, such as *Everyman*. From these it was but a short step to a play like Marlowe's *Doctor Faustus,* and thence began the modern stage."[38] On the musical side, within a century of the composition of the piece, vernacular verses were being interpolated between the Latin stanzas in Germany. From them grew the pre-Reformation Chorale, *Christ ist erstanden,* utilizing phrases of the earlier melody. Luther loved this Hymn, and based upon it a still closer imitation of the Sequence in his Chorale, *Christ lag in Todesbanden,* translated in 1539 by Bishop Miles Cover-

[38]Athelstan Riley, *Concerning Hymn Tunes and Sequences,* p. 93. See also Carl Lange, *Die Lateinischen Osterfeiern,* Munich, 1887, and W. Meyer, *Fragmenta Burana,* pp. 49, 76.

dale in England. And in turn, Bach used the music in Chorale Preludes, and the whole piece in his noble Cantata of the same name, composed for use on Easterday, 1724.

Illustrative Records:

2000-Jahre Musik Album, Berlin Academy Choir.
    Parlophon B 37026, *Christ ist erstanden*, Heinrich Fink, 1500.
Victor Album M 120, Orfeo Catalá.
    Cantata, *Christ lag in Todesbanden*, J. S. Bach.
Odeon 166147, Organ, Louis Vierné.
Victor 7437, Philadelphia Orchestra, L. Stokowski.
    Chorale Prelude, *Christ lag in Todesbanden*, J. S. Bach.

The melody of the Easter Sequence also inspired Adam, Canon Regular of St. Victor in Paris, by common consent the greatest of all Sequence writers: from whose skilled pen we possess some forty-five poems which bring the mediæval rhymed rhythmical verse to its highest perfection.[39] Adam wrote his Sequence for Easter Eve for the tune of *Victimæ paschali*.[40] Later he composed new melodies of his own; one of which he liked so well that he wrote eleven Proses for it. Four of these were for the springtide Feasts of Holy Cross,[41] Ascensiontide, Whitsuntide, and Trinity Sunday; which gives us the key to the form of the masterly *Corpus Christi* Sequence, *Lauda Sion Salvatorem*. St. Thomas Aquinas wrote it in 1263 A.D., to fit this melody by Adam of St. Victor, who had died ninety years earlier.

Illustrative Record:

Christschall 139, Steyl Fathers' Choir.

[39]A faint imitation of Adam's manner is found in our Hymn No. 288, *Come, pure hearts.*
[40]E. Misset et Pierre Aubry: *Les Proses D'Adam de Saint Victor*, Paris, 1900, pp. 256, 257.
[41]The genesis of this melody was the *Alleluia, Dulce lignum* for May third.

Mention of two further Sequences included in *The Hymnal* must close our consideration of the form. They are *Dies iræ*, No. 65, and *Stabat Mater*, No. 161. Both reflect characteristic features of the new feeling which came into Western Christianity with the transforming Franciscan movement, in a world filled with a sense of impending doom, where terror must be mitigated with pity and sorrow and love: where a new family of God, the Brothers Minor, must go forth in poverty under its grand Pauline motto, *Mihi absit gloriari nisi in cruce Domini*,[42] to combat not only corruption in high places, but also wide-spreading heresy veiled as asceticism. Both were probably by Franciscan authors; the first by Thomas of Celano,[43] the friend and biographer of the Poverello: the second by Jacopone da Todi[44] whose *Laudi* in the Umbrian dialect were among the earlier vernacular praises in the new trend of life and thought.

The *Dies iræ* stems from Zephaniah i:14–15; "The great day of the Lord is near . . . that day of wrath, a day of clouds and thick darkness." This was closely reflected in one of the most majestic examples of liturgical prose produced by the Church during the Middle Ages, the Respond sung at the Absolution of the Dead.[45] From the music of this Respond, at the Verse *Dies illa, dies iræ*, is derived the amazing melody (the second tune in *The Hymnal*) which has become a sort of *leitmotiv* suggesting death in modern secular music, as well as sacred.

Illustrative Records:

Victor 21621-A (a little too fast!), Palestrina Choir, Philadelphia.
Victor Album M 177, Pius X Choir: disc 11530-A.
Parlophon E 3212, Westminster Cathedral Choir.
Christschall 66, Treves White Fathers.

[42]Galatians vi:14.   [43]Thomas of Celano, b. late 12th cent., d. about 1255.
[44]Jacomo Benedetti, or Jacopone of Todi, d. 1306.
[45]For words and music, see *The American Missal*, pp. 575, 576.

I have found it in over forty compositions. Because of this unique musical derivation, the piece is called a Sequence only in a very loose and inexact way; as it is not the extension of an Alleluia Jubilus, but is merely sung in the Eucharist between Epistle and Gospel. Only the sonorous majesty of the original Latin sung to its profoundly imaginative music unaccompanied by any harmonies can make us fully aware of its transcendent perfection. No translation is adequate for this: that which appears in *The Hymnal* is the best; and can at least present the noble and moving sequence of thought in singable lines, from the awe-inspiring picture of Judgment Day in the first six verses to the deeply personal pleading of the rest. Thomas of Celano's poem ended with stanza 17. This translation was made under highly dramatic circumstances. The revolutionary year 1848, like the times of St. Francis, and like the present age, was marked by dire uncertainty, terror, and death. In Paris, the culminating horror was the shooting of the Archbishop at the barricades of the Place de la Bastille, while he was trying to put an end to armed conflict. At his Requiem in Notre Dame, the priests of the diocese sang *Dies iræ* with overpowering effect. Doctor William Josiah Irons, an English priest, was present. Profoundly moved both by the service and the tragic circumstances, he began this translation at once. Stanzas 18 and 19 were not part of the original poem; the final couplet, now happily restored to its original form as a prayer for the dead, was translated by Isaac Williams.

The Latin of the *Stabat Mater,* written a little later, is of almost equal beauty: but it is the pathetic beauty of tenderness, of love and of pity, rather than that of sublimity. We do not possess its contemporary music. That given in *The Hymnal,* at

No. 161, was composed four centuries later: and the Plainsong of the Roman *Graduale* is the work of a contemporary of our own, Dom Fonteinne, O.S.B. Our book contains only a part of the Sequence.[46] The division is of interest: for it calls to mind that early in the fifteenth century, at Cologne, was instituted a Commemoration of the Seven Sorrows of the Blessed Virgin Mary; for which *Stabat Mater* was divided to form the Office Hymns at Vespers and Lauds respectively. Thus the two streams of Liturgical Hymnody, for the Office and for the Eucharist, are at last united in one: and the Sequence has become a Hymn. This tendency found its final expression in England, just before the Reformation, when the Hymn *Jesu, dulcis memoria*[47] was adopted as a Sequence, and sung to a melody found only in the early printed Sarum Graduals, the last of which was issued in the year that Henry the Eighth appointed Cranmer Archbishop of Canterbury.

We have now traced the growth of the Latin Liturgical Hymn from its beginnings in primitive Christianity to those changes which were the immediate forerunners of Post-Reformation vernacular Hymnody, and of the specifically eclectic Hymnody of the Anglican Communion. The Latin Hymn has passed away from the public worship of the Anglican Communion: but let us not forget that we need, for the right completion of our worship, the Liturgical Hymn, forming an integral part of a specific service in the Christian Liturgy, to be used as inevitably as its Proper Psalms, Lessons, or Prayers.

[46]Full translations may be found in *The Monastic Diurnal*, pp. 506, 507; *The American Missal*, p. 583; and *The Midnight Mass*, Douglas, pp. 63, 64.

[47]Long attributed to St. Bernard, but now known as a work prior to his time. Excerpts in *The Hymnal*, Nos. 316, 328.

ILLUSTRATIVE RECORDS

Additional records illustrative of the Plainsong Hymn:

Victor Album M 87 II, Solesmes Abbey Choir:
Victrola 7352-B, *Virgo Dei genetrix. O quam glorifica.*

Victor 20897-B, *Ut queant laxis,* Palestrina Choir, Philadelphia.
Victor 24820-B, *Ut queant laxis,* American School Children.

The names of the notes of the scale were taken from the first syllables of six lines of this Hymn.

UT queant laxis	O for thy spirit,
RE-sonare fibris	Holy John, to chasten
MI-ra gestorum	Lips sin-polluted,
FA-muli tuorum	Fettered tongues to loosen;
SOL-ve polluti	So by thy children
LA-bii reatum	Might thy deeds of wonder
S-ancte I-oannes	Meetly be chanted.

The S and I make *Si. Ut* was later changed to *Do.*

Victor Grand Séminaire Album, Montreal.
Tantum ergo, O salutaris, Lucis Creator.
Semen S. A. I, II, Averbode Abbey Choir.
Sanctorum meritis, O salutaris.
Christschall 58, Treves White Fathers.
Stabat mater.
Christschall 64, Treves White Fathers.
Pange lingua gloriosi.
Semen, Schola of Maredsous Abbey.
S. M. IV, *Ave maris stella.*
S. M. VIII, *Vexilla regis.*
Semen, Phonedibel Choir.
S. N. 1001, *Tantum ergo.*
S. N. 1001, *Tantum ergo* (Spanish).

CHAPTER VII

ANGLICAN ECLECTIC HYMNODY
LATER PRE-REFORMATION SOURCES

INTRODUCTION

Contemporary Anglican Hymnody

THE contemporary Hymnody of the Anglican Communion, of which *The Hymnal* is a fairly good representative, is the richest treasure of St. Augustine's *Laus Dei cum cantico*, "the Praise of God with song," which the world has ever seen in use. To it have contributed every age since Augustine's own; practically every country which has accepted the message of the Gospel; and not only every main religious movement within the limits of Christianity, but also some sincere efforts outside the bounds of the Christian faith, but actuated by the Christian spirit. Within it are distilled the precious essences of countless human lives: lives of men, women, and even children, lives of clergy, of religious, of reforming prophets, of poets, of musicians, who were in some sense 'the lights of the world in their several generations.' They form a large part today of the great Apocalyptic[1] "multitude, which no man can number, of all nations, and kindreds, and people, and tongues, who stand before the throne and before the Lamb, and cry, Salvation to our God which sitteth upon the throne, and unto the Lamb."

After the Bible, and the Book of Common Prayer, which

[1]Rev. vii:9, 10.

is the Bible co-ordinated for practical use by the Church, its inspired interpreter, the Hymnal is our most precious spiritual treasure and spiritual tool. For true effectiveness with his people, both in rendering the services of the Prayer Book, and in relation to his preaching, the parish Priest must study the Hymnal, and continue that study his whole life long. The Choirmaster and organist cannot even secure the proper functioning of his Choir unless with equal care he continually studies the Hymnal and tries to bring it, little by little, to fullest effect in the singing of the Congregation. The Metrical Hymn had its origin in the need of the Congregation, as we saw in the last chapter. In whatever age or place the congregational character of hymn singing has been neglected, the Church has suffered inevitable spiritual loss. The Congregation itself must therefore be encouraged and helped to use the Hymnal. To that end, we need to effect a change in a matter wherein we Episcopalians lag far behind our Protestant brethren. We need to work toward no smaller an end than the *personal ownership* of a Bible, a Prayer Book, and a Hymnal *with music,* by every communicant of the Church. Probably I should not now feel so intense an interest in the Hymns of the Church if my Presbyterian father had not, out of his poverty, provided a Hymnal for each of his children. My mother's Hymnal, Lowell Mason's fine *Sabbath Hymn and Tune Book,* is beside me, as I write: and later, we shall see how important a factor it was in American Hymnody.

The passive indifference of many Congregations to the Hymns will seem less strange when we realize that to the English Church, from the fourteenth century to the eighteenth, the Congregational Hymn was practically unknown; except as barbarously represented by crude metrical versions of the Psalms after the year 1559. The old art of the Latin Liturgical Hymn was dying, because it had ceased to be the Hymn of the people. But throughout this long period of decline in one vehicle of the Praise of God, new and varied expressions which would in time gloriously expand it were slowly forming from the people themselves all over Europe. As a rising tide seems often to be flowing out of this or that inlet by the sea's margin, and only after some time is seen to be visibly higher, as through many another channel it pours in, so we can perceive that Christian Hymnody became far richer and fuller both in the Catholic and Protestant bodies as a result of the readoption, in various forms, of the poetry and music of the people.

Let us follow, in order, the gradual decline of the Latin Hymn, and then the rise of this great surge of vernacular song.

THE DECLINE OF THE LATIN HYMN

An Age of Imitation

AFTER its high climax with *Dies iræ* and *Stabat mater*[2] in the thirteenth century, Latin Hymnody and sacred verse began to lose its distinctive qualities. It became more artificial or more commonplace. Its exquisite rhythms deteriorated. An age of imitation, and of inferior imitation, had set in. There was a vast increase in the number of poems and in that of writers: but quality fell off. One reason for the spate of new Latin Hymns was the very chaotic condition of the liturgical services in the Western Church. Almost every Diocese in northern

[2]See pp. 186–188.

Europe had its own Breviary, its own Missal. The Religious Orders, sometimes individual Convents, had the like freedom. One early instance of this is called to mind by our Hymn 544, "O what the joy and the glory must be." The tragic Peter Abailard composed *O quanta qualia* as the Saturday Vespers Hymn in a complete series "for the whole cycle of the year," which he sent to Héloïse at her request for the use of her nuns at the Convent of The Paraclete; which had been the hermitage of his 'consolation' after his condemnation in 1121 A.D. The nuns of The Paraclete sang them daily till after his death, and that of Héloïse in 1164 A.D.

In her letter requesting the Hymns, she complains of the lack of Proper Hymns for certain Feasts. If this were the case early in the twelfth century, how much more after the fourteenth, as new Festivals multiplied in the hundreds of Diocesan and Monastic liturgies! For them, literally hundreds of Office Hymns and Sequences were written. They have continued to be written in the Roman Church on this account down to the present day. Two of the anonymous Hymns composed for the new Office of Our Lord Jesus Christ the King within the last decade have come into Anglican use both here and abroad. I cannot refrain from citing the second stanza of the Lauds Hymn, because of its terribly needed evangelical message to the world as it is today.

Non ille regna cladibus,	He hath not won his kingdom here[3]
Non vi metuque subdidit:	By devastation, force, or fear;
Alto levatus stipite,	But on the Cross uplifted high
Amore traxit omnia.	By love alone draws all men nigh.

Many of these Hymns are devout, useful, and poetical, and

[3]Winfred Douglas, *The Monastic Diurnal,* Oxford University Press, 1932.

have come into common Christian use in translations. In fact with some of them, translation has added a poetic or devotional quality stronger than that of the original: for Latin poetic composition deteriorated in the sense of beauty during this long period, and became academic. *The Hymnal* contains twelve translations of late Breviary Hymns. I append a list of them,[4] including two from the earlier "Joyful Rhythm on the Name of Jesus" which, as we have seen, came late into Breviary use.[5]

[4]285 O wondrous type! O vision fair	*Cælestis formam gloriæ*	
	Sarum Breviary	1495
316 Jesus, the very thought of thee	*Jesu, dulcis memoria*	
	Sarum Breviary	1495
110 Alleluia, song of gladness	*Alleluia, dulce carmen*	
	Antwerp Breviary	1496
39 To the Name of our salvation	*Gloriosi Salvatoris*	
	Meissen Breviary	1512
178 At the Lamb's high feast we sing	*Ad regias Agni dapes*	
	Roman Breviary	1632
Recast under Urban VIII from the ancient	*Ad cœnam Agni providi*	
328 Jesus, thou Joy of loving hearts	*Jesu, dulcedo cordium*	
	Paris Breviary	1680
30 As now the sun's declining rays	*Labente jam solis rota*	
	Paris Breviary	1736
88 The ancient law departs	*Debilis cessent elementa legis*	
	Paris Breviary	1736
91 Conquering Kings their titles take	*Victis sibi cognomina*	
	Paris Breviary	1736
282 On Jordan's bank the Baptist's cry	*Iordanis oras prævia*	
	Paris Breviary	1736
47 On this day, the first of days	*Die parente temporum*	
	Le Mans Breviary	1748
17 The sun is sinking fast	*Sol præceps rapitur*	
	French Office of the Most Holy Will of God	1805

[5]See page 188, *Jesu dulcis memoria.*

THE DECLINE OF THE LATIN HYMN

Baneful Effect of Italian Humanism

It will be observed that the later Hymns in the foregoing list are no longer in accentual rhythm, but in an imitation of quantitative classical verse: they are artificial, not spontaneous. "No one writes poetry in a language which he has not learned from his mother, but from books."[6] The origins of this artificiality go back to the rise of Humanism in the fourteenth century. Man and nature became the center of thought and of literature, instead of God, as of old; and such human ideas, as expressed in the superb artistry of the Augustan classics, made its votaries despise mediæval poetry as barbarous. It was a secularist movement always, and as it progressed, the Italian Renaissance became increasingly pagan. We see its evil side today in the lowered sense of moral relations, especially in the field of sex; and in the national and international political ethic which then found expression in Niccolo Machiavelli's *Il Principe*.

But God overrules the affections of sinful men, and among the manifold changes of the world, the wheat grows with the tares till the day of reaping. Vast good was to enrich the world through the restoration of ancient learning and literature, and especially through the revival of Greek, the language of the New Testament and of the noble heritage of the philosophers. Education in every field was to become more normal, more natural; and its scope was to expand with fresh vitality. A new poetry in the precisely contemporaneous vernaculars which then attained complete coherence; a new music springing from popular song in those vernaculars, which we will presently consider, more

[6]Reverend Matthew Britt, O.S.B., *The Hymns of the Breviary and Missal*, New York, Benziger Brothers, 1922.

than made up for the disastrous influence of Humanism on Latin Hymnody.

It was Giovanni de'Medici, son of Humanism's notable patron, Lorenzo the Magnificent, who as Pope Leo X (A.D. 1513–1521) entrusted his friend Zaccharia Ferreri with the task of recasting the Breviary Hymns in classical Latin: which he did, with the naïve introduction of a pagan terminology. Leo's cousin Giulio de'Medici, who had been educated by Lorenzo, became Pope Clement VII in 1523 A.D. The following month, on December 11, he recognized and approved the revised Hymnal. From that day to this, the Roman Church has suffered a barbarous mutilation of the superb mediæval Hymns.

Urban VIII

OTHER changes were made in the sixteenth century: and finally, Urban VIII, the last of the Humanist Popes, appointed four learned Jesuits in 1629 to "correct" the Hymns. They made 952 alterations in 81 of the Hymns, and far exceeded their instructions. Nevertheless Urban set forth their work in the Roman Breviary of 1632: in this connection, it may be fairly said of him, as was said at the time for another reason, *Quod non fecerunt barbari, fecerunt Barberini.* An example illustrates the nature of the changes. Our beloved Hymn 457 is from the seventh century.

Angularis fundamentum
  Lapis Christus missus est,
Qui parietum compage
  In utroque nectitur,
Quem Sion sancta suscepit,
  In quo credens permanet.

Christ is made the sure foundation,
  Christ the head and corner-stone,
Who, the two walls[7] underlying,
  Bound in each, binds both in one:
Holy Sion's help for ever
  And her confidence alone.

[7]The heavenly and the earthly Church.

[196]

Urban's *literati* made of this the following: happily they refrained from calling God the Father Jove!

Alto ex Olympi vertice	From the high summit of Olympus
Summi Parentis Filius	came the sovereign Father's Son,
Ceu monte desectus lapis	like a stone cut from the mountain
Terras in imas decidens,	descending to the lowest plains, and
Domus supernæ, et infimæ,	joined together either corner of the
Utrumque junxit angulum.	celestial and lower abodes.

It occasioned widespread disappointment when the desires of Pius X were not wholly carried out in the Breviary of 1911, but the mutilated Hymns retained. However, the original Office Hymns with their music were added as a supplement to the *Antiphonarium Vaticanum;* and it is significant that they are sung in St. Peter's and in St. John Lateran, the Cathedral of the Roman Bishops. They are also retained by the Benedictines, the Dominicans, the Cistercians, the Carthusians, and others of the older Religious Orders; in which, of course, they are still congregationally sung in a language understood by all.

Polyphonic Settings

THE Hymns, as such, entered but little into the field of Polyphony, although single strains from their music were widely used as the foundation of other compositions, especially Masses. But charming three and four part settings of Hymns were made in England at the height of Polyphony by such composers as Whyte, Tallis, and Byrd, and by Hassler and others in Germany. Palestrina, however, composed a masterpiece in his *Hymni totius anni* published in 1589 A.D. Victoria also set the Hymns in 1581 and 1600.

Illustrative Records:

> Roycroft 161, The English Singers.
>> Byrd, *Christe qui lux est et dies.*
>>> O Christ, who art the Light and Day.
> Columbia 4970, London Catholic Chorus.
>> Palestrina, *Veni, Creator Spiritus.*
> Parlophone E 3185, Westminster Cathedral Choir.
>> Palestrina, *O salutaris hostium.*
> Parlophone E 10804, La Scala Chorus.
>> Victoria, *Tantum ergo sacramentum.*

These Polyphonic settings suggest a valuable modern practice comparable to the use of alternate Faux-bourdons in the Psalmody of the Canticles.[8] It is that of more elaborate arrangements of individual stanzas of Hymns for the Choir, sometimes with the melody in the tenor or bass, alternating with the unison stanzas for the Congregation. The use of Descant, an occasional independent melody for trebles, rising above the Congregational tune, is also widely practiced today. This, however, should be used but sparingly for its most refreshing effect.

The Jesuit hymnological expert Clemens Blume, writing of the Latin liturgical Hymn, says, "That this once so flourishing art should have declined and finally died out cannot be wondered at, if it be considered that in all human undertakings the period of growth is followed by a period of decay *unless a new spirit pours fresh life into the old forms.*" The italics are mine. Let me suggest that 'a new spirit *has* poured fresh life into the old forms.' What has prevented the exercise of its proper function by the Latin Hymn during recent centuries has been the death of the Latin tongue. It is no longer spoken, even in Universities,

[8]See pp. 114, 115, 140.

once its refuge. This has led to the movement of the Roman Church tentatively begun in England with the English Primer of 1534 A.D., and continued, with accelerated movement during the past few decades, to provide her children with adequate vernacular translations of all her services, including the Hymns. But these will never regain their power over Christian congregations till they are again *sung* in the vernacular, as they were throughout so many centuries.

NEW BEGINNINGS IN VERNACULAR HYMNODY

GREEK ceased to be a familiar tongue in Rome, and the services, with much of their music, were translated into the popular Latin. By the beginning of Renaissance times, Latin had likewise ceased to be a European vernacular, and had been supplanted in Northern Europe by languages chiefly of other origin, and of different characteristic rhythms. We must now examine the surge of new life expressing itself in these tongues, in those elements which have chiefly contributed to our Hymnody.

The Carol

THE Carol was not only an outcome of the irresistible desire for vernacular song in the Middle Ages: it was also the introduction of a wholly different kind of music into a freer Praise of God; namely, the Folksong, with its rhythms springing from the long neglected Dance impulse,[9] which re-entered Western Christianity with infectious zest. This is involved in the very word, "carol," from the late Latin *caraula,* a dance-song. The

[9]See p. 8.

theatre, the dance, the popular song, had been sternly and rightly repressed in early Latin Christianity, because they were not only connected with pagan religion, but also with gross immorality. The need of denying this impulse continued long. At Rouen in the seventh century, we find St. Ouen writing in the biography of his lifelong friend St. Eloi, *Nullus in festivitate Sancti Joannis, vel quibuslibet sanctorum solemnitatibus, solstitia aut ballationes vel saltationes aut caraulas aut cantica diabolica exerceat.*[10] Men might not observe the old heathen festivities of Midsummer Day by dancing and leaping and diabolical carol singing; nor might they do this at any Saint's Day celebration.

But the dance is one of the normal activities of mankind: and with the passing away of its pagan connotations, was inevitably to bring back merriment into Christian praise. The puritanism which succeeded license gradually yielded to better balanced thought, as it has in America since the Pilgrims sacked Merry-mount in 1628 for carol singing and Maypole dancing. Eventually, Jacopone could describe an Angelic Carol in that loveliest of his Umbrian *Laudi,* worthy of the brush of Botticelli, which runs: "See how the *Bambino* kicked in the straw; his mother covered him, and put his little mouth to her breast; . . . with her left hand she rocked him, and with holy songs lulled her dear Love to sleep . . . and all around danced the Angels, singing verses most sweet and speaking of naught but love." Here is the first suggestion of the tender cycle of cradle songs of the divine Babe that was to culminate in the Christmas Oratorio of Bach. A little later Dante could speak of the Choir

---

[10]Dom Luc d' Achery, O.S.B., *Spicilegium* V, ii:15.

of Saints dancing in heaven:[11] and we are back in the spirit of the Ambrosian Hymn *Jesu, corona virginum,* where the Virgin Saints "follow the Lamb whithersoever he goeth."[12]

Post te canentes cursitant,	In blessed troops they follow thee
Hymnosque dulces personent.	With dance and song and melody.[13]

A well-known hymnologist, Canon Dearmer, has said that the Carol was "a creation of the fifteenth century," citing Professor Saintsbury's statement that the oldest English Carol was not earlier. But the form originated long before on the Continent of Europe. *The Hymnal* has several examples of earlier date, which we will examine briefly.

The tune of No. 115 takes us back to Sens and Beauvais in France in the early thirteenth century. It was then sung, not in the prosaic and conventional rhythm to which the indefatigable arranger Richard Redhead tamed it in 1853, but in merry triple dance time. Pierre de Corbeil became Archbishop of Sens in 1200 A.D. He set forth an Office of the Circumcision for the use of his newly restored Cathedral, the immediate architectural progenitor of Canterbury Cathedral. It contains the delightful and naïve Prose of the Ass, soon part of a popular ceremony in that region, especially at Beauvais. It began with a quaint dramatic procession through the town, in which a richly caparisoned ass bore a maiden and child, typifying the Flight into Egypt. To the Latin stanzas of the ecclesiastical choir, the people responded in Old French, "Hey, Sir donkey, Hey."

[11]*Paradiso,* Canto XXIV. *Così quelle carole differemente danzando.*
[12]Rev. xiv:4.
[13]John Mason Neale's translation: note implication of *cursitant.*

Returning, the ass with his symbolic burden was led before the High Altar, and Mass was sung. Before the Epistle, the piece was sung again at Beauvais in three part counterpoint.

Orientis partibus	From the East
adventavit asinus	came an ass,
pulcher et fortissimus	fair and very strong,
sarcinis aptissimus.	most ready for his burden.
Hez, sire asnes, hez.	Hey, Sir donkey, hey!

Merriment, drama, popular song, and the spirit of the dance have returned in France into the very Cathedral itself.

Doubtless these gay strains were still heard in central France when Blessed Henry Suso, the Dominican mystic, was born, toward the close of the century. The transforming thought of Abailard,[14] that ideas are not entities, but conceptions of the human mind, lay back of many and divergent religious movements from his time on; wherein now the reason, now the intuitive faculties, lead to the myriad ways in which God reveals himself to man's spiritual consciousness. Among these ways was that of such mystics as Eckhard, Tauler, St. Catherine of Siena, and Heinrich Suso (d. 1365), who avoided some questionable speculations of his master Eckhard.

From this devout German monk, we receive the most joyous Carol, Hymn 549, as is indicated by a contemporary manuscript.[15] Whether, as there told, he danced with the Angels to its happy lilt or not, it has set millions of hearts dancing ever

[14]See p. 193.

[15]Cited in Cardinal Melchior von Diepenbrock's biography, *Heinrich Suso's Leben und Schriften*, Regensburg, 1829, as follows: "Wie eines Tages zu Suso himmlische Jünglinge kamen, ihm in seiden Leiden eine Freude zu machen; sie zogen den Diener (himself, God's servant) bei den Hand *an den Tanz,* und der eine Jüngling sing an ein frohlickes Gesänglein von dem Kindlein Jesus, das spricht also, *In dulci jubilo.*

since. The original words are what is called macaronic: a mixture of Latin and the vernacular, such as we have in the fifteenth century English Carol (*The Hymnal* 547) "When Christ was born of Mary free." Here is the original first stanza.

In dulci jubilo	*In dulci jubilo*
singet und sit vro	Now sing with hearts aglow!
Aller unser wonne	Our delight and pleasure
layt in presepio,	Lies *in præsepio,*
Sy leuchtet vor dy sonne	Like sunshine is our treasure
matris in gremio	*Matris in gremio*
qui alpha est & O.	*Qui Alpha es et O!*

The words in our Hymnal are original with Doctor Neale.

Illustrative Records:

His Master's Voice, C 2070, Royal Choral Society.
Odeon O 6501 AA, Berlin Academy Choir.
Polydor 90160, St. Thomas Choir, Leipzig.

This Carol was introduced into England in 1708, through a little book of twenty-four Hymns called *Lyra Davidica.* It began

In dulci jubilo
To the house of God we'll go.

It came to America but little later. It was sung at the newly opened Moravian Mission in Pennsylvania on Christmas Eve, 1741, under the leadership of Count von Zinzendorf, who had so strongly influenced the Wesleys. On the same night another Carol

Not Jerusalem;
rather, Bethlehem

[203]

gave the name to the new settlement and the present city. There, on September 14, four years later, the old mission diary records that *In dulci jubilo* was sung simultaneously in thirteen languages, European and Indian, accompanied by an orchestra. Surely the macaronic trend could go no further!

The tune *Puer nobis*, No. 556, calls to mind another and characteristic use of Latin in a vernacular Hymn. The Latin Lauds and Vesper Offices closed with the V and R, *Benedicamus Domino, Deo gratias:* "Let us bless the Lord, Thanks be to God." In the fourteenth century many Carols were made which included the Latin Versicle and Response in the last two stanzas. They were sung at the close of the Offices, thus actually bringing popular vernacular song into the services. This was undoubtedly among them, with its original Christmas words, although our first manuscript of it is in 1410.

Another "Trope on *Benedicamus*," as such songs are technically called, is Hymn 555, *O filii et filiæ*. This *Alleluia du jour de Pasques* was written by a Franciscan friar in Paris, Jean Tisserand, toward the close of the fifteenth century. He was the founder of an Order for penitent women, risen from the death of sin to the life of righteousness. Perhaps he had been in the lyric South, for the form of the Carol is Provençal. The tune is restored in our version to its original simple form. This happy dance of the spirit was printed in Philadelphia in 1787, and has voiced the Easter joy of Americans from that time to the present.

The year that Tisserand died, 1494 A.D., Jean Mauburn, Abbot of Livry, wrote the swan-song of mediæval rhythmical Latin poetry in his *Eia mea anima*,[16] of which three stanzas appear

[16] *Analecta Hymnica* xlviii, p. 515.

as No. 550 in *The Hymnal*. He entitled it *Carmen . . . ad præsepii visitationem, canendum sub nota:* Dies est leticie. This latter is the Latin title of a popular German Carol[17] first found in a manuscript of the twelfth century. Its music became an inspiration to later composers, including Bach, who wrote two Chorale Preludes on the theme. Our regret for its absence from *The Hymnal* is lessened by the tender expressiveness of Doctor Noble's tune, so well paralleling the verse.

Whence came this exquisite tenderness, this praise of holy poverty, this touching quasi-dramatic dialogue between the Babe of the manger and the individual soul? Mauburn's title tells us: "To be sung on visiting the Crib." We are carried back to Christmastide at Greccio in 1223, when the loving heart of St. Francis gave the Church the devotion of the Manger, which makes the Gospel of the Incarnation vivid throughout the world today. At the very culmination of mediæval culture, the Church was assailed without by worldly corruption, and infected within by the false spiritualism and asceticism of heretical movements that spread like wildfire among the poor. Then God raised up Francis: and spiritual joy, the fruit of love and the seed of peace, entered afresh into the world. After the black oppression of the humble by five centuries of misrule in Church and State, men learned anew that *Deus est Deus pauperum*. Spiritual poverty found God, not by abandoning the Church, but by a direct personal bond which could overthrow corruption, turn heresy to living faith, and communicate a joy that dared face the realities and implications of the Passion of Christ. This was the true 'Kingdom of the Spirit,' not the distorted one predicted by such false prophets as Joachim of Flora. "This

[17]*Ein Kindelein so lobelich.*

spiritual and emotional renewal of Western and especially of Italian Christianity was the main influence which made itself felt . . . in the vernacular and Latin poetry of the thirteenth and fourteenth centuries."[18]

In this new springtide, the soil of all Europe blossomed with fresh song, the *Laudi spirituali* of Italy, the *Cantus Mariales* of Spain, the *Noëls* of France, the *Piæ Cantiones* of the North. Carol and Folksong blended into a new type of popular Hymnody, relying more on melodic grace and beauty than on rhythm. *The Hymnal* illustrates these allied trends of religious song.

Laudi Spirituali

Two melodies of precisely this period in Italy may be familiar to you. The fine A Cappella Choir of Evanston, Illinois, has often sung *Alta Trinita beata* in its antique Italian. Another example is the well-loved melody *Divinum Mysterium,* Hymn 74. Its later history is so typical of the ways in which a real tune can pass through long historical and linguistic changes, and still exercise its potent charm, that I must tell it in part.

In 1580, Didrik Pedersen, a young Finlander, left Åbo in the province of Nyland to attend the University of Rostock. In his sophomore year, he published *Piæ Cantiones,* a collection of school and sacred songs which he had gathered among his collegiate friends for future use as a school Hymnal.[19] Among them was a form of this tune, which had found its way from Franciscan Italy to Germany and so to Finland. In 1853, a copy

[18]F. J. E. Raby, *Christian Latin Poetry,* p. 417.

[19]Very many of these songs are still sung in the schools of Helsingfors. I possess a collection recently edited by Heikki Klemetti, the Finnish choral conductor.

of *Piæ Cantiones,* now unique, was brought to England, and came into the possession of Thomas Helmore: by whom our tune was edited for English use with the words of Prudentius, "Of the Father's love begotten." *The Hymnal* has restored the rhythm to its earlier form: and probably more people sing it in America than ever did in Europe, for it has recently been included in several Protestant Hymnals.

Spanish Melodies

OUR only representative is the smooth fluent melody, *Tantum ergo,* No. 338^{III}, anciently associated with the same words in Spain. This old tune became the theme of a famous motet by Victoria, at the height of classical Polyphony.

Noëls

THE popular Christmas refrain Noël became the familiar name of the French Carol, and was early adopted in England as Nowell.[20] Most Noëls are strongly rhythmed Folksongs. Hymn No. 339 is sung to *Picardy,*[21] a Noël whose expressive grace was first heard in this country at the recitals of the distinguished artist, Madame Yvette Guilbert.

Piæ Cantiones

THE title of Didrik Pedersen's book, just mentioned, was simply the common designation of songs of this type in the Germanic and Scandinavian countries. Some fifteen hundred

---

[20]See *The Hymnal,* 551. The term may be derived from natalis, "birthday," or possibly from *novella,* "news."

[21]It may well be sung, also, to the words of *Tantum ergo* on the previous page.

of them were written and composed in Germany alone before the Reformation. We may illustrate the type by two. The tune *Rosa Mystica,* Hymn 82, was traditional in the Rhineland with its original words, *Es ist ein' Ros entsprungen,* a canticle of loving honour to the mystic Rose-tree springing from the root of Jesse

> That bore a Blossom bright
> In depth of chilly winter
> About the dead of night.

The setting by Michael Praetorius, now in *The Hymnal,* has been a favourite among American *A Cappella* choirs for thirty years.[22]

Illustrative Records:

Victor 21623-B, Palestrina Choir.
Polydor 95376, St. Thomas' Choir, Leipzig.
Polydor 22390, German School Children.
Polydor 21694, St. Hedwig's Choir, Berlin.
Odeon O 6451, Irmler's High School Choir, Berlin.

The tune *Ravenshaw,* Hymn 59, came from the south, where it was early adopted with German words by the Bohemian Brethren; representing the first of the Separatist movements in mid-Europe. Bohemian Hymnody powerfully influenced Lutheran, and led the way to the next great type, the Lutheran Chorale.

[22]When this Hymn is sung the organist may well play as a voluntary that exquisite posthumous Prelude of Brahms, in which the several parts twine themselves into a veritable wreathen garland of musical roses about the tender theme.

CHAPTER VIII

ANGLICAN ECLECTIC HYMNODY
POST-REFORMATION SOURCES

At the beginning of the sixteenth century, it is evident that Europe had a very considerable treasure of exceedingly varied religious song in the vernacular. This normal process of enrichment in the Praise of God came to a sudden and violent end in various countries with the Reformation movement. Wholly new methods of Hymnody arose on all sides after 1520. We will consider them in order.

THE LUTHERAN CHORALE

Before examining the actual music of the Chorale, we must remember that a new and revolutionary factor, especially in Central Europe, began to speed and increase the dissemination of Hymns with their melodies. I refer to the invention of printing from movable types. Comparatively little in the way of popular Hymnody is found among the *incunabula:* but in 1501 a book of eighty-nine Hymns was printed for the Bohemian Brethren at Prague, the first musical outcropping of the Continental Reformation. It was followed by others; and in 1531 Michael Weisse, a monk who abandoned his convent on reading some of Martin Luther's early writings, and joined the Bohemian Brethren, printed a German Hymnal,[1] partly translated from

[1]This book was the source of Tune 59, Ravenshaw. See p. 208.

both Latin and Czech. Luther thought him "a good poet." Our Hymnal of 1892 contained an Easter poem of his, "Christ the Lord is risen again." This vigourous movement was soon merged with the greater one of Lutheranism. Long before the Reformation, such Office Hymns as *Pange lingua, Veni Creator, Lauda Sion,* and *Jesu, dulcis memoria* had been translated into German. Luther made even better translations, as we have noted in speaking of the Prose *Victimæ paschali.*[2] Moreover, he skilfully adapted ancient melodies of varying type to German speech and tempo. He practically created the Chorale. Like a second Ambrose, he possessed in a pre-eminent degree a gift for writing Hymns of the liturgical type. Even his paraphrases of parts of Holy Scripture were so free, so poetically powerful in the idiom of the people, that they are really new creations. "He had an extraordinary faculty for expressing profound thought in the clearest language. . . . He never leaves the reader in doubt of his meaning. He brings the truth home to the heart of the common people."[3] When there is added to this a positive genius for trenchant and forceful melody, supported by adequate musical training, and an almost unparalleled personal force, we are no longer surprised at the tremendous hold that Luther's Hymns soon obtained in Germany, or at their influence on the Christian world, which is still increasing. I recently heard his Christmas Chorale *Vom Himmel hoch* sung in the Basilica of the Sacred Heart on Montmartre, Paris, by five thousand French Roman Catholics. Luther himself wrote his friend Georg Spalatin, Court Chaplain to the Elector Frederick, "It is my intention to make German psalms for the people, spiritual songs

[2]See p. 184.
[3]Philip Schaff, Art. "German Hymnody," in Julian's *Dictionary of Hymnology.*

whereby the word of God may be kept alive in them by singing."
This note must never be forgotten in the use of Hymns. They
do keep alive the religion of those who can learn to sing them
from the heart, and not merely with the lips.

In 1523 Luther wrote his paraphrase of the *De profundis,*
Ps. 130; *Aus tiefer Noth schrei ich zu dir,* which was later
sung at his burial. The following year he produced no less than
twenty-one of his thirty-seven Hymns. Five years later, he
published the greatest and most famous of them, *Ein' feste
Burg,* a very loose paraphrase of Psalm 46. Let us briefly consider this masterpiece, Hymn 213, and our other examples of
the type. An English translation of *Ein' feste Burg* by Bishop
Miles Coverdale was sung in England within ten years of its
publication: yet not till 1916 did it enter the American Hymnal.
The melody has there been restored to correspond with the
form in a manuscript part-book which belonged to Luther in
1530, and bears his signature. It is without doubt the most
important musical addition yet made to *The Hymnal.* Its
tonic and virile strains disperse the miasma of sentimentalism
as the sun scatters the morning mist.[4] An inferior translation
of the words was formerly set to our tune 64, *Luther.* This was
published at the same time, but is not by Luther. In the part-
book just mentioned is also found our tune 410[II]; the name *Old
112th* betokens its adoption in the Anglo-Genevan Psalter of
1561 with that Psalm. But Luther set it to his versification of
the Lord's Prayer, *Vater unser.* He probably composed the tune,
which is only less great than *Ein' feste Burg.* Unlike that unique

---

[4]For ordinary occasions, it is better to use only the first two stanzas. The alleged
derivation of this tune from the *Kyrie de Angelis* is absurd. A few notes coincide,
in a quite different rhythm.

pæan, it has been the vehicle of many poems to the present day; among them, Charles Wesley's profound Eucharistic Hymn, which we should have retained:

> O thou, before the world began
> Ordained a Sacrifice for man.

John Wesley loved this tune, and called it "pure psalmody."[5]

Another great tune now believed to be Luther's composition was composed for his charming Christmas Hymn, *Vom Himmel hoch,* in 1539. It is our No. 484. In that same year a Scottish priest, John Wedderburn, fleeing from Dundee under suspicion of heresy, came to Wittenberg. On his return to Scotland, he published a translation of this Hymn into old Scots in his *Gude and Godlie Ballates.* It is a pity that we have no Long Metre Christmas words for this justly famous Christmas melody.

Two other pieces first published in 1539 illustrate the vernacular adaptation of both sacred and secular music. In the *Deutsch Evangelisch Messze* of 1524, *Gloria in excelsis* in Latin was set to its customary Easter Plainsong, still sung in Roman Catholic Churches. But for the *Geistliche Lieder* of 1539, Nicolaus Decius converted both words and tune into a German Hymn; as he did also with *Sanctus* and *Agnus Dei.* It is our tune 424, there set as harmonized by Mendelssohn in his Oratorio of *St. Paul.*

The second example is a secular Folksong, one of a collection of similar pieces.[6] The old words were, *Innsbruck, ich muss dich*

---

[5]He sang it to his words, "Thou hidden love of God, whose height," our Hymn 227.

[6]*Alte und newe Teutscher liedlein,* Nürnberg, 1539.

lassen. Heinrich Isaak, the first great German musician, who had been a protégé of Lorenzo de'Medici in Florence, and of the Emperor Maximilian at Innsbruck, evidently loved this melody. Not only did he make the beautiful setting, printed twenty-two years after his death in the booklet just mentioned, but he also used the tune in the *Christe eleison* of what has been called the first Folksong Mass: his *Missa Carminum.* Isaak's setting was later utilized with sacred words in what was called a *contrafactum:* that is, an adaptation of a serious and beautiful secular poem to sacred purposes. The deeply felt farewell to Innsbruck became a farewell to earthly life: *O Welt, ich muss dich lassen.* The tender melody has been the vehicle of many beloved Hymns: we use it for the resurrection of Jesus, "The First-begotten of the dead," Hymn 174.

Thus, at the very beginning of the English Reformation, Germany offered an example of superbly developed vernacular praise including original Hymns, both words and tunes, scriptural and liturgical paraphrases which were practically new poems, tunes adapted from familiar Plainsong, and tunes adopted from beloved Folksong.

Records illustrating the early Lutheran Chorale:
>   *Aus tiefer Noth.*
> Parlophon B 37026, in 2000-Jahre Musik Album.
> Columbia G 4057 M, Lotte Lehmann.
>   *Ein' feste Burg,* tune 213.
> Victor 35920, St. Olaf Choir.
> Victor 1692-A, Philadelphia Orchestra.
> Columbia G 50147-D, Berlin Cathedral Choir.
> Polydor 19953, Cologne Teachers' Chorus.
>   *Vater unser,* tune 410[II].
> Columbia DB 506, Bach Cantata Club.

Vom Himmel hoch, tune 484.
Polydor 21020, St. Hedwig's Choir, Berlin.
Columbia G 9045 M, Richard Tauber.
   Allein Gott in der Höh' sei Ehr, tune 424.
Polydor 22030, organ, Kurt Grosse.
   Innsbruck, ich muss dich lassen.
Polydor 19882, Berlin Teachers' Chorus.
   O Welt, ich muss dich lassen, tune 174.
Kantorei 22, Praetorius Society Chorus.

Contemporary English Versions

THIS glorious treasure was well known to the English Reformers, and much of it was put into English dress by no less a person than Miles Coverdale, first translator of the whole Bible into English, and editor of the first translation printed in England, which embodied Tyndale's work with his own. His Hymnal entitled *Goostly Psalmes and Spiritualle Songs* was printed at this time, and prohibited a little later, perhaps on the fall of his patron, Thomas Cromwell. He meant it to be popular: saying in his Preface, "Would God our carters and ploughmen (had none) other thing to whistle upon save psalms: and if women spinning at the wheels had none other songs, they should be better occupied than with hey nony nony, hey troly loly." No tra-la-la-ing for Coverdale: he was not a gay person, nor a better poet than was Cranmer. But in his book were versions of thirty-six Chorales with their music, including several of those mentioned above, and five original pieces, the last a bitter diatribe against Rome beginning "Let go the whore of Babilon." The book was relicensed in 1546, but never came into general use. Our next section will show why not.

GENEVAN PSALMODY

Clément Marot

THE beginnings of metrical Psalmody in French afford an amazing contrast to the German movement we have been considering. Instead of the profound seriousness, the deep human passion for righteousness which produced the Chorale, we find the atmosphere of a frivolous and dissolute Court in Paris. Against the dominant and portentous figure of Luther we must set that of a slender lad of twenty-one, Clément Marot: who, after five years as page in a noble house, became *valet de chambre* to Marguerite de Valois in 1518. His intense admiration for her as a woman, as a poet, and as a Christian, led him to a very real piety, and a sympathy with the Calvinist movement. He was a fellow captive with Francis I after Pavia, and later, his *valet de chambre*. Marguerite is better known for her Boccaccian *Heptameron* than for her really devout *Cantiques Spirituels*: but she was an excellent poet, and her protégé followed and surpassed her. He contributed a purely religious instruction and a metrical version of the sixth Psalm to a work of hers[7] published after she became Queen of Navarre. Later on, he finished in 1539 a translation of thirty of the Psalms in the fluent and graceful rhythms characteristic of French lyrical verse at that period. They were immediately circulated at court in manuscript; a little later they were published in many editions, for their popularity was great. At court they became a game; for lord and lady vied with each other in finding tunes for them. The Dauphin chose a hunting song. His wife, Catherine de'

[7] *Miroir d'une âme pécheresse,* Alençon, 1531, Paris, 1533.

Medici, alluded to her husband's notorious unfaithfulness in the air *Des bouffons,* to which she sang the beautiful paraphrase of the sixth Psalm mentioned above, *Ne veuillez pas, ô Sire.* His mistress, Diane de Poitiers, thought of a lively dance tune from her native province, *Le branle*[8] *de Poitou,* for *Du fond de ma pensée,* Psalm 130, the *De profundis:* which Luther had sung fifteen years before to the tragically eloquent strains of *Aus tiefer Noth;*[9] soon to be his burial Anthem. St. Hilary, first Bishop of Poitiers, could use the *versus popularis*[10] to the glory of God: but these impious and frivolous worldlings could not

Make the soul dance upon a jig to heaven.[11]

Catherine, for all her sacrilegious toying with Calvinist Psalmody, was later to bring about the St. Bartholomew massacre of the Huguenots. Marot was soon obliged to flee for safety to Geneva. He had already met Calvin; who presently encouraged him to go on translating the Psalms, fifty of which were published there in 1543, with a characteristic dedication, "To the Ladies of France."

Louis Bourgeois

THE musical indignities of the Parisian Court were made good at Geneva: for there Marot met Louis Bourgeois, one of the best melodists who ever lived, a man whose unsurpassed musical contribution to Hymnody is only now coming to general appreciation, after centuries of neglect. Bourgeois set

---

[8]*Branle,* a round dance in two time. Illustrative record, *l'Anthologie Sonore,* 5b.
[9]See p. 211.   [10]See pp. 163, 174.   [11]Alexander Pope.

all of Marot's Psalms, and others by Théodore de Bèze, or Beza, who completed the versification of the Psalter. Among Bourgeois's melodies are very beautiful and reverent settings of the two Psalms just mentioned. Our only reasonably accurate representative of Bourgeois is *Old Hundredth,* as printed at Hymn 250, although even there the rhythm of the last line has been modified, as in most modern Hymnals. Tunes 88, *St. Michael,* and 451, *Toulon,* are so altered from Bourgeois's originals as to be almost unrecognizable. A musical duty to the Christian world is to adopt for future use the finer examples of the unaltered melodies: of which Robert Bridges,[12] who with the Reverend George R. Woodward[13] has made them familiar in England, can say, "Historians who wish to give a true philosophical account of Calvin's influence at Geneva ought probably to refer a great part of it to the enthusiasm attendant on the singing of Bourgeois's melodies."

Illustrative Records:

l'Anthologie Sonore Vol. II, 12: Psalms 19, 25, 42, 69.
Columbia 9165, *Old Hundredth,* Rochester Cathedral Choir.

But although this musical treasure and the corresponding excellence of Marot's exceedingly varied and fluent metres were to be the real contribution of the Genevan Psalter to Anglican Hymnody, Calvinism reverted to a principle which had been tested and rejected in earlier Christian times, last of all by the Diocese of Rome, in the ninth century: namely, that only ma-

[12]*The Yattenden Hymnal.*
[13]*Songs of Syon.* Many of these tunes may be found in *The English Hymnal,* in *Songs of Praise,* in *The Yattenden Hymnal,* in *The Church Hymnary,* in *The Oxford Hymnal,* and in *Hymns of Western Europe;* all pub. Oxford University Press: also in *The Pilgrim Hymnal,* the Pilgrim Press, Boston.

terial drawn accurately from the Bible, the inspired word of God, might be used in public worship.

THERE was a brief period in the reign of Henry VIII when the rich Lutheran Hymnody began to influence the English, as we have just seen in the mention of Miles Coverdale's Hymnal translated from the German. But the Genevan influence became paramount among the Reformers.

Calvinist Influence Forbids Hymns

CALVINISM was not only to affect the doctrinal formulas and the life of the English Church disturbingly, until the Long Parliament abolished Episcopacy and the Prayer Book a century later: but it was also to keep English Metrical Psalmody in the Egyptian bondage of slavery to the letter of the Bible for a hundred and fifty years, and deny the power of the Holy Ghost to inspire men afresh in the Praise of God. The Act of Parliament which authorized the first English Prayer Book in 1549 provided "that it be lawful to use openly any Psalme *taken out of the Bible* . . . not letting or omitting thereby the service or any part thereof mentioned in the said book."

This, of course, referred to the congregational singing of metrical versions of the Psalms, then thought to be nearer to the Hebrew originals than the superb prose translation of the Prayer Book, whose use was nevertheless required in the actual service. There was nothing novel in the mere translating of Psalms into metre; from Paulinus of Nola, who versified Psalms in Virgilian hexameters in the days of St. Ambrose, to Racine, who paraphrased St. Paul in classic French poems, the thing was done as a literary exercise. But the adoption of such translations as the sole vehicle of congregational sung praise began with John Calvin.

Sternhold and Hopkins's Metrical Psalms

IN England no stirring poet like Luther, no skilled versifier like Marot, was available to make the translations. The poetic dawn which heralded Elizabethan day shone elsewhere than in church. Indeed, it is one of the tragedies of Hymnody that so few great poets have contributed true hymns, and that the Church has failed to make use of the available work of those few. It remained for Thomas Sternhold, the pious but prosaic Groom of the Robes to Henry VIII and Edward VI, to try an unaccustomed hand at rendering Psalms into popular ballad form, and thus set the stamp of monotonous metrical uniformity which was later to degenerate into sanctimonious mannerism. Sternhold, however, *sang* his crude versions to his own organ accompaniment. Poor little pious King Edward overheard them and liked them; as a result, nineteen were published and dedicated to him. Sternhold died in the year of the first Book of Common Prayer, 1549, having completed 37 Psalms. Others,[14] notably John Hopkins, took up the work, eventually concluded in Elizabeth's reign by *The Whole Booke of Psalmes . . . with apt notes to sing them withal,* printed by John Day in 1562. By then, metrical Psalmody had become a powerful agent of religious change. It was strictly congregational: we read (in John

---

[14]Doctor Tye, mentioned on pages 73 and 84, set metrical versions of the first fourteen chapters of the *Acts of the Apostles*. His note for note counterpoint paralleled Merbecke's syllabic melodies. See the tune *Windsor*, Hymn 221.

Strype's *Life of Grindal,* page 27) that "before the new Morning Prayer, a Psalm was sung after the Geneva Fashion, all the congregation . . . men, women, and boys, singing together." Apparently the little girls 'kept silence in the Churches,' or probably at least in St. Paul's, where the Psalmody was then introduced!

Elizabeth's Injunctions Permit Hymns

THE intricate story of Psalms in metre may not be told here: although it is interesting to note that in 1544 the future Queen Elizabeth, at the age of eleven, put into English verse the fourteenth Psalm from the French metrical translation of Marguerite of Navarre.[15] But more germane to our purpose is the fact that in her *Injunctions* of 1559, she included the significant phrase, still echoed in the American Prayer Book, "In the beginning, or in the end of Common Prayers, there may be sung *an hymn,* or such like song to the Praise of Almighty God, in the best sort of melody and music that may be conveniently devised." From this little liberating sentence has arisen the whole slow growth of Anglican Eclectic Hymnody, with its rich treasure of poetry and music. In Day's Psalter, "alowed according to the ordre appointed in the Quene's maiesties Iniunctions," are included paraphrases of the Canticles, Athanasian Creed, Commandments, and Lord's Prayer: and seven Hymns, including one from the Breviary, *Veni Creator,* and a Thanksgiving after

[15] *A Godly Medytacion of the Christen sowle, concerning a love towardes God and hys Criste, compyled in frenche of Lady Margarete Quene of Navarre, and aptely translated into Englysh by the right vertuouse Lady Elizabeth, doughter to our late sovereyne Kynge Henri the VIII.* Hans Luft, 1548; also Asher, London, 1897. Elizabeth's mother, Anne Boleyn, had been lady in waiting to the Queen of Navarre.

[220]

Holy Communion, thus continuing the ancient Irish tradition mentioned in the sixth chapter.[16] Lutheran influence returns by way of Strassburg, whither some of the Marian exiles had gone: it is represented by three Hymns, one set to the great melody *Vater unser,* Hymn 410[11]. The Genevan melody of the *De profundis* is retained.

It has taken the Anglican Communion a very long time to decide that it is neither Lutheran nor Calvinist, but Catholic. The whole process may be studied in its changing Hymnody: but already, in Day's Psalter, known as the Old Version, the eclectic principle of utilizing excellence from whatever source is recognized, however timidly and tentatively.

No trace remains in contemporary practice of the Old Version, as regards its words, except Psalm 100, No. 249 in *The Hymnal.* But it gave us certain permanent results: the reassertion of the primary importance of congregational singing, now again endangered by the predominance of professional choirs; the principle of using Hymns, both original and translated from any worthy source; and finally, certain admirable tunes, such as *Old Twenty-fifth,* No. 189, and *St. Flavian,* Nos. 56, 134, and 299. Similar tunes from other Psalters of the following hundred years are still in common use.[17] They should not be sung like modern Hymn tunes, but slowly, with grave dignity, not neglecting the proper pause for breath at the end of each line.

Worship of the letter of Holy Scripture kept the Old Version in use long after its absurdities were evident to the unprejudiced. Wesley could call it "scandalous doggerel." In 1696, the New

---

[16]See p. 176.
[17]Such as *Windsor,* No. 124; *London New,* 216; *Dundee,* 269; *St. James,* 279; *Tallis' Ordinal,* 344; and *Dunfermline,* 431.

Version of Tate and Brady began an epoch of change for the better, artificial as much of it seems today. The quality of the two may be illustrated by their respective first stanzas of Psalm 42.

Old Version:

> Like as the hart doth breathe and bray
> The well-springs to obtain,
> So doth my soul desire alway
> With thee Lord to remain.

New Version:

> As pants the hart for cooling springs
> When heated in the chase,
> So longs my soul, O God, for thee,
> And thy refreshing grace.[18]

The Psalm is becoming a Hymn; the letter is yielding to the spirit. This gradual transformation was characteristic of the next hundred years' growth. Psalms were imitated, not translated.

George Wither: Orlando Gibbons

But original Hymns appeared from time to time before this. George Wither published *Hymnes and Songs of the Church* in 1623, on the liturgical principle. It contained Hymns for the Festivals, Seasons, and Holy Days of the Church, and a Communion Hymn. No less a person than the last great polyphonist, Orlando Gibbons, provided sixteen tunes of distinguished beauty.

---

[18]For this was composed the glorious tune *St. Anne,* now fittingly sung to "O God, our help in ages past."

The Hymnal is enriched by three of them, *Gibbons,* Nos. 219 and 447; *Angel's Song,* 490; and the exquisite *Fletcher,* 405, second tune. But Wither was no poet;[19] the book was bitterly attacked as "Popish, superstitious, obscene, and unfit to keep company with David's Psalms." As with all this period, only the superb music remains, for us to use more fittingly.

THE DAWN OF THE EIGHTEENTH CENTURY

THE impulse toward Hymnody began to accelerate its movement in the very first decade, both in words and music. Great men had yielded to it a little earlier. John Donne, Dean of St. Paul's, had heard his touching song of contrition, "Wilt thou forgive that sin," sung there: Bishop Ken had written his Morning and Evening Hymns, and the Winchester schoolboys had sung them, though they were not to be included in a public Hymnal till 1782:[20] Bishop Cosin's paraphrase of the *Veni Creator* had found its place in the Prayer Book. But after 1700, the trickle became a flowing tide. In that year, a fresh edition of the New Version appeared, with a Supplement containing a Christmas Hymn, "While shepherds watched their flocks by night"; two Easter Hymns; and three for Holy Communion. The tremendous controversy over the respective merits of Old and New Versions stirred up healthy public interest, both in the Church and among the Dissenters. Musicians felt the stimulus, and invented new types of song.

---

[19]A later edition included Hymns When Washing (the original bathtub song!); On a Boat; for Sheepshearing; for a House-warming; for Lovers, Tutors, a Jailer, a Prisoner, a Member of Parliament!
[20]The Evening Hymn somewhat later.

Jeremiah Clark: Playford's "Divine Companion"

AMONG them, we must pay belated honour to the name of Jeremiah Clark, the true inventor of the modern Hymn tune. Examine, in *The Hymnal,* the tunes *Bishopthorpe,* 351, and *Bromley,* 11, second tune.[21] The plaintive grace of their flowing melodic line, the modern richness of their original harmonies, sprang from a feeling far less abstract, far more personal, than that of the old Psalter tunes. Robert Bridges says of them, "They are the first in merit of their kind, as they were the first in time; and they are truly national and popular in style, so that their neglect is to be regretted." May I add, and to be remedied. Many of Clark's tunes were published in 1701 in Henry Playford's *The Divine Companion, or David's Harp New Tun'd,* which contained Hymns of a higher literary quality by such writers as George Herbert, Richard Crashaw, and Drummond of Hawthornden, the first adequate translator of many ancient Breviary Hymns. This little Hymnal was several times reprinted with additional Hymns and tunes. It introduces the name of William Croft, organist of St. Anne's, Soho, whose vigourous tunes *St. Anne,* No. 445, and *Hanover,* No. 255, were first printed in the 1708 edition of the *Supplement to the New Version.*

Lyra Davidica

THAT same year, 1708, appeared a little book, *Lyra Davidica,*[22] whose preface announces the musical aim of providing music in a freer style than the old Psalm tunes. One such melody is the

[21]Both of the year 1700. *Bromley* was undoubtedly the source from which Doctor Miller adapted the tune *Rockingham,* which is inferior to its original.

[22]See p. 203.

original form of our Easter tune, No. 172,[23] for "Jesus Christ is risen today." But this book not only illustrates the new trend of composition in England: it also provides significant translations from the Latin and especially from the High German. Luther's *Ein' feste Burg* with its tune appears again. But more indicative of the fresh awakening of praise, two great Chorales composed many years before in Germany by Philip Nicolai,[24] *Sleepers Wake,* No. 62, and *Frankfort,* No. 98,[25] enter English Hymnody.

The second edition of *The Divine Companion,* in 1709, gave us Robert King's most expressive melody, *David's Harp,* No. 230, which almost immediately came into American use. Even the Metrical Psalm changed its character and became lyrical. For instance, Joseph Addison contributed two paraphrases to *The Spectator* in 1712, which we still sing with delight to their highly characteristic contemporary tunes: Psalm 19 to John Sheeles' *Addison's,* No. 252; and Psalm 23 to the exquisite pastoral melody No. 317, by Henry Carey, who wrote *Sally in Our Alley.*

But the new renaissance of praise within the Church of England was to receive its greatest development outside her borders. We must briefly recount the incalculable debt which the Church owes in this field to Independency and to the Methodist Movement.

Illustrative Records:
    While shepherds watched, *Winchester Old.*
    Columbia DB 1248, St. Mary's Choir School.
    His Master's Voice B 4304, Royal Choral Society.

[23]Misnamed *Worgan.* Doctor Worgan was not yet born in 1708.
[24]See p. 229.   [25]See pp. 229, 253.

[225]

O God our help, *St. Anne's.*
Columbia DX 498, Nicholson Festival Choir.
Disposer supreme, *Hanover.*
His Master's Voice B2543, Canterbury Cathedral Choir.
Jesus Christ is risen today, *Worgan.*
Columbia DB 749, St. George's Chapel Choir.

THE CONTRIBUTION OF NONCONFORMITY

In Commonwealth times, all the Nonconformist bodies were united in rejecting Hymns: but they were also united in rejecting Sternhold and Hopkins' Old Version of the Psalms. The Presbyterians eventually adopted the Scottish Psalter; the Baptists, Barton's Psalms. The Independents alone took the forward path in God's Praise, led by that great and lovable Presbyter who for conscience' sake could refuse a bishopric and rebuke a Lord Protector; Richard Baxter, to whom may God grant 'The Saints' Everlasting Rest.' Although he imposed upon himself a strict literalness in paraphrasing the Psalms, he says in the Preface to his posthumous volume,[26] "I durst make Hymns of my own, . . . Doubtless Paul meaneth not only David's Psalms, when he bids men sing with grace in their hearts, Psalms, Hymns, and Spiritual Songs: yea, it is past doubt, that Hymns more suitable to Gospel-times may and ought now to be used."

Isaac Watts

A new and doughty champion of unfettered praise, young Isaac Watts, who unknowingly was a true Catholic Reformer, not only defended and advanced these ideas, but also brought about a return to the ancient conception of the Church Fathers,

[26]*Paraphrase on the Psalms.* And see Hymn 392, "Lord, it belongs not to my care."

that our Psalmody must be Christian, not Jewish; a conception already mentioned in this book.[27] In 1707, the youthful pastor of the Independent congregation in Mark Lane, London, put forth a statement of principles, *A Short Essay toward the Improvement of Psalmody,* and an embodiment of those principles in a volume of *Hymns and Spiritual Songs.* He believed that Congregational praise should spring from the free movement of hearts and minds toward God; that the whole body of Church song should be truly Evangelical, expressing the Gospel, not the Law; lest "by keeping too close to David in the House of God, the Vail of Moses be thrown over our Hearts"; that the Psalms, as being God's word to us, should be chanted in prose as in the Cathedrals, but that from them we may draw Hymns of our own time and place and personality. When he averred that "the land of Canaan may be translated into Great Britain," he adumbrated a later and greater poet, William Blake, whose prophetic *Jerusalem* has become the battle-cry of Christian social reform in England.

> I will not cease from mental fight,
> Nor shall my sword sleep in my hand,
> Till we have built Jerusalem
> In England's green and pleasant land.

Illustrative Records:

Columbia 9763, The Sheffield Choir.
His Master's Voice B3125, Royal Choral Society.
His Master's Voice RC2362, sung by the audience at a meeting of the National Council of Social Service, London.

Throughout forty years of invalidism, Watts kept up his brave mental fight for a more worthy Praise of God. Over four

[27]See page 153.

hundred of his Hymns are still sung. Although he was not a major poetic genius, and often applied his principles ineffectively, he was really the "creator of the modern English Hymn; which is neither an Office Hymn . . . nor yet a metrical Psalm, nor again a close paraphrase of Scripture, but a new species, evolved from the last named, and acquiring in the process a novel liberty of treatment and a balanced artistic form."[28] To be convinced of this, we need only sing two of his deathless masterpieces, a Hymn and a Psalm. At the precise age of Jesus crucified, he published Hymn 154, probably written earlier:

> When I survey the wondrous cross
> Where the young Prince of glory dy'd.

We mar its perfection by omitting stanza four:

> His dying crimson, like a robe,
>   Spreads o'er his body on the tree;
> Then am I dead to all the globe,
>   And all the globe is dead to me.

A few years later came the greatest paraphrase ever written, that for Psalm 90, our Hymn 445, "O God our help in ages past." These two, the very summit of English Hymnody, have irresistibly drawn to themselves their perfect musical counterparts, *Rockingham* and *St. Anne's*.

THE CONTRIBUTION OF THE EVANGELICAL REVIVAL

WATTS achieved the development of Calvinistic praise toward greater fullness of Christian content: let us now turn to the

[28]Bishop Frere: Introduction to the Historical Edition of *Hymns Ancient and Modern*.

significant contribution of the Wesleys; which must necessarily be preluded by an excursus on

The Hymnody of German Pietism

A NEW strain of Christian Praise developed slowly in Germany in the seventeenth century, and, by means of a seemingly fortuitous contact with two young Anglican Priests, John and Charles Wesley, profoundly affected our Hymnody for two hundred years. Its purely musical effect is still increasing. We owe it many of our finest tunes, and many great Hymns: for whose sake we must forgive certain devotional distortions now happily diminishing.

The note of manly vigour and God-centered worship through the incarnate Son, characteristic of early Lutheran praise, is well sustained in the first of the two great Chorales published by Philip Nicolai in 1599, our Hymn 62.[29] It is the culmination of the series of 'Watchman Songs' begun four hundred years earlier by Wolfram von Eschenbach, the epic poet of the Holy Grail. We have a similar piece in Sir John Bowring's "Watchman, tell us of the night," Hymn 106.[30] Our Lord's parable of the Wise and Foolish Virgins is objectively sung to this classic melody, which is even more effective with the words of Hymn 262.[31] But in the so-called 'Queen of Chorales,' No. 98, Nicolai struck a different note, not apparent in the strong paraphrase by William Mercer which we now sing to the tune. In Nicolai's

[29]See p. 225.

[30]This may be sung with superb effect to the tune *Aberystwyth*, No. 130[II], Illustrative Record, His Master's Voice, B8229.

[31]By James Montgomery, the greatest of Moravian Hymn writers.

original, we have the first of a long series of intensely personal songs of love to the heavenly Bridegroom. It is

> My Bridegroom, King divine.
> My heavenly Bridegroom, passing sweet.

The Hymn has become personal and subjective; it even fore-shadows "Rock of Ages":

> In thy side,
> Thy living member let me bide.

These majestic tunes, although published in England,[32] had to await a better translation of the first text and a complete altera-tion of the second, before they attained their present favour.

Illustrative record of both tunes: Polydor 27027, organ.

In 1613, a song of suffering human love by Hans Leonhard Hassler was adapted for sacred words: later it was chosen as the moving expression of Paulus Gerhardt's Hymn of love to our crucified Saviour, translated from a Latin original;[33] and became the incomparable *Passion Chorale,* Hymn 158, the per-fect union of words and music.

Illustrative Records:

Polydor 22105, Choir of St. George's, Berlin.
Polydor 23583, St. Cæcilia Choir, Berlin.
Polydor 22589, Paderborn Cathedral Choir.
Victor 35920, St. Olaf's Choir, Minnesota.
Victor Album M 138. The St. Matthew Passion of Bach contains these great Chorales sung by the Choir of St. Bartholomew's Church, N. Y.

[32]See p. 225.
[33]*Salve, caput cruentatum.* Attributed, without conclusive proof, to St. Bernard of Clairvaux: more probably by Arnulf von Loewen, 1200–1251.

Gerhardt was second only to Luther as a writer of Hymns: but his poems are of the subjective type. Sixteen of them begin with the word, "I." His subjectivism, however, was not morbid or unwholesome. A charming example is found in Hymn 545, with its fresh cheerful original tune, *Ebeling*.

The agonies of the Thirty Years' War intensified the deep need of personal consolation and help in German religion. Johann Heerman, pastor of Köben, his little parish repeatedly sacked by Wallenstein's troopers, all of his own property destroyed, contemplated "the bitter sufferings of Jesus Christ" as set forth in an old meditation attributed to St. Augustine, but really by St. Anselm of Canterbury; and transcribed it in his Hymn, *Herzliebster Jesu*, our No. 155, presently set to the sapphic tune of Johann Crüger, with its solemn downward movement. An earlier period would not have spoken of "Heart's Dearest Jesus." Nor does Robert Bridges retain the expression in his touching translation, a masterpiece of penitential devotion. Hymn 340 is set to Crüger's chorale melody, *Jesus, meine Zuversicht* (Illustrative record, Columbia G 4057 M), "Jesus, my reliance sure," another deeply religious tune. Hymn 356, *Schönster Herr Jesu*, anonymously expressed this intimate tender devotion in 1677. Our translation, "Fairest Lord Jesus," which restores to us the very beautiful original music, was made in Philadelphia in 1850.

Such Hymns were the outward signs of a slowly gathering movement against the crystalizing scholastic tendency which had been spreading in Lutheranism. It was a Revival rather than a Reformation. Philip Jakob Spener made it articulate with his *Pia desideria* in 1675, and August Hermann Francke, his disciple, became its organizer, from his point of vantage at the new University of Halle, whence over six thousand graduates in theology spread the ideas of Pietism throughout the land. Francke, though a theologian, sought "not to build up *scientia,* but to arouse *conscientia."* The pietists specially emphasized emotional feeling, and cultivated "enthusiasm" in worship toward God and in practical philanthropy toward men. These forces culminated in Count Nicolaus Ludwig von Zinzendorf, a godchild of Spener, a disciple of Francke at Halle, and a keen advocate of religious individualism. In whatever confessional body men found a *Herzensreligion,* a religion of the heart founded on individual personal experience of the Saviour, von Zinzendorf considered that they had attained the fulness of God's purpose for their own salvation. This profoundly pious but mentally confused man gave charitable hospitality to the Moravian refugees of the old *Unitas Fratrum,* the Bohemian Brethren whose effort at reform had preceded Luther's.[34] He sought to make Lutherans of them; but in the end, accepted their views, and threw himself heart and soul into their extensive missionary activities. Before his death, there were forty-nine Moravian Mission Stations in North America.[35] In the endeavour to preserve the ancient Episcopal order of the *Unitas Fratrum,* David Nitschmann was consecrated Bishop in 1735. On October 14th of that year he set sail from London with twenty-six companions to evangelize the Creek and Cherokee Indians.

On the same ship were the two young Anglican Priests, John and Charles Wesley, whom God raised up to revive in the

[34]See pp. 208, 209.

[35]Among them the great Mission at Bethlehem, Pa., mentioned on page 203. This became a real center of American musical development in every field, and is the present home of the Bach Festival.

Anglican Communion a life which was being choked by formalism, frigidity, and Erastianism. The Wesleys, accustomed to the singing of Hymns in their father's rectory at Epworth, brought with them many volumes for such domestic worship. The Moravians had the treasures of Pietistic Hymnody from Halle as well as their own older traditional airs. They sang together daily. On the third day out, John began the study of German. Within a fortnight, he was translating from Count von Zinzendorf's Herrnhut *Gesangbuch* of 999 Hymns, whose music and words profoundly affected him. Thus, on the tossing Atlantic, German and English traditions blended in the heart and mind of a young high Churchman who was to startle the Anglican world with a spirituality which did not disdain "enthusiasm," and which depended upon personal, individual religious experience: and John Wesley was to bring about a practical eclectic Hymnody which neither Coverdale nor the editor of *Lyra Davidica* had been able to achieve.

Johann Sebastian Bach

BEFORE passing on to its consideration, the loftiest musical result of Pietism must be mentioned. We have recently observed with reverent honour the two hundred and fiftieth anniversary of the birth of Bach. That supreme religious musician, in his youthful days as organist of St. Blaise's Church, Mühlhausen, served under Pastor Frohne, a follower of Spener. Although he avoided all ecclesiastical controversy, his profound and simple faith never departed from the purest ideals of Pietism. He was educated in strict Lutheran orthodoxy; and as a musician, sided with the greater stress on art characteristic of that school. But the depth of his emotional religious experience, the personal

devotion to Jesus evident throughout his entire life, reveal themselves not only in his letters; they shine through the vast mass
of that music most characteristic of the man, his treatment of
the German Hymn. From boyhood to his very deathbed[36] the
Hymns formed the center of his art. His hundreds of masterly
harmonizations for Church use; his more extended treatment·
in the Passions, Oratorios, Cantatas, and Motets; his composition of original Hymn tunes; and greatest of all, the vast treasure
of organ music drawn directly from a devotional interpretation
of the words of Hymns in the Chorale Preludes:[37] these make
the greatest of all contributions to the Praise of God through
the Hymn. Every modern Hymnal uses Bach's versions increasingly. Every wise organist learns to enrich his own religious
and artistic experience and that of his congregation by playing
the Chorale Preludes in church. Twelve of our Hymns are
sung to the music of Bach and twenty-two of our tunes have
been the themes of numerous compositions by him.[38] Their
constantly growing use yearly augments the great multitude

[36]A few days before Bach's death in 1750, he composed and wrote out with his
own hand twenty-six bars of a Chorale Prelude for the organ on the beautiful
melody by Louis Bourgeois, *Leve le cœur*. Most modern Hymnals sing to this,
Ellerton's "The day thou gavest, Lord, is ended." Bach bade his son-in-law write
in the title of his dying Hymn, *Vor deinen Thron tret ich hiemit;* and dictated
the rest of the marvellous music. It is recorded for the phonograph in H.M.V.
C1543, by Albert Schweitzer. Here is the Hymn in English:

Before thy throne, my God, I stand, Grant that my end may worthy be,
Myself, my all are in thy hand;   And that I wake thy face to see,
Turn to me thine approving face,   Thyself for evermore to know!
Nor from me now withhold thy grace. Amen, Amen, God grant it so!

[37]See list of records, p. 240.

[38]59, *Ravenshaw;* 62, *Sleepers, Wake;* 64, *Luther;* 98, *Frankfort;* 123, *Heinlein;*
143, *St. Theodulph;* 155, *Herzliebster;* 158, *Passion Chorale;* 174, *Innsbruck;* 213,
Ein' feste Burg; 250, *Old 100th;* 340, *Luise;* 375, *Veni, Creator;* 383, *Cana;* 410[11],
Old 112th; 422, *Deo Gratias;* 424, *To God on high;* 484, *Yule;* 545, *Ebeling;* 549,
In dulci jubilo; 561, *Nassau;* 577, Chant, *Tonus peregrinus.* It will be noticed that

who give Bach "the thanks we render only to the great souls to whom it is given to reconcile men with life and bring them peace."[39]

The Influence of the Wesleys

LET us return to the Wesley brothers in America. John Wesley was not a successful missionary. He had not yet learned sound judgment in his dealings with men; nor had either he or his brother Charles, who acted as secretary to Governor Oglethorpe, experienced that profound conversion which was to transform their lives three years later in England. But both exemplified that devotion to "method" in study, prayer, and work, which had gained for Charles in his college days at Oxford "the harmless name of Methodist,"[40] later to attain such vast significance. John worked in Georgia with singular diligence to prepare a Hymnal for local use. It was tested from manuscript, and printed without his name: *A Collection of Psalms and Hymns. Charles-town, 1737.* Its immediate effect seems almost comic today. He was at once charged before the Grand Jury with "making alterations in the metrical Psalms" and with "introducing into the Church and service at the Altar compositions of psalms and hymns not inspected or authorized by any proper judicature." But this little book of seventy Hymns was the first real Anglican Hymnal: and it established more firmly the eclectic principle enunciated in *Lyra Davidica*

they include music of the Gregorian Chant, Plainsong Tune, Carol, Folksong, Lutheran and Pietist Chorale, and Genevan Psalter. Bach was the true eclectic, whose principles today characterize Christian praise.

[39]Albert Schweitzer, *J. S. Bach*, Chap. XX. For a full list of Records illustrating Bach's uses of the Hymn melodies, see *The Gramophone Shop Encyclopedia of Recorded Music*, 1936.

[40]Louis F. Benson, *The English Hymn*, New York, 1915, p. 222.

twenty-nine years earlier. His own translations from the German, poems by his father and his brother Samuel, and by such poets as Addison and Herbert, were combined with many Hymns by Watts, the Dissenter. John Wesley returned to England soon after: Charles had already done so. Whitsunday 1738 brought the spiritual conversion of Charles, followed by that of his brother: the real beginning of that momentous Revival called Methodism, which was only lost to the Church through ecclesiastical blindness and folly. Hymn-singing characterized the Methodist societies from the first. The American book was enlarged and republished. A larger collection soon followed, and began the memorable work of Charles Wesley, greatest and most prolific of Anglican Hymn writers, who gave its fullest development to the Hymn of personal experience.

At first, the Methodist movement was close to the Moravian. John Wesley visited Herrnhut, and translated in part a Hymn of Count von Zinzendorf, the last and best known of those "Bridegroom" songs previously mentioned,[41] the famous *Seelen-bräutigam,* whose beautiful tune, *Rochelle,* No. 449, is still popular. It is recorded in Odeon O 11054 A, *Jesu, geh voran.* But as will be seen in Hymn 119, Wesley modified or omitted those expressions, more characteristic of human love than of divine, which were already enfeebling Moravian Hymnody. Because of this, and of its over-emphasis on the physical sufferings and wounds of our Lord, Wesley broke with the Moravian tendency. He never included in his own publications his brother's greatest Hymn, "Jesus, lover of my soul," deeming it too intimate in its emotional feeling for general use. Spiritual reserve such as this safeguarded the Wesleyan Hymn of Christian experience.

[41]See p. 230.

It also characterized John Wesley's life-long direction of the music to be used and the manner of singing it. He knew, loved, and sang, the fine German melodies, and English tunes which could be heartily congregational, but were neither dull nor florid; the faults of the period. He printed the *tune only* without harmonies for the people's use, an example which would double the effectiveness of our singing if we would follow it.[42] He gave the following succinct rules for the Congregation: "Learn these tunes . . .; sing them exactly as printed; sing all of them; sing lustily; sing modestly; sing in time; above all, sing spiritually, with an eye to God in every word."[43] He would stop a noisy Hymn, being sung carelessly, by asking the people, "Do you know what you said last? Did it suit your case? Did you sing it as to God, with the spirit and understanding also?" If our clergy would dare to overcome their conventionality and do likewise, our worship would be the better. John Wesley's great influence was always against the cheap, the showy, the sentimental, the unreal, in the music of the Hymns, as in their words.

Few of the Hymns of this period have come to us unaltered. Thus the Deacon, George Whitefield, altered Charles Wesley's famous Hymn composed as he heard the pealing bells on his way to make his Christmas Communion,

> Hark! how all the welkin rings
> Glory to the King of kings

to the poorer and cheaper

> Hark! the herald angels sing
> Glory to the new-born King.

[42]*The English Hymnal* is now offered in an edition with the melody only.
[43]*Sacred Melody,* 1761. Preface.

Again, Charles Wesley changed for the better the Hymn of John Cennik, the first Methodist lay preacher, who later became a Moravian, from

> Lo, he cometh, countless trumpets
> Blow before his bloody sign

to the familiar

> Lo, he comes with clouds descending,
> Once for our salvation slain.

Another Methodist, Thomas Olivers, wrote for this the famous tune *Helmsley,* which we unfortunately lack. We also owe to Olivers that magnificent Christian paraphrase of the Jewish poetic Creed, the *Yigdal;*[44] our Hymn 253. The stately melody *Leoni* is named for Meyer Lyon, the Hebrew singer from the Great Synagogue, Duke's Place, London, who supplied it to Olivers in 1770. It was then traditional, but is probably not very ancient. We have no finer congregational Hymn than this.

Notwithstanding the calamitous exclusion of the Wesleyan revival from the Church of England, there *did* ensue the slow growth of an Evangelical movement, still following the traditional Calvinistic trend, as did Wesley's earlier disciple, George Whitefield. Its influence, little by little, slowly modified the Anglican clinging to Metrical Psalms. Augustus Montague Toplady, Wesley's bitter Calvinist opponent, could nevertheless include in the first Evangelical Hymnal[45] his own unapproached "Rock of ages" and Charles Wesley's "Jesu, Lover of my soul."

[44]A metrical form, written by Rabbi Daniel ben Judah Dayyam in 1404, of the thirteen Articles of Maimonides, 1130–1205 A.D.
[45]*Psalms and Hymns for Public and Private Worship,* London, 1776.

Church music is a great irenic force. Whatever may be men's mental divergencies, they must inevitably, when they join in the Praise of God, glorify him "with one heart and with one mouth."

Olney Hymns

A STRANGE friendship brought about another important increment to Evangelical Hymnody: that of the timid melancholy poet Cowper with the adventurous converted slaveship captain John Newton, his pastor at Olney. Together they published the famous *Olney Hymns* in 1779; which brought up the body of Hymns in the Church of England to something like equality with those of Calvinist Independency and of Methodism. Among them high place must be awarded to such beloved songs as "How sweet the Name of Jesus sounds" and "Glorious things of thee are spoken"; given to the Church by one who described himself as "John Newton, Clerk, once an Infidel and Libertine, a servant of slaves in Africa."

Few numbers in this growing collection retain today their original melodies. But throughout the eighteenth century, many sturdy tunes of solid worth,[46] mostly composed for metrical Psalms, were added to the musical treasure, whose full richness was to be gathered and put to better use in the coming Century of Reform.

[46]The reader may well go through such tunes of this period as have not already been mentioned. The best among them are *Wareham** No. 9; *Duke Street*, 32; *St. Stephen*, 70; *Yorkshire*, 76; *Bangor*, 102; *Moscow*, 104; *Rockingham*, 154; *Isleworth*, 156; *Truro*, 187; *Miles Lane*, 192; *St. Bride*, 246; *Darwall*, 264; and a striking group from English Roman Catholic sources; *Melcombe*, No. 1; *St. Thomas*, 57; *Dulce Carmen*, 110; *Veni, Sancte Spiritus*, 196; and *Consolation*, 388.
*Illustrative Record, Columbia DB215, Nicholson Festival Choir.

Records illustrative of the Chorale Prelude:

Johann Pachelbel †1706

l'Anthologie Sonore, Vol. I. *Vater unser* (tune 410).

Johann Sebastian Bach †1750

His Master's Voice, E 471 (organ), Marcel Dupré.
Wachet auf (tune 62).
Christ came to Jordan.

His Master's Voice, C 1543 (organ), Albert Schweitzer.
Passion Chorale (tune 158).
Vor deinen Thron tret ich hiemit.

His Master's Voice, B 2927 (organ), Doctor W. G. Alcock.
Liebster Jesu, wir sind hier.

His Master's Voice, D 1873 (organ), Marcel Dupré.
In dir ist Freude.

His Master's Voice, B 3483 (organ), G. D. Cunningham.
Nun freut euch, lieber Christen Gemein.

Victrola 11159 A (organ), Doctor E. Bullock.
St. Theodulph (tune 143).

Odeon, O 4112 (organ), Louis Vierne.
In dir ist Freude.
Christ lag in Todesbanden.

Odeon, O 2363-A (organ), Paul Mania.
Ein' feste Burg (tune 213).
Nun danket alle Gott.

Victrola Album M 120, *Orfeo Catala.*
Wachet auf (tune 62).

Brunswick 90105, Berlin Philharmonic.
Komm, Gott Schöpfer (tune 375).
Schmücke dich.

Victor Album M59, Philadelphia Orchestra, 7089-B, *Wir glauben alle an einen Gott.*

Victor Album M 243, Philadelphia Orchestra.
8494-B, *Nun komm der Heiden Heiland.*
6786-B, *Ich ruf zu dir.*
7437-B, *Christ lag in Todesbanden.*
7553, *Aus der Tiefe* (tune 123).

THE CHORALE PRELUDE

Max Regert †1916
Victrola 11159 B, *Wachet auf* (tune 62) organ, Bullock.
Sigfrid Karg-Elert b. 1879
His Master's Voice, C 2059 (organ), Ellingford.
In dulci jubilo (tune 549).

Many additional recordings of Chorale Preludes are listed in *The Gramophone Shop Encyclopedia of Recorded Music* under the names, Bach, Buxtehude, Pachelbel, Reger, and Scheidt.

Attention should be drawn to the pamphlet, *Hymn-tune Voluntaries for the Organ,* by Henry Coleman (Oxford University Press, 1930), which lists about 300 Preludes specially suited for use in worship, and based on familiar Hymn-tunes.

CHAPTER IX

A CENTURY OF REFORM

In a previous chapter,[1] the statement was made that we are in the very midst of the Reformation initiated in the sixteenth century. Whatever were the human errors and misconceptions which distorted that movement, whatever were the political and secular adulterations which debased it, among both Catholics and Protestants, its primary spiritual purpose was the revival and restoration in Western Christianity of a pure Catholic belief and life. Music cannot be separated from life: and as we consider the past Century of Reform in Church Music, we must necessarily think also of the vital religious movements toward truer and fuller Catholicity which have chiefly affected the Praise of God.

WHAT IS A CATHOLIC

The high name of Catholic cannot be truly appropriated by merely reciting it in the liturgical use of the ancient Creeds, which nevertheless embody its full significance; nor yet by its etymological use emptied of its historic content: still less as a shibboleth of partisanship in the Church of God, or as the insufficient coda of a hyphenated title. The One Holy Catholic and Apostolic Church requires of its members an effort for Unity in a charity which flows from the heart of Jesus Christ, and in a love of truth founded on faith in the Holy Spirit, who

[1]See p. 124.

[242]

can guide us into *all* truth. She requires an effort for Holiness which must both underlie and transcend all forms of external worship. She requires an effort for Apostolicity which may not rest in any policy of a mere convenient "historic Episcopate," but rather in a divinely constituted order and authority in her organic being, of whose very essence is the Apostolic Commission, "Go ye into all the world and preach the Gospel to every creature." The universality of the Catholic name must include each of these elements and efforts. Everyman, rightly to assume it, must be becoming

> the catholic man who hath mightily won
> God out of knowledge and good out of infinite pain
> And sight out of blindness and purity out of a stain[2]

through Jesus Christ, the Maker and Ruler of men, the Head of his living Mystical Body the Church: of which, pray God, all who praise him may be Catholic members indeed. No mere being a high Churchman or a low Churchman or a broad Churchman: an Episcopalian or a Roman Catholic or a Baptist or a Methodist or a Presbyterian, can give us a right to that lofty name. "It is for us to live, not an incomplete, but a Catholic life, claiming for ourselves and our day all the noble characteristics, the mystic beauty, the irresistible power, which have adorned the individual Christian centuries or epochs, but which we would gather into one galaxy of glory for all the people and for all time. . . . The vicious habit of referring everything to the Reformation of the sixteenth century is the antithesis of Catholicity."[3]

[2]Sidney Lanier, *The Marshes of Glynn.*
[3]Bishop Charles H. Brent in *The Return of Christendom*, Macmillan, 1922.

Three Vital Religious Movements

No. All Christendom is today in the midst of that revival and restoration of Catholic life begun so long ago. No *Church* can be truly Catholic which neglects the souls of men, or their bodies, or their minds. Jesus is full Humanity as well as full Deity. We must attain toward "the measure of the stature of the fulness of Christ,"[4] and neglect none of the surging waves of religious renewal and advance which have carried the tide of Praise to its present height in the Anglican Communion. They were primarily three. The first was the Evangelical Revival, with its intense desire to win the souls of men. The Wesleys, who never abandoned their allegiance to the English Church, or to its sacramental principles and liturgical methods, began the movement as missionaries. Its result was the vast missionary expansion of the Anglican Communion throughout the world early in the nineteenth century. The Tractarian Movement followed, stressing a return to the fulness of ancient faith and practice. Its profound care for the salvation of souls led to sacrificial effort for the building of the Kingdom of Heaven on earth in social and economic justice for man, both in body and soul. Last of all, in this present time, came a wide but confused movement, which I dislike to call either Modernist or Liberal because of the common secularist implication of these words, but which, in its essence, cares for the minds of men as well as for their souls and bodies; and boldly asserts that *all* truth is necessarily Catholic truth, and that "the truth shall make you free."[5] In the freedom of that liberating truth, Churchmen have long been rising from the partisanship of a

[4]Eph. iv:13.   [5]St. John viii:32.

maimed and incomplete Christianity to utilize for the work of God the good results of these three waves of Reform.

Let us trace their influence in Church Music: first going on with the Hymns, then with the music of the Eucharist and of the other services; not forgetting parallel movements in other Communions which have blended with the life of Praise in our own.

THE TRIUMPH OF ANGLICAN ECLECTIC HYMNODY

METRICAL Psalms continued to hold their unduly predominant place in Anglican praise right down to a hundred years ago, both among the Evangelicals and among the old-fashioned obstinate 'High Churchmen.' But a forgotten Evangelical preacher, Basil Woodd, took a step forward in 1794, and published a collection of Psalms and Scripture paraphrases, with a few Hymns, "arranged according to the order of the Church of England." Each Sunday and Holy Day was supplied with a metrical Psalm to serve as the Introit, provided in the first Prayer Book. It will be observed that *The Hymnal,* following this precedent, has grouped sixteen metrical Psalms under the heading, Introits. Of course the appended Doxologies should always be sung, just as is *Gloria Patri* with the prose Psalms. Woodd also appointed proper Psalms or Hymns suited to the Epistle and Gospel for each day; and followed with Hymns for Communion, Holy Baptism, and other occasions.[6] We owe to this obscure Evangelical the present *form* of our Hymnal.

John Wesley was not the last to be sued at law for the irregularity of publishing a Hymnal. The conservative Bishops con-

[6]Louis F. Benson, *The English Hymn,* N. Y., 1915. Page 351.

tinued their opposition to the Hymn: and in 1819, Thomas Cotterill, the Evangelical Vicar of St. Paul's, Sheffield, was sued before the Archbishop of York for endeavouring to introduce into his parish Church a book containing, in addition to the conventional 150 metrical Psalms, no less than 367 Hymns. The book was printed by Cotterill's friend, James Montgomery, the Moravian editor of *The Sheffield Iris*, who also contributed fifty of the Hymns. Montgomery had the old Moravian missionary spirit, and was a fighting liberal, who had suffered fines and imprisonment in York Castle for printing a poem celebrating the fall of the Bastille, and a militant article on local politics. He was also one of the best English Hymn writers, a true religious poet. We sing 17 of his Hymns, and they are among the perennially useful ones. The Chancellor of York decided that Cotterill had no authority to publish the book, but postponed sentence, and called in Archbishop Harcourt, who effected a masterly compromise. The book was withdrawn, and the Archbishop paid for a new edition, prepared with his assistance. St. Paul's was supplied with copies, each inscribed, "The gift of his Grace the Lord Archbishop of York."[7]

Bishops continued to issue formal charges to their Dioceses against the introduction of Hymns into parochial worship. The Bishop of Exeter even forbade the use of Bishop Ken's well-loved Morning and Evening Hymns. But the long battle for Hymns was won, and thenceforth Hymnals, too many Hymnals,[8] entered the service of the Church of England without ecclesiastical litigation.

[7] Louis F. Benson, *op. cit.*: and other sources.
[8] One hundred and twenty were published between 1800 and 1850 in England.

The Hymnody of Romanticism: Reginald Heber

THE most important of them for many years was the work
of Reginald Heber, Vicar of Hodnet, although it was not published until after his death. Like other works of salient importance, it both utilized the past and, in its own fresh achieve-
ment, foreshadowed the future. Its growth was most interesting.
Heber was from the first a cultured poet and author, the friend
of Scott, Southey, Milman, and other leaders of the swiftly
growing Romantic movement in English letters. He was
familiar with the *Olney Hymns,* and early in his ministry sought
to introduce them in his parish. His own Hymn writing was
soon merged in a growing collection, in manuscript, for which
he had the most definite ideals. It was to be of high literary
quality, to embody the new lyric spirit of Romanticism, together
with the earlier work of Jeremy Taylor, Ken, Pope, Dryden,
Addison, Cowper, Watts and Wesley. It was to draw on the
old Latin treasure in the translations of Drummond of Hawthornden. In these two particulars, it fulfilled the promise of
that significant little book, *Lyra Davidica,* two centuries earlier.
In his own words, it was to contain "no fulsome or indecorous
language; no erotic addresses to him whom no unclean lips can
approach; no allegories, ill understood and worse applied." He
also originated a new and useful form, the Metrical Litany.[9]

But one further ideal needs our special attention. Heber
arranged his Hymns to provide definite relationship to the
Epistle and Gospel of each Sunday and Holy Day: and it was
his practice to *preach* on the Epistle and Gospel. His *Sermons*
of 1822 are the first published on the liturgical services of the

[9]See Hymn No. 41.

Church. Here we have the clearest indication of the desirability of unifying Liturgical Service, Sermon, and Hymns. Many Priests fail to make their selection of Hymns spiritually effective by neglecting to do this simple thing. Heber sought authorization of the complete work, first from the Bishop of London, then from Archbishop Sutton of Canterbury. Authorization was refused. In this attitude toward an official Hymnal, the Church of England has remained, I think wisely. And although it is not the historic position of the American Church, I earnestly hope that greater freedom in the choice of Hymns, the necessary condition of normal advance, may be won among us: always safeguarded by the *jus liturgicum*[10] of the Bishops to reject what is undesirable.

The fruition of Reginald Heber's interest in India came when he was made Bishop of Calcutta, with all British India for his See. Three years of apostolic labour exhausted his vitality, and he died a few moments after recording his final Confirmation, "Trichinopoly, April 3, 1826." The following year his book was published: *Hymns written and adapted to the Weekly Church Service of the Year.* We smile at the incongruities of "Greenland's icy mountains," written long before he left England. A somewhat unneighbourly English editor has even patriotically sought to uphold the prestige of the British Empire by substituting "Java" as the isle of pleasing prospect "where only man is vile." But Reginald Heber heard the call of those benighted men, and laid down his life to bring them the Light of the world: and whenever we sing a Hymn of his, we should

[10]"The Bishop's *jus liturgicum* is limited to the sanctioning of services" (hymns) "additional to those in the authorized service books and doctrinally in harmony with them." W. K. Lowther Clarke, in *Liturgy and Worship,* Macmillan, p. 4.

remember that no man can be a healthy Christian who does not lay down *something* that costs self-denial, in order to spread among men the knowledge of the "Holy, Holy, Holy, Lord God Almighty" whose praise Bishop Heber so nobly sang.

The Hymnody of the Oxford Revival

THE Oxford Tractarian Movement followed at once. John Keble published *The Christian Year,* in 1827, precisely contemporaneous with Heber's book. Six years later, he preached the famous Assize Sermon, regarded as the beginning of the movement. In 1834, he re-opened a mine which was to yield great riches to the Praise of God, in translating a Greek Hymn, the famous φῶς ἱλαρόν :[11] which in another form, is No. 12 in *The Hymnal.* Let us trace the progress of Tractarian Hymnody.

I Revival of the Latin Hymn in Translation

THE characteristic appeal to antiquity which was a distinguishing feature of early Tractarianism very naturally led to an increased interest in the old liturgical Latin Hymn, which, as we have seen, had never quite disappeared from the attention of translators. Bishop Heber's inclusion of earlier versions was the prelude to many fresh translations: notable among them were those of Bishop Mant[12] and of John Chandler[13] in 1837; of Newman[14] in 1838; of Isaac Williams[15] in 1839; of Frederick Oakeley,[16] 1841 and of Edward Caswall,[17] 1849: those of Newman, Oakeley, and Caswall were made prior to their entering the Church of Rome.

[11]See p. 161.   [12]Hymns 146, 161, 375.   [13]Hymns 30, 91, 282, 458.
[14]Hymns 5, 8.   [15]Hymn 509.   [16]Hymn 72.
[17]Hymns 17, 63, 93, 196, 316, 331.

None of these translators was concerned with the music of his versions. They were made from a literary point of view, as poetry. The next great step in the forward progress of Hymnody was to be an increasing attention to the use of the Proper Tune: not merely metrically possible, but in all ways suitable; for a Hymn being "the Praise of God with song," it makes vast difference what particular song is employed.

Before we follow this next step, let us pause for a moment to look at the tunes of the period. Many of them were very dull, but a few names stand out, such as the serene melody *St. Peter*,[18] No. 232, composed by Alexander Reinagle, Vicar of St. Peter's-in-the-East, Oxford, in 1836; the tune *St. Michael*, No. 88, skilfully adapted by Doctor Crotch from Bourgeois the same year; and S. S. Wesley's *Harewood*, No. 559, the first of a fine series by the best English composer of his time. In the next two decades, tunes of a high type and of enduring usefulness were written by William Horsley,[19] Sir John Goss,[20] Henry John Gauntlett,[21] and Charles Steggall.[22]

II Revival of the Folksong Carol

BUT in the very year of the Oxford Movement's beginning, another element, long neglected, returned to be a permanent part of Anglican Hymnody; namely, the Folksong Carol. Carol singing had fallen either into complete disuse, or into such dis-

[18]This tune is almost always sung too fast, to its great detriment as music expressive of the words to which it is set.

[19]*Horsley*, 159.

[20]*Bevan*, 463; *Lauda anima*, 258; Illus. Record, H.M.V., B 3047, Temple Church Choir.

[21]*St. Alphege*, 69; *University College*, 116; *St. Albinus*, 176; *Newland*, 261; *St. George*, 276; and *Irby*, 349.

[22]*Christchurch*, 182; *St. Edmund*, 298.

tortion as to make the name meaningless in its true sense. In 1833, William Sandys, a lawyer interested in antiquarian research, published his *Carols Ancient and Modern.* Note the significant title. It contained among other things, *The First Nowell* (Hymn 551) with its authentic traditional Folktune in the Phrygian Mode. From this timid beginning (for Sandys thought the Carol "more neglected every year") has sprung a vast revival of true Carol singing, and an adoption of Folksong as a legitimate and expressive source of music for many of our Hymns.[23]

Illustrative Records: *The First Nowell:*

Columbia 4579, St. George's Chapel Choir.
H.M.V. B3977, Royal Choral Society.

III *Revival of the Plainsong Hymn*

LET us return to the revival of Proper Tunes, mentioned above. Translations from the Latin had thus far been sung to any available modern tune, except for a few Lutheran Chorales adapted from Plainsong. The antiquarian interest of English Romanticism speedily began to show itself in an interest in Pre-Reformation Hymn melodies. Doctor Gauntlett, the hymn composer, left the profession of the law for that of music in 1844. He devoted himself ardently to the reform of Church music. In that same year he published a *Gregorian Hymnal,* restoring some of the ancient music to use. And now we come to one of the greatest names in the whole history of Hymnody: that

[23]Note the following tunes in our Hymnal: *Silician Mariners,* 51; *Picardy,* 339; *Sussex,* 345; *Luke,* 350; *St. Elisabeth,* 356[11]; *Noël,* 362; *Lew Trenchard,* 417; *Im Babilone,* 522[11]; *St. Patrick,* 525, pt. 1; and *Deirdre,* 525, pt. 2. A far greater proportion of Folksong is found in recent English Hymnals. *The Cowley Carol Book* and *The Oxford Carol Book* are notable collections of Folksong Carols.

of the learned scholar, the distinguished poet, the humble and holy Priest, John Mason Neale. The only work offered this brilliant and devout spiritual leader was that of warden of an almshouse for old men, at a salary of £27 a year: and there, from 1846 to 1866, in a holy poverty like his Lord's, he lived his short life, issuing his learned studies in Church History and Liturgiology, his notable Commentary on the Psalms, and above all, his very faithful and beautiful translations of both Latin and Greek Hymns, of which thirty-three are now to be found in *The Hymnal*. In 1850 he wrote a most fruitful essay on *English Hymnody, its History and Prospects,* pointing out the serious blemishes which defaced it, and pleading especially for more adequate treatment of the old Breviary Hymns. Shortly after, with Thomas Helmore, Master of the Children of the Chapels Royal, as his musical editor, he prepared, and issued in two parts, in 1852 and 1854, *The Hymnal Noted,* containing 105 of the ancient Office Hymns translated in their original meters and set to their proper Plainsong tunes.[24] The book had a very limited adoption, as was but natural. When we look back at it now, we readily see that the music was barbarously distorted, for Plainsong notation was then but little understood. But Neale's ideal thus boldly set forth has never again been lost to the Church. Practically every modern Hymnal contains such Hymns, and in several the entire ancient cycle is provided. The Plainsong and Mediæval Music Society provided authentic versions of the tunes later on. Other translators such as G. R. Palmer and M. J. Blacker increased the number of adequate versions. As recently as 1932 *A Plainsong Hymnbook* edited by Doctor Sydney H. Nicholson, and containing 163 Hymns,

[24]Ten of our Plainsong Hymns were first printed in this book.

has obtained wide sale in England. Our own little modicum of 14 in *The Hymnal* will undoubtedly be increased. The growing popularity of this music is shown by its increasing adoption in Protestant Hymnals,[25] as well as by its more frequent appearance in our own service lists.

IV Revival of the German Chorale

1854 saw also the publication of William Mercer's *Church Psalter and Hymn Book,* notable for several reasons. It was the first important general Hymnal to include the tunes as well as the words, for the use of the congregation, as had originally been done by Coverdale and by Day at the Reformation. The music was edited by that sturdy upholder of excellence, Sir John Goss. It was used for nearly twenty years at St. Paul's Cathedral, and widely adopted elsewhere; and it re-introduced into Anglican use the German Chorale, in which a fresh interest had been shown during the previous decade. It is to Mercer that we owe the version of the "Queen of Chorales," *How bright appears the morning star,*[26] which appears with its proper tune in *The Hymnal* as No. 98. This lead was magnificently followed by Miss Catherine Winkworth[27] in the two volumes of *Lyra Germanica,* and in the famous *Chorale Book for England,* an attempt to provide a complete Hymnal from German sources, such as Neale and Helmore had constructed from the Latin. Both, of course, failed as practical books: but every practical book since them has drawn upon their contents; and

[25]Such as, *The Presbyterian Hymnal, The Oxford American Hymnal, The Pilgrim Hymnal, The Scottish Mission Hymnal.*
[26]See pp. 225, 229.
[27]Miss Winkworth's translations appear in Hymns 62, 186, 342, 414, 422, 440, and 545.

the German Chorale[28] is an essential part of every modern Hymnal.

V Hymns Ancient and Modern

AT last these various streams of Praise merged in a wise effort to provide a book not for special groups, but for the whole Church. The number of Hymnals in the Church of England now exceeded 150. In 1858, on the initiative of the Rev. Francis H. Murray, the proprietors of many of these books agreed to withdraw them, and combined to produce a new Hymnal in their place. A Committee was formed in 1859; it began its work by invoking the aid of the Holy Spirit with the *Veni Creator*. Some two hundred clergy cooperated in the enterprise. John Keble gave the wise counsel, "If you wish to make a Hymn Book for the use of the Church, make it comprehensive." At the suggestion of the Rev. Sir Henry W. Baker,[29] the Secretary of the Committee, William Henry Monk was made musical editor. He suggested the famous title, *Hymns Ancient and Modern,* which so tersely conveys the eclectic character of the collection. The book was published in 1861. It contained 131 Hymns of English origin, 132 of Latin, and 10 of German. Its success was immediate and overwhelming. In a few years, 114 new Hymns were added, mostly modern. Several translations from the Greek were included. Other revisions followed. By 1895, 10,340 Churches in England alone were using the collection, besides the entire British Army and Navy. Before the World War, over 60,000,000 copies had been sold. The triumph of the first important eclectic Hymnal was complete.

[28]See pp. 209–214. *The Hymnal* contains fifty-three tunes of German origin, besides some arrangements.

[29]Composer of *St. Timothy,* No. 6, and *Stephanos,* No. 386: author of Hymns 6, 59, 323, 326, 436, 515: translator of Hymns 47, 74, 158.

Musically, also, the book was significant, for it accustomed England to a new sort of Hymn tune, wholly unlike any that had been known before. Doctor Dykes was the characteristic representative of the new school: others who became prominent were Joseph Barnby and John Stainer. It adopted the methods of the secular part song very largely, and obtained its effects less by a strong Congregational melody than by elaborate and luscious sounding harmonies for the Choir. It tended to make of the Hymn a pretty thing to be heard: not a vital expression of religious faith to be uttered. It was inevitable that this phase should appear. A general movement such as Romanticism has its weak elements as well as its strong ones: and an age that could express its feeling for antiquity by building artificial ruins in parks would be sure to fall into musical and religious sentimentalism as well. The trouble with sentimentalism in either sphere is that it releases no spiritual energy for the work of God, but wastes itself in pleasant personal satisfactions.

Thus at the very moment of the triumph of Hymnody, a "weak and beggarly element"[30] kept it from spiritual completeness. But nowadays, in the reaction from Victorianism, we find those who condemn all the work of such composers as Dykes, Barnby, and Stainer; which is folly. They gave us many beautiful, strong, and well-loved tunes. I cite among them Dykes's tunes *St. Cross,* No. 153, *Nicæa,* 205, *Hollingside,* 223, and *Dominus regit me,* 326: Barnby's *Laudes Domini,* 37, and *Winkworth,* 229, a noble tune: Stainer's *Beati,* 198, and his tender childlike *Evening Prayer,* 343. Other excellent tunes of the period are Monk's *Merton,* 63, *St. Philip,* 122, and *St. Constantine,* 361: Smart's *Regent Square,* 80, and *Heathlands,* 312:

[30]Galatians iv:9.

Elvey's *St. George's Windsor,* 421: Redhead's *Petra,* 217, and *St. Prisca,* 409: and S. S. Wesley's *Aurelia,* 464, composed for *Jerusalem the golden.*

Records illustrative of the Victorian Hymn:

Victor 22626, *Laudes Domini,* Barnby, Hymn 37.
Columbia DB 749, *Hollingside,* Dykes, Hymn 223.
    4490, *Aberystwyth,* Parry, Hymn 130[II].
    9745, *Eventide,* Monk, Hymn, 18.
DB 1206, *Aurelia,* Wesley, Hymn 464.
    4209, *Nicæa,* Dykes, Hymn 205.
DB 934, *Ewing,* Ewing, Hymn 511.
DB 582, *St. Chrysostom,* Barnby, Hymn 228.
His Master's Voice B 3491, *Eventide,* Monk, Hymn 18.
    B 3746, *Aurelia,* Wesley, Hymn 464.
    B 3981, *Nicæa,* Dykes, Hymn 205.
    B 3992, *Ewing,* Ewing, Hymn 511.
    B 3047, *Lauda anima,* Goss, Hymn, 258.
    B 4279, *Horsley,* Horsley, Hymn 159.

When you select Hymn tunes, sing the words unaccompanied: do not play the harmonies on the piano and think how sweet they are. *Never* encourage the habit of *listening* to Hymns instead of singing them; or of singing them in the secular spirit of the social college song. Keep them, and their music, on a high spiritual plane.[31]

Peter Christian Lutkin wrote fully and sympathetically of the Victorian School in the Hale Lectures of 1908–9. In a later publication, he says, "The former strength and vigour have

[31]A contributing cause to the poor condition of congregational hymn singing in America is found in the almost universal misuse of the radio, which not only offers people bad examples of the so-called hymn crudely and sentimentally sung, but also accustoms them to a merely passive rôle. The musical experience is not primarily passive but active. Only those who themselves make music up to at least a part of their capacity can rightly enter into it by mere listening.

given place to more sinuous melodic curves, and more seductive but weaker harmonies of a chromatic tendency. The hold of these tunes is gradually loosening in England; and the latest Hymnals are stressing German Chorales, adaptations of Folk-songs, Gregorian melodies, and new tunes of a more solid style than the Dykes-Barnby type." What are some of these recent Hymnals which represent the swing away from an outworn Romanticism?

VI Twentieth-Century Hymnals

ROBERT BRIDGES, later poet laureate of England, was a most distinguished worker in the field of Church Music reform; a great poet, a great editor, a great hymnologist. In 1899, he completed *The Yattenden Hymnal* for his village Church. It was published in a sumptuous folio with the antique types of Peter Walpergen and Bishop Fell. H. Ellis Wooldridge was his musical editor. The book has well been called "the most distinguished of individual pioneer contributions to modern hymnody."[32] It contains but 100 Hymns: but they are of the highest devotional, literary, and musical quality. It enunciates and exemplifies a new principle; that it is just as important to supply fitting words to a great Hymn melody, as to supply a tune to a great Hymn. Every modern Hymnal has been enriched through this book, including our own.[33]

Another scholarly work which should be in the library of every Church musician is *Songs of Syon,* published by the Rev. G. R. Woodward in 1910.[34] This notable book carries further

[32]*Songs of Praise Discussed.* Oxford University Press, p. 394.
[33]See Hymn 155, and Tunes 11[11] and 490.
[34]Schott and Company, London.

the principle set forth by Bridges, of providing fitting words for the work of many of "the finest melodists in Europe," and contains 414 absolutely authentic unaltered versions of the nobler Hymn tunes of many lands.

The English Hymnal, originally published in 1906, but much revised and enlarged in 1933, carries the ideas of the books just mentioned into the practical sphere, and, under its distinguished musical editor, Ralph Vaughan Williams, the first composer in England, adds a valuable element of Folksong, which has won both popular and artistic approval. It is, all things considered, the completest and most practical of Anglican Hymnals. Its provision for the liturgical services of the Church is full: including the translated text of the ancient Eucharistic Propers. Its general editor, the Rev. Percy Dearmer,[35] whose services to the cause of Hymnody have been invaluable, had at heart three needed things: the publication of the Hymns as their authors wrote them, as far as possible; the inclusion of Hymns of literary excellence, bringing the true poets into the service of the Sanctuary; and the gathering of adequate Hymns of Social Service. In the 1904 edition of *Hymns Ancient and Modern,* the writer of the Preface said, "Few (Hymn writers) apparently have been inspired by the social and national aspects of Christianity which appeal so largely to our time." The need of such Hymns is great if the Church is to do her appointed work of doing God's will on earth as it is in heaven. We little heed, even we of the Church, our own Whittier's great word,

O brother man, fold to thy *heart* thy brother.[36]

[35]Canon Dearmer of Westminster died in 1936. May he rest in peace.
[36]*Poems,* 1850.

Instead, we fall into an insufficient and distorted humanitarianism, which seeks to relieve the suffering of mankind primarily by scientific techniques: to alleviate the material symptoms resulting from our common sin, without either the insight or the courage to attempt its radical cure by living contact with the sacred Humanity of our blessed Lord, and the inevitable social and economic earthquakes which would necessarily follow the free flow into human relationships of that Almighty power of love. Great transforming movements call for inspired song. We do not even sing the prophetic words of our own American poets in this field: and although we followed *The English Hymnal* in adopting a few such Hymns,[37] how often do we have the opportunity to sing them either in Church or in public meetings? Our Hymnal indicates that we are more concerned with war than with the welfare of our fellow men.

Songs of Praise, published in 1925 and enlarged in 1931, carries out Canon Dearmer's ideas even more fully. It is a national song book, rather than a Church Hymnal; but its wealth of hitherto unused religious poetry will undoubtedly enrich future Hymnody; and its musical editors, Vaughan Williams and Martin Shaw, have assembled an impressive group of those sturdier modern tunes alluded to by Dean Lutkin. Many of them are strong unison tunes, with free accompaniment, such as Hubert Parry's superb setting of William Blake's *Jerusalem*. Indeed, the editors direct that "the congregation must always sing the *melody,* and the *melody* only," wise and sound

[37]432, Judge eternal, throned in splendour, *St. Leonard;* 433, Once to every man and nation, *Tony-y-botel;* 442, God of the nations, *Pax veritatis;* 492, Rise up, O men of God, *Festal Song;* 494, Where cross the crowded way of life, *Gardiner;* 496, O Lord and Master of us all, *Walsall;* 499, Our Father, thy dear Name doth show, *Bethlehem;* 501, When wilt thou save the people, *Kendal.*

advice. Another characteristic is a rhythmical freedom which gets away from uniform barring in threes or fours. Such freedom occurs in all of the older Chorales and Psalter tunes, when the proper pauses are made at the close of lines, as well as in Plainsong. It now reappears in modern composition, with stirring effect. Note, in our own Hymnal, the rhythms of *Rosa Mystica*, No. 82, and of *Egbert* or *St. Dunstan's*, No. 117.

Illustrative Records:

His Master's Voice:
B 2615, *For all the Saints*, Vaughan Williams.
B 3125, *Jerusalem*, Parry.
Columbia:
9763, *Jerusalem*, Parry.
4647, *The King of Love*, Irish Folksong.

Thus the complete cycle has been made in Hymnody. Age after age has made its characteristic contribution; and it is our high privilege to live in an age which offers for our intelligent use in the Praise of God the chief treasures of them all.

GROWTH OF THE AMERICAN EPISCOPALIAN HYMNAL.

OUR own Church has usually followed English practice, at the natural interval of some years. But a few distinctive points should be mentioned.

Metrical Psalmody, either the Old or the New Version, had an even stronger hold on the Colonial Church than in England. We have seen the prompt rejection of Wesley's book.[38] But when, after the attainment of national independence, the infant National Church met in Convention at Christ Church, Philadelphia, in 1785, it authorized a Committee to "publish, with

[38]See p. 235.

the Book of Common Prayer, such of the . . . singing Psalms
. . . as they may think proper." William Smith, a member
of the Committee, inserted in the Preface of the "Proposed
Book" (which was never ratified) the following: "A *selection*
is made of the . . . singing Psalms . . . and a collection of
hymns are (*sic*) added." 84 Metrical Psalms and 51 Hymns
were printed in the book, *followed* by the significant phrase,
"End of the Prayer Book." This was the first official proposal
in the Anglican Communion to include Hymns as an authoritative, instead of a permissive, part of divine worship. Doctor
White (later Bishop White), who never permitted a Hymn in
Christ Church except on Christmas Day,[39] objected; but later
wrote, "I give up my sentiment respecting ye hymnifying ye
Psalms." But the book failed. In 1789 when the New Prayer
Book was finally adopted, the House of Bishops, consisting of
Bishops Seabury and White, restored "The *whole* Book of
Psalms, in meter," and cut down William Smith's Hymns to the
number of 27. These were *officially* set forth when the Prayer
Book was ratified; and the American Church, unlike the English, which, as stated before, has never adopted a Hymnal, has
kept to the policy of an authorized book ever since. In 1820,
however, the Psalms and Hymns were no longer included as a
part of the Prayer Book; which made revision somewhat easier.

But the Church was little satisfied with so meager a provision. Trinity Church, Boston, set forth its own Hymns in 1808,
152 of them, 57 by Anne Steele. We inherit Hymn 396,
"Father, whate'er of earthly bliss," from it. General Convention added thirty more Hymns that same year. Later, after

[39]Probably "While Shepherds watch their flocks by night," from the *Supplement
to the New Version.*

[261]

publishing and using his own sacred poetry,[40] that doughty advocate of Hymn singing, Doctor William Mühlenberg, forced the consideration of the subject, and the Convention of 1826 authorized 212 Hymns, of which over 40 were scriptural versions other than Psalms. This purely Evangelical selection was the Episcopal Hymnal until after the Civil War.

Musically, little can be said for this whole period. American praise had started with the Bay State Psalter, furnishing a common tune for each of the metres used. Such tunes, given out and repeated line by line, with appalling lethargy, must have taxed the human spirit severely. Later, very elaborate "fuguing tunes" with successive melodic imitations in the separate parts were fashionable. As late as 1846, a tune was publicly sung which compelled the poor congregation to say

> And ever in this calm abode
>   May thy pure Spirit be—*rit be,*
> And guide us on the narrow road
>   That terminates—*minates*—in thee.

In the Episcopal Church, a higher standard had long been maintained. Its music was profoundly influenced for good by the work of a great religious musician in mid-century who was not a churchman; Lowell Mason, whose remarkable *Sabbath Hymn and Tune Book,*[41] published in 1858, was musically superior to most of the seven versions of our own Hymnal of 1892. Mason collected an extraordinary library of Hymnology, now the property of Yale University; and made himself conversant with the historical treasures and traditions of his art. His influence is shown in the Reverend George T. Rider's *Plain Music*

[40]See Hymns 75 and 343.   [41]See p. 191.

for the Book of Common Prayer (1854), the first Manual making "full provision for the music of our Liturgy, in a form that congregations can easily use."[42] Among its fifty Hymn tunes can be found practically every type described in these chapters: Plainsong, Psalter Tunes, Chorales, and fine English tunes. Most of them are in our Hymnal today, and many of them were restored to it in the last revision.

A word should be said of Frederic Dan Huntington, who, as a Unitarian minister in Boston, included versions of the Breviary Hymns on the one hand, and on the other, German Chorales, translated by his colleague Frederick Hedge,[43] in a Hymnal ahead of its time. Doctor Huntington, later the saintly Bishop of Central New York, was a quietly pervasive force for all that was highest in Hymnody.

The influence of *Hymns Ancient and Modern* soon led to the Hymnal of 1872, which followed Bishop Huntington's lead in including 37 translations from the Latin, and other eclectic features. The type has remained unchanged to the present day, through the revisions of 1892 and 1916. It would be pleasant to recall the musical labours of Tucker and Hutchins, of Messiter and Parker, and of others who edited successive musical editions; but time forbids. Much of their work is embodied in the present Hymnal, which is also enriched by so much of the musical treasure previously described. But any future revision should involve the simultaneous consideration of both words and tunes: the lack of which has caused many blemishes in our present book. The *chief* preparation for revision should be the enthusiastic *use* of what we now possess, a Hymnal filled with

[42]The congregational melody is printed on a separate line. See p. 237.
[43]Translation of *Ein' feste Burg,* Hymn 213.

the devotional and musical treasures of the Christian ages.

But let us return to a brief review of other musical reforms during the century past.

THE OXFORD MOVEMENT AND CHURCH MUSIC

A HUNDRED years ago, musical worship in England and in Europe was at a low ebb. The Cathedrals, save Durham and Exeter, had no sung Eucharist.[44] The Daily Offices were slovenly and careless. The art of chanting was almost lost. The music of the Chapels Royal was showy and dependent on instrumental brilliancy. The old traditions set up at the Reformation had practically disappeared from the Parish Churches. On the continent, things were as bad. Listen to Welby Pugin, the great Roman Catholic architect, writing in 1858: "There exists a *want of reality* in the present services of the Churches in this and many other countries; and from what does it proceed but the corrupt and artificial state of ecclesiastical music? The clergy and the people have been precluded from taking any real part in the service of Almighty God. They are reduced to the position of *listeners* instead of worshippers: so that in lieu . . . of clergy and people uniting in one great act of adoration and praise, the service is transferred to a set of hired musicians, who *perform* in a gallery, while the congregation is either amused or wearied."

What influences have changed all this? Primarily two: the Oxford Movement and the Benedictine Revival. We will consider the first. Its purpose was the restoration of full Catholic belief and life in the Church of England, as taught by the ancient fathers: the recognition of the Church, not as a depart-

[44]See p. 85.

ment of the State, and subject to it; but as the living Mystical Body of Christ, in which alone might men find a right relation to God and to their fellow men. The early years of Tractarianism were devoted to questions of principle, based on the study of the undivided Church of the early centuries. Parallel with this appeal to Christian antiquity, we find in the first musical publications inspired by the Movement a similar turning back to the ancient principles of choral worship; but especially through the Reformation restatement exemplified in Merbecke. William Dyce, in 1843, published a complete adaptation of the Merbecke book to the Prayer Book of 1662, with extensive critical essays covering the scope of the work. In it he says, "Above seven hundred years ago, the Church of England, under the guidance of St. Osmund, Bishop of Sarum, agreed that the Gregorian method of chanting, brought in by St. Augustine of Canterbury, should be continued in preference to the more modern. . . . Merbecke's book affords positive proof that he understood the injunction made as to the use of music in the reformed service to require the use of that very music which had been customary in the Church of England ever since the Sarum *Consuetudinarium.*"

It is positively startling to find this sudden reappearance for use of a book which for three centuries had been regarded as a mere antiquarian curiosity, and an extremely rare one. A demand for the reprinting of the original *Book of Common Prayer Noted* arose at once; and in 1844 Pickering issued his very beautiful facsimile Merbecke. Thus the ancient principles we have been considering were promptly reasserted early in the Movement. Their outward practical expression soon followed. Dyce's book was not in convenient form for use; in 1845, the

Reverend Thomas Helmore began the publication of a series of really serviceable music-books. He became Master of the Children of the Chapels Royal in 1846. In 1850 appeared his complete and very useful *Manual of Plainsong,* which not only perpetuated and disseminated the work of Merbecke, but also extended it, in drawing more fully upon the ancient treasures.

Since then the influence of Merbecke has been twofold. First, his music for the Eucharist has been studied from many points of view, and arranged for use by many editors. It has found its way into our own Hymnal, and is sung in churches ranging from village Chapels to metropolitan Cathedrals. Second, Merbecke's Psalm chants inevitably turned men's minds to a study of their ancient prototypes. Both Dyce and Helmore set forth clearer principles of chanting. But some eager editors turned to contemporary Continental practice, then at its lowest ebb of corruption. Psalters edited by Doran and Nottingham, Redhead, Baker, and Monk, copied these vitiated methods.

Recent Plainsong Service Books

EVENTUALLY a very great scholar, the Reverend George Herbert Palmer, by masterly analysis of the ancient music of the Sarum Rite, fully restored English Psalmody to its lovely and perfect completeness in *The Sarum Psalter.* Somewhat later, in 1888, Harry Bembridge Briggs and others founded The Plainsong and Mediæval Music Society, of which Sir John Stainer became president. Stainer, Briggs, and the Reverend W. H. Frere, later Bishop of Truro, re-edited the old *Manual of Plainsong,* in full accord with Palmer's results: and in America, General Convention has now authorized and set forth a Psalter on similar lines, using the revised translation of the present Prayer Book. Briggs and Palmer met at the French Benedictine Abbey of Solesmes, to be mentioned later. The Plainsong Society has carried on a vast work for Church Music on the old principles. Its many publications bear witness to its great activity during fifty years. They include phototype facsimiles of the ancient Sarum musical service books, learned studies by such scholars as Bishop Frere and Dom Anselm Hughes, textbooks, and many practical editions based upon all this material. The Joint Commission on Church Music of the Episcopal Church, after still further study of original sources, has incorporated in its official publication, *The Choral Service,* the whole of the ancient music involved in the dialogue between Priest and People, both at the Holy Eucharist and in the various Offices.

Thus, through the Oxford Movement, the great principle of a liturgical music at one with the words of the service, and providing for each member to have his due active share in the praise of the whole Body, as first set forth in the sixth century, transmitted to the English Church, and revived at the Reformation, has been restored throughout the Anglican Communion and authoritatively accepted and set forth by the American Episcopal Church.

Music of the Religious Orders

ONE of the major spiritual results of the Oxford Movement was the revival of the Religious Life for men and women. The existence of over sixty monastic Orders in the Anglican Communion has involved a special musical development. The Communities are of quite varied types, ranging from those chiefly occupied in external works of mercy to those called by God to a cloistered life of prayer. But in all of them, in some degree, goes on the great work which St. Benedict called the *Opus Dei*, the Work of God; the monastic family as an organic whole praising God in choir; and so through an ever-increasing Vision of God, preparing for the service, by labour or by prayer, of their fellow men.

Very soon after the beginnings of the Anglican Religious Communities, it was perceived that the whole round of the ancient Offices, with a considerable portion of their music, should be made available. In 1852, a book was published in London entitled, *The Psalter, or Seven Hours of Prayer, according to the Use of the Illustrious and Excellent Church of Sarum*. It contained much of the old Offices. The music, to be sure, was crudely and experimentally adapted to the English text; but the work was a brave, pioneer effort which, impracticable in itself, led to the development of greater skill. The long, patient labour of the Rev. G. H. Palmer eventually produced, in the Wantage Vesper Book and the Diurnal now being printed at Wantage, a complete English Antiphoner; a wonderful treasure for future liturgical enrichment. And in this country has been prepared a parallel version of the text and music of the Benedictine Diurnal; the most venerable of all such monastic Office books.

THE BENEDICTINE REVIVAL

THREE days before John Keble preached his Assize Sermon in 1833, a young French priest, Prosper Guéranger, left his home in Sablé, Sarthe, and, with a few companions, walked a mile or more to the unoccupied tenth-century Priory Church of St. Peter, Solesmes. There they knelt in the presence of God, and dedicated themselves to the restoration of the Monastic life in France, deprived of it since the Revolution. The new Benedictine Community founded by them devoted itself to liturgical studies, and eventually, to an intensive examination of all the existing remains of early Christian music. They also entered upon the older ways of spiritual life and endeavour. The result was a vast reform in the Roman Communion of which the world is as yet little cognizant. Dom Guéranger, whose early studies gave the world a priceless commentary on the old services, *l'Année Liturgique,* soon found the necessity of reforming the utter confusion and corruption of the liturgical chant. He evolved the principle that "when manuscripts of different periods and countries agree in a given version, it may be affirmed that the true form of a melody has been recovered."

Comparative Study of Ancient Manuscripts

THIS was the beginning of the comparative criticism of the ancient musical manuscripts, which has developed at Solesmes and elsewhere, that precise, thorough, systematic scholarship which is essential to sound practice. The Benedictines photographed every important musical manuscript in Europe. The vast labours of copying melody after melody in tabular form from all of them has gone on for many decades, under the skilled guidance of Dom Pothier, Dom Mocquereau, Dom Gajard. The secrets of all of the old notations have been revealed, and published in the vast *Paleographie Musicale* of Mocquereau, the *Paleografia Gregoriana* of Suñol, the *Monumenti Vaticani di Paleografia* of Bannister. From this long study finally emerged practical editions.

A CENTURY OF REFORM

The "Motu Proprio" of Pius X

THE world became aware of all this when Pius X issued in 1903 his famous and much misunderstood *Motu Proprio* on Church Music, which does *not* banish all music from the Roman Church save Plainsong, but, in its own words, "admits to the service of religion everything good and beautiful discovered by genius in the course of ages," but always with due regard to the purposes of the Liturgy itself.

In accordance with this reform there has been a great revival of the wonders of classical Polyphony; new types of purely religious music for the Eucharist have sprung forth in Spain, in Italy, in Germany, in France; and the long labour of the Benedictines has found expression in the official publication of the restored Plainchant by the Roman Church. I was present with the Vatican Commission at Appuldurcombe in 1904, and can testify to the spiritual ardour which actuated all of its work. The most recent fruit of the Benedictines' labour is the *Antiphonale Monasticum* issued in 1933, the complete restoration of the ancient Office Music to its purest forms.

ENGLISH AND AMERICAN COMMISSIONS ON CHURCH MUSIC

BUT the great surging wave of musical betterment has affected other Churches than the Roman. The Archbishops of Canterbury and York assembled a Committee in 1922, whose admirable Report, *Music in Worship*,[45] should be studied by every Priest and organist in America: as should the three Reports

[45]To be had of The Macmillan Company, New York, and the S. P. C. K. in London.

of the Joint Commission on Church Music of the Episcopal Church, issued in 1930 in a single pamphlet.[46]

These documents do not merely indicate careful study; they reflect a vast advance already made. Their recommendations remove any excuse for the continuance of such indifference to the art of musical worship as still persists in many Churches.

PRESENT TREASURES AND FUTURE HOPES

WE must thankfully acknowledge that a restored knowledge of the original ideals and principles of Christian Choral Worship has clarified the musical objectives of the Anglican Communion, and encouraged it to purge away whatever dross has mingled with the fine gold of its offerings of praise. The treasures of the Church's own Chant, of the Hymns of the ages, of the Classical Polyphony, of the superb liturgical music of the Russian Church, are now ours in English dress. An ever increasing company of religiously-minded musicians is not only spreading their effective use in our Parish Churches and Cathedrals, but also composing new and worthy music in the devotional spirit of the old, but in the idioms of our own time. Once more thousands of devout choristers and solo singers are exercising what they regard as a ministry to Almighty God; not as a display of their own skill as entertainers. Again Congregations both great and small join actively in that music of God's Church whose sweet sound so thrilled the soul of St. Augustine at Milan. Still the Holy Spirit moves in the hearts of men to create new songs consonant with the old. We can thank God that he has led us so far toward a pure worship where the prayer will sing

[46]To be had of The H. W. Gray Co., 159 W. 48th St., New York.

and the music will pray; where each member of the Mystical Body of Christ will be taken up into the heavenly worship and actively participate in it with heart and mind and voice. But our gratitude for God's blessings in this matter must spur us on to fresh effort, to greater patience, to stronger love: for there is still vast indifference and conventionality and misunderstanding to be overcome before God's Church on earth will be as his Church in heaven in the utter sincerity and splendour of its united praise.

MEMENTO MEI, DEUS MEUS, PRO HOC; ET PARCE

MIHI SECUNDUM MULTITUDINEM

MISERATIONUM

TUARUM

PROGRAMS DURING THE LECTURES

Choral Compositions Sung by the Northwestern University
A Cappella Choir, Oliver Seth Beltz, Conductor

Hymn 74, Of the Father's love begotten	Plainsong
Motet, *Ave, verum corpus natum*	William Byrd
Respond, Are ye come out as against thieves	Tomás Luis da Victoria
The Cherubic Hymn	Alexander Gretchaninoff
Ascension Invitatory and *Venite*	Winfred Douglas
Sursum corda, followed by *Sanctus* in E	Peter Lutkin
Hymn 155, Ah, holy Jesus	Sarum Plainsong
Motet, Let all mortal flesh keep silence	Peter Lutkin

Organ Compositions Played by Lester W. Groom, F.A.G.O.

Diferencias sobre el Canto del Caballero	Antonio de Cabezon
Chorale Preludes	Johann Sebastian Bach

> *Kyrie, Gott heiliger Geist*
> *Aus tiefer Noth schrei' ich zu dir*
> *Liebster Jesu, wir sind hier*
> *Wenn wir in höchsten Nöthen sein*
> *An Wasserflüssen Babylon*
> *O Mensch, bewein' dein' Sünde gross*
> *Schmücke dich, o liebe Seele*

Chorale Preludes	Johannes Brahms

> *Es is ein Ros' entsprungen*
> *Herzliebster Jesu*

Fugue in E flat, known as *S. Anne's*	Johann Sebastian Bach

THE HALE LECTURES

The Rt. Rev. Charles Reuben Hale, D.D., LL.D., Bishop of Cairo, Bishop Coadjutor of Springfield, was born in 1837, consecrated Bishop on July 26, 1892, and died on Christmas Day in the year 1900.

In his will he bequeathed to Western Theological Seminary, now Seabury-Western Theological Seminary of Evanston, Illinois, a fund to be held in trust "for the general purpose of promoting the Catholic Faith, in its purity and integrity, as taught in Holy Scripture, held by the Primitive Church, summed up in the Creeds, and affirmed by the undisputed General Councils, and, in particular, to be used only and exclusively for . . . the establishment, endowment, printing, and due circulation of a yearly Sermon . . . and . . . of Courses of Lectures."

The subjects of these Lectures were to be:

(*a*) Liturgies and Liturgics.
(*b*) Church Hymns and Church Music.
(*c*) The History of the Eastern Churches.
(*d*) The History of National Churches.
(*e*) Contemporaneous Church History: *i.e.,* treating of events happening since the beginning of what is called "The Oxford Movement," in 1833.

The Trustees of the Seminary accepted the generous bequest of Bishop Hale and have endeavoured faithfully to carry out its provisions. A full list of the Hale Lectures thus far delivered and published appears at the front of the present volume.

BIBLIOGRAPHY

BIBLIOGRAPHY

Books of exceptional usefulness are marked with an asterisk.*

GENERAL

DAVISON, ARCHIBALD T., *Protestant Church Music in America,** E. C. Schirmer, Boston, 1933.
FLEMING, GEORGE T., *The Music of the Congregation,* The Faith Press, London, 1923.
GARDNER, GEORGE, AND NICHOLSON, SYDNEY H., *A Manual of English Church Music,** Macmillan, New York, 1923.
GARDNER, GEORGE, *Worship and Music, Suggestions for Clergy and Choirmasters,** Macmillan, New York, 1918.
GRACE, HARVEY AND DAVIES, H. WALFORD, *Music and Worship,** Eyre & Spottiswoode, London. (H. W. Gray Co., New York, 1935.)
HADOW, SIR W. H., *Church Music,* Longmans, Green & Co., London, 1926.
LUTKIN, PETER CHRISTIAN, *Music in the Church,** The Young Churchman Co., Milwaukee, 1910.
Music in Worship, Report of the Archbishops' Committee S. P. C. K., London, 1922 (Macmillan, N. Y.). Revised Edition, 1932.
NICHOLSON, SYDNEY H., *Church Music, A Practical Handbook,** The Faith Press, London.
POPE PIUS X, *Sacred Music, Motu Proprio,* The Catholic Education Press, 1928.
Reports of the Joint Commission on Church Music, 1930, Wallace Goodrich, Secretary, New England Conservatory of Music, Boston, Mass.
RICHARDSON, A. MADELEY, *Church Music* (Handbook for the Clergy), Longmans, London, 1904.
SHAW, MARTIN, *The Principles of English Church Music Composition,** London, 1921.
SHORE, S. ROYLE, *The Church and Her Music,* Birmingham Printers, Birmingham.
STEELE, J. N., *Importance of Musical Knowledge to the Priesthood of the Church,* Pott, New York, 1895.
TERRY, SIR RICHARD RUNCIMAN, *A Forgotten Psalter and Other Essays,* Oxford University Press, London, 1929.
——*The Music of the Roman Rite,* Burns, Oates & Washbourne, London, 1931.

HISTORY OF CHURCH MUSIC

AIGRAIN, REV. RENÉ, D. D., *Religious Music,** Sands & Co., London, 1931 (J. Fischer & Bro., N. Y.).
BRIGGS, H. B., *Recent Research in Plainsong,* Charles Vincent, London, 1898.
The Catholic Encyclopedia, The Encyclopedia Press, New York, 1913.
DAVEY, HENRY, *History of English Music,* Curwen & Sons, London, 1922.

BIBLIOGRAPHY

DICKINSON, EDWARD, *Music in the History of the Western Church,* Charles Scribner's Sons, New York, 1902.

GEVAERT, F. A., *Les Origines du Chant Liturgique de L'Eglise Latine,* Ghent, 1895.

GRATTAN-FLOOD, W. H., *Early Tudor Composers,* Oxford University Press, 1925.

GROVE's *Dictionary of Music and Musicians,* Macmillan, New York, 1935.

The Oxford History of Music, Oxford University Press, London, 1929.

SHORE, S. ROYLE, *The Choral Eucharist Since the Reformation,* Faith Press, London, 1914.

WAGNER, PETER, *Origine et Developpement du Chant Liturgique,* Desclée, Lefebvre & Cie, Tournai, 1904.

WEINMANN, REV. DR. KARL, *History of Church Music,* Pustet, New York, 1910.

WYATT, E. G. P., *St. Gregory and the Gregorian Music,* Plainsong and Mediæval Music Society, London, 1904.

WORSHIP

CABROL, RT. REV. FERDINAND, O. S. B., *Liturgical Prayer, Its History and Spirit,** Burns, Oates & Washbourne, London, 1925.

CLARKE, W. K. LOWTHER, *Liturgy and Worship,** Macmillan, London and New York, 1932.

DUCHESNE, L., *Christian Worship: Its Origin and Evolution,** S. P. C. K., London, 1903 (Macmillan, N. Y.). Fifth Edition, 1919.

FISKE, GEORGE WALTER, *The Recovery of Worship,* Macmillan, New York, 1931.

HEILER, FRIEDRICH, *Prayer,* Oxford University Press, 1932.

HERWEGEN, RT. REV. ALPHONSE, *Art Principle in the Liturgy,* Benziger Bros., New York.

HISLOP, D. H., *Our Heritage in Public Worship,** Charles Scribner's Sons, New York, 1935.

KIRK, KENNETH E., *The Vision of God,** Longmans, Green & Co., London and New York, 1931.

MORTIMER, ALFRED G., *The Development of Worship in the Rites and Ceremonies of the Church,* George W. Jacobs & Co., Philadelphia, 1911.

OTTO RUDOLF, *The Idea of the Holy; Religious Essays,* Oxford University Press, 1931.

SPERRY, WILLARD L., *Reality in Worship,** Macmillan, New York, 1926.

UNDERHILL, EVELYN, *Worship,** Mowbrays, London, 1936 (Harper, N. Y.).

VOGT, VON OGDEN, *Art and Religion,* Yale University Press, New Haven, 1921.

HEBREW MUSIC

BOX, REV. G. H., *Judaism in the Greek Period,* Oxford University Press, London, 1932.

FRIEDLANDER, ARTHUR M., *Facts and Theories relating to Hebrew Music,* Reeves, London, 1924.

—— *Hebrew Music,* article in *Oxford Dictionary of Music.*

IDELSOHN, A. Z., *Jewish Music,** Henry Holt & Co., New York, 1929.

MOORE, GEORGE FOOT, *Judaism,* Harvard University Press, 1927.

OESTERLEY, REV. W. O. E., *Music of the Hebrews* in *Oxford History of Music.*

BIBLIOGRAPHY

—— *The Jewish Background of the Christian Liturgy,* Oxford University Press, London, 1925.

SAMINSKY, LAZARE, *Music of the Ghetto and the Bible,** Bloch Publishing Co., New York, 1934.

GREEK MUSIC

MACRAN, H. S., *Greek Music* in Grove's *Dictionary.*

REINACH, TH., *Le Musique Grecque,* Paris, 1926.

TORR, CECIL, *Greek Music* in *Oxford History of Music.*

LATIN MUSICAL PALEOGRAPHY

BANNISTER, REV. H. M., *Monumenti Vaticani di Paleografia Musicale Latina,* Leipsic, 1913.

Benedictines of Stanbrook, *Gregorian Music, An Outline of Musical Paleography,* Benziger Bros., New York, 1897.

MOCQUEREAU, DOM. ANDRÉ, *Paléographie Musicale,* Series I, II, Desclée & Cie, Tournai.

SUÑOL, DOM GREGORI M., *Paleografia Musical Gregoriana,* Abadia de Montserrat, Spain, 1925.

AMBROSIAN CHANT

Antiphonarium Ambrosianum, Milan, 1898.

Grammatica di Canto fermo Ambrosiano, Ambrosius, Milan, 1929.

Manuale di Canto Ambrosiano, Sten, Turin, 1929.

Melodie Ambrosiane, Ambrosius, Milan, 1929.

MOCQUEREAU, DOM ANDRÉ, *Paléographie Musicale,* articles and reproductions in two volumes.

PLAINSONG TEXTBOOKS

By a Benedictine, *A Grammar of Plainsong,** Stanbrook Abbey, Worcester.

BRIGGS, H. B., *The Elements of Plainsong,** Quaritch, London.

BURGESS, FRANCIS, *The Rudiments of Plainchant,* Office of Musical Opinion, London, 1923.

FRERE, RT. REV. W. H., *Plainsong,** in *Oxford History of Music.*

—— *The Sarum Gradual and the Gregorian Antiphonale Missarum,** The Plainsong and Mediæval Music Society, London, 1895.

GATARD, DOM AUGUSTIN, *Plainchant,* The Faith Press, London, 1921.

JOHNER, REV. DOMINIC, *A New School of Gregorian Chant,** Fr. Pustet & Co., New York, 1925.

MOCQUEREAU, DOM ANDRÉ, *Le Nombre Musical Grégorien,* Desclée & Cie, Tournai: Part I, 1908, Part II, 1927; English edition, 1932.

MOCQUEREAU, DOM ANDRÉ; GAJARD, JOSEPH; DESROCQUETTES, J. HÉBERT; POTIRON, H., *Monographies Grégoriennes,* 10 volumes, Desclée & Cie., Tournai.

POTHIER, DOM JOSEPH, *Les Mélodies Grégoriennes d'après la tradition,* Desclée & Cie, Tournai, 1888.

SUÑOL, DOM GREGORI M., *Text Book of Gregorian Chant,** Desclée & Cie, Tournai, 1930.

BIBLIOGRAPHY

PLAINSONG, MUSIC

Antiphonale Monasticum pro Diurnis Horis, Desclée & Cie, Tournai, 1934.
Antiphonale Sarisburiense, The Plainsong and Mediæval Music Society, London, 1901–24.
Cantorinus Romanum, Editio Typica Vaticana, Rome, 1911.
DOUGLAS, WINFRED, *The St. Dunstan Kyrial,* H. W. Gray Co., New York, 1933.
—— *The Ceremonial Noted,* St. Mary's Convent, Peekskill, 1923.
GOODRICH, WALLACE, and DOUGLAS, WINFRED, *The Choral Service,* H. W. Gray Co., New York, 1927.
Graduale (Dominican), Rome, 1904.
Graduale Romanum, Desclée & Cie, Tournai, 1908.
Graduale Sarisburiensis, The Plainsong and Mediæval Music Society, London, 1895.
Liber Antiphonarius pro Diurnis Horis, Vatican Press, Rome, 1912.
Liber Usualis Missae et Officii, Desclée & Cie, Tournai, 1921.
Officium Majoris Hebdomadae, Desclée & Cie, Tournai, 1923.
PALMER, REV. G. H., *The Offices, or Introits,* St. Mary's Convent, Wantage, 1904.
—— *The Wantage Vesper Book,* 1919.
—— *The Order of Compline,* 1919.
—— *The Diurnal Noted,* 1926.
—— *The Antiphons upon Magnificat,* 1930.
Pars Antiphonarii, The Plainsong and Mediæval Music Society, London, 1923.
Plainsong and Mediæval Music Society, *The Plainchant of the Ordinary of the Mass,* Tenth Edition, The Faith Press, London, 1937.

PLAINSONG, ACCOMPANIMENT

ARNOLD, J. H., *Plainsong Accompaniment,** Oxford University Press, 1927.
BRAGERS, ACHILLE P., *Plainsong Accompaniment,* Carl Fischer, New York, 1934.
BURGESS, FRANCIS, *The Teaching and Accompaniment of Plainsong,** Novello & Company, London, 1914.
GROOM, LESTER W., *Accompanying Harmonies for The Plainsong Psalter,** The H. W. Gray Co., New York, 1933.
MATHIAS, DR. FR. X., *Die Choralbegleitung,* Pustet, Regensburg and New York, 1905.
MOLITOR, P. GREGOR, *Die Diatonisch-Rhythmische Harmonisation der Gregorianischen Choralmelodien,* Breitkopf & Härtel, Leipsic, 1913.
PARISOT, J., *L'Accompagnement Modal du Chant Grégorien,* Paris.
POTIRON, HENRI, *Cours d'Accompagnement du Chant Grégorien,** Paris, 1927.
SPRINGER, MAX, *The Art of Accompanying Plain Chant,* J. Fischer & Bro., New York, 1908.

DESCANT AND FAUX-BOURDON

BENNETT, J. LIONEL, *English Hymnal Organ and Choir Book of Varied Accompaniments and Descants,* Oxford University Press, 1926.
GRAY, ALAN, *A Book of Descants,** Oxford University Press, 1926.
SCEATS, GODFREY, *Plainchant and Faburden,* The Faith Press, London.

BIBLIOGRAPHY

PSALTERS AND CHANTING

Articles in *The Oxford Dictionary of Music* and in *The Prayerbook Dictionary.*

BRIDGES, ROBERT, *Collected Essays, XXIV–XXVI,* Oxford University Press, 1935.

BRIGGS, H. B., AND FRERE, W. H., *A Manual of Plainsong,* Novello & Co., London, 1902.

DOUGLAS, WINFRED, *The Canticles at Evensong,* The H. W. Gray Co., New York, 1915.

DOUGLAS, WINFRED; NOBLE, T. TERTIUS; HALL, W. H.; FARROW, MILES, *The American Psalter,** The H. W. Gray Co., New York, 1930. The only Anglican Psalter with the Psalm text of the American Prayer Book.

DOUGLAS, WINFRED, AND WILLIAMS, WALTER, *The Plainsong Psalter,** H. W. Gray Co., New York, 1932.

HEYWOOD, JOHN, *The Art of Chanting,** William Clowes and Sons, London, 1893.

MARSHALL, WALTER, AND PILE, SEYMOUR, *The Barless Psalter,* Novello & Co., London.

PALMER, REV. G. H., *The Sarum Psalter,** St. Mary's Convent, Wantage, 1916.

RICHARDSON, A. MADELEY, *The Psalms, Their Structure and Musical Rendering,* Vincent, London, 1903.

TREMENHEERE, REV. G. H., *The English Psalter, with the Canticles,* Faith Press, London, 1915.

See Page 127 for earlier Psalters. See also, *Plainsong Textbooks,* above.

HYMNOLOGY

Historical Notes on Words and Music

BACON, LEONARD WOOLSEY, *The Hymns of Martin Luther,* Charles Scribner's Sons, New York, 1883.

BENSON, LOUIS F., *Studies of Familiar Hymns,* Westminster Press, Philadelphia, 1903.

—— *The English Hymn,** Doran, New York, 1915.

BROWN, THERON, AND BUTTERWORTH, HEZEKIAH, *The Story of the Hymns and Tunes,* George H. Doran Co., New York, 1906.

DAVISON, ARCHIBALD T., *The Harvard University Hymn Book,* Harvard University Press, 1926.

DEARMER, PERCY, AND JACOB, ARCHIBALD, *Songs of Praise Discussed,** Oxford University Press, London, 1933.

DOUGLAS, WINFRED, *A Brief Commentary on Selected Hymns and Carols,* Northwestern University, Evanston, Ill., 1936.

DUFFIELD, SAMUEL W., *English Hymns,* Funk and Wagnalls, New York, 1888.

Historical Edition, *Hymns Ancient and Modern,* William Clowes and Sons, London, 1909. Contains Bishop Frere's invaluable Historical Introduction.

JULIAN, JOHN, *Dictionary of Hymnology,** John Murray, London, 1915 (Scribners, N. Y.).

METCALF, FRANK J., *American Writers and Compilers of Sacred Music,* Abingdon Press, New York, 1925.

BIBLIOGRAPHY

MOFFATT, REV. JAMES, *Handbook to the Church Hymnary,** Oxford University Press, London, 1927.

PRICE, CARL F., *The Music and Hymnody of the Methodist Hymnal,* Eaton and Mains, New York, 1911.

RILEY, ATHELSTAN, *Concerning Hymn Tunes and Sequences,** Mowbrays, London, 1915.

WOODWARD, G. R., *Piæ Cantiones,* The Plainsong and Mediæval Music Society, London, 1910.

LATIN HYMNS

BRITT, REV. MATTHEW, *The Hymns of the Breviary and Missal,** Benziger Bros., New York, 1922.

DREVES, DR. GUIDO MARIA, *Die Kirche der Lateiner in ihren Liedern,* Munich, 1908.

HUGHES, DOM ANSELM, *Anglo-French Sequelæ,* The Plainsong and Mediæval Music Society, London, 1934.

HUGHES, REV. H. V., *Latin Hymnody,* Faith Press, London, 1922.

MEARNS, JAMES, *Early Latin Hymnaries,* Cambridge University Press.

MISSET, E., AND AUBRY, PIERRE, *Les Proses d'Adam de Saint Victor,* H. Welter, Paris, 1900.

RABY, F. J. E., *Christian Latin Poetry,** Oxford University Press, Oxford, 1927.

TRENCH, ARCHBISHOP RICHARD CHENEVIX, *Sacred Latin Poetry,* London, 1874.

WALPOLE, A. S., *Early Latin Hymns,** Cambridge University Press, Cambridge, 1922.

WRANGHAM, DIGBY S., *The Liturgical Poetry of Adam of Saint Victor,* Kegan Paul, Trench, & Co., London, 1881.

PLAINSONG HYMNALS

A Daily Hymn Book, Burns, Oates & Washbourne, London, 1931.

Cantate Domino, Rushworth & Dreaper, Liverpool, 1932. (Excellent harmonies.)

*Hymn-Melodies and Sequences,** The Plainsong and Mediæval Music Society, London, 1920.

The New Office Hymn Book, Novello & Co., London, 1908.

NICHOLSON, SYDNEY H., *A Plainsong Hymnbook,** W. Clowes and Sons, London, 1932.

The Office Hymn Book, Pickering and Chatto, London, 1891.

CAROLS

DEARMER, PERCY; WILLIAMS, R. VAUGHAN; SHAW, MARTIN, *The Oxford Book of Carols,** Oxford University Press, London, 1928.

MAITLAND, J. A. FULLER, *English Carols of the Fifteenth Century,* Charles Scribner's Sons, New York.

WOODWARD, G. R., *The Cowley Carol Book,* Mowbrays, London, 1902.

J. S. BACH

PARRY, C. HUBERT H., *Johann Sebastian Bach,* G. P. Putnam's Sons, New York, 1909.

SCHWEITZER, ALBERT, *J. S. Bach,** Breitkopf & Härtel, New York, 1911.

BIBLIOGRAPHY

TERRY, CHARLES SANFORD, *Bach,** Oxford University Press, London, 1928.
—— *Bach's Chorales,** Cambridge University Press, 1915 (Putnams, New York).
—— *J. S. Bach's Four-Part Chorales,* Oxford University Press, London, 1929.
—— *J. S. Bach's Original Hymn-tunes,* Oxford University Press, London, 1922.

THE CHORAL PRELUDE

COLEMAN, HENRY, *Hymn-tune Voluntaries,* Oxford University Press, London, 1930.
GRACE, HARVEY, *The Organ Works of Bach,** Novello & Co., London. (H. W. Gray, N. Y., 1922.)
HULL, A. EAGLEFIELD, *Bach's Organ Works,** Musical Opinion, London, 1929.
SCEATS, GODFREY, *The Liturgical Use of the Organ,* Musical Opinion, London, 1922.

RECENT HYMNALS, ENGLISH

The Church Hymnary, Oxford University Press, London, 1927.
The English Hymnal, Oxford University Press, 1933.
Hymns Ancient and Modern, Revised Edition, William Clowes and Sons, London, 1904.
Hymns of Western Europe, Oxford University Press, London, 1927.
The Oxford Hymn Book, Oxford University Press, London, 1908.
The Scottish Mission Hymnbook, Oxford University Press, London, 1912.
Songs of Praise, Oxford University Press, 1931.
Songs of Syon, Schott & Co., London, 1910.
The Yattenden Hymnal, Oxford University Press, London, 1920.

RECENT HYMNALS, AMERICAN

Harvard University Hymn Book, Harvard University Press, 1926.
The Hymnal (Episcopalian), The Church Pension Fund, New York, 1930.
The Hymnal (Presbyterian), Presbyterian Board of Religious Education, Philadelphia, 1933.
The Methodist Hymnal, The Methodist Book Concern, New York, 1935.
The Oxford American Hymnal, Oxford University Press, N. Y., 1930.
The Pilgrim Hymnal, The Pilgrim Press, Boston, 1931.
Selected Hymns and Carols, Northwestern University, Evanston, Ill., 1936.

INDEX I

SUBJECTS AND PROPER NAMES

INDEX I

English Polyphonic School, 73, 74, 75, 77, 79, 80, 84–85, 124, 138–139, 143, 146, 147, 148
Ephesians iv:13, 244
Ephesians v:14, 22, 157
Ephesians v:19, 94
Ephraem, St., 161
Epictetus, 156–157
Epiphany, Feast of the, 33, 37
Epiphany, Second Sunday after the, 35, 37
Epistle, The, 19, 32, 34, 39, 43, 100, 112, 247
Epistle, Chant of the, 43
Epworth England, 233
Errors in Church Music (see Abuses in Church Music)
Eschenbach, Wolfram von, 229
Ethelbert, King of Kent, 55
Etheria, 45, 94
Eufronius, Bishop of Tours, 170
Eusebius, 18
Evanston, Illinois, 206
Evelyn's Diary, 129
Evening Prayer, 102, 103, 112, 115, 122, 125, 138, 142, 144, 146, 154, 175
Everyman, 184
Exeter Cathedral, 85, 246, 264

FAFNER, 66
Farsed Kyrie, 61, 80
Fauré, Gabriel, 90
Faux-bourdon, 114–115, 140, 198
Fell, Bishop, 258
Fellowes, Canon Edmund Horace, 85
Ferias in Advent and Lent, 48
Ferreri, Zaccharia, 196
Finland, 206
Florence, Italy, 213
Folksong, 14, 17, 64, 69, 110, 161, 163, 174, 199, 202, 207, 212, 213, 216, 235, 250, 251, 258
Fonteinne, Dom O. S. B., 188
Fortunatus, Venantius, 170–172, 174, 178, 182
Francis I, King of France, 215
Francis of Assisi, St., 187, 205
Franciscan movement, 96, 186, 187

Francke, August Hermann, 231–232
Frederick, The Elector, 210
Frere, Bishop Walter Howard, 60, 67, 83, 179, 228, 258, 266
Friedlander, Arthur, 42, 159
Frohne, Pastor Johann Adolph, 233
Fulbert of Chartres, St., 173

GAJARD, Dom Joseph, O. S. B., 269
Galatians xi:14, 186
Galerius, 52
Gallican Hymnal, 168
Gallican use, 26, 40, 49, 175, 178, 182
Garrett, George M., 146
Gauntlett, Henry John, 250, 251
General Convention, 160, 260, 261, 262, 266
Genevan Psalmody, 215–218, 220
Georgia, 235
Georgian Jews, 16
Gerbert, von Hornaw, Martin, 51
Gerhardt, Paulus, 230–231
Gibbons, Orlando, 85, 138, 139, 146, 151, 222
Gill, Thomas H., 11–12, 92
Glinka, Mikhail, 91
Gloria in excelsis, 42, 44, 46, 47, 50, 59, 62, 63, 70, 71, 72, 80, 81, 87, 115, 157, 159, 160, 175, 212
Gloria Patri, 33, 38, 99, 106, 115, 139, 153–155, 159, 161, 245
Gloria tibi, 43, 58
Gnosticism, 161
Golden Sequence, 182–183
Good Friday, 76, 101, 115, 117, 118, 158, 178, 182
Gospel, The, 19, 32, 34, 39, 43, 100, 112, 247
Gospel Canticles, 97, 111–112, 115, 121, 124, 157
Gospel Chant, 43
Goss, Sir John, 151, 250, 253
Goudimel, Claude, 115
Gounod, Charles, 90, 145
Gradual Respond, 34–35, 39, 97, 98, 100, 141, 179
Graduale Romanum, 188
Graduale, Sarum, 188

[290]

SUBJECTS AND PROPER NAMES

[291]

INDEX I

SUBJECTS AND PROPER NAMES

INDEX I

Levitical Choir, 15
Liber Pontificalis, 32
Liège, Belgium, 113
Limerick, Ireland, 86
Lincoln Cathedral, England, 85
Litany, English, 79, 121
Litany, Processional, 121
Little Hours, 97, 98, 167
Liutward, Bishop of Vercelli, 181
Loewen, Arnold von, 230
Lord's Prayer, The (see Pater noster)
Lotti, Antonio, 75
Low Sunday, 36
Lowe, Edward, 127
Loyola, St. Ignatius, 73
Luke i:3, 157
Lully, Jean-Baptiste, 144
Luther, Martin, 72, 73, 121, 163, 184,
 209–212, 215, 216, 219, 225, 231,
 232
Lutheran Church, 102, 121, 142
Lutkin, Peter Christian, Dedication,
 256, 259, 273
Lydian mode, 25
Lyon, Meyer, 238
Lyra Davidica, 203, 224–225, 233, 235,
 247
Lyra Germanica, 253

MACARONIC verse, 202, 204
Machaut, Guillaume de, 70, 71, 74
Machiavelli, Niccolo, 195
Madrid, Spain, 74
Magnificat, 111, 115, 146, 157
Magrephah, 13
Maimonides, Moses, 238
Mainz, Germany, 172
Mant, Bishop Richard, 249
Marguerite de Valois, 215–216, 220
Maria, Empress of Spain, 74
Mark Lane, London, 227
Marlowe, Christopher, 184
Marot, Clément, 215–217, 219
Martin, George C., 146
Mary Tudor, Queen, 84
Mason, Lowell, 191, 262
Mass, Concert, 71, 88–89, 90
Mass, Musical, 70–72, 74–75, 84–87

Matins, 82, 100, 101, 112, 160, 167, 184
Matthew, George, 134
Mauburn, Jean, Abbot of Livry, 204–
 205
Mauduit, Jacques, 153
Maundy Thursday, 34, 112, 117
Maximilian, Emperor, 213
Medici, Catherine de', 215, 216
Medici, Giovanni de', 196
Medici, Giulio de', 196
Medici, Lorenzo de', 196, 213
Megilla, 17
Mendelssohn-Bartholdy, Felix, 149, 151,
 212
Mensurable rhythm, 67–68, 76–77, 116
Merbecke, John, 47, 80–82, 83, 84, 87,
 124, 125, 265, 266
Mercer, William, 229
Messiter, Arthur H., Mus. Doc., 263
Metre, comparison with rhythm, 23,
 162–164, 195–197
Metrical Litany, 247
Metrical Psalters, 113, 217–222, 223, 224,
 226, 260–262
Metz, 55, 170
Meyer, Wilhelm, 160
Migné, France, 170
Migné, Jacques Paul, 170
Milan, Italy, 32, 95, 104, 161, 164, 168,
 271
Milan, Edict of, 12, 52
Milanese music (see Ambrosian music)
Miller, Doctor Edward, 224
Milman, Henry Hart, 247
Miracle Plays, 184
Mishnah, 14, 15
Missale Mixtum Mozarabicum, 46
Misset, E., 185
Misuses of music in church (see Abuses
 in Church Music)
Mocquereau, Dom André, O. S. B., 269
Monastic Diurnal, The, 188, 194, 268
Monk, William Henry, 127, 254, 255,
 266
Monotone, inflected, 19, 43, 103
Monotone, recitation, 43, 102, 104
Monte Cassino, Italy, 53, 68
Montgomery, James, 229, 246

INDEX I

SUBJECTS AND PROPER NAMES

INDEX I

Elaboration at the Eucharist, 31–32, 112

Genevan, 215–219

Metrical, 215–222

Office compared with the Mass, 32, 112

Responsorial, 32, 34–36, 37, 98–101, 116

Psalmus in directum, 97

Psalters (see Index II)

Pugin, Welby, 264

Purcell, Henry, 144, 151

QUENTIN, Church of St., Cambrai, 71

Quiñones, Francisco, Cardinal, 73, 122–123

RABANUS Maurus, Magnentius, 172–173

Raby, F. J. E., 24, 206

Rachmaninoff, Sergei, 91

Racine, Jean, 218–219

Radio, 256

Rebellion, The Great, 126–127

Recitation in Chanting, 18, 98, 102, 126, 133–134

Redhead, Richard, 201, 256, 266

Reform documents in Church Music, 69, 76, 79, 80–82, 121, 124, 143, 218, 220–221, 254, 270–271

Reformation, 72–74, 113, 114, 117, 120–124, 143–144, 208, 209, 213, 214, 242, 243, 253, 265, 267

Anthem-services, 137–140, 146

Cranmer's principles, 79–82

English, 77–85

Influence on continental polyphony, 72–77

Simplicity, desire for, 59–61, 80, 121–123, 181

Uniformity, desire for, 120, 123–124, 248

Vernacular, urge to use of, 58, 77, 78, 120–122, 143, 178, 195, 198–208, 209, 210, 212–214, 215

Reinagle, Alexander, 250

Religious Orders, Anglican, 267–268

Remigius of Auxerre, 21, 56

Renaissance, 195–198

Reproaches, The, 76, 115, 158, 182

Requiem, 33, 34, 38, 48, 50, 62, 75, 80, 81, 82, 89, 90, 105, 186–187

Respond, 19, 34–35, 36, 37, 97, 98, 100, 101, 116–118, 123, 141

Respond, Short, 97, 98–99

Responsorial Chant, 32, 34, 35, 36, 37, 97, 98–101, 116–118, 134–135

Restoration, The, 127, 129, 144

Revelations vii:9–10, 190

Rhadegonda, Queen, 170

Rheims, France, 70

Rhineland, The, 208

Rhymed Offices, 113, 121

Rhythm, 7–10, 19, 23–26, 28, 57, 67, 68, 76, 77, 107, 109, 110, 116, 124, 126, 129, 130, 131–132, 138, 139, 159, 162–164, 174, 192, 195, 199, 201, 207, 260

Mensurable, 67–68, 76–77, 116

Metre, comparison with, 23, 162

Prose, 19, 28, 106–109, 126, 130, 131

Word accent vs. classical metre, 23, 24, 162–164

Rice, Elmer, 5

Richards, G. Darlington, 134

Rider, Rev. George T., 262

Riley, Athelstan, 184

Robert the Pious, King of France, 182

Rodkinson, M., 17

Romance languages, 120

Romanticism, 87, 247–249

Rome, Italy, 16, 20, 21, 24, 26, 31, 32, 36, 44, 48, 49, 51–54, 71, 73, 95, 122, 123, 174, 178, 199, 214, 217, 244, 249, 270

Rossini, Giacomo, 89

Rostock, University of, 206

Rouen, France, 200

Round, 69

Rudinger, Gottfried, 149

Russian Church Music, 65, 90–91, 271, 273

SABLÉ, Sarthe, France, 268

St. Anne's Church, Soho, London, 224

St. Bartholomew, 18

St. Blaise's Church, Mühlhausen, 233

SUBJECTS AND PROPER NAMES

INDEX I

TALLIS, Thomas, 73, 84–85, 114, 125, 126, 127, 128, 130, 138, 197
Talmud, 15, 16
Tamid, 14
Tate, Nahum, 222
Tauler, Johann, 202
Taverner, John, 77, 80
Taylor, Bishop Jeremy, 247
Tchaikovsky, Peter Ilyich, 91
Tchesnokoff, Paul, 91
Te Deum laudamus, 6–7, 42, 46, 47, 112, 121, 124, 146, 147, 158–160, 184
Temple in Jerusalem, 13, 14, 15, 17, 22, 95
Tenebræ, Office of, 101, 117, 118
Tennyson, Alfred, 172
Teresa, St., 74
Terry, Sir Richard R., 89
Tersanctus (see *Sanctus*)
Tertullian, 20
The Lord be with you (see *Dominus vobiscum*)
Theodosius I, Emperor of Rome, 168
Theodulf of Orleans, St., 177
Thirty Years' War, 231
Thomas Aquinas, St., 173, 174, 178, 185
Thomas of Celano, 186, 187
Tiflis, 17
Tisserand, Jean, 204
Todi, Jacopone of, 186
Toledo, Third Council of, 49
Tombs, Captain, 133
Tomkins, Thomas, 138
Tonarium of Montpellier, 57
Tonic accent, 24–26, 107–108
Toplady, Augustus Montague, 238
Tours, France, 48, 170
Tract, 36–37, 39, 98
Tractarian movement, viii, 86, 87, 244, 249–253, 264–268
Trajan, Emperor of Rome, 94
Tralles, Asia Minor, 21
Trans-Caucasia, 17, 18
Trench, Richard Chevenix, Archbishop, 164, 183
Trichinopoly, India, 248
Trinity, Feast of the Holy, 113, 121, 185

Trinity Church, Boston, Mass., 261
Trisagion, 158
Tropes, 59–61, 67, 70, 80, 181, 204
Troy, N. Y., 127
Tucker, Rev. J. Ireland, 263
Turle, James, 127, 146
Tutilo, 70
Tye, Christopher, 73, 84, 219
Tyndale, William, 214

UMBRIA, Italy, 200
Unitas Fratrum, 208, 209, 232
Urban VIII, Pope, 196–197

VATICAN Commission on Church Music, 270
Venantius Fortunatus, 170, 172, 174, 178, 182
Veni, Creator Spiritus, 172, 173, 198, 210, 220, 223, 234, 249, 254
Venite, exultemus Domine, 99, 100, 127, 128, 134, 135, 146, 273
Verdi, Giuseppe, 89
Vernacular, change to the, 16, 19, 24, 45, 58, 77, 78, 79, 80, 120–122, 124, 143–144, 158, 162–164, 178, 184, 187, 195, 198–208, 209, 210, 212–214, 215, 220, 223, 224, 233, 247, 249–254
Versicle and Response, 27, 39–41, 43, 44, 81–82, 102–103, 112, 114, 124, 125, 160, 204
Versus popularis, 163, 216
Vespers, 94, 96, 97, 98, 100, 101, 112, 167, 188, 193, 204
Victoria, Queen of England, 87
Victoria, Tomás Luis, 73–74, 75, 76, 117, 118, 147, 148, 197, 207, 273
Victorian age, 145, 255–257
Viennese school, 88, 89
Vigils, 100
Virgin, Mass for a, 38
Visitation of the Sick, Office of, 102, 142
Vulgate, 31

WAGNER, Peter, 158
Wagner, Richard, 9, 66

INDEX II

MUSIC, BOOKS AND TEXTS

T indicates name of Tune: *R* indicates Phonograph Record

INDEX II

INDEX II

INDEX II

MUSIC, BOOKS AND TEXTS

Joint Commission, The Plainsong Psalter, 109, 133
Nicholson, The English Psalter, 146 R
Palmer, The Sarum Psalter, 266
Redhead, Psalter, 266
Scottish Psalter, The, 226
Sternhold and Hopkins, The Whole Booke of Psalmes, 219, 221, 223, 226
Tate and Brady, The New Version, 222, 223, 224
Turle, S. P. C. K. Psalter, 127
Watts, Paraphrase on the Psalms, 226
Puer natus est, 33 R
Puer nobis, T, 173, 204

Qui sedes, 34
Quinque prudentes, 38 R
Quomodo sedet, 112

RAMAULX, *T,* 178
Ravenshaw, *T,* 208, 209, 234
Regent Square, *T,* 255
Reges Tharsis, 37 R
Regina cæli, 105 R, 143 R
Rejoice in the Lord alway, 151 R (Purcell)
Remember not, Lord, our offences, 151 R (Purcell)
Reproaches, The, 76 R, 115 R
Requiem æternam, 33, 34 R, 75 R
Requiem Mass, 33 R, 34 R, 37 R, 38 R, 48 R, 50 R, 62 R, 75 R, 80, 82, 89 R (Verdi), 90 R (Fauré, Mozart)
Resurrexi, 338
Rise up, O men of God, 259
Rochelle, *T,* 236 R
Rock of ages, cleft for me, 238, 256
Rockingham, *T,* 224, 228, 239
Rosa Mystica, T, 208, 260

ST. ALBINUS, *T,* 250
St. Alphege, *T,* 250
St. Anne's, *T,* 222, 224, 226 R, 228
St. Anne's Fugue in E flat (Bach), 273
St. Bride, *T,* 239
St. Crysostom, *T,* 256 R
St. Columba (Irish Folksong), *T,* 260 R

St. Constantine, *T,* 255
St. Cross, *T,* 255
St. Dunstan's, *T,* 260
St. Edmund, *T,* 250
St. Elisabeth, *T,* 251
St. Flavian, *T,* 221
St. George, *T,* 250
St. George's, Windsor, *T,* 256
St. James, *T,* 221
St. Leonard, *T,* 259
St. Matthew Passion (Bach), 230
St. Michael, *T,* 217, 250
St. Patrick, *T,* 251
St. Paul, Oratorio, 212
St. Peter, *T,* 250
St. Philip, *T,* 255
St. Prisca, *T,* 256
St. Stephen, *T,* 239
St. Theodulph, *T,* 234, 240 R
St. Thomas, *T,* 239
St. Timothy, *T,* 254
Sally in our alley, 225
Salve, caput cruentatum, 230
Salve, festa dies, 176
Salve Regina, 105 R, 143 R
Sancte, venite, Christe corpus sumite, 176
Sanctorum meritis, 189 R
Sanctus, 44, 47, 48 R, 50, 59, 62 R, 70, 71, 72 R, 74 R, 75 R, 80, 85, 86, 157, 159, 212, 273
Sanctus ex quo sunt omnia, 60
Sarum Psalter, 266
Saviour, who thy flock art feeding, 262
Schmücke dich, o liebe Seele, T, 240 R
Schönster Herr Jesu, T, 231, 273
See the destined day arise, 249
Seelenbraütigam, T, 236 R
Shema' Israel, 110
Shout the glad tidings, 262
Si iniquitates, 105 R
Sicilian Mariners, *T,* 251
Sicut cervus, 76 R
Sine Nomine, T (Williams), 178, 260 R
Singet dem Herrn, 150 R (Bach)
Sleepers Wake, *T,* 225, 230 R, 234, 240 R
Sol præceps rapitur, 194, 249

[309]

9–55